'Prue Leith knows about colour and flavour and this has lots of both . . . a delicious family saga' *Daily Mail* on *The House at Chorlton*

'Perfectly captures the Sixties' scene' *Choice* on *The Prodigal Daughter*

'Leith has really hit her stride as a writer and uses her own considerable catering experience . . . skilfully interweaving emotional drama with food fashions' *Daily Mail* on *The Prodigal Daughter*

'A delicious mix of romance and cookery . . . a fascinating insight into the restaurant and hospitality business, [with] well-sketched characters [and] vivid flashes of period detail' *My Weekly* on *The Prodigal Daughter*

'An unmissable read packed with secrets and revelations' *OK!* on *The Lost Son*

'Uplifting and gripping, a must for a spot of al fresco reading this summer' *Cotswold Life* on *The Lost Son*

'Amiable, absorbing and satisfying, with some sensitive things to say about adoption and addiction' *Daily Mail* on *The Lost Son*

As a cook, restaurateur, food writer and business woman, Prue Leith has played a key role in the revolution of Britain's eating habits since the 1960s. She is now a judge on Channel 4's *The Great British Bake Off*. Prue is the author of seven romantic novels as well as a memoir, *Relish*, and after a long break from food writing has returned to writing cookery books alongside her fiction. She lives in Oxfordshire. Follow her on Twitter @PrueLeith.

ALSO BY PRUE LEITH

The Gardener
Leaving Patrick
Sisters
Choral Society
A Serving of Scandal

THE ANGELOTTI CHRONICLES

The House at Chorlton (previously published as *The Food of Love*)
The Prodigal Daughter

AUTOBIOGRAPHY

Relish

Prue Leith
The Lost Son

Quercus

First published in Great Britain in 2019 by Quercus
This paperback edition published in 2019 by

Quercus Editions Ltd
Carmelite House
50 Victoria Embankment
London EC4Y 0DZ

An Hachette UK company

A CIP catalogue record for this book is available
from the British Library

PB ISBN 978 1 78747 195 5

10 9 8 7 6 5 4 3

Typeset by CC Book Production

Printed and bound in Great Britain by Clays Ltd, Elcograf S.p.A.

For Lyn and Francisca

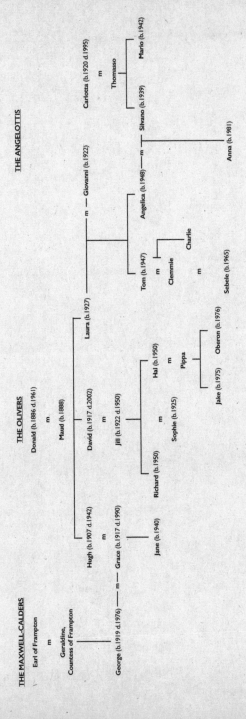

THE MAXWELL-CALDERS

THE OLIVERS

THE ANGELOTTIS

Earl of Frampton (b.1886 d.1961)
m
Geraldine, Countess of Frampton

George (b.1919 d.1976) —— m —— Grace (b.1917 d.1990)

Donald (b.1886 d.1961)
m
Maud (b.1888)

Carlotta (b.1920 d.1995)
m
Thomasso

Mario (b.1942)

Silvano (b.1939)

Giovanni (b.1922)
m

Angelica (b.1948) —— m —— Silvano (b.1939)

Anna (b.1981)

Hugh (b.1907 d.1942)
m

David (b.1917 d.2002)
m

Laura (b.1927)

Tom (b.1947)
m
Clemmie

Charlie

Jane (b.1940)

Richard (b.1950)

Jill (b.1922 d.1950)
m
Sophie (b.1925)

Hal (b.1950)
m
Pippa

Sebele (b.1965)
m

Jake (b.1975)

Oberon (b.1976)

THE STORY SO FAR

In the aftermath of the Second World War, an illegitimate baby boy is born to Laura Oliver and given up for adoption. She elopes with her Italian lover, former prisoner of war Giovanni Angelotti, from her Cotswolds family home, Chorlton, to London. The rift with Laura's parents takes years to heal. Meanwhile the young couple marries. They have a second child, Angelica, and start to build a catering business. They begin with a tiny café in Billingsgate fish market and develop a chain of Italian cafés and delicatessens, ice-cream parlours and a high-end restaurant, in London.

Laura still yearns for her lost son and bears the secret knowledge that the reason she agreed to the adoption of her baby was not because she and Giovanni were homeless, jobless and broke. It was because she knew that he could be the son, not of her husband but of her former lover, the Polish prisoner of war, Marcin. Laura tries to put this to the back of her mind. She becomes the matriarch of the family, living with Giovanni in a sprawling row of converted cottages in Paddington that also houses Giovanni's sister, Carlotta, and her two sons, Mario and

Silvano, as well as other members of the family if they are up from the country.

Angelica grows up as passionate about food and cooking as her parents are. She becomes the first female pastry cook in the Savoy Hotel kitchens and eventually a successful chef, caterer, food writer and television cook. However, her love life runs less smoothly. As a cookery student in Paris she falls disastrously in love with her charismatic but irresponsible cousin, Mario. It is years before she realises she has given her heart to the wrong brother. Eventually she marries Silvano, by now the proud tenant of a successful pub belonging to her grandparents' neighbour in the Cotswolds, the Earl of Frampton.

PART ONE

2001

CHAPTER ONE

'You OK, darling?' Angelica looked at her husband. He's exhausted, she thought, and the day hasn't begun. 'Shall I drive?'

Silvano shifted in his seat, pulling himself up a little. 'I'm fine. Be glad to get home, though. I'm less and less keen on jaunts to London.'

'Mm, but we could hardly skip Papa's birthday.'

Her watch said it was six thirty in the morning. 'We'll be home by eight,' she said, 'and you'll be at the Crabtree before anyone else.'

They were both working hard. The Crabtree, a mile from their home, was Silvano's new pub-turned-restaurant. It was due to open in two months. That meant he was deep into the organizational detail of a new venture: appointing suppliers, planting the garden, overseeing the website design, setting up training programmes, and all the while harrying the builders and decorators.

Angelica had no time to help him because her catering company, Angelica's Angels, was so busy. They had a near monopoly on the weddings and parties in the Cotswolds and had a dozen more events – weddings, barbecues, and garden parties – to cater for before the summer was over. Then there would be a steady flow of dinners, dances and parties until things hotted up at Christmas. Boxing Day was likely to be her first day off.

Angelica glanced again at Silvano's profile. He was clenching his jaw, a sure sign that he was fretting. By way of comfort she laid her hand on his thigh, patting it. He shot her a rueful smile, silently acknowledging his anxiety and her awareness of it.

When they rattled over the cattle grid – a relic from the days when Holly Farm was a working farm – and swung round the bend, they saw at once half a dozen cars parked in front of the house, only two of them familiar: Angelica's Honda hatchback and their daughter's ancient Subaru Justy.

'What the hell?' exclaimed Silvano.

Angelica knew at once. 'Oh, God,' she said. 'Anna. She must have had a party.' Silvano leapt out of the car and marched up to the front door. Angelica ran after him. 'Darling, don't be angry with her. It's her house too.'

Silvano turned to her, his key in the lock. 'Of course I'll be angry with her. If she wants a party she can at least tell us in advance, not wait for us to disappear and then . . .'

Angelica took her husband by the shoulders and forced him to meet her gaze. 'Darling, please. You're imagining a drunken orgy with the youth of the county comatose everywhere. It might not be like that at all.'

'Even if it isn't, having your friends to stay without telling your parents is bloody bad manners, isn't it?'

'Silvano, please, just let me deal with it. You go to the Crabtree and get on with the builders. Don't go into the house. Even one empty bottle will make you furious, and I'd like to have a calm discussion with Anna, not a blazing row. Please, sweetheart.'

Silvano opened the door for her, then got back into the car.

Angelica stood in the gloom of the hall for a minute, steadying herself. She hoped her stressed-out husband would have returned to his calm and gentle self by the time they met for supper. The only person ever to upset him was his daughter.

Angelica looked at her solemn face in the hall mirror. Silvano and I never used to quarrel, she thought, but for the last four years we've frequently been at odds, and always about Anna. She sighed, then walked through to the sitting room. The after-party fug of beer, cigarettes and marijuana, was thick, and there were sleeping bodies on both sofas. She went into the dining room and found one young man, wrapped in a duvet, on the mahogany table. He was snoring gently. Full ashtrays, dirty plates, glasses, wine and beer bottles were everywhere. No one stirred as she moved through the house.

Upstairs in the spare bedroom, a fully clothed couple was asleep on top of the covers. She opened her and Silvano's bedroom door, praying that their bed would be empty. But, no, it was occupied by another pair, this time between the sheets, their clothes strewn over the floor. Her chest tightening, Angelica stared at the dark head against Silvano's pillows, and a young woman's leg protruding from the bedclothes. How dare Anna let anyone sleep in their bed?

Swallowing her mounting anger, she headed for Anna's bedroom. It crossed her mind that she might find her daughter tucked up with a man, and she hesitated as she reached the door. How would she deal with that?

Then she thought, She's twenty, a lot older than I was when I had my first lover. She squared her shoulders and opened the door.

Two bodies occupied Anna's big bed, both young women. Anna was nearest to the door, and her friend Helen – Angelica recognized her short spiky hair – stirred in her sleep, then snuggled down again. Anna was lying on her back, her dark hair, wavy and thick, spread over the pillow, her full-lipped mouth half open. She was breathing softly and evenly, a picture of innocent beauty.

The familiar anguish that assailed Angelica every week, almost every day, blotted out her fury: how could someone so beautiful, so talented, so loved, so privileged be so wild? Somehow it had to be her fault, hers and Silvano's, but what had they done wrong? Anna had been a model child. True, she'd always been mischievous, insouciant and carefree, but she'd done well at school. She was out-going, happy. She'd been a joy to them. Her nature and her behaviour had completely disproved the doomsayers – Angelica's doctor, her mother, every expert she'd read on adoption, all of whom had warned against taking a near-silent four-year-old from a Romanian orphanage.

Perhaps they'd spoilt her, an indulged only child. Or maybe they shouldn't have sent her away to school. Perhaps she'd needed another kind of mother, one who hadn't worked so hard, who had been at home all the time.

Anna had been fine until puberty when, almost overnight, she'd put on a lot of weight, had become difficult and moody, unpredictable and obviously unhappy. A poisonous gang of girls had teased her mercilessly, while the school had denied any bullying, and then there'd been that truly awful business with the music master. He'd been sacked, but not before half a dozen girls had complained of him fondling and kissing them, telling each of them they were exceptionally talented, and he would make them famous music stars.

Angelica had never got to the bottom of what had really happened, and Anna had resolutely refused to talk about it, even to the counsellor the school had brought in to help the girls. After that it had been downhill all the way. Anna was expelled for smoking weed and had gone to a sixth-form crammer where she had done no work, but, as Silvano put it, had 'studied the bottom of a beer glass.'

With a heavy heart, Angelica left the girls undisturbed and went downstairs. She put the electric and the Aga kettles on to boil. There was only one clean mug in the cupboard, so she took a tray and collected all the dirty ones she could find, washed them and set them to drain. She took a sliced loaf from the freezer and started making toast.

One of the boys ambled into the kitchen. He looked bemused to see her, and she didn't bother with introductions. 'Hello,' she said. 'Could you do me a favour? Wake everyone on the ground floor and tell them to get dressed. I need you all out of here. Meanwhile I'm making everyone coffee and toast. OK?'

She carried a tray with two cups of strong coffee up to Anna's room and put it on the dressing-table. Then she knelt beside the bed and shook Anna's shoulder. Anna's large eyes, a surprisingly clear dark brown, opened, blinked, and stared straight into hers.

'Anna, there's coffee on the dressing-table. Get up and shoo everyone out as quickly as you can.'

Anna sat up with a jerk and looked around wildly, then registered Helen in the bed. She stared at her mother. 'Mum, why are you . . . ? You were going to London. I thought . . .'

Angelica could feel her anger returning. 'You thought you'd get away with it. Well, bad luck. We came home.' She stood up. 'But now is not the time to discuss it. We'll talk later. Just get up.' She turned to Helen, now awake and gazing at her, clearly horrified. 'Both of you. Right now.'

She went downstairs and cleared the kitchen table of bottles and glasses to make room for the coffee. She put out butter and marmalade, made a stack of toast, then picked up her briefcase and called up the stairs to her daughter.

'Anna, I have to go to work. There's coffee and toast in the kitchen. I'll come back at lunchtime, and by then I hope you'll have sorted the house.'

CHAPTER TWO

Helen jumped out of bed and began pulling on her clothes. 'Do you think she guessed?'

'Guessed what? About us? Nah. It wouldn't occur to her. Don't worry.'

'But, Anna, even so, you'll be in such trouble!'

Anna forced a grin. 'I'll be fine. Daddy will sulk for a day or two, and Mum will act hurt and disappointed. But it'll blow over.'

When everyone was dressed, with coffee and toast inside them, Anna called for volunteers to clean up the house. Some of her friends were patently too hungover to be of any real help and she rejected their half-hearted offers.

The half-dozen who stayed looked surprised, and faintly put out, at Anna's bossiness. She insisted that they change the sheets in her parents' room, that everything was put back in the sitting room as before, that each surface was cleaned, that the dining-room table got a rub of polish to diminish the couple of rings caused by beer cans. She made them put all the empty bottles and plastic glasses, takeaway pizza boxes, ice-cream cartons and other debris into crates and bin bags and help her load them into her car. It was a struggle, but she lowered the back seats and crammed everything in. She'd take it all to the tip later.

A few minutes later, she was doing the washing-up with her back to the door and the tap running. She didn't know anyone had come in until she felt Helen's arms go round her waist and a kiss on the nape of her neck. She turned, keeping her wet hands away from her sides as they kissed briefly.

'Hi, lover,' Helen said. 'Last night was good, wasn't it?'

'It was. Pity about my mother's rude interruption.'

'Mm. It *was* a bit hairy.'

'Never mind. There can always be a next time – but let's not get serious. I'm no good at serious.'

'Don't worry,' said Helen, reaching for a tea-towel. 'I'm never serious. Usually I'm a one-night-stand girl. But a short fling might be nice.' She picked up a mug from the draining-board to dry it. 'Where do these go?'

Anna indicated the row of hooks along the dresser and they dried the mugs, then hung them up. 'Anyway,' Helen resumed, 'will you be at the club next Friday? We could go together.'

'I'm not sure. I may be working.'

Anna knew she wouldn't be but she hated to commit to anything. Helen was great, and she liked her as a friend, even as an occasional lover, but she wasn't The One.

As she went back into the house having said goodbye to the last of her volunteers, Anna had a moment of anxiety. Her mother, she hoped, would be soothed by the transformation of the house, though she'd still be angry. But, really, what harm had they done? They'd not damaged anything. Well, not much anyway. The red wine stain on the sofa barely showed, and she'd hidden it with a cushion so she could choose her moment to confess. The ring-marks on the dining-table had all but disappeared with energetic polishing. And they'd not had any of her parents' drink. The boys had brought the booze.

Yet an uneasy clutch of anxiety persisted. What if she'd missed something – evidence of coke or weed? No, she'd scanned every inch of the house. It was fine.

Maybe, she thought, if I make an effort at repentance, rather than insisting I've nothing to be sorry for, the storm will blow over faster. She had no idea if her father would come back with her mother, but she would make lunch for the three of them – a cheese soufflé, her mother's favourite.

She laid the kitchen table and made a green salad, then turned on the oven, putting a baking tray onto the middle shelf to heat. It would give the soufflé a boost from underneath – a trick she'd learnt from her grandmother. As she made the thick white sauce she began to feel less anxious. Cooking always calmed her and lifted her spirits. She grated cheese and stirred it into the sauce until it melted, then added black pepper, Dijon mustard and paprika. The egg yolks loosened the mix a little and she left the saucepan standing in a basin of hot water, so it wouldn't cool and solidify. She put the bowl of egg whites into the Kenwood but didn't turn it on: she'd whisk and add them at the last minute. She greased the soufflé dish with butter and put it on top of the Aga to warm. If Mum was here, she thought, and I wasn't in the dog-house, she'd be impressed.

Twelve forty-five. Her mother generally returned at one. If she put the soufflé into the top oven on her arrival and took it out at one thirty, they could get the unpleasant conversation over with while it baked. Meanwhile she'd do one more thing . . .

She shrugged into her dad's Barbour and pulled on her wellies. Taking her mother's secateurs, she went out to find what she could for a conciliatory bouquet.

She'd just put the vase of pink, purple and white cosmos onto the coffee-table in the sitting room when she heard her mother's car. She hurried into the kitchen and turned on the Kenwood at full speed. Through the kitchen window she saw her mother still sitting in the driving seat. Was she listening to *The World at One*? Or girding her loins for a fight?

Anna was folding the egg whites into the cheese mixture when she heard the front door opening and her mother's keys landing in the bowl on the sideboard. She put the soufflé into the oven and swung round, forcing a big smile. But her mother didn't come into the kitchen. Anna heard her steps on the hardwood floor of the dining room, and then nothing as, presumably, she inspected the sitting room. Her steps echoed again as she crossed the hall.

'Hi, Mum.' Her heart banged, and her voice wasn't quite steady. 'Am I forgiven, do you think?'

'Oh, Anna, what is the matter with you? You're twenty, for goodness' sake, not fifteen. Why didn't you tell us you wanted a party?'

'Because I didn't know. Honestly, Mum, it just happened. We were all in the pub, and then I remembered you and Daddy were in London so I invited everyone home. We stopped off to buy pizza and ice cream . . .' As she talked Anna began to relax and her smile became less tentative. 'And, Mummy, it was such fun. We rolled up the carpet and Jamie and I taught them all to do the tango. Don went home and got his decks, and—'

'Anna, stop! Didn't it occur to you to ring us up and tell us? A quick call wouldn't have killed you.'

Anna shook her head. 'I did think of it. But I decided Dad would spend the whole night convinced we'd wreck the place, that we'd all be snorting coke and throwing up, and it would just ruin your evening.' She could see her mother softening. 'It's true, isn't it, Mum?'

Angelica smiled reluctantly. 'I suppose so. And you've obviously put in Herculean efforts to clear up. And the flowers, I presume, are by way of apology.'

Anna grinned. 'They are. But I'd have cleaned up anyway, Mum, like I usually do, before you came home. I just thought you'd go straight to the office and not be here until lunch.'

'What do you mean, like you usually do? Have you done this before?'

Anna laughed. 'Yes, of course. It's more fun to have friends here when you're away. You can see that, can't you?'

'But it's so deceitful. Surely you can understand that not telling us is wrong.'

'Even if it saves you, or at least Dad, a heap of worry? I just don't think he can handle that sort of info. He can't, can he?'

Briefly her mother closed her eyes, then shrugged.

It was going to be all right, thought Anna. Her mother would square her father and they could all forget about it. Although Dad was bound to chalk it up as more evidence of her fecklessness, like not getting a proper job, rejecting university, refusing to train as a chef. Why does he rate success so highly anyway? she wondered.

*

13

Anna's confidence in her mother's ability to soothe Silvano proved misplaced. She overheard them talking in the kitchen.

'You shouldn't indulge her, Angelica. She twists you round her little finger.'

'That's not true, darling. But I understand her better than you do. I was a wild child at her age.'

'Exactly and look what happened to you. If your parents hadn't let you run off to Paris, you might have escaped my brother.'

Anna knew the story of her mother falling in love with Uncle Mario in Paris, then ditching him and marrying her dad, but she didn't like to think of it. That her mother had actually *lived* with Mario upset her somehow. The thought of them in bed together made her feel sick. Mario could be good fun, but he was too confident of his charm, too flamboyantly Italian. That way he had of looking at you with his eyes half closed, like a cat – it was creepy.

That he and her quiet, serious dad were brothers was hard to believe. If Mario had been her father, he wouldn't have disapproved of anything. He'd have encouraged her – even wanted to join in. Anna shuddered. That would have been worse. But why did Dad have to be so strait-laced, so boring? What did it *matter* if she lacked ambition? He seemed to think she owed the world something. But that was nonsense. The world didn't need any more people jostling on the greasy pole.

One lunchtime, a few days after the party, her friend Don drove her home. She'd stayed with him and his partner, Jamie, at their flat in Tewkesbury and she had a hangover. She was still wearing last night's high heels and short, now crumpled, skirt.

She let herself into the house and made for the kitchen. She needed coffee and toast. Her father was sitting at the table, a bowl of pasta in front of him. He looked up, said nothing and gave just the slightest shake of his head. Hardly a welcome.

'Where's Mum?'

'Working. Where have you been?'

'Does it matter?'

'Yes, it does. We worry about you. Your mother barely slept.'

'But why? If I was at uni, you wouldn't worry about me. I'd be out of sight and out of mind and you'd have no idea if I didn't get home at all.'

'But if you were at university, you'd have work to do, some aim in your life.'

'Oh, Dad! You never give up, do you? What's wrong with just aiming to make enough money to keep going?'

'In a pub? Waitressing? Anna, you can't do that all your life.'

Oh, God, thought Anna, I'm not up to this. Next he'll be telling me how bright I am, how talented. How I could do anything I liked if I'd only try.

She put a hand on the side of the half-full cafetière. Still warm. Good. She poured a mug of coffee and turned to the door. She'd have a shower and come back for the toast when her father had gone.

CHAPTER THREE

Angelica came up from the country at least twice a month to see Laura and Giovanni. She told herself she was being a dutiful daughter, visiting her parents, but she knew it was more for her sake than theirs. It was a break from Angelica's Angels, Anna's waywardness and Silvano's frustration with his daughter.

They were in Laura's kitchen trying to bring an antique copper fish kettle back to life. Laura had found it in a junk shop in Goldbourne Road. It was tarnished to a deep brown, with not a glimmer of copper. But, thought Angelica, it was a beautiful thing. It was five feet long and ten inches wide, with an inner tray that was perforated with drainage holes and had handles at each end.

Angelica stretched her arms wide to reach the handles and lift out the tray. 'It's perfect,' she said. 'You could lift a forty-pound salmon out of the *court bouillon* with this, couldn't you?'

'But who would order one? Modern customers are so squeamish they can't look at a whole fish with head and tail intact.'

' Oh, I don't know. My hunting and shooting customers would be up for it, I'm sure.'

'Well, I couldn't resist it,' said Laura, 'and it'll be useful for your catering business, won't it?'

'It certainly will. We'll use it all the time. I have to get the Christmas puddings made next week, before the autumn parties take off, and it'll probably hold six or seven big ones.'

Laura mixed more flour, vinegar and salt. She claimed the paste did the job and was cheaper than copper polish. They rubbed it all over the sides and lid of the kettle, then Angelica made coffee. They drank it sitting at the kitchen table, while the paste did its work, softening the grime of years.

As so often, Angelica found herself telling her mother her troubles. 'She's twenty, Mamma, but she's behaving like a teenager.'

'Darling, she's a lovely girl underneath all that bluster. You know that.'

'It's hard to believe it at the moment. She's not happy, though she insists she is.'

'Does she have a boyfriend? I've never met one.'

'She's never had one. There've been plenty of lads sniffing around her, and she has lots of friends, girls and men, but no boyfriend. No.'

'Maybe that's why she's not happy.'

'Maybe. I don't think she likes herself much. Sometimes I think she doesn't even like us much . . . She behaves much better with you. I know she loves her *nonna*, at least.'

'Well, you know she can always come here. I'd love to have her.'

'Thanks, Mamma. Maybe it'll come to that.'

They returned to cleaning the fish kettle, Laura using a Brillo pad on the bottom while Angelica scrubbed round the handles with a toothbrush and a lot of elbow grease. Gradually the copper began to show.

Half an hour later, Laura stood back. 'I think that's the best we can do. Now we need to get rid of the muck.'

The kettle was too big for the sink, so they carried it up to the bathroom, washed off the paste and dried it with an old towel.

Back in the kitchen Angelica surveyed their handiwork. 'Pretty good. At least you can see it's copper now.'

Laura produced a tin of Brasso. 'Yes, and proper polish will give it a glow. That homemade stuff works a treat, but it doesn't make it shine.'

While they rubbed the sides and lid of the fish kettle, Laura returned to the subject of Anna. 'You have to remember she had the worst possible start in life. That must leave some scars.'

Angelica nodded. 'The consultant we spoke to before we adopted her warned us of the likely problems with a child as ill-treated as those babies in Romanian orphanages. He warned us she might not speak for years, that she might be claustrophobic from being confined in a cot for years, might be undersized and grow very slowly, might have eating disorders. And, Mum, we felt so pleased with ourselves when none of it happened. She was such an excited, lively, smiling child, wasn't she? It's only now that she's so difficult. I don't know how we went wrong.'

'You did nothing wrong, darling,' said Laura. 'Anna is a lovely girl, and she'll come right. She's given you years of happiness and she's healthy, strong, and still here. Adoption can never be plain sailing, I'm sure.'

Something in her mother's voice made Angelica look up. Laura was staring at the fish kettle, her mouth tight.

'Mamma,' said Angelica, slowly, 'did you worry about the baby you gave away? My brother?'

When her mother didn't answer Angelica regretted the

question. They'd hardly ever spoken of that baby. Giovanni had only told Angelica about him when she was grown-up, and he'd warned her then that her mother never spoke of it.

Angelica had once suggested they try to find him, but her mother had cut her off. 'No,' she'd said. 'We promised to stay out of his life. If adoption is ever going to work, it needs the child to see their new mother as their only mother.'

'But he's grown-up now,' she'd argued. 'I'd love to find him.'

'No.' Laura's voice had brooked no argument. Giovanni had caught his daughter's eye and shaken his head.

Now Angelica leant over the table and touched her mother's forearm. 'Did you, Mamma? Did you worry about him?'

Laura looked up at her. 'I still do,' she said. 'He'd be fifty-four now.'

CHAPTER FOUR

Tom stood at the window of his Docklands penthouse, thirty storeys above the Thames. He'd been there a while, idly watching the river traffic. The tourist cruisers crept along, giving the guides time to describe the sights: the Millennium Dome, the Maritime Museum, the *Cutty Sark*. He watched a barge, stuffed with refuse, moving slowly downstream, then the speedy river-bus, efficiently disgorging its City-suited passengers.

A young woman in an orange dress stood out in the predominantly dark-suited male crowd. She jumped off the ferry ramp, strode away from the other passengers and set off across the square. She looked like a child's toy from up there, and he couldn't see her face, but he admired the speed and confidence of her walk. I bet she's good-looking too, he thought, feeling a little flush of interest.

He reached for his binoculars to get a better look. As he focused on the woman, she lifted her head to look up the wide steps that formed a spacious plinth to his apartment building.

Tom burst out laughing. She was Susan, his girlfriend. The twinge of lust for a stranger, strong enough to make him peer at her through binoculars, had been sparked by the woman he'd been with for four years. The woman he'd not slept with for, what, a month? Six weeks?

The laughter had been genuine. He'd been laughing at himself, caught out, a fifty-four-year-old man ogling a young woman in secret. But as he put down the binoculars, guilt overtook amusement. Poor Susan, she so badly wanted them to get married. 'The trouble with you, Tom, is you're married to Ajax,' she'd said. 'That company owns you, body and soul. You've less and less time for us.'

There was some truth in that. But signing up to a lifelong commitment just seemed so unnecessary. Until about a year ago Susan had never mentioned marriage – she'd always declared herself bored by the idea of domesticity. She never cooked anything, had never ironed a shirt in her life and hated the idea of children, which suited him fine. He'd never risk another child. Not after Charlie.

Susan had her business selling picture copyrights to travel companies and ad agencies and she was definitely 'a woman of independent means'. Although, thought Tom, with wry affection, that doesn't prevent her dipping into my pocket for a new pair of Manolo Blahnik shoes or a Jean Muir coat.

Tom knew he was the cause of her discontent, but it puzzled him. They had a good relationship, they seldom quarrelled, they'd had some great holidays together in fancy places, and he always felt proud to have her on his arm. True, they weren't besotted with each other, but she'd never before had this (mostly unspoken but always there) need to be told she was beautiful, that he loved her. Her wanting constant reassurance was quite recent, since she'd turned forty. It irritated him a little. He did love her, as much as he could. But he knew perfectly well, which he couldn't tell her, that he'd never love anyone as much as he'd loved Clemmie.

By the time Tom heard the lift doors to their penthouse open and Susan's heels on the floor, he had the shaker of margaritas in one hand and two chilled glasses, rimmed with salt, in the other. He walked across the wide stretch of polished stone to kiss her. 'I was watching you get off the ferry. I thought, That's one good-looking bird in the orange dress, then you looked up and I saw it was you.'

She smiled and dropped her briefcase on a chair. 'Was it a disappointment?'

'Of course not. Just shows my taste hasn't changed, and you look as sexy as ever.' Her face lit up and she came close again for a more serious kiss, but he avoided it, waving the shaker and glasses by way of excuse. He put the glasses on the coffee-table and poured the cocktails, rather regretting his gallantry. Why had he said that about her being sexy? Out of guilt? Because he wished he still found her so?

'How was your day?' He must have asked her the same question five times a week for the past four years.

'Oh, OK. Exhausting.' She sank into the sofa and pushed off her shoes. 'I bought a great archive of war pictures from the widow of an Israeli photographer.'

'War photos?'

'Uh-huh. Lots of blood and guns and action stuff, which will be good for book jackets and DVDs. Other than that, we've just been very busy selling photos.'

Tom handed her a drink and she took a sip. 'Lovely,' she said. 'You did the salt thing.'

Tom smiled. 'It's hardly difficult when the fridge produces

the crushed ice and Yen leaves everything else ready to go.' Yen was their Filipina help. He sat down and reached for his drink. 'Maybe we should tell her not to whizz the mangoes for daiquiris as well. We hardly ever drink them any more.'

'I know, but then she makes the juice into smoothies for breakfast. Which I like.'

'She's a marvel. She does everything like a pro. My shirts look as if they've just arrived from Turnbull & Asser.'

'She was doing fourteen-hour days at her last job, babysitting and the school run as well as everything else. Coming here must be a relief.'

'Well, long may she last.' Tom took a gulp of his drink. 'So, back to your day. How's the new assistant?'

'OK, I think. She worked for the Hulton Picture Library so I guess she knows what she's doing.'

They chatted on, Tom telling her about a deal he was working on, advising a medium-size pharmaceutical client on the acquisition of one of its key competitors. 'If we close tomorrow, which with luck we will, I'll be out with the boys in the evening, getting smashed. I'm really too old for such shenanigans, but since I'm the boss . . .'

'Will you get a bonus?'

'Not directly. It goes into the team's pool and will be a million and a half. But I'm not complaining. My bonus is based on overall profits, which are obscene, according to the *Guardian*. I do see their point.'

It was nine thirty by the time they got to the new Mark Stone restaurant, with a long bar and probably a hundred people at tables. The bar was packed with none-too-sober City types drinking champagne and braying at the top of their voices. Tom's heart sank, but Susan was in her element. She swung in, smiling, waving, air-kissing. Ten minutes ago, she'd declared herself exhausted but, thought Tom, the sound of conspicuous consumption had revived her.

The noise was deafening, and even though they had a table to the side, Tom was having trouble hearing her across it. He switched his seat to sit closer to her.

'You're going deaf, Tom,' she teased.

'Don't think so, but this joint's too noisy, that's for sure.'

'We could have gone to Pétrus. It's all holy hush and gastronomy there.'

'And it means a jacket, a taxi into the West End and leaning on Marcus to give us a table. Too much hassle.'

They ate grilled duck breasts with Szechuan pepper and parsnip mash, occasionally interrupted by a colleague of his or Susan's. Then, over the panna cotta, Susan came back to the question of marriage. 'It wouldn't kill you, Tom. We get on better than most of the married couples we know, don't we?'

'Of course we do.' Here we go again, he thought. How many times have we had this conversation? But somehow it was like stepping onto an escalator: once on the first step, there was no going back. 'But what's changed, Susan? You were never one for wedding bells. I thought we were alike in that. It was part of the reason we were attracted to each other, wasn't it?' He spoke gently. He'd no wish to hurt her but marrying again would seem a betrayal of Clemmie. He dismissed the thought. Plenty of people got married without the kind of love he'd had with Clemmie, total and all-encompassing. But he couldn't tell her she'd be second best, that he could never really, really love her.

'I want to be married, Tom, that's all. Is that so bad? All my friends are married. I feel like an old maid. And it wouldn't change anything for you. I don't want to give up work and be a little housewife or anything. I just want a bloody ring on my finger!'

'Are you sure it's not that you want the wedding day? Big party, white dress, centre of attention. I can understand that, but it's marriage we're talking about . . .' He stopped. 'No, that was unfair. I'm sorry.' He held her gaze and reached for her hand. 'Or is it because you've changed your mind and want children? Because if it's that, darling, I'm not the man for you.' He didn't like to suggest it might be too late for her anyway.

'Hell, no. Of course not,' she snapped. 'I've never wanted them. I'm not about to lose my figure or my independence for kids, that's for sure.'

'Wouldn't you lose your independence with marriage?'

'Of course not.' Her laugh had an edge of harshness. 'This is 2001, not 1901.'

He looked at her flushed face, her eyes bright with anger or distress. Both, he suspected. He lifted the bottle of burgundy, but it was empty. 'Would you like another glass?' She shook her head, and he signalled for the waiter, ordering one for himself.

The little interruption seemed to calm her, and also to fortify her. She took a breath. 'Oh, Tom, you have to give in. It's just not fair, is it?'

'What's not fair, darling? I've never been unfair to you, have I?'

'No, not you personally. But, well, you can go on pulling the birds, can't you? Probably till you're eighty. You look great, slim, and not a grey hair in sight. Like some model for hair dye. Meanwhile I'm in the hairdresser touching up my colour every three weeks.'

'You know very well I'm not after any birds,' Tom said, 'and you look ten years younger than you are. You're absolutely gorgeous.'

He meant what he was saying. She was a classic beauty, with her wide mouth, straight nose, blonde hair cut like a boy's to show off her long neck and perfectly shaped head.

Gratified, she smiled a little foolishly, her eyes softening and meeting his in the old intimate promise he knew so well. Yes, he thought, we'll make love tonight.

They walked home along the empty streets, his arm around her. She was silent, her head tucked into his shoulder. He could smell her hair, clean and delicious.

She had a point. He was being unfair. If he lacked the courage to leave her, he'd no right to keep her dangling. She was the same woman she'd always been, as good-looking, cool and hard-working as always. And he felt for her. There was such a negative ring to 'spinster' or 'single woman' that didn't apply to bachelors, even to men of his age. Of course I don't love her as I loved Clemmie, he thought. But does it matter? Hearts and flowers were not essential for marriage. So why not just do it?

Her heels clicked on the stone slabs as they walked. He tightened his arm round her, smiling to himself. Perhaps, he thought, I'll give her a ring in some swanky restaurant in Paris or something. Make up for all my hesitation and churlishness. But then he had a sudden memory of the night he'd given Clemmie a ring in Giovanni's and knew he couldn't do that.

Still, he could leave the ring on her pillow. No getting down on one knee, though. There were limits.

*

A fortnight later Tom was at his desk eating a sandwich and checking the firm's expenses on his screen. Could they really have spent that much in a month? There were only eight London partners, but between them their expenses amounted to almost as much as the total salary bill. His own exes were a lot less than his partners' and he'd like to think that was because, as the senior partner, he was setting a good example. But the truth was that even his claims were phenomenal. Did existing clients and targets, FTSE chairmen and CEOs really have to eat in Michelin-starred restaurants all the time, and did he need to hire private jets to save a few hours?

He scrolled down to bring up the New York office expenses. As usual Gerard's claims were moderate, even modest. How did he do it, in a city even better known for its excesses than London? Tom found himself smiling. I love that guy, he thought.

He and Gerard had been through a lot together. They'd met at Eton, taken their degrees at Edinburgh, cut their teeth in investment banking in the City. They'd shared a flat while at Harvard Business School and ended up together at Merrill Lynch. The only time they'd really been apart was when Tom had left to set up Ajax and Merrill Lynch had sent Gerard to their New York office. But they still saw a lot of each other as they criss-crossed the Atlantic for work. Then, when Ajax needed a New York base, Gerard had resigned from Merrill Lynch to head up the office. Brothers could not have been closer.

Tom was the man with the energy and ideas while Gerard was the intellectual, who did the research and got the deals right, working away tirelessly on the detail. Tom knew Ajax would never have done so well without him. He'd said so once, and Gerard had laughed.

'Nonsense. You'd have found some other geek to do my bit. It's your talent for networking and your big smile that bring in the punters.' Gerard had grinned and punched his arm. 'Plus you're a past master at bullshit.'

Gerard's downtown office was modern and smart, but not grand. His New York acquaintances regarded him as an English eccentric, mainly because he didn't drink, gamble, or take clients to nightclubs. He went home to his family at six o'clock, did not work at weekends, and preferred to entertain clients, if he had to, at a neighbourhood seafood restaurant where he encouraged them to have the lump crab, a glass of Sauvignon Blanc and be done with it. He liked to be back in his office at two thirty. Gerard had always had a quiet charisma that allowed him to break the mould.

Tom thought now, as he often did, how much he owed Gerard. After Clemmie and Charlie's deaths, he had been near-useless for a month. Gerard had run both offices, steadying the ship with good sense and calm, while also being the best friend a man could have. Not a day had passed without Gerard calling him. 'Just checking on you, pal,' he'd say.

Clemmie had liked Gerard's wife almost as much as he liked Gerard. Born in Virginia, Jemima could have played a Southern belle in *Gone With the Wind*: classic features, flawless skin, tall with a wasp waist and a Southern drawl. When Gerard had first shown him a picture of her, Tom had fallen into the trap of assuming beauty went with brainlessness. But when he and Clemmie met her – Gerard had brought her to dinner at their London house – he had realized her modesty concealed a formidable intellect.

The two families enjoyed at least one holiday a year together.

As a foursome they'd travelled together in South Africa as well as India. When the children arrived, they went to Disney World, on safari, and to stay on a ranch in Montana. Christmases were spent together, skiing. But Tom had not seen Jemima or the girls since he'd lost his wife and son. He couldn't face it. Imagine holiday snaps without Clemmie and Charlie.

Tom wrenched his mind back to his partners' expense accounts. Damon was the worst offender. Last month alone his client-schmoozing had included grouse-shooting, trips to the opera, dining in posh restaurants and staying in the best hotels in Dubai, Paris and Shanghai. It made Tom feel faintly sick but there wasn't much he could do about it. Next to him, Damon brought in the most business. He was gold. If Tom tried to clip his wings, there were half a dozen firms in London, Geneva or New York who would snap him up, give him an eye-watering golden hello, unlimited expenses and twice the money he earned at Ajax.

The City, thought Tom, has gone mad. People talked about working hard and playing hard as if it were a sort of religion. The young traders were high on bonuses, snorting coke and quaffing Dom Pérignon. The senior partners, like those at Ajax, were older and soberer, but they still lived like kings and worked ridiculous hours. No wonder Damon's marriage had fallen apart. Come to think of it, all his partners were on their second or third marriages, except Gerard, who'd been happily married to Jemima for more than twenty years.

Suddenly the screen on the wall opposite Tom's desk, usually set to City prices, was showing a picture of a skyscraper belching smoke with an excited American voice reporting '. . . causing a massive explosion in the North Tower of the World Trade Center. Oh, my God . . .'

Tom's door burst open and Damon rushed in with Eliza, Tom's PA, and several others. 'Christ, Tom, someone's flown a fucking plane into the World Trade Center!'

Tom jumped up and flipped the channel to the BBC, which had the same pictures of billowing black smoke from near the top of the building.

The men watched, transfixed, as more pictures revealed great rolling balls of orange flame. No one spoke as smoke poured out of a dozen or more floors three-quarters of the way up the tower.

And then realization hit Tom, like a gut punch. 'Oh, Jesus. Gerard! Gerard's office is in there!'

They were all talking at once, 'It's OK. They'll be fine. The office is in the South Tower.'

'Are we sure it's not the South that's hit?'

'No, no, it's the North. Isn't it? I'm sure he said the North Tower.'

Tom was pressing Gerard's name on his phone. 'It's engaged. Oh, Jesus, I guess he's calling Jemima.'

As they watched the screen, they saw tiny figures appear at the windows, more and more of them, black smoke above and beside them. They were a hundred or more storeys up, waving frantically for help. The hopelessness of their plight was desperate to watch. 'Where the hell are the helicopters? They could lift them off the roof, surely!' cried Damon.

Tom kept trying Gerard's phone. He tried the landline too and could hear it ringing but no one answered. And then, suddenly, he heard Gerard's voice. 'Hi, Tom, I was about to ring you. You know what's happened?' He sounded almost normal.

'Yes. Where are you?'

'I'm in the Sky Lobby. It's OK, Tom. We've had an announcement from the security guys. This building is secure, and they say to go back to our desks. I guess they have enough to do evacuating the North Tower.'

The relief made Tom's legs weak. 'He's OK, everyone,' he said to the others. 'Do you know what's going on, Gerard? It's . . .'

'Yes, we're watching CNN. Apparently, it was a plane, not an internal explosion. I just hope . . .' Tom could hear someone shouting in the background. Gerard went on, talking quickly: 'Tom, I'll call you back. I just need to check we're all present and correct. If we do evacuate I'd like all our guys together. At the moment we're missing Jo and Paula.'

Tom put his phone back into his pocket. 'They're fine. They're in that lobby near the top of the building. Gerard wants to get them all together and he's just trying to locate Paula and Jo.'

Tom looked across at Eliza. She and Paula, Gerard's assistant, were best friends. She was staring wide-eyed at the screen, tears running down her face as people began to leap out of the North Tower windows. One after another, over and over, people were jumping to their deaths. They all stared, mesmerized at the tiny figures falling, falling, one after another, sometimes two or three together, twisting and turning as they fell past floor after floor.

'Oh, God,' whispered Eliza. 'No one on the upper floors will get out.'

Tom put an arm round her. 'It's unbelievable. Horrific. But at least the South Tower is OK. Our guys will be fine.'

No one sat down. No one answered the landlines. All eyes remained glued to the television screen. Occasionally someone would glance at their mobile phone and answer briefly or deflect the call.

31

And then, just after two o'clock, about three-quarters of an hour after the disaster, Tom's phone buzzed.

It was Gerard.

'Gerard, hi. What's up?'

'Just thought I'd tell you we're evacuating after all. Just been told to make an orderly exit, and we're all present and correct. But I guess it'll be chaos down there so don't expect to hear from me soon. I'll speak to you when I can.'

'Sure, old chap. Good luck.'

'We'll be fine. I'll call you.'

Tom had just relayed this information to the others when they saw a silver passenger plane flying steadily across the screen. And straight into the South Tower. Gerard's building.

Everyone cried out or gasped, but no one said a word. They all watched, appalled, as the plane ploughed deep into the building, erupting into flame, igniting everything in its path. A huge lump of something, maybe part of the plane, fell away, out of the building and somersaulted to the ground.

Tom stared in horror at the building. The camera was in close-up, trained on those waving, jumping, falling people. Then another picture showed the whole South Tower and the reporter's voice identified the plane's entry point as between the seventieth and eighty-fifth floors.

Tom was the first to speak, 'What floor is the Sky Lobby? Does anyone know?'

'Seventy-eighth, I think,' said Damon.

Tom spent the rest of the day and evening watching the continuing horrors unfold as both towers collapsed, taking desperate calls from relatives of his staff, from colleagues, clients and business friends. He told everyone the same thing: that he'd spoken to Gerard less than two minutes before the plane hit, when he and the rest of the Ajax team were on the seventy-eighth floor about to evacuate the building. The worst call was with Jemima.

'I know, Tom,' she said, 'but I've watched the film of the plane over and over. It didn't hit the middle of the building, did it? It went in skewed, near a corner. Maybe they got down on the other side. We don't know where on the Sky Lobby they were.'

She was clutching at straws, her voice pleading for agreement, for him to tell her she might be right. 'Darling Jemima, I don't think they could have got out, and the whole building collapsed an hour later. Of course, we don't know for certain. We can do nothing but wait.'

She didn't want to believe him. She kept saying she'd spoken to him just as he was about to leave the building. The lifts were very fast: surely they could have got out in time. But why hadn't he called? Maybe he was helping with the rescue operations. Maybe he'd forgotten his cell phone.

Tom didn't press it. The horrendous truth would make its way through her resistance soon enough. He told her he would be with her as soon as planes were taking off again and he could get on a flight.

For the next three days Tom was on auto-pilot, spending almost all his time in the office. He couldn't relate to Susan and found himself hoping she'd be asleep when he got home. If she was still up, he went to bed, unable to talk about it.

She did her best to be comforting. 'You should get some sleep, darling. You're going around with the weight of the world on your shoulders. But it's not your fault.'

Tom shook his head. He couldn't explain.

33

He concentrated on three things: to give what information and comfort he could – mostly financial – to the relatives of his five dead colleagues; to try to assess the damage to the business; and to do his best to rally the London staff. Meanwhile he was going from one crisis meeting to the next.

He tried to hold despair at bay. The business, he hoped, would survive the disaster because, to put it brutally, they'd only lost one partner out of nine, and the New York business was as yet only eight per cent of the total. Gerard's main value had been in his information and advice, which would be hard to replace, but not impossible. It wasn't as if Ajax's head office had been wiped out with all its staff, like that of Cantor Fitzgerald – they'd occupied five floors and lost at least six hundred people.

All Ajax's New York work was backed up in London, so information wasn't the problem. It was a question of assigning the work to the London partners, discovering what damage any of their New York clients or associates had suffered, and deciding with them the way forward.

But for all his encouraging words, he couldn't be sure they'd survive. The New York Stock Exchange had closed and no one had a clue what would happen next.

He made himself put aside his grief at the loss of his best friend and concentrate on the practicalities. He got Eliza to sit on the phone and move heaven and earth to get him on the earliest possible flight to New York. It seemed flights might resume by 14 September, but every American in Europe was desperate to get home, and all flights were booked. He abandoned his new resolution not to charter planes, but there wasn't one to be had. Eliza finally got him an economy seat on American Airlines five days after the disaster, by which time Jemima had accepted that Gerard was dead. They were all dead.

New York was in a state of shock. On Monday the NYSE reopened, 12 per cent down. Tom spent a week with Jemima and the girls in the Connecticut house. Each morning he set off to visit one or other of the bereaved families. He uttered the same platitudes, watched the widows' or parents' (or, in Paula's case, boyfriend's) tears, and felt his heart wrenched with pity, his soul racked with guilt.

He hadn't expected to feel guilty, but he did. Guilty for being alive when the others were dead. The five who'd died hadn't wasted their lives, as he suspected he was wasting his. They'd had real reasons to live: people they loved, people who depended on them.

Once, on a train back to Connecticut, he let out a gasping sob, and then he was crying, hiccuping like a child, scrabbling for a handkerchief, saying, 'Sorry, sorry,' to his fellow travellers. A woman handed him a packet of tissues and he accepted them, unable to speak, even to say, 'Thank you.' The man sitting next to him patted his shoulder. No one asked what was wrong. New York was full of devastated people breaking down in public.

When his tears subsided, Tom sat looking out of the train window. He hadn't ever cried like this, not even when Clemmie and Charlie died. He remembered snivelling quietly in the dormitory when bullied by the bigger boys in the Swiss holiday home. He'd been six then. Gerard's death had cleaved him open.

Calmer now, he tried to work out why he'd been sobbing. The loss of Clemmie and Charlie? The loss of Gerard? His own loneliness? The pointlessness of his existence? All of it.

On the red-eye back to London, Tom thought he'd be exhausted enough to sleep. But his mind kept returning to the unfairness of Fate. If he'd died in that inferno, what would it have mattered? Not to anyone, except perhaps Susan, who would miss the security and status that came with a well-heeled fiancé.

How had he been so weak as to agree to marriage? He'd finally bought Susan a ring, the day before the disaster. Why, for God's sake? Because she wanted it so much and he'd run out of reasons to duck and dive. But he saw now, with absolute clarity, that he didn't love her, that their relationship was about form and convenience, not love.

I'm not cut out for love, he thought. Until Clemmie blasted into my world and lit it up, I'd no bloody idea what love was.

Did he love his parents? He didn't think so. He was grateful to them, of course: they'd adopted him, given him a good home and a smart education. But why had they taken him on? he wondered. They were so distant: his dad formal and strict, with that ramrod stance and disapproving mouth, giving him a formal handshake on his arrival home from school or university, his mother dispensing the occasional brief hug to signify hello or goodbye.

There'd been a succession of nannies, some cruel, some kind, but none had stayed long enough for him to remember their names now. Not surprising, really: he'd been at boarding school from the age of seven and spent most holidays in that children's holiday hotel in Switzerland. At least he'd learnt to ski in winter and got a taste for walking alone in summer. He was grateful for that. He didn't think he minded the lack of affection. He didn't feel deprived, maybe because he'd never really known love. His mum and dad had done their best, he supposed.

Tom seldom drank on transatlantic flights. He needed to

be alert for early-morning or late-night meetings. But now, exhausted yet sleepless, he pressed the service button and ordered a whisky. The attendant brought him two miniature double-shot bottles of Johnnie Walker. He was about to refuse one but changed his mind. Maybe he'd need both. He drank one with water and closed his eyes.

While they were alive he'd dutifully visited his parents in their retirement home. They'd had a double bedroom and sitting room, and predictably kept themselves to themselves. When he'd got engaged to Clemmie he'd taken her to meet them and was annoyed when Clemmie's friendliness and obvious happiness did not disturb their habitual coolness. After they were married Tom had offered to let Clemmie off the duty visits. But she'd said, 'No, poor things, they don't mean to be cold. They're just proud, hanging on to their dignity. I bet they're lonely underneath.'

From then on, it was Clemmie who insisted on more frequent visits. When Charlie was born, Tom thought if anything could crack though his parents' reserve, their adorable baby would. But no. His father barely looked at the baby, and when Clemmie put Charlie into his mother's arms, she promptly gave him back.

When, a few years ago, they'd died within months of each other, a year after Clemmie and Charlie, he'd felt nothing, except alone, and oddly grateful that he hadn't loved his adoptive parents. He could not have borne more grief.

After the second whisky, Tom slept, but woke bleary-eyed and desperate for a shower. Unable to face Susan, who might still be at home, he climbed into his waiting Mercedes and was driven straight to his office. He would shower there.

As he rubbed shampoo into his head and face and let the hot

water course down his body, he told himself he should somehow change his life. There must be more to it than work, money and a decorative fiancée? There had to be.

On the Sunday morning after he returned from New York, he and Susan were sitting in the conservatory on the penthouse deck, eating breakfast. It was a sun trap in summer but there'd been no sun for weeks and now it was raining.

Susan was flipping through the *Sunday Times* Style magazine while Tom watched the raindrops running down the glass in uneven lines, as if in a race to the bottom. Sometimes drops would bump into each other, join and go faster. It was hypnotic.

He should talk to her. He'd promised her he wouldn't go to the office, and here he was, sitting in silence. The only thing he wanted to say was that he couldn't marry her, but he hadn't the energy, or the heart, for that conversation.

Since their engagement Susan had been much more relaxed. At first he'd been amused by her delight in her ring, a horrendously expensive diamond. She would stretch out her hand and twist it so that the stone caught the light. She did that now and he read her thoughts. She was about to talk to him about the wedding, the date, her dress, the venue. He couldn't face it. He stood up. 'I'm sorry, Susie, but I must go to the office after all.'

CHAPTER FIVE

Angelica had hoped to avoid a big family party at Christmas. She spent so much of her time cooking for the catering company, and the run-up to Christmas was so busy, she felt she wanted never to see another turkey or smoked-salmon canapé. Her plan was to have a quiet Christmas Day with Silvano and Anna, and that would be that. They'd probably eat veal or duck – certainly not turkey. But then an invitation had come from Aunt Sophie at Chorlton to a slightly delayed Christmas lunch party on 29 December. They couldn't celebrate on Christmas Day, said Sophie, because so many of them were working over Christmas.

This would be Sophie's first Christmas without David, Laura's late brother. Angelica knew they'd have to go.

David had died a year ago, on Millennium night. His death hadn't been totally unexpected – a stroke thirty years earlier had put him in a wheelchair and by eighty-three he'd been very frail – but it was still a horrible shock. Everyone had been at Chorlton for the Millennium party, three generations of Angelottis and Olivers. She remembered the family group standing on the terrace, heads back and mouths open to emit prolonged aahs as rockets exploded overhead, sending repeating bursts of white stars into the black sky.

After the last chime of Big Ben, they'd all hugged and kissed each other. Happy New Year. Happy New Year. They'd shuffled into a ragged circle, arms crossed and linked, and begun to sing 'Auld Lang Syne'.

They'd hardly got through two lines when Angelica noticed Sophie's daughter-in-law, Pippa, bent over David's wheelchair. She'd watched her straighten up and turn towards the singers, her face distraught. Then Pippa was shouting, and everyone turned towards her, the singing trailing away to silence. David's head was thrown back, his face contorted, his eyes open. He was already dead.

Angelica reread Sophie's email. She'd invited the whole extended family. With the events of that horrible night brought back so vividly, Angelica closed her eyes, steeling herself. Poor Sophie. Of course they must go.

Angelica was still worrying about Anna. Since her unsanctioned party earlier in the year her daughter and Silvano had barely spoken. Silent and moody, Anna had been out of the house, working or with friends, or holed up in her bedroom, refusing to be drawn.

'I'm fine, Mum. Leave me alone.'

But then, a few days before Christmas, she had seemed almost back to her younger self, cheerful and even helpful. Angelica had promised Sophie she'd bring a Christmas pudding to Chorlton, thinking the business still had some left over from the ones they'd made in September, but had then found they'd all gone. Resigned to making one, she was surprised when Anna firmly took over. 'I'll do it, Mum. You need a holiday from cooking,' she'd said, 'and since Richard has a week off from cheffing at Giovanni's, he'll be doing the turkey. So you're off the hook for once.' Anna drove to the village shop, bought all the ingredients, and made a huge, perfectly round cannonball of a Christmas pudding that took six hours to steam. She made brandy butter and vanilla ice cream too.

Angelica couldn't believe it. Her daughter hadn't once complained about anything, had done her own washing-up, and seemed altogether relaxed and happy. She and Silvano exchanged a surreptitious glance of shared content. Maybe Anna was coming out of whatever had ailed her.

On Christmas Day, Anna was still cheerful, helping with roasting the duck and pleased with her presents, a Nokia mobile phone and a fake fox-fur jacket.

On the day of the Chorlton party, Anna came downstairs wearing a red dress, high heels and her new fur jacket. She spun round in a circle. 'What do you think?'

She'd curled her long hair into loose ringlets that lifted as she turned. Her eyes were made up and she was wearing a glossy red lipstick, the colour of her dress. Silvano, who'd been polishing his shoes at the kitchen sink, put cloth and shoe down to kiss her. 'You look lovely.'

Angelica, her heart lifting at the sight of them smiling at each other, said, 'You do look good. Red suits you.'

They arrived to find the lovely old farmhouse decorated in the old-fashioned way, just holly and ivy from the farm, with red apples, bowls of walnuts and candles everywhere. It looked mellow and inviting.

The whole family was there. Hal, Angelica's cousin who farmed Chorlton, and his son, Jake, were pouring drinks. Her parents,

Laura and Giovanni, had come down from London a couple of days before, and Richard, Hal's twin brother, had arrived yesterday with a car full of food, plus his enormous lurcher, Tatiana, and Silvano's renegade brother, Mario. Everyone except Richard, who was busy doing last-minute preparation in the kitchen, was in the sitting room drinking champagne.

Angelica looked at Mario, wondering how she could ever have been in love with him. That she'd very nearly married the wrong brother still gave her an occasional shudder of horror, followed by a wash of relief, like waking from a nightmare. Although, if you didn't know about his mood swings and depression, Mario could be exhilarating company. She listened to him complaining, only half joking, about the dog fogging the car windows and trying to usurp him from the passenger seat. 'She's a canine JCB, that dog. She just shoves her snout under your thigh and burrows away until you shift. She's spoilt rotten,' he said, heaving the lurcher off the sofa and shooing her towards the kitchen.

'No, Mario, don't put her in the kitchen!' cried Sophie. 'Richard's cooking and she'll make off with the turkey.' She lowered her voice: 'Last night she snatched the ham. I rescued it, gave it a rinse, re-glazed it with sugar and mustard and whacked it back in the oven. It was delicious.'

Richard came in. 'We have lift-off, I think,' he said.

'No, darling,' said his mother, 'we're waiting for Jane.'

That woman is always late, thought Angelica. If she can find a way of being annoying, she will. She arrives last at any gathering, like the Queen.

When Lady Jane did arrive, she made no apology, and stood near the door, forcing everyone to come to her. Anna was nearest, and Angelica was pleased to see her daughter give Jane a warm smile, a kiss on the cheek and wish her a cheerful happy Christmas.

'It's a bit late for that, isn't it?' said Jane.

God, the woman's ungracious, thought Angelica. She stepped closer, about to protest that there were twelve days to Christmas, but Jane seemed to regret her rudeness and quickly said, 'It's good to see you, Anna.'

'How are things at Frampton?' Angelica asked. 'I saw the stacks of Frampton Christmas hampers in Browns. That looked like a good idea.'

'Did you buy one?'

'Er, no. Sorry.' Angelica put an arm round Anna. 'My eco-friendly daughter insists I buy organic.'

'Huh.' Jane snorted. She turned back to Anna. 'Don't tell me you're like Jake here, banging on about greenhouse gases and saving the planet, are you?'

She was smiling, but Angelica detected the malice. She opened her mouth, but Anna got in first. 'Yes, or, rather, I would be if anyone would listen. Jake and Hal are principled farmers, but with most producers pooh-poohing the evidence and continuing to screw more money out of the earth by poisoning it, there's not a lot of point.' Anna gave Jane a tight smile and turned away. Angelica watched her daughter link her arm through Jake's, saying something in his ear. They both smiled, and Jake looked across at Jane and her. But Jane, now being welcomed by Sophie, didn't notice.

There were thirteen for lunch, so Sophie had laid a place for Richard's teddy bear, his feet and cheeks bald from too much loving fifty years ago. Richard's delight at the reunion made everyone laugh. He lifted the bear, looked into his face and nuzzled him into his neck. 'Well, old Ted, still with us!' He looked fondly at Sophie. 'Where did you find him, Mum?' His lurcher, jealous, sprang up on her hind legs to lick his face. Richard, laughing, pushed her down. 'Don't, Tatty.'

'I was clearing out your dad's things,' said Sophie. 'Ted was on the top shelf of his wardrobe. God knows why he kept him.'

Angelica noticed the slight tremor in Sophie's last words. Poor thing, she thought. It's only been a year.

Lunch was delicious, of course. Sophie had checked that the Angelottis would be eating Italian on the twenty-fifth, leaving her free to serve the traditional English turkey and plum pud they'd had for fifty years. Nearly everything came from Chorlton Farms: the turkey, potatoes, carrots, sprouts, all cooked to perfection by Richard. The conversation was light-hearted and merry, getting noisier as they reached the Christmas pudding and port.

Angelica was pleased with Anna's pudding. It was perfectly balanced between firm and crumbly, and the Christmassy aroma of nutmeg, cloves and cinnamon filled the room.

Now Sophie was offering second helpings. 'Where's Anna?' she asked. 'She's been gone for ages, and she made this pudding.'

Anna's plate was untouched. Angelica felt a little current of anxiety. She stood up. 'I'll go and see.'

She met Anna on the stairs and saw with relief that she was fine. Indeed, she bounced down the stairs, brushing past her mother. 'Hi, Mum,' she said. 'Is everyone getting up? Have I missed the pudding? Was it all right?'

Angelica followed her daughter back into the dining room. Anna sat down and glanced round the table. She was flushed, excited and extraordinarily beautiful. Angelica watched her as she talked animatedly to her grandfather. She'd obviously had a glass or two too many, but it was a pleasure to see her happy. Giovanni was clearly relieved, and delighted by her lively energy. Angelica caught Silvano's eye and tipped her head towards their daughter, now holding forth to Jake's brother, Oberon, about the joys of salsa dancing. Silvano smiled, as pleased as she.

Half an hour later, Angelica noticed Anna raking through her Christmas pudding with her spoon and fork, looking for five-pence pieces. She found one and, laughing, sucked it clean. She pushed the pudding away. She doesn't eat enough, thought Angelica. She leant across the table. 'Eat your pud, darling. Then we can clear away.'

Anna's face darkened. 'Oh, Mum, stop fussing and telling me what to do! I'm twenty years old, for God's sake.' Her voice was louder than it needed to be.

Everyone's conversations stopped. Anna, unaware of any embarrassment, stood up. 'C'mon, Oberon,' she said, 'let's go. I'll teach you to salsa. You, too, Jake. You'll love it.'

'Maybe later, Anna,' said Oberon. 'I think the plan is to all play games. Like always.'

'Stuff that.' Anna pushed back her chair and grabbed Jake's arm. 'You don't want to play charades and consequences, do you?'

She's drunk, thought Angelica. Jake, obviously aware of that too, allowed Anna to pull him up, then put his arm round her and led her out of the room. As they left, he looked over his shoulder at Angelica, signalling reassurance.

The three young people, Oberon, Jake and Anna, did not join the rest of them in the sitting room. They must have gone to Jake's room across the farmyard, thought Angelica. She was still smarting from Anna's rudeness and found she could not concentrate on Trivial Pursuit. Her mother sat next to her, a comforting hand on her arm. After an hour or so, the game ran out of steam, and Sophie suggested they go for a walk round the farm and visit the pigs with leftover potatoes.

Angelica stayed behind with her mother. As soon as they were alone, Laura said, 'Don't worry, darling. Anna will be all right. She's interesting and talented and she'll find her way sooner or later.'

'I hope you're right, Mamma. But in the meantime, it's pretty stressful at home. Sometimes she's fine and reasonable, but mostly she's so headstrong, so contrary. Anna drinks too much and sleeps too much. And doesn't eat enough. I've no idea how to shake her out of it.'

'Maybe she should get away from Holly Farm for a bit. She could come to us in London. Papa dotes on her, as you know.'

'That would be such a relief, especially for Silvano. But if I suggest it, Anna will instantly refuse.'

'Leave it to me, love. Just don't let her know that we've had this conversation. Let her think it's her decision.'

As they climbed into the car and waved goodbye, Angelica prayed: Please, God, don't let Silvano and Anna have a shouting match on the way home.

But, of course, they did. Silvano spoke over his shoulder to his daughter in the back seat. 'Anna, listen to me. That was really embarrassing. You're drinking too much, that's the problem.' He spoke in a measured tone, not loudly, but Angelica knew it would enrage their daughter. She turned to see Anna sink down in her seat while pushing her fingers into her hair, her eyes raised to the car ceiling.

'Oh, Dad, you're easily embarrassed, aren't you?' Her words were a little slurred. 'What did I do to trigger your embarrassment this time?'

'You know perfectly well. Or maybe you were too drunk to remember. You bit your mother's head off when she suggested you eat your pudding, and you insisted on breaking up the lunch party, dragging your cousins off to dance, pooh-poohing Sophie's idea of games and disappearing altogether.'

'We went to Jake's place.' Anna's voice was now loud with indignation. 'Surely I can spend time with my cousins. We'd done the boring happy families bit for hours. It was time to have some fun.'

Silvano's voice remained steady but he was gripping the steering wheel tightly. 'This boring happy family,' he said, 'is what puts the clothes on your back.'

Angelica had told herself not to join in. She longed to tell Silvano to leave it for now and Anna to behave with more respect towards her father. But whoever she supported, the other would feel betrayed.

Suddenly she had to know. 'Darling, it's not just the drink is it? Were you taking drugs? Is that what you were up to with the boys? Is that why you wouldn't join us?'

There was a little silence. Then Anna laughed. 'Well, yes, but we only had a few joints. And some champagne – I nicked a bottle as we went through the sitting room.'

Does she even know right from wrong? Angelica wondered.

'I'm sorry I took Jake and Oberon away,' Anna continued, her voice still truculent, 'but you must admit that Aunt Jane is about as friendly as a snake while poor Aunt Sophie and the rest of you aren't exactly a bundle of Christmas cheer, are you?'

They were turning into the Holly Farm drive. Silvano pulled up at the house and stopped the car. He made no effort to get out but swung round in his seat to face Anna. 'I need to get this straight, Anna. You're smoking marijuana. Are you taking other drugs? If so, what kind?'

Again, Anna laughed. 'Oh, Dad, you make it sound so criminal, but—'

'It is criminal. It's against the law.'

'But it's harmless. Everyone knows that. Pot and hash will be legalized one day. Maybe even all drugs.'

'What else do you take, Anna?'

'I'm not on heroin, Dad. Or crack. Relax.'

'Answer the question. What do you take?'

Angelica wanted to know the answer too, but she hated to see Silvano pinning Anna down. She'd begun to look defensive and trapped.

'Well, if you must know,' said Anna, 'mostly I smoke weed, when I can get it. And I've snorted coke a few times.' She stopped for a second then blurted out, 'And, yes, I had a line today to help me get through lunch with my smug middle-class happy family.' She opened the car door, jumped out and slammed it after her.

She walked to the front door, fast and almost steadily. Silvano and Angelica sat in silence. Oh, Christ, thought Angelica, I don't know how to cope with this.

She resolved to ring her mother in the morning to plan Anna's move to London.

CHAPTER SIX

The move to Paddington had been surprisingly easy. Laura had suggested to Anna that she might like a change of scene and Anna had leapt at it.

'I'd love that, Nonna,' she'd said. 'Mum and Dad are driving me mad.'

'I must talk to them first. I expect you're driving them mad too, are you?' Her voice was amused rather than judgemental, and Anna found herself smiling.

'Yeah, I guess so. But I won't be a pain, I promise. I'll get a job and be out of your hair.'

Laura had proposed that Anna stay in Sophie's cottage in the Paddington mews with Oberon. Since David had died, their grandson had had it mostly to himself. Sophie, on her rare visits to London, tended to stay with Laura rather than in her own cottage with Oberon. She and Laura had been friends for sixty years, since they were schoolgirls. It was easier, she said, than competing for space with the clutter of Oberon's business, which he ran from the kitchen and garage, sometimes using the sitting room and bedrooms too.

'But what about Oberon? Will he mind?'

'Of course not, darling. Everyone loves you.'

Other than at Chorlton after Christmas, Anna hadn't seen her cousin much lately. He'd been travelling. But she'd always liked him. And, she thought, if he's been hitching through India he'll be fine with the smell of pot. Might even share a joint with me.

She drove into the Paddington mews at nine in the morning. The row of seven cottages belonged to the family, ruled by her grandparents, Laura and Giovanni, who had restored the first three in the 1950s. Now it was like an Italian commune.

As she humped her suitcase out of the car, Oberon came out of the garage that took up most of their ground floor. He was wearing an apron, a disposable hat, like a shower cap, and bright blue latex gloves, which he stripped off as he approached. Stuffing them into his pocket, he held out a hand to take hers.

'Hi, Anna,' he said, kissing her cheek. 'So the country mouse has come to town?'

'Yup. It was getting a bit desperate at home,' she said lightly. She didn't want to discuss her parental troubles. 'What on earth are you doing? You look like a butcher. Or maybe a pantomime dame.'

'I'll show you in a sec. Let's get your bag in first.'

She followed his lanky frame as, carrying her case, he climbed the stairs two at a time to the second floor. He opened the door into a large, airy room with a big double bed. 'It's my gran's,' he said, 'but she stays with Laura, so it's all yours.'

When Anna came downstairs, she found Oberon in the garage. He was working at a trestle table on which stood a row of open brown paper bags. 'So, tell me how it all works. What's this?' she asked.

Oberon didn't answer. He was cutting a roll of goat's cheese into thick slices – or, rather, trying to. The cheese was sticking to the knife, then crumbling and breaking. His frustration was obvious. 'I've tried chilling the cheese and heating the knife but look at it. What a mess.'

He sounded so cross that Anna hesitated a second before she said, 'Don't you have a cheese wire?'

'Cheese wire?'

'Yes. Wire will go through the cheese without splitting it.'

'Really?'

'Do you have any thin wire? Fuse-wire? Picture wire?'

A rummage through the tools and electrical bits on the garage shelves revealed none.

'Your gran will have wire, I bet,' Oberon said. Anna went down the mews to number one, where, after hugging her granddaughter surprisingly tightly, Laura produced a pack of fuse wire.

'Nonna, do you have a couple of corks? To make the handles?'

Laura pulled a cork out of the half-finished bottle of red wine on the kitchen sideboard, then fetched a full bottle and a corkscrew.

'Don't open another. I'll find a bit of stick or a teaspoon or something.'

'It's fine darling. We'll be bound to open a second bottle tonight. And if you and Oberon join us for supper we'll probably open a third.'

Anna tied a cork to each end of a short length of wire. Pleased with herself, she returned to Oberon, who was now putting an onion and a clove of garlic into each bag.

'You really need a proper cheese-cutting board with a slot in it so the wire can go right through the cheese,' she said, 'but you should manage with this if you cut from the bottom up.' She positioned the wire under the roll of cheese. Then, holding it down with one hand, she grasped the two corks in the other and slowly pulled the wire up through the cheese. It came through clean as a whistle, the slice still whole. She looked up at Oberon, pleased with herself.

'You're a marvel,' he exclaimed. 'Brilliant. That's so cool. How did you learn that trick?'

'Mum taught me. In the days when I was interested in cooking.'

'Aren't you still?'

'Not really. Or not much.'

Anna started to cut another slice, but Oberon stopped her. 'If you're going to help me, you'd better dress the part,' he said, rummaging in a cupboard to find an apron and a hat. He handed them to Anna and pushed a box of latex gloves at her.

'That's a bit neurotic, isn't it? I'm only going to slice the cheese.'

'Yeah, but we'd better obey the rules. This is a business, and I don't want to be shut down by Health and Safety before I've really begun.'

She donned the apron, but hesitated over the Basely cap. It was so hideous. Did she really have to wear it? But then she thought, No one will see me, and who cares anyway? She pushed her hair into the cap, pulled on the gloves and retrieved the board with the goat's cheese roll on it.

They worked together to cut and wrap twenty-three slices of the cheese, and then to pack the rest of the ingredients for a goat's cheese and beetroot risotto into the bags.

Anna wanted to know about the business.

'It's pretty simple,' Oberon replied. 'The customers look at the week's dishes on the website – they're for two or four people.

They pick what they want. We deliver packs for Monday, Tuesday and Wednesday on Monday afternoon, and on Thursday for the rest of the week. I prepare the stuff, pack the bags, and the courier collects them.'

'How do you decide how much prep to do for them? Why are we shredding the beetroot but they have to chop their own onions?'

'Well, we promise preparation time is no longer than half an hour and peeling and cutting a raw beetroot into tiny julienne strips is a big ask without a machine. So I shove it through the Robot-Coupe and it takes seconds. But chopped onion or garlic smells horrible after a while, and it doesn't take long to do at home.'

'What about oil? You haven't given them the oil to fry the rice and sweat the onion.'

'The only things I expect them to have in their store cupboard are salt, pepper and olive oil. Everything else I send.'

They didn't talk much as they worked, and Anna rather enjoyed it. Oberon was so peaceful, quietly explaining stuff or showing her how to do things.

When the packed risotto bags were chilling in the huge refrigerator beside the chicken kormas that Oberon had packed before she'd arrived, they went through to the kitchen and Oberon printed out address labels and recipe cards. The cards, along with the bags, went into polystyrene delivery boxes. They stuck the labels and delivery notes on the lids.

'You shouldn't use polystyrene, Oberon,' said Anna. 'It can't be recycled and it doesn't degrade.'

'Well, thanks for the info, madam, but I knew that already. What else can I use that will keep everything cold?'

'No idea. There must be some paper product that would do the job. I could find out for you, if you like.' Anna made some coffee and persuaded Oberon to sit down for a minute. 'Is it working, do you think?' She picked up a label to peer at it. 'Is Oberon's Recipe Boxes going to take off?'

Oberon looked up at her through hair that bounced in messy curls over his forehead. 'I think so. I've been going less than two months and I've almost a hundred regular customers who order once or twice every week. Getting into profit is going to take a while, though. I might just drop dead from exhaustion before then.' He was laughing, but Anna could see it was no laughing matter.

'Don't you have *any* help?'

'Can't afford any. Mum lent me some money to get going and she lets me live and work here for nothing, so I've got to pull it off.'

Anna didn't get it. How extraordinary Oberon was! He'd been offered a lucrative job in computers but had opted for working like a slave on this venture. He'd told her he'd been up since six that morning and they still had the Swedish meatball recipe to pack before the delivery company arrived at noon. He was bonkers. Nice, but bonkers.

A few days later Anna found her grandmother on the floor in her kitchen, surrounded by cooking machinery – a battered fondue set, some aluminium saucepans, an ancient mixer, a mincer, and a scattered pile of attachments. She had come to share the news that she'd got a job.

'That's good to hear. Tell me.'

'It's the big pub on the corner, the Duck and Dog. It's not great but it's convenient. Five nights a week, Tuesday to Saturday. I start tomorrow. But what are you doing down there, Nonna? What are you looking for?'

Laura sat back on her heels. 'I'm having a sort-out. Half this stuff I haven't used for years and Oberon doesn't want it. Can you take it to the tip for me this afternoon?' Anna nodded. 'Better take my car – all this junk won't fit into yours. The recycling centre's in Wandsworth. And on the way back, could you stop at Waitrose for me and do a shop?'

As Anna drove Laura's ancient Renault van, now stuffed with boxes of kitchen gear, old clothes, blankets, a broken chair and a child's cot, she thought how odd it was that she seldom helped her mother but was happy to do stuff for her grandmother. She quite liked it really.

At six o'clock she was back with five Waitrose carrier bags, which she helped Laura unpack.

'Darling, now you've got a job, should you be paying Oberon, or should I say his mother, some rent?'

Anna lifted her eyes to meet her grandmother's. It hadn't even occurred to her. 'I don't know. No one's said anything. Do you think Aunt Sophie will want rent?'

'Probably not. But that doesn't mean you shouldn't repay them in some way. If they won't take money it becomes even more important to show you appreciate their generosity. Even a small present occasionally. It's not a good idea always to be on the receiving end of someone's kindness.'

Three weeks later Anna found, rather to her surprise, that she seemed to be working for Oberon two mornings a week. She helped him pack measured amounts of spices, sauces (mostly

Worcestershire, soy, balsamic or chutney) into tiny plastic pots, sprigs of fresh herbs into small packets, pheasant breasts or lamb chops into boxes. It was fiddly work, but somehow satisfying, and she enjoyed being with Oberon, whose work ethic, she thought wryly, was exactly what her parents wished she had.

As they watched the courier's van doing the three-point turn necessary to get out of the dead-end mews, Oberon put his arm round her shoulders and gave her a brief hug. 'You're a godsend. I'm so grateful. Thank you.'

'I enjoy it. Do you want me next week?'

'Of course I do. It makes all the difference in the world. But I can't pay you, Anna, and you should be getting at least the minimum wage.'

'Stuff that, Oberon. Consider it rent.'

'Rent?'

'Something Nonna said about me not being on the receiving end of Aunt Sophie's kindness without reciprocating in some way.'

'So you're working for me to pay back my mum?' His eyebrows, black and thick, were raised in enquiry.

Anna laughed. 'Sort of, yes. Anyway, it makes me feel better.'

CHAPTER SEVEN

While Clemmie and Charlie were alive, Tom had had purpose: he told himself he worked hard so they could continue to enjoy the great life they had.

After their deaths, he'd continued the long working hours, champagne-filled evenings and early starts. The rollercoaster of ever-bigger deals had helped to distract his mind from the heartbreak. Before the tragedy, his self-image of a successful City tyro with the golden touch was only part of the story. Now it had become the whole story.

After the Twin Towers disaster, a different kind of hard work took him over. It was a rescue operation. He'd spent the months following 9/11 transferring the New York business to London, motivating his traumatized workforce and persuading clients to hold firm and not panic. He was labouring without the shot-in-the-arm of winning or the exhilarating danger of losing. Prices had slumped all over the world and the merger-and-acquisition frenzy had sunk into a slowly bubbling pool of under-valued deals.

Tom sat at his desk, reluctant to go home. Cold January rain was hitting the windows and the thought of his vast glass flat,

with its minimalist wasteland of grey and white, chilled him.
He ran his hands over his face, rubbing hard in an effort to
shake himself out of his gloom, to banish the thought that he
was living a grey life. It had been anything but grey before he'd
lost his wife and son. He rocked slowly back and forth. If only
he could remember the wonderful times without this aching,
suffocating sadness. His mind spooled back twenty-five years to
his thirtieth birthday.

He'd booked a table at Giovanni's, which, according to *Time Out*,
was the best Italian restaurant in London. He'd never been there,
but tonight he wanted to push the boat out. Ajax, his investment
company, had just pulled off their fourth major international
deal, netting the firm a cool eight million. And, most impor-
tantly, he was going to ask Clemmie to marry him. He had the
ring in his pocket.

He was early and was shown to a corner table in a little
alcove, with a semi-circular banquette against the wall. Good,
he thought. We won't be overheard, and if she cries, as I know
she will, I can slide onto the banquette next to her and hold her.
Maybe kiss the tears from her cheeks. He smiled, thinking he
could almost taste the salt and smell her clean-laundry scent.
He would tease her into laughing.

That was what was so great about Clemmie. She was hopeless
at concealing emotion. She was utterly without guile. Any emotion – concern, happiness, amusement, consternation – chased
across her face, like clouds in the wind.

He took the jeweller's box out of his jacket pocket and opened
it in his lap. He felt furtive, but he didn't want the waiters to
see. The ring was a large square-cut aquamarine in a modern

platinum setting. It was undoubtedly handsome and stylish, but would it be too showy for her? Clemmie was such a funny girl. She wore the simplest things, mostly from C&A or Marks & Spencer, and she kept them for years. She didn't see the point of designer clothes, she said.

Now that he could afford almost anything, he'd have liked to take her into Asprey or Garrard and let her choose a whacking great diamond. Show off a bit, treat her like a princess. But she'd never have agreed. Maybe I'll have to pretend this is a bit of coloured glass set in silver, he thought.

He snapped the box shut and dropped it into his pocket. When they married, he'd give her a platinum wedding ring to go with it.

Clemmie was late. She hurried in, her skirt swishing round her lean frame, her bag swinging on her shoulder. She dropped a kiss on his cheek and slid into the seat opposite him. 'Oh, darling, I'm so, so sorry,' she said, pushing falling hair behind her ear. 'I'd forgotten it was parents' evening. I escaped as soon as I could.'

God, she was beautiful. Her face, still a little tanned after their Indian holiday, was unmade-up except for a clear brownish lipstick, the kind you could see through, which emphasized the soft fullness of her mouth. As she smiled he saw, with familiar pleasure, her slightly uneven teeth, as clean and white as a puppy's. He wanted to run his thumb over her bottom lip, push it into her mouth.

'Don't be silly. I was quite happy sitting here, thinking how lucky I am. How good life is. How I love you. Stuff like that.'

She smiled her big wide smile, brown eyes alive. 'Good,' she said. She looked about her, taking in the ample space between the tables, the deep turquoise carpet on one wall, the heavy silver and elegant glasses, the tablecloth, which felt as if it had a padded quilt beneath it. 'Wow, this is a bit upmarket, isn't it?'

'Uh-huh. But it is my birthday.'

The waiter handed Clemmie the menu.

'Choose for me,' said Tom.

She chose tagliatelle alle vongole to start, then lamb steaks, grilled with rosemary and garlic.

As they ate, Tom, conscious of the ring in his pocket and with half his mind on picking the right moment to produce it, was barely aware of his food, but Clemmie was eating with her usual pleasure and concentration. He loved to watch her eat. She did so with such enthusiasm, and so efficiently, neatly clearing her plate from one side to the other. When she looked up her eyes were alight.

'I wish it was the sight of me that makes you look so happy,' he said, 'but I suspect it's the food.'

She laughed. 'Both,' she said. 'And why wouldn't I be happy? I have everything I could wish for. Job I love, man I love . . .'

'Nothing more you want? Not this, perhaps?' He put the little box on the table.

He'd managed to get her to agree to wait a while to have children. 'How about we aim at five years together to have fun, then have all the babies you want?' he'd said. The truth was he didn't like the idea of sharing Clemmie with anyone, not even children. She'd agreed but stipulated that then they'd have to get on with it. She'd be thirty, her fertility dropping like a stone, and she wanted at least three, maybe four.

The five years were wonderful. They'd both had jobs they

enjoyed. They had good friends, wonderful holidays, plenty of money, a nice house. But the deep content, he knew, came from their loving each other. They were so happy it frightened him sometimes. The way her face lit up as she saw him never failed to send a shot of pleasure through him. Until he'd met Clemmie he'd had no idea marriage could be so deeply satisfying, that a mate could be the be-all and end-all of your existence.

He'd have been content to go on like that for ever, but Clemmie wanted children, and when the five years were up, she binned her pills and they confidently expected she'd soon be pregnant. But four years later, they were still childless. He felt so sorry for Clemmie. He knew she thought of little else now, though she did her best to hide her sadness behind a cheery smile. He didn't feel the lack of a child as she did. They had a great life, but he knew it was no longer enough to make Clemmie completely happy.

It wasn't for lack of trying. Clemmie got pregnant readily enough, but she couldn't keep her babies. She'd had five miscarriages, three of them under twelve weeks. The worst were much later, at over five months.

And then, in the summer of 1986, she was pregnant again. Convinced she would, as usual, miscarry, Clemmie decided to take no notice of her doctor's advice to take it easy, not work, not drink, watch her diet. But this time she didn't miscarry. She had a trouble-free pregnancy, and just before Easter, their miracle baby boy, Charlie, was born – when Clemmie was thirty-five and Tom was forty.

He held the baby in one arm, a tiny red and rumpled five and a half pounds of lusty yelling, his open mouth taking up most of his face. Tom looked from the baby to Clemmie, tears running down his unshaven cheeks. 'I've never felt anything so emotional in my life,' he said. 'I swear, darling, I'll kill anyone who ever hurts a hair on his head.'

In the days that followed, Tom's super-charged emotion stayed with him. Both he and Clemmie were hollow-eyed with exhaustion, but he felt he could still climb Everest if Charlie or Clemmie needed him to. 'I thought it was just mothers who felt like this,' he said.

Lying awake, listening to the gentle rhythmic snuffling that meant Clemmie was still feeding the baby, Tom thought, for the first time in years, about his own mother, his birth-mother. He knew nothing about her, except that she'd given him up for adoption. His parents had made it sound commonplace, no big deal. It was just after the war, his mother said, and she couldn't have children, so they'd collected him from the hospital the day he was born. His real mother had signed the papers.

How could she just give him away? He could no more have given Charlie away than fly to the moon. At last he understood why Clemmie had wanted a family. His family, Clemmie and Charlie, were more important than life itself. Sounded melodramatic, but it was the truth.

When Charlie was nine they went to St Moritz for Easter. But Clemmie seemed more anxious than she had on previous skiing holidays. 'I don't know why I thought this would be a restful break. I should know by now it's full-on skiing all day, mostly spent worrying about you two, hurtling out of sight down the mountain, you reckless and him fearless. Horrible combination.'

They were having breakfast at the Hotel Kulm and Charlie was in a sulk. Tom felt for him. He knew Clemmie was right to be cautious, but he understood Charlie's need to kick off parental shackles.

'But why? Why can't I go off-piste?' said Charlie. 'I'm a better skier than half the people who do.'

It was true, thought Tom. After four years of alpine holidays he was probably the best skier of the three of them. Watching him ski was like watching a bird fly or a fish swim: he did it without thinking, as if the skis were part of him.

'You know why, Charlie,' said Clemmie. 'It's too dangerous and nine is too young.'

Clemmie agreed that Charlie would be allowed off-piste when he was twelve. Tom thought that was fair: he would have four or five more skiing holidays under his belt by then and would have learnt some caution. Charlie thought two and a half years was a lifetime away, but he also knew that his mother was implacable on the matter.

As it turned out, Charlie didn't have to wait until he was twelve. The very next year Tom's old friend Erik Sorenson invited Tom, Gerard and their families to go heli-skiing in Iceland, all expenses paid. He wanted them to check out his new venture, an exclusive and stupendously expensive mountain resort.

Since Easter week was a comparatively quiet time for Ajax, both he and Gerard leapt at the chance to have a week's holiday together. None of them had been heli-skiing before, but both families were good skiers, and the opportunity was too good to miss.

It was a relief to be travelling without cumbersome skis and snowboards. The lodge would have everything in every size, skis, poles, goggles, helmets, the lot. 'Just bring yourselves,' Erik had said.

Gerard, Jemima and their children flew from New York. The

two families met at Reykjavik airport where they walked through Customs, then across the tarmac to Erik's private plane.

It was a brilliantly clear day. They flew over vast wastes of blinding white, the shadow of their plane on the snow below keeping pace with them. Tom listened to Charlie's excited English accent vying with the American tones of Gerard's two. He'd been worried that the girls, now eleven and twelve, would consider themselves too grown up to consort with a ten-year-old but they were fine.

He felt Clemmie's hand on his knee and looked at her. She smiled at him, intimate and happy. She'd been listening to the children too. 'They'll be fine,' he said. 'Aren't we lucky, darling?'

'We are,' she replied. 'Amazingly lucky. But, Tom, I'm probably being silly, but aren't we being reckless? We said we'd not let Charlie go off-piste until he was twelve.'

'Erik would never do anything reckless. He'll look after us. We won't get lost and be skiing off a cliff, I promise.'

Erik's team was impressive. As well as a housekeeper and two village girls, there were ski instructors for those skiing on the gentle slopes, ski guides for the powder snow aficionados, pilots for the two helicopters, and a lodge manager, Magnus. He kitted them all out with skiing gear and was the only person who used the satellite phone. He checked the weather forecasts and decided where on the mountain the helicopter would drop the skiers. He'd go with them to the drop-off, he said, and instruct the guides who led the skiers down the mountain. He's like a headmaster, thought Tom. Everyone respects him and no one will dare gainsay him.

The children were clamouring to go on a helicopter. Magnus

organized a ride for them, but he would not allow them, or indeed anyone else, to heli-ski until he'd seen them on the slopes.

After the first morning he declared that Tom, Clemmie, Charlie and Gerard were cleared to heli-ski but Jemima and her two girls should stay on the lower slopes for a couple of days. Then they could be dropped halfway up the mountain to ski down with a guide.

Charlie was triumphant, and Tom ticked him off sharply. 'Be quiet, Charlie. Of course you ski better than the others. You've had much more practice. Boasting is very unattractive.'

The next day, before they put their kit on, Magnus fitted them each with a transceiver, adjusting the straps and making sure they wore them under their jackets. 'Never wear it on top,' he said. 'If you fall it could get yanked off.' He checked each one was tuned to transmit. 'Never, ever, turn it off. Golden Rule Number One.'

Tom could see that Clemmie was nervous. He put an arm around her. 'It's just a safety precaution,' he said. 'It emits a little beep so they can locate you if you disappear.' If anything, that seemed to make her more anxious.

The helicopter took them halfway up, with their skis and poles carried on a basket attached to its side. Once there, it took a little while to get skis and goggles on but finally everyone was ready.

'We're going to stick like limpets to the guide, aren't we?' Clemmie said.

'Darling, we'll all be fine. Just enjoy it.'

Then they were off, skiing down virgin snow. It felt so good. Tom's lungs expanded in the cold air, which seemed to sparkle like diamonds. He felt light and glorious.

For two days the helicopters repeatedly flew them up the

mountain and they skied down. Charlie, Clemmie and their guide made frequent stops because Charlie wasn't strong enough for the two hundred-odd linked turns it took to get down the longest runs in one go. But he managed forty or fifty and earned the admiration of his guide.

On the fourth night, there was a fresh fall of snow and they spent a fabulous morning on a sunny slope to the west of the lodge. They must have done fifteen or sixteen runs, arriving at the bottom, legs aching, out of breath and deliriously happy.

After lunch Magnus decreed they should ski the longest run on the mountain. It was directly behind the lodge and they could ski almost onto the terrace. 'It also has some of the steepest slopes. It's the best,' he said.

As they flew over the areas they would soon be skiing down Tom had a moment of anxiety. Parts were really steep. He looked at Clemmie and she pulled a mock-scared face. Erik saw her and leant into her ear to shout over the noise of the chopper. 'It's fine. Don't worry.'

They decided that Erik, Gerard and Tom would set off first. It would take them several minutes to get down to the lodge, where the helicopters would be waiting to take them up again. Clemmie and Charlie would follow a little more slowly with the guide. Charlie tried to object: he wanted to go with the men. But Tom silenced him with a shake of his head. 'No, you'll need at least two stops, we'll only have one. You look after your mum. Show her how it's done. We'll wait for you at the first stop.'

When they stopped a third of the way down, and Clemmie arrived with the other two, Tom was relieved to see his wife laughing. 'Oh, Tom, this is amazing, isn't it?' she said.

'It is.' He turned to his son. 'How was that, Charlie?' The boy's face was flushed with excitement and he couldn't stop grinning. 'Great, Dad. Just so cool.'

When the advance party skidded to a halt behind the lodge, Tom had to bend over to wait for the ache in his thighs to subside. His legs were trembling. He was breathing hard. He grinned at the other two. 'Fantastic,' he said. 'Maybe the best two minutes of my life!'

Erik seemed as happy as he and Gerard were. 'Good, isn't it? Shall we go straight up again or have a beer?'

They opted for the beer and sat on the wooden deck. It was warm in the sun and they shook off their jackets. 'We can watch the others with binoculars,' said Erik.

Erik scanned the slopes but couldn't see them. 'They'll have stopped behind that outcrop, where it flattens out. They'll emerge from the right, over there.'

They chatted on, drinking cold Icelandic beer in the sun and passing the binoculars between them. Suddenly they heard an odd sound, like a whip-crack, but loud. Puzzled, Tom jerked his head up and saw something behind the ridge. A cloud maybe, like a puff of smoke.

Erik leapt up. 'Shit. Avalanche.' He dashed into the lodge, shouting for Magnus.

Tom and Gerard jumped up too. Tom could not take his eyes off the mountain. He watched calmly, not connecting what he saw – the cloud flattening out, moving fast down the slope – with Erik's word: avalanche. Then they heard the rumble, deep, distant, but unmistakable. It sounded like an approaching express train. Christ, it *is* an avalanche, Tom thought. That's the sound of tons of snow tumbling down the mountain. And Clemmie and Charlie are up there.

Suddenly he saw a tiny black figure, skiing fast down the slope below the ridge, to the right of what looked like the mountain moving. Relief swept through him, melting his legs. He had to lean against the table. Thank God, thank God.

His eyes were glued to the ridge above the little figure hurtling down the mountain. Tom let out a choking gasp. He'd been holding his breath, his brain paralysed. There should have been three of them.

Erik ran past him to the ski rack, grabbed his skis and shouted, 'Tom, Gerard, come. *Now!* We're going up there. Bring your jackets.'

Tom stood, not really understanding what Erik had said. He repeated to himself, 'Bring your jacket.' Then his brain clicked in and he reached for it. They ran to the heli-pad. Both helicopters' blades were already turning, and Magnus was climbing into one of the machines. Erik shouted to Gerard to join him, then took Tom's arm and pushed him into the second helicopter. Tom could feel his calm turning to panic and he forced himself to be quiet, do as he was told. He sat in one of the back seats, Erik next to him. He watched the pilot and one of the guides dropping skis and poles into the basket on the side of their helicopter, shifting them around to fit them all in. Suddenly he could bear it no longer and he was shouting, out of control, through the Perspex window. 'Jesus, will you guys fucking get on with it? My wife could be dying up there . . .Why can't—'

And then he couldn't shout any more because Erik's huge hands were around his head, pulling his face away from the window. Then Erik slid his arms round him and held him. 'It's all right, Tom,' he shouted, above the noise of the engines. 'We'll be off in a second.'

The two helicopters flew up the mountain, one on each side of the path of the avalanche. It was still now, the run-off stopping where the slope flattened out. He scanned the bright snow for any dark object, any sign of life, anything other than snow. It was impossible to tell how deep it was. The thought of Charlie choking, pressed down by tons of it, made him retch. His hand over his mouth, he closed his eyes, fighting for control.

When he opened them, a few seconds later, he saw that the other helicopter was lower than they were and seemed to be dropping down. It was landing. Tom's heart somersaulted. Maybe they'd seen Clemmie or Charlie. But then he realized the figure on the ground was the skier they'd seen racing down the mountain. Clemmie and Charlie's guide. He'd managed to ski to the side of the avalanche. Now he was skiing across to where the helicopter was landing, a flattish slope beyond the path of the avalanche.

What Tom felt was overpowering fury. How could the man have left them to be swallowed by an avalanche? How dare he save his own skin? 'I'll kill the bastard!' he shouted. 'I'll—'

Erik took his wrists and squeezed them so hard it hurt. He shouted over the noise: 'Tom, he'll be able to tell us where they are. If they were buried by the avalanche.'

'Why aren't we landing too? I want to ask him—'

'No, we need to stay up. Landing and taking off will lose us time. Look, he's getting in. He'll be able to guide them, tell them what happened.'

The pilots were talking to each other as both helicopters flew further up the mountain. Erik signalled to their pilot to open the mike. They heard Magnus's voice.

'. . . their guide. He heard the avalanche and shouted at

Clemmie and Charlie to follow him out of its path, but either they couldn't hear or they misunderstood. They tried to race it, but that's impossible.'

That night was the worst of Tom's life. His thoughts would not turn from his wife and son up there on the mountain under tons of cold snow, dead, while he was under a warm featherweight duvet. Were they yards apart, separated, broken? Or together? He imagined them as he'd seen them so often, Charlie cradled in Clemmie's arms. But he knew that was nonsense.

The next day the Icelandic mountain rescue team dug them out. Tom didn't ask whether they were close to each other when they died.

It took a week to get authorization to bring the bodies home, during which Tom was silent, barely existing. Gerard made all the arrangements, and Jemima mothered Tom. He obediently ate soup, drank whisky, went to bed, took a sleeping pill. The only time he came to life was when the undertaker wanted to put Clemmie and Charlie in separate coffins. 'No!' he yelled. 'They must lie together.'

CHAPTER EIGHT

Tom shook himself out of his reverie and dragged his mind back to the present. It was seven p.m. and he was still sitting at his desk. He must focus. Was it wise, he wondered, to take a punt on the medical catheter start-up? It would be expensive, would not be in profit for four years and depended heavily on the guy that had invented the stuff the tubes were made of. He was a genius, but also a nutter.

But if it all worked, it would make a fortune. They could sell it on and repay themselves a hundred times over. Still Tom hesitated.

Suddenly irritated with himself, he stood up and reached for his jacket. What's the matter with you? he thought. You never used to be so chicken, so risk averse, so wet. Ajax was built on your instinct for a good deal. And even if this one fails, we can afford it. Ajax's balance sheet is still healthy, the company's still worth millions, you're still absurdly rich. For God's sake, get up and go home. You're useless here.

Riding down in the lift, looking in the mirror, he thought, You're useless at home too. Poor Susan.

As the lift doors to the penthouse flat opened, the homely

smell of cooking cheered him. 'Hi, darling. Sorry I'm late. Something smells good.'

'I ordered cannelloni.' said Susan. 'It's in the oven, heating. And chestnut cake. Bad for you, but it's so miserable out.'

He put an arm briefly round her thin shoulders, the cashmere jersey – pale grey, of course – soft as a kitten under his hand. He kissed her cheek. 'Wonderful.'

The cannelloni was good. Very good. 'Is it from Deli-Calzone downstairs?' he asked.

She nodded. The fashionable Italian café in the modern square (grey stone flags, shallow grey canal, indecipherable stainless-steel sculpture) was open from seven a.m. until midnight and ran a thriving delivery service.

Susan had taken a tiny portion and not eaten all of it. She was picking at her undressed salad leaves without enthusiasm. Why did it irritate him that she was always on a diet? If she would just tuck into food with gusto and pleasure, he thought, maybe I'd love her more.

But the food seemed to lighten his mood. After two slices of chestnut cake and a brandy, he felt almost expansive. When, once again, she raised the question of the wedding date, he smiled, if a touch wryly, at her. 'When would you like?'

Her expression registered at first surprise – as well it might since he'd always dodged the question before – and then delight, her face opening like a flower, eyes wide, mouth smiling. I've done it now, he thought. No going back.

'Oh, darling, let's do it this summer,' she said. 'We'll have time to make all the arrangements, invite everyone.'

Tom felt the beginning of panic compress his chest. He leant across the table and took her hand in both of his. 'Darling, let's make it summer next year, can we? Now is too soon. I'd like the business to be truly over 9/11, to know our future is secure. Right now, a couple of bad deals and we'd be done for.'

She pulled back a little. 'What do you mean? Are you saying Ajax could go belly up?'

'It's unlikely. I think we've weathered the storm very well. But, still, you don't want to marry a bankrupt, do you?'

He was teasing her. Susan would never marry a bankrupt. He could see her mind calculating: financial uncertainty against her dream of marriage this summer. She forced a smile, nodded. He had to hand it to her, she was a brave loser.

He felt a clutch of guilt. He was lying to her. Ajax was quite safe – or as safe as any investment business ever is. To assuage the guilt, or perhaps to console her, he said, 'And then I'd have time to plan with you. For the next six months I doubt I'll have a day free.'

Her eyes still reflected her disappointment. 'But I could do all the planning,' she said, lamely. 'You needn't be bothered with it.'

'Of course you could, but I'd like to be free to do it with you. Plan where we'll go for a honeymoon, where we'll get married . . .' As he spoke he knew he was being a hypocrite. He'd no desire to help with any wedding plans. He was playing for time. It was despicable.

The next day, on the Docklands Light Railway to the City, he picked up a discarded *Daily Mail* and flipped through the pages, paying little attention until his eye was caught by the headline: *How I found my real mother and forgave her.*

Tom scanned the story, reading a predictable tale of an abandoned baby, now a young man, tracking down his mother, a former prostitute, and finding a whole new welcoming family.

He studied the photograph for a long time. It was of a large family group. The adopted twenty-year-old was in the middle and the caption beneath the photo detailed his newly discovered grandparents, both in their seventies, four or five middle-aged people, including his parents and their siblings, and nine younger ones, among them several children.

The young man said his acceptance by his birth-family had changed his life. He hadn't known the meaning of love before, blah-blah-blah. Tom tossed the newspaper aside and forced himself to be serious, think about the upcoming meeting with Damon and the team.

But the thought of that man, the unknown adoptee, wouldn't go away. All morning Tom debated whether finding his parents would be a good or bad thing. What if they were dreadful? What if they were broke and became leeches, sucking him dry, or trying to? What if his mother rejected him a second time?

He knew almost nothing about his real parents. His mother hadn't told him he was adopted until just before he went to Eton at thirteen. He'd spent his first weeks at the college looking at the other boys in his house, wondering if he was the only adopted one. The first time he went home, he cornered his mother. 'Mother, why didn't my real mother want to keep me?'

She'd shrugged. 'I expect because she was ashamed. She could hardly pretend she was married without a husband to prove it. Everyone would know you were illegitimate, wouldn't they?'

He'd thought about that for a second. Illegitimate. A bastard. And there was I thinking I was the son of a decorated brigadier. 'She could have pretended to be a war-widow.'

Again she'd shrugged. 'I don't think so. The war was long over by the time you were born. Anyway, she didn't have any money. She had to give you up because her father had kicked her out of the house.'

He remembered feeling a little rush of sympathy. Poor woman. It also upset him that his mother was so matter-of-fact, almost brutal, about it. Suddenly he hadn't wanted to know any more and had left the room.

Over the next five years he'd gradually absorbed more small bits of information. Any questions to his father always got the response 'Ask your mother. Her department,' but his mother seemed to know very little.

'You were born in the Middlesex Hospital,' she'd told him, 'and your mother's name was Laura Oliver, I remember that. She was very young, nineteen or twenty. She wasn't married. We never spoke to her, or even saw her.'

'But did she want to give me up, do you think?' He had felt a bit pathetic asking this.

'She must have. I don't think she had anywhere to live either. She'd been in a home for "fallen women" in Soho.'

'But what happened to her?'

'I've no idea.' She'd carried on adding newly laundered napkins to the neat pile in the linen cupboard, replacing the lavender bag on top and closing the door. 'Now run along and forget about her. Just think that you'd never have gone to such a good prep school or to Eton if she'd kept you. You should be grateful to her for having the sense to give you a good chance in life. You're a lucky boy, Tom.'

He'd seen the logic of this. She was probably right, but he hadn't felt lucky.

*

When Tom got to his office he closed the door, telling his secretary not to disturb him and to deflect all calls. Then he rang the Middlesex Hospital.

After a few blind alleys – the human-resources department, patient welfare, and obstetrics – he was finally put through to the secretary of the administrator.

'I know this is an unusual request but I'm trying to trace my real mother who gave birth to me in your hospital fifty-five years ago.'

'Ah. I'm not sure that I can help you. Have you tried Norcap?'

'Norcap? Who are they?'

'It's the National Organization for Counselling Adoptees and Parents. That's what they do – help adopted children find their birth-mothers, and vice versa.'

'But they won't know anything about me, will they? They'll just do what I'm doing, and ring you up.'

'I don't know how they work, but we don't have any historical records here. Norcap should know how to trace people. We do occasionally get similar requests and we always refer people to Norcap.' She gave him an address and a telephone number.

Tom hesitated, conscious that he might be about to set in train a series of events, or a stream of knowledge, that he might regret. He sat for perhaps a minute, thinking. Then he grabbed the phone and dialled the number.

'Norcap, good morning. Can I help?' The woman sounded friendly and bright.

'I hope so. The Middlesex Hospital told me you might help with finding my birth-mother. I'm adopted.'

'Well, Mr . . . ?'

'Standing. Tom.'

'Well, Mr Standing, let me put you through to someone who may be able to help you.'

A few seconds later he was talking to another intelligent-sounding, friendly woman. He told her all he knew: his mother's name, the date he was born, that he was given to his adoptive parents immediately. 'It's not much to go on, I'm afraid.'

'On the contrary. That's a lot of information and I'm sure we can help you.'

'Really? That's excellent. What happens next?'

'We'd assign a case officer to you and she would do the research and keep you informed of progress. If she tracks your mother down, you can decide together how best to approach her.'

That night, as they got ready for bed, he told Susan what he planned to do. 'My adoptive parents are dead so they can't be upset or hurt. And since it's much easier to trace people nowadays, and Norcap does nothing else, why not? It might be interesting, don't you think?' He spoke in a deliberately casual tone. For some reason he didn't want her to know that he felt a little scared and quite emotional. I suppose, he thought, I'm looking for her support and encouragement.

He didn't get either. Susan's eyes narrowed, and when she spoke, her voice was hard. 'But why? Why do you want to open such a can of worms, dig up some poor woman who'll just become a leech?'

'What makes you say that? We don't know anything about her. She might be perfectly delightful. And, anyway, she's my mother.' As he said the word 'mother', he realized he really did want to find her. Why didn't Susan see that?

'And I thought you said you were too busy to concentrate on our wedding,' she snapped. There was a mean set to her gorgeous mouth. 'But not too busy to go on a wild-goose chase for someone who'll drain you dry.'

He resisted the temptation to point out that if it was a wild-goose chase she wouldn't be there to drain him dry. 'Susan, Susan,' he pleaded, stretching his hand out to cover hers, 'don't be like this. Why do you mind? It won't affect our relationship, will it? It could be a fascinating quest that we'll undertake together. Aren't you at all interested in who my real parents might be?'

Susan stood up. 'No, I'm not. And nor should you be. Why are you looking for your mummy when you're about to get a wife? What does that say to me? That I won't be enough, that's what.' She picked up her nightdress and made for the bathroom, banging the door shut.

Tom stayed sitting on the end of the bed. He felt suddenly exhausted. Now I'll have to follow her, comfort her, make love to her, he thought.

But he didn't. He just climbed, naked, into bed, pulled the duvet round his shoulders and closed his eyes.

He couldn't sleep, alternately telling himself to go to her, and to leave her be. After perhaps half an hour of indecision, he was at last sliding into sleep when he heard the bathroom door click open. Seconds later he felt her climb into bed and cuddle up to his bare back. She was naked too. At first he thought, Oh, no, please, I want to sleep. But almost at once desire overrode everything else and he turned to her, holding her head as he kissed her mouth. Her body against his felt hard and bony, just her small high breasts deliciously feminine.

They made love fast and in silence. There were no reproaches, no apologies, but they fell asleep at peace with each other.

Two days later he received a phone call. 'I'm Jeannie MacDonald.' She spoke with a Scots accent. 'From Norcap. I'm your case officer.'

Tom asked her to meet him at his office. Susan sometimes came home unexpectedly during the day and he didn't want to reopen the subject with her. Since the night he'd told her of his intention to look for his birth-parents, he hadn't mentioned it again and neither had she. He suspected she knew he would continue with it, but there was no point in upsetting her by trying to involve her.

Jeannie MacDonald was middle-aged, her round face framed by a straight dark bob. Her fringe almost met her eyebrows. She had a cheerful, straightforward manner and Tom liked her immediately. 'I've checked the St Catherine's House Register – that's where all London births are recorded,' she said. 'They were really helpful. Your birth was registered a fortnight after you were born, and your mother's name, Laura Oliver, is there. But not your father's.'

'Did she register the birth herself?'

'We don't know, but I'm pretty sure it would have been your adoptive parents. You're named Thomas Andrew Standing, not Oliver or your birth-father's name. Also, mothers of illegitimate children don't generally admit to not knowing who the father is.'

'So they'd have given me my first name too. Tom?'

'It's likely. Since the registration was two weeks after your birth, and you have told us you were handed to them as soon as you were born, I imagine they named you Thomas Andrew Standing.'

Tom nodded. 'Andrew was my adoptive dad's first name, so I guess that's right. I never asked where the Tom came from.' He sat silent for second, then looked up. 'Do we know where my mother lived?' he asked.

'There's no full address on the record, just Oxfordshire. I imagine that's because your parents didn't know your birth-mother but were aware that she came from Oxfordshire. Presumably she was living in London to get away from home. In 1946 illegitimacy was still something shaming, to be hidden. Do you know how old she was when you were born?'

'Nineteen or twenty, I think Mum said.'

'Excellent. That gives me something to go on. That would make her born in . . .' she closed her eyes to calculate '. . . nine-teen twenty-six or -seven. There can't be that many Laura Olivers born in Oxfordshire in those two years. It's back to the official records for me. Her birth records should tell us exactly where the family lived.'

Jeannie left with a promise to report back as soon as she knew more. Tom ushered her to the lift, then went back to his desk. Eliza asked if she could put calls through, but Tom said, 'Not yet. Give me ten minutes.'

His thoughts were whirling. He was excited by the search. Now that it looked possible to find his mother, his competi-tive instinct was engaged and he wanted to win. But there was more to it than the thrill of the chase. He now felt emotionally connected with the young woman who had given birth to him. Nineteen, penniless, unmarried, disowned by her family – his heart went out to her. If nothing else, he'd like to tell her he'd fared well, to relieve her of any guilt or worry about him. Of course she might be dead, or have disappeared or gone abroad.

Maybe her parents never registered her birth and the trail would peter out.

When he'd first started on this, his feelings, if any, were a mix of curiosity and indignation at her abandoning him. But now he saw things differently. He was aware of what a burden he'd been to her. If he hadn't come along, maybe her boyfriend – if that was what he was – wouldn't have left her. Maybe he'd have married her. Maybe they'd have lived happily ever after. As it was, she'd lost everything – lover, home, family, presumably job if she'd had one. Maybe, if he ever found her, she'd refuse to see him. Why would she want to meet the cause of such unhappiness?

He sat at his desk, aware that the train had left the station and if he didn't want it to arrive at its destination he had to pull the emergency cord right now. But he knew he couldn't. Or wouldn't.

He buzzed through to Eliza. 'I'm free now, Eliza. I need to speak to Damon, and then to Whatshisname at Goldman Sachs.'

That evening he and Susan were going to hear the Young Musicians' Symphony Orchestra at St John's, Smith Square. Tom was a patron of the orchestra and seldom missed one of their concerts. He'd agreed to meet her at the Footstool Restaurant in the basement of the concert hall for supper first. Susan was there when he arrived, looking, as ever, polished and smart. He bent to kiss her cheek. 'Did you order?' he asked.

She nodded. 'Baked seabass. Salad on the side. And two glasses of white.'

'Perfect.'

When they were halfway through supper, Tom told her about

meeting Jeannie MacDonald. 'She says it will be possible, even easy, to find my mother.'

His eyes had been on her face as he spoke, but she didn't look up to meet his gaze. He saw her mouth tighten a little, and then she shut her eyes for a second, briefly shaking her head. She looked up at last, her face unyielding. 'You're going ahead with it, then?'

'Yes. I thought I would.' He made an effort to keep his voice gentle, but he didn't feel gentle. 'Do you have some objection to my looking for my parents?'

'Too right I do. It's ridiculous. It's pathetic, Tom.'

'Pathetic?'

'You don't need a long-lost mother.' Her voice was rising. 'You're fifty-five, for Christ's sake. You're self-sufficient and successful. Why do you suddenly want to open a can of worms like that?'

'I'm not exactly sure. Because it's interesting? Because I'm curious about my origins? Maybe because life is short, and I think, if I have parents, sisters and brothers, I'd like to know them. Or at least know of their existence.'

'So it's the sad whim of a fifty-five-year-old.'

'That's a bit rough, Susan. But, yes, if you like, it's the sad whim of a fifty-five-year-old.' He looked at her unhappy mouth, her eyes devoid of sympathy. Why are we still together? he thought. What's the use? Sometimes I think we don't even like each other much. And she's already told me her real objection. She thinks the time spent searching will be time stolen from her. And she doesn't want the competition of another woman in my life.

He paid the bill and they left the table. The circular stone steps, originally built to connect the church – now a concert hall – and the crypt below were not wide enough to climb side by side so he walked behind her. Her slim round bottom was at his eye level, and he watched her gym-toned glutes moving beneath her tight skirt. Usually he found her bum erotic but now he felt only irritation.

Their enforced silence while the musicians played was a blessing. At first, he barely listened to the music, his brain running fretfully over the discussion at supper. He couldn't answer Susan's question as to *why* he wanted to find his parents, though he'd stated the obvious reasons. Somehow, he thought, it was tied up with the loss of the three people he had loved most in the world, in the avalanche and then on 9/11. Maybe I'm hoping to hear that my mother loved me. Unlikely, since she gave me away as soon as she could. Was that the start of a life of losing the people I love?

Gradually the sweeping music of Beethoven's Pastoral Symphony caught him up and calmed him. He wondered how sound could be so moving.

When they rose at the interval he saw that the music had had its effect on Susan too. She commented on the performers and the conductor with lively interest. And then, when he'd got her a glass of wine, and they were standing in a corner by themselves, she stretched up and kissed his cheek. 'I'm so sorry, Tom, darling. I don't know why I mind. I just want you to myself, I suppose. But it's wrong of me. Of course you must find your parents, if you can.'

Tom looked into her open face, her eyes wide and pleading. Immediately he regretted his anger. 'No,' he said, 'I should have involved you from the start. It's natural to feel resentful.'

'I can be such a bitch, Tom. I don't know why you put up with me.'

The second half of the concert was Elgar's Cello Concerto and the young cellist was the best he'd heard. Not for the first time, Tom thought that young professionals sometimes played with more heart and more soul – more love – than experienced top performers who never hit a duff note. He came out of the concert energized and uplifted. Something had settled in him and he felt a sense of peace. He must somehow make a go of it with Susan. Once they were married, she'd be less needy and demanding. Plenty of people had good marriages without being head over heels in love.

CHAPTER NINE

'That was the biggest order we've had,' Oberon told Anna, looking at his watch. 'It took us seven hours. We'll need help if this goes on.'

They were sitting on plastic chairs in the garage drinking Coke.

'And more refrigeration, and more space,' said Anna.

'And I should be paying you more than the minimum wage. We'd never have got this far if you hadn't been working for free. But if I paid you what I ought to and we hired more help, had better refrigeration and more space, we'd be back to making no money. It's Catch-22. If we work like slaves and do it all ourselves in dreadful conditions, we do really well – we've been in profit now for months. But if we expand, the surplus will be gobbled up by the costs.'

Anna stood so she could get her hand into the pocket of her tight jeans. She pulled a Rizla roller and cigarette papers out of one pocket, tobacco and marijuana out of the other. She sat down again and started to roll a joint.

'You shouldn't smoke so much of that stuff, Anna,' said Oberon, mildly.

'Why?' She offered him the joint, but he shook his head.

'It rots your brain. I don't have any great moral issues with that – it's your brain, not mine – but it also makes you careless. Fine if you smoke like now, after we've packed all the boxes, but when you smoke before we start, you're a bit of a liability.'

His voice was pleasant and matter-of-fact. Anna, who usually resented any suggestion that she change her ways, found she didn't mind the criticism. 'Really? she said. 'Can you tell if I've been smoking?'

'Yes, absolutely. But it's worse when you've been snorting coke.'

'I've never done that before work!'

'Yes, you have.'

'I haven't! When?'

'A fortnight, maybe three weeks ago. Don't you remember? You'd been rowing with your mum on the phone. Ten minutes later you were all energy and enthusiasm, and then you stormed off in a strop because I pointed out you were using the wrong bags for the sweetcorn.'

Anna was about to protest, but then she realized Oberon was right. Her mother had been moaning that she never came home at weekends any more, and implying, as ever, that she was wasting her life: 'You can't want to pack boxes for Oberon and pull pints at the pub for ever, darling, can you?' she'd asked.

Something in her mother's measured, reasonable tone always stoked her up. She answered with more heat than she'd meant to, and as she spoke, she got angrier still. 'I can if I want to, Mum. It's my life, remember? You should be glad I'm not dependent on you any more. Isn't that what Dad wanted? To get me off his payroll?'

She'd stayed angry for the first half-hour of work with Oberon. She couldn't concentrate, so she'd slipped upstairs and snorted a quick line.

Now she laughed. 'OK, OK. Guilty as charged. I'd no idea you were monitoring my illegal-substance intake.'

'I'm not. I'm monitoring your efficiency, which does vary from brilliant to pretty bloody useless, Anna.'

Reminded of her mother, and particularly of her complaint about not coming home, Anna rang Holly Farm. Her father answered. 'Hello, darling,' he said, his voice soft with affection. 'How nice.'

'I thought I'd come home this weekend.'

'Excellent. Your mother will be so pleased.'

'I've got Monday off too.'

'All the better. Come in time for supper on Friday.'

At the end of the week, driving down to Holly Farm, she felt slightly apprehensive. Did anyone, she thought, have an open relationship with their parents? Did anyone confide in their mother? She'd always felt she didn't quite belong, and she used to think it was because she was adopted. But it couldn't be: she loved her parents and was fully conscious of the debt she owed them. They'd given her a life, and a good one, rescued her from the cruelty, uncertainty and probably unhappy future in Romania.

She didn't remember a lot about the orphanage, but she did remember being frightened of the dark, and the sound of the little girl in the next cot, as she rocked forwards and backwards, forwards and backwards, tugging the bars with each lurch of her body. The cot had creaked in unison with the rocking and her keening.

And the nurses were so mean, one in particular. Anna clearly remembered how the light would be suddenly blotted out as a woman with a lot of black hair around her face loomed over the cot to lift her out. And the cringing fear, not knowing if the nurse was going to beat her for wetting the bed, or kiss and cuddle her.

Anna shuddered at the memory. She'd never talked to the girls at school about those early days. They'd never have understood anyway. Her parents were just like theirs, middle class, well educated, civilized, but she'd assumed her early life was what somehow made her an outsider.

But now, she thought, that wasn't it: it was her being gay that had set her apart from her schoolmates – they'd never talked of the possibility of homosexuality at school and she'd quickly sensed that to admit to feelings they didn't share would make her isolation worse. Her parents were liberal-minded, intelligent and loving. But she was sure they'd be horrified if they knew.

She did love her parents but, these days, conversations so often turned into full-blown rows. This weekend, she thought, has to be different. She determined not to rise, to go with the flow, to remember that, whatever they said, they meant well.

Once home, she wondered why she'd been so anxious. Indeed, why she'd found her parents impossible. She helped her mother make supper and enjoyed it. She'd loved cooking as a child but had lost interest when she was fourteen or so. For years now, her mother had tried to re-inspire her, but she'd resisted. Now, as they fried mushrooms and garlic, then tossed in a handful of spinach and slices of ripe avocado, she thought how rich and delicious it smelt, and how vibrant the colour of wilting spinach and avocado was against the velvety dark mushrooms. It made your mouth water to look at it. She tipped the contents of the pan onto three slices of toasted ciabatta and felt a buzz of pride as she set them in front of her mum and dad.

Maybe things were better, she thought, because no one mentioned drugs or alcohol, her future or lack of it. Or asked her if she'd 'met anyone', by which they meant did she have a boyfriend? Of course, it never occurred to them that she might have a girlfriend.

Anna smiled wryly at the thought. The answer would be the same. No. No one special. Plenty of friends, most of them gay, and the occasional one-night stand or brief affair.

They talked of her job. Her mum and dad seemed interested, for once, so she told them of Oberon's obsession with good ingredients. They discussed how impossible it was to stick to buying organic when it was so expensive, and how much they'd love to be wholly sustainable.

Afterwards she met Jamie and other friends in the pub. She was careful not to drink too much and was home by midnight. On Saturday morning she went to see her cousins at Chorlton. It was a lovely day, perfect April weather, warm in the sunshine. She and Jake were lazing on the terrace, chatting and half listening to Robbie Williams.

They had tea in the Chorlton kitchen and her great-aunt Sophie told them about life as a young doctor after the war. Anna was amazed at how little she knew of her family history. She'd known that Jake's real grandmother, Jill, had died when Hal and his twin brother Richard were born, but she hadn't known Sophie had been the doctor at the birth.

'It was just dreadful,' she said. 'We didn't have the drugs or the knowledge we have now. It was worse for your grandfather because at least I had something to do, trying to save her, but he was just pushed out of the room.'

'When did you stop doctoring, Gran?' asked Jake.

'I went part-time at once so that I could look after your dad and Richard. And when they were two, David and I married. I left the practice when David had his stroke, but I still did a lot of locums, both for my old practice and others. But I've not practised for the last five years at all. I'm out of touch anyway, medicine moves so fast. When I started I used to visit patients on my bicycle and give injections with a syringe the size of a bicycle pump.'

Sometime after five, Anna asked if she could use the landline to ring her parents: her mobile-phone battery was dead, and she wanted to tell them when she'd be back. 'They're such fusspots, they'll probably think I've crashed my car if I don't tell them I'm still here.'

'Yes, of course,' said Sophie. 'Use the one in my study.'

While Anna waited for her mother to answer the phone, she idly examined the neatly stacked papers on the shelf above the desk. Why don't old people chuck stuff away? she wondered. She lifted a wooden bowl full of paperclips off a pile of pads and booklets. The one on the top was an NHS doctor's prescription pad.

Almost without thinking, Anna slipped it into her trouser pocket and pulled her top down over it. I probably won't do anything with it, she thought, but Sophie'll never miss it, so why not nick it? It might be useful one day, if I get desperate.

On Saturday night, she had dinner with her parents at the Crabtree. She had to admit her father had done a great job. The place was packed. Silvano had turned what had been an old coaching inn into a super-smart 'restaurant with rooms'. The food was excellent, executed by an ambitious young chef bent on gaining a Michelin star. The décor had been designed by the style queen Nina Campbell. She had stipulated a complete break with the traditional chintz of the country-house hotel: the furniture was a mix of expensive shabby chic (mostly old oak or mahogany tables and chairs rubbed down and painted in pale blue-grey), some antique chests and cupboards fitted with modern interior hinges so that the drawers and doors opened and shut silently at a touch, expensive art objects perfectly lit, thick white curtains held back by large silk cords and tassels. The beds were huge, with soft-as-gossamer duvets, pale cashmere throws and silk cushions. The bathrooms had free-standing antique baths, double basins and sometimes a sofa or an armchair.

The garden had had a designer's attention too, with a selection of topiary in tubs, neatly edged lawns, slate terraces and classy flowers, mostly white with grey leaves.

It wasn't Anna's taste. Too conventional, safe and posh. But it was impressive. 'Wow, Dad, I can't believe how this has come on. It's amazing. And doing well, obviously.'

'Yes, thank the Lord. It cost enough, so it had to be a success. But it looks as though it will be. The restaurant is booked up weeks ahead and the hotel's full every weekend. It's a huge relief. With luck we'll pay the bank out in three years.'

'Not so fast!' cautioned her mother. 'The real test will be next winter. Summer in the Cotswolds is one thing . . .'

'What about your events business, Mum?'

'It's doing really well, too. We have to turn down work at busy times but at least we can steer smaller events here. We plan to convert the old coach house and stables at the back for parties, conferences and so on.'

'God, you two. You never stop!' As Anna said this, she realized it was a mistake. And, of course, her dad couldn't resist the opening.

'True, we both work hard. And in jobs we love and can make something of. It's hugely satisfying. Not like . . .' He tailed off, and Anna saw her mother glare at him.

'Not like dead-end jobs such as packing boxes and pulling pints,' Anna said. 'That's what you wanted to say, isn't it?'

'Well, yes, I suppose it was. Something like that.' He leant across the table. 'Anna, I only want what would make you happy. You say you're happy, but I don't believe you. You need a proper career.'

Anna felt her anger mounting. She always did when her parents cornered her like this. She could cope with one of them at a time, but both together made her feel bullied and trapped. 'Oh, for Christ's sake. Can't I come home for a weekend without the pair of you getting at me?'

'Anna darling, don't be cross.' Her mother reached to touch her arm. 'If your father can't talk to you, advise you, who can? And I agree with him. I honestly believe that the only two things that matter in life, that can make anyone happy, are satisfying work and love. Love of a partner, family, something. You seem to be doing nothing to advance either.'

'Jesus, Mum. What is it with you two? You complain I never come home. Well, are you surprised?' Her voice was rising, and she made an effort to control it. 'How often do I have to tell you I'm *fine*? I may not be ambitious and driven like you two, but I like working with Oberon. I'm perfectly happy. I'm earning my living. I have friends. Non-judgemental friends who take me as I am. So will you just bloody well back off?'

She saw her mother glance round the dining room. Obviously, her voice had risen to a height unacceptable to the prim and proper diners at the Crabtree. It made her sick, everyone looking down at their plates, pretending that the owners weren't having a domestic with their daughter.

Anna stood up, the chair making a loud scraping noise on the wooden floor, just as the waiter arrived with their main courses. 'Oh, darling,' her mother said, 'your duck's here. Looks delicious.'

Silvano, his voice very low, spoke into his lap: 'Sit down, Anna. You're making an exhibition of yourself.'

But Anna had had enough. 'Fuck the lot of you,' she muttered, as she dropped her napkin on her chair and walked out.

Angelica started to stand up, but Silvano restrained her. 'Let her walk. It's only a mile. It'll give her time to calm down. If we drive her, we'll only continue the quarrel and when we get home she'll jump in her car and drive to London.'

Silvano motioned for the approaching waiter to put their plates down. 'I think you can take the duck away, Franco. I don't think she's coming back.'

Six weeks later, Angelica was getting breakfast when the telephone rang. It was her mother. Laura's voice was urgent but controlled. 'Angelica darling, I'm afraid Anna's in trouble.'

'Oh, God, what?' Her heart contracted as images of her daughter drunk in the pub, or maybe hit by a car, flashed into her brain. 'Is she all right?'

'She's not hurt. But she's been arrested.'

'Oh, no! Oh, Mum, I can't believe it. What's she done?'

'We don't know exactly. The police called Oberon, and he and

Giovanni went to the police station. She's been charged with theft, fraud, possession of drugs and dealing.'

Angelica groped for the chair back with her free hand and sat down abruptly. Her mother was still talking. 'She has to stay at Oberon's, and not go to the pub or see any of her friends there. Giovanni has found a lawyer to represent her. She's to appear in court on Wednesday.'

When she told Silvano about Anna's arrest and proposed they drive up to London, he'd looked more weary than worried. 'Maybe it would be kinder to let matters take their course,' he said. 'Let her suffer the consequences. In the end, as she constantly reminds us, it's her life.'

'But we can't just give up on her, can we?'

'I'm getting close to the point of *wanting* to give up on her. These months without her here have been good, haven't they? It's been great not worrying about her, not pussyfooting round her moods, quarrelling with her all the time.'

'But she's our daughter! We're responsible for her.'

In the end, Angelica drove up alone, feeling let down by her daughter and her husband.

When she arrived at her mother's house in Paddington, Anna wasn't there. She was at Oberon's and the lawyer was with her. Laura gave Angelica a mug of coffee and they sat in the kitchen. She told Angelica what she knew, which wasn't much. Giovanni's lawyer had established that Anna had taken a prescription pad belonging to Sophie from Chorlton, and had been using it to get hold of methadone, which she traded for marijuana in the pub. It could carry a prison sentence.

When Anna and the lawyer appeared, Anna looked terrible.

There were smudges of yesterday's makeup under her eyes; her hair was dirty and hadn't been brushed.

The lawyer, Mr Appleton, a skinny young man with prematurely grey hair, explained that, due to the severity of the charges, the case was unlikely to be tried on Wednesday. 'The intrinsic value of the prescription pad,' he said, 'could make this an indictable offence, which could carry a longer prison sentence than six months. If that is so, then the initial hearing will be short, and Anna won't have to enter a plea. The magistrate will send it to the Crown Court and we'll have to wait a few weeks.'

Angelica stayed in town for the next three days. Anna was subdued and obedient, even agreeing to a trip to Marks & Spencer to buy her a sober jacket and trousers for her court appearance. She barely spoke and spent most of the time in her bedroom, sleeping. On the second day, over a cup of tea, Angelica tried to get her to open up a little. 'Darling, I hope you've been absolutely truthful to Appleton, even if you can't talk to me,' she said.

Anna relaxed a bit and began to speak. The only explanation she could give for having stolen the pad was that it was there. 'I didn't set out to take it,' she said. 'When I saw it in Aunt Sophie's study, I just picked it up. I don't think I even planned to use it then, and I didn't for ages. But when I told Duggie I had it, of course he wanted it. I should have just given it to him. But he said I would make a more believable patient, and he told me what to fill in for the methadone.'

'Appleton says the charge is that you traded the methadone for marijuana.'

Anna's expression was resigned, beaten. 'I know. It looks like that, because I get my weed from Duggie. But honestly, Mum, it wasn't really a trade. I bought weed from Duggie long before

I got the pad. And I could buy it anywhere – it's not expensive. Methadone on the street is worth much more. If I was really dealing, I could have got much more for it than a few packets of grass.'

That night Angelica lay in her childhood bedroom, her sanctuary when unhappy as an adult. And here she was again. *Plus ça change,* she thought, staring at the ceiling. She couldn't help blaming herself. Anna's waywardness must have started because she'd neglected her daughter for her business. Maybe an adopted child with a troubled background should have gone to a more traditional family where the mother was at home all the time. Maybe they shouldn't have sent her to boarding school.

Or maybe Silvano was right. Maybe they were mollycoddling her. Maybe they should cut her loose, let her sink or swim. As long as the family housed her, employed her, picked her up when she fell down, she'd never find out whether she could cope on her own.

The hearing was in the Westminster magistrates' court in Marylebone. Anna, looking tired but calm, stood in the dock, next to a security officer wearing a navy jumper with epaulettes. Handcuffs and a bunch of keys hung at his waist. Catching sight of her mother, Anna gave her a small apologetic smile.

Angelica steeled herself to listen to the evidence, but the case, as Mr Appleton had predicted, was promptly referred to the Crown Court, and they all went home in a taxi. No one spoke much. The anticlimax was deflating, and worrying.

Angelica went home to Holly Farm. She'd have liked to take Anna with her, but the terms of her bail would not allow it. At least Anna had promised she wouldn't flout the bail conditions: she would stay away from the pub and off drugs.

Three weeks later they were all back in court, this time with Silvano. On the advice of the lawyer, Anna pleaded guilty to all the charges, her voice barely audible, eliciting a bark from the judge to speak up.

The judge, an overweight woman with large glasses and a downturned mouth, looked barely interested as she listened to the police evidence.

'The facts of this case are not contested, Your Honour. The pharmacist, Mr Aziz Halim, of Halim Pharmacy in Praed Street, has confirmed that he filled four repeat prescriptions for the drug methadone to Ms Anna Angelotti, the defendant. But on being presented with the fifth prescription, he followed NHS guidance for repeat prescriptions of controlled drugs and questioned Ms Angelotti. She was unable to provide details of her treatment or of her doctor. He informed the police.

'When questioned by DC James Mathews, the defendant admitted that she had stolen a prescription pad from her great-aunt, a former GP, and used it, at the request of her friend Douglas Entebe, to obtain methadone, which she gave to him in the Duck and Dog public house. Unfortunately, Mr Entebe has absconded, and the police, in a separate investigation, are following up possible illegal activities in the Duck and Dog.'

Angelica watched Anna's face, but Anna was staring at the floor in front of her.

Mr Appleton was next. He checked his notes and looked up. 'Your Honour, we do not contest the facts of the case,' he said, 'but I would like to put some matters of mitigation before the court. This is my client's first offence. Ms Angelotti does admit to the occasional personal use of marijuana but has never taken methadone or hard drugs.'

Angelica, who had heard her daughter admit to snorting coke, did not dare look at her. The lawyer continued; 'My client took her great-aunt's prescription pad on the spur of the moment in an unpremeditated act. When she told a friend, Mr Douglas Entebe, who works with her in the same public house, that she had the prescription pad, he persuaded her to use it to obtain methadone. She admits supplying the methadone to Mr Entebe but she did so, not for profit, but as a friend and at his request. Had she been truly "dealing" she would not have exchanged it for marijuana, which has a street value of far less than that of methadone. She realizes that she has been foolish and weak to give in to pressure to use the prescription forms. She finds it difficult to say no when she is under the influence of alcohol.

'Ms Angelotti is of good family, and her parents are here in court today. I will put before the court testimony of her good character from her employer, Mr Oberon Oliver, for whom she works when not waitressing in the pub, and also from her grandparents, who are the well-known and respectable Angelottis, proprietors of the Deli-Calzone café chain, Laura restaurants and Giovanni's. My client deeply regrets her actions. I suggest that a non-custodial sentence would be appropriate punishment.'

The judge tapped her pencil on her pad, apparently thinking. Then she looked across at Anna. 'Ms Angelotti,' she said. 'Would you say you have an addiction problem?'

Anna looked confused. 'I don't know,' she said.

'Do you drink alcohol every day?'

'I . . . I . . . Yes. Probably.'

'How often do you smoke marijuana?'

Anna looked at her lawyer, obviously not sure what to say. He nodded. 'Quite often,' she said.

'Whenever you are offered some, or can get hold of it?'

'I suppose so.'

'Well, I'm going to give you a suspended sentence of nine months in prison. The suspension of the sentence is conditional on your doing one hundred hours of community service as well as attending a drug-and-alcohol-awareness course. If you fail on either the community service or the awareness course, you will serve your full sentence in prison.'

PART TWO

CHAPTER TEN

Tom discovered that trying to trace his birth-mother was a long, slow process, and he wasn't Jeannie MacDonald's only client. For two months there was no news and Tom tried to put his quest to the back of his mind. When Jeannie eventually came back to him it was to tell him that his mother had not been born in Oxfordshire, but in Hampshire. Her birth, if this was the right Laura Oliver, was registered in Andover. Of the other Laura Olivers born in those two years, one had been born in Scotland, and two in Wales. There were a few other Olivers, but not with a first name of Laura.

'In some cases, Laura was a middle name, so I've parked them for the moment and concentrated on the Hampshire Olivers.'

'Are they still living in Hampshire, though? They must surely have moved if my mother came from Oxfordshire?'

'Yes, any time after Laura's birth. Unfortunately there are scores of Olivers living in Oxfordshire.'

'So what do we do?'

'Well, I thought I'd try to narrow it down a bit, so I looked for any brothers or sisters born to the same parents. Your mother, if she is your mother, had two elder brothers, Hugh and David.

What's particularly surprising is that there appears to have been a ten-year gap between each of the siblings.'

'How do you know that?'

'This is partly why it's taken me so long. I looked for the same parents in all the Oliver birth records for thirty years after and thirty years before our Laura was born. Women generally give birth between the ages of fifteen and forty-five, but as Laura might have been born at the beginning or the end of her mother's fertile period, I had to look over a sixty-year period to find any siblings. And I found her brothers, Hugh and David.'

Tom listened to this explanation, but he wasn't really following. He was thinking of that picture in the paper of the adopted man surrounded by an extended family. You set out trying to find your mother, and suddenly there are two uncles to contend with as well. Did he want any uncles? He wasn't sure. He jerked his thoughts back. 'Did you find the brothers?' he asked.

'Not yet.'

'OK. So, what now?'

'What I suggest is this,' she said. 'I write to them all, the Oxfordshire ones, asking if the siblings Hugh, David and Laura Oliver, born 1907, 1917 and 1927 respectively were or are part of their family. I'll just say I'm writing on behalf of a friend who would like to contact any of them.'

'They'll all be dead I expect, won't they?'

'Hugh will be, I imagine – he'd be ninety-five. And maybe David. He'd be eighty-five. But Laura, at seventy-five, may well be alive.'

'But if she doesn't want anything to do with me, or anything that reminds her of her life back then, she'll not answer, surely.'

'There is that risk, but by now there might be younger Olivers in the family. They may answer out of curiosity, or in the hope there is to be money in it, or out of concern for Laura. We won't address a letter to any Laura yet. Not till we know for sure we've got the right one.'

A month later, Jeannie was back to visit Tom, smiling from ear to ear. 'We've found her, Tom. And she's alive and well.'

'Oh, my God.' His heart thumped, and he felt oddly weak. 'How did you do that?'

Jeannie pulled a letter out of her bag and handed it to him. 'You read it while I go and talk to Eliza. Shall I ask her for some coffee and to block your calls for a bit?'

Tom nodded. 'Thank you.'

His heart continued to pound as he opened the letter. It was a single sheet in a neat, round hand. The writing paper had a printed address at the top, Chorlton, near Frampton, Oxfordshire, with a postcode and two telephone numbers, one for the office, one for the house. He ran his eyes to the bottom. It was signed Sophie Oliver.

Tom went back to the top and read, deliberately slowly.

Dear Miss MacDonald,

Of course, I have no idea of the reason you wish to contact the Oliver siblings you mention, but I am assuming, for the moment at least, that your intentions are benign.

I can tell you that both Hugh and David are dead. I am David's widow. Laura is alive and well.

She is, and has been since we were little, my close friend, and in order to decide whether to put you in touch with her, I need to

know your reasons for wanting to contact her. I would be happy
to meet you, either here or in London, or you could telephone me
on the house number above.

Yours sincerely,

Sophie Oliver

When Jeannie returned with the coffee, Tom was still holding the letter. She sat down opposite him and pushed a cup towards him. 'I think I should contact her,' she said, 'and then we should meet her together. What do you say?'

'I agree. I'm rather glad Laura has a protectress, a kind of filter. It means she doesn't have to deal with me if she wants nothing to do with me. The last thing I want is to add to her guilt or grief.'

'Tom,' said Jeannie, 'you don't know that she has any guilt or grief.' Tom was surprised at her steely tone. 'It's true you might have caused her either, but we just don't know. But I agree it's good if Sophie is in the picture and she'll be a better judge of what's good for Laura than either of us.'

The three met in the cheerless public area of the Paddington Hilton Hotel. When a short, oldish woman walked through the revolving door, stopped and stood looking around the entrance area, Jeannie jumped up, telling Tom to stay put, and walked towards her. Tom watched the two women shake hands and smile. Jeannie gestured to where he was sitting, and he rose as the two women approached. Sophie had dropped her smile for a serious expression and held out her hand rather tentatively, examining Tom with what seemed more like suspicion than curiosity.

'Tom Standing,' he said.

'I've ordered tea,' said Jeannie. 'Mrs Oliver, it's very good of you to come.'

'Please call me Sophie,' she said.

Tom examined her as she added milk to her tea. She had slightly reddened hands with neatly trimmed nails. Her hair was still thick, a short, wiry mass of salt-and-pepper curls. They framed a face surprisingly unlined for someone who must be in her seventies. She was a little plump, but she looked healthy, like a farmer's wife advertising butter.

Tom liked her at once. He found himself wondering if his mother would be anything like her friend.

Her gaze was very direct. 'And you are?' she asked.

Tom hesitated, and Jeannie prompted, 'Go on, Tom.'

'Well, here goes.' He tried to smile at Sophie. 'I think I'm Laura's son, born in the Middlesex Hospital in January 1947.'

Sophie stared at him. 'Oh, my God,' she said, her voice hardly more than a whisper.

No one said anything more. Tom watched Sophie process the information. She gazed at him intently, shook her head slightly, and said again, 'Oh, my God. I can't believe it.'

'The thing is,' said Tom, suddenly finding his voice, 'I don't want to frighten Laura. Or even see her if she wants me to just disappear again. But I would love to meet her if she's willing.'

'I . . . I don't think she would be, but I don't know. We never talk about you. Haven't for years and years. At first, she couldn't stop talking about you, the loss of you, how she'd given you up. But then Angelica came along . . .'

'Angelica?' asked Jeannie.

Sophie wasn't listening. She had a question of her own. 'But how did you track us down?'

Jeannie explained that she worked for Norcap and that she helped parents find their children or children find their parents. 'I do the legwork, looking through official records, and advising clients on how to proceed. Or whether to proceed. Sometimes it's obvious that finding your mother would only make you miserable.'

Tom wanted to get back to his new-found sibling. 'Sophie, please would you tell us about Angelica?'

'Yes, Angelica. Laura and Giovanni got married after you were born and then they had another baby, Angelica.'

Information was coming foo fast for Tom. 'Giovanni? Is that Italian? Is he my father?' His mind was spinning.

'Yes. He's Italian. He was a prisoner of war. I don't think he'd want to see you either.' She stopped. Tom and Jeannie looked at her, waiting for more. 'They're happy you see. They've got used to not having a son, I think. And they adore Angelica. But . . . but . . .' She put her head in her hands. 'I just don't know. I don't know what's best.'

'Angelica! I have a sister called Angelica?'

'Yes,' said Sophie, raising her head again. 'She's a chef. Like her parents.'

'They're chefs?'

Jeannie interrupted. 'Tom,' she said, 'enough questions! Poor Sophie. It's all too much for now.' She turned to Sophie, almost cutting Tom out. 'You need time to consider what to do. Obviously we'd like you to put us in touch with Laura. But only if you think that's the right thing to do. Maybe I can ring you in a day or two.'

She peered into her handbag and took out a sheet of paper. 'This is a little précis about Tom here. Just to reassure you that he's not a crook, that he doesn't need money from Laura or anyone, and that if Laura doesn't want to meet him, he'll go away and not bother her again. If you want to ask any questions, give me a ring.'

Sophie did ring Jeannie, but only to tell her that she felt too close to Laura, too involved in the family, to know what to advise. She didn't want to tell Laura she'd met Tom because she felt Laura herself should decide if anyone in the family met him or not. But she would pass on a letter from Tom or Jeannie to Laura. They should write the letter addressed to Laura Oliver, at Chorlton, of the kind Jeannie would normally write to suspected birth-mothers of adopted children, making no mention of their meeting with her, Sophie, or admitting to knowing anything that she'd told them. She would send the letter on. That way they would not have Laura's address if Laura decided she wanted no more to do with it, and Sophie would not be influencing her friend one way or the other.

CHAPTER ELEVEN

The following Monday morning, Laura was picking through her post, putting the boring bills to one side, when she found a white envelope addressed in an unfamiliar hand to Laura Oliver at Chorlton. Sophie had re-addressed it. Laura recognized her friend's familiar round writing, and Sophie had put a row of Xs and the initial S on the back of the envelope.

Who would call me Laura Oliver? she wondered. She was Laura Angelotti to everyone. She slit open the envelope to find a hand-written letter from a private address in Cheam, someone she'd never heard of called Jeannie MacDonald. Frowning, she read it.

Dear Laura Oliver,

I apologize for bothering you out of the blue, but I have been asked to help a friend of mine trace you. Of course, I may not have found the right Laura Oliver, and I do apologize if that is so, but my friend says the last time you saw him was on 19th January 1947. If that date means anything to you, I would be most obliged if you would let me know.

Yours sincerely,

Jeannie MacDonald

The room seemed to tilt and Laura felt the blood drain from her face. She tried to stand but her legs were suddenly unable to support her. Abruptly she sat down again at the kitchen table: 19th January 1947. The day she'd given away her baby.

Oh, my God, this was about that baby. Or, rather, about the man he'd become. He would be grown-up now. A year older than Angelica. They were both in their fifties.

She started to stuff the letter back in the envelope. She wanted not to have opened it, to pretend it had never arrived. For all those years she'd fretted daily, wondering where that baby was, what sort of child, then adult, he'd become. All those miserable hours speculating on whether he was happy, healthy, doing well. Whether that couple had treated him kindly, really loved him as she would have. Then later: was he good at school? Did he go to university? What kind of a career was he having? Was he happily married? Were there children? Did she have grandchildren she didn't know about? Was he alive?

But the pain and anxiety had gradually lessened. Angelica at least half filled the gap, and she'd been the balm that had made Giovanni forgive her for parting with the boy. But she'd still wished she had both of them. She often dreamed of the two as siblings, playing together, quarrelling, ganging up to defend each other, growing up, maybe both in the business. Giovanni never said so any more, but she knew he'd sorely missed the son he'd never had to work with, to train and bring into the business.

For years now, she'd managed not to allow thoughts of that baby to overwhelm her. She adored her grandchild, Anna, and she could see that adoption sometimes worked and sometimes didn't, and maybe the parents you grew up with didn't necessarily dictate success or otherwise. Her boy might be miserable or brilliantly happy. But he might have been either of those things if she'd kept him. She no longer suffered from deep guilt and depression about abandoning her baby to strangers. She'd become calmer, more like Giovanni, whose philosophy was not to fret about something you could do nothing about.

And now this. It threw her right back fifty-five years. She couldn't bear it.

She pulled the letter out of the envelope again and ran upstairs to her desk. She took a sheet of letterhead from her drawer and sat down to write. No! The woman would have her address if she used that. She stuffed the paper back into the drawer, crumpling it as she did so, and extracted a plain sheet. She held her breath for a moment, telling herself to be calm.

She wrote the date on the top right corner, but no address.

Dear Miss MacDonald,

The date you mention means nothing to me. I have no money and I do not want to meet your friend.

Laura hesitated about whether to write Laura Oliver or Laura Angelotti. She signed it simply *Laura.*

She sealed the envelope, stamped it and went straight to the post office in Praed Street. She thought if she delayed she might change her mind.

When Giovanni came home he kissed her as usual, then looked hard at her face. He always picked up on her mood. 'What's up, *cara mia*?' he said. 'You look strained. One of your migraines?'

'No, I'm fine,' she said, and burst into tears. As he held her, his arms right round her and his big hand on her head, pulling her to him, she made a decision. The temptation to tell him was almost overwhelming, but she mustn't do that. She absolutely must not. She'd be opening Pandora's box, and out would come all that old wretched unhappiness. Giovanni had never understood why she'd given away the baby, and she couldn't tell him that she'd had to, not just because they were broke and homeless but mainly because she'd feared the baby wasn't his.

She pulled away from him. 'Maybe I'll go and lie down,' she said. 'I do feel a migraine coming on.'

'But something has upset you. Talk to me, *cara*.'

She shook her head, still fighting tears. She forced a smile. 'I'll be fine.' She turned and hurried upstairs, away from her beloved husband before she broke down and told him everything.

Laura spent the next week telling herself she had done the right thing, that to meet her fifty-five-year-old son would be too painful, and too dangerous. What if he looked like the lover she'd had before she'd fallen in love with Giovanni, big and blond and obviously not Giovanni's son? Suddenly all the anxiety and misery she'd suffered when she'd given up the baby for adoption came flooding back. She'd not been able to tell Giovanni of her fears because she'd allowed him to believe she'd been a virgin, and she'd feared he'd abandon her.

She made a huge effort not to seem distracted or anxious, indeed not to think about the matter at all. Giovanni remarked on her pallor once, then suggested she was doing too much, but after a fortnight she began to relax. She began to hope she'd got away with it, seen off the danger.

But then she received another letter, again forwarded by

Sophie from Chorlton. I should just throw away the envelope, unopened, she thought. But as she hesitated, a feeling of inevitability – she could not hold back the waves – closed in on her. And curiosity overwhelmed her. She took it up to her bedroom, sat on the bed, and opened it.

It wasn't from the MacDonald woman. It was long and typewritten. The printed letterhead was a company she hadn't heard of with an east London postcode.

She dropped her eyes to the signature. Tom Standing. She went back to the beginning.

Dear Laura,

I realize that hearing from me after fifty-five years must be a shock and if you don't want to meet me then you only have to say so and I won't trouble you again.

But before you decide, I should tell you something of my life.

I was very lucky. My adoptive parents gave me an excellent home and a good education (I went to Eton, then Edinburgh University). I wanted for nothing.

My career has been in the City and thirteen years ago I set up an investment company, Ajax, of which I am the senior partner. It has made me a rich man.

I married a wonderful girl called Clemmie when I was thirty-five and we had a son, Charlie. When he was just ten, he and his mother were killed in an avalanche, skiing in Iceland.

I have known I was adopted since I was thirteen and I don't think it has ever bothered me. But recently I have begun to wonder about you and my father, and whether I have any siblings, cousins, other family.

I am not looking for anything from you, except to know something about you and to meet you. Of course, we might not get on, and you might not want to know me. I accept that. But if you do want to meet, I would be so pleased.

If I don't hear from you, I will assume you don't, and I won't write again.

Tom Standing

PS I now live in a flat in Docklands, London.

Laura crumpled up the letter and put it in the wastepaper basket at her feet. Then she fished it out, smoothed it flat, and put it under the tray on her dressing-table.

Two days later a third readdressed envelope arrived from Chorlton. On the back Sophie had written. *What's going on? XX Sophie.*

She felt a wave of despair. Would this never stop? On top of the anxiety of the letters, Laura felt badly about Sophie. She longed to talk to her and tell her what was going on, tell her everything about Marcin and Giovanni. Sophie was too hon-ourable to have opened the letters. She'd obviously just passed them on. If she could just talk to Sophie it would be a relief. Sophie would understand and advise her. But she couldn't tell Sophie and not Giovanni. Again, she took the envelope up to the bedroom to open it. Inside was a folded plain sheet of paper with a handwritten line: *I'm so sorry, I forgot to enclose these. Tom.*

There were two photographs. One was a black-and-white head-and-shoulders shot of a broad-faced man with dark hair. He was smiling at the camera. The second picture was in colour, of the same man and a young woman with long hair, sitting on a boat, with a skinny lad, perhaps eight or nine, standing between them. All three were laughing at something to the left of the camera.

Laura could not take her eyes off them. She looked from one picture to the other, thinking, That's my son. The son I gave away because I didn't know if he was my husband's. She looked long and hard at the close-up of Tom. Did he look like Marcin, the Polish prisoner of war she'd had a secret affair with, making love in haystacks and hedgerows when she was eighteen? Or Giovanni, the love of her life who'd taught her what real love was, and wooed her away from the bullying Marcin? The broad face looked more like Marcin's; the dark hair could be Giovanni's. But in truth she could see no resemblance, except that he looked a bit like the framed photo of her long-dead brother Hugh, shot down in the Channel when she was a teenager. She studied the picture of the family, then hugged both photos to her chest while she rocked back and forth on the edge of the bed.

What am I doing, she thought, mourning two people I've never met? Longing to pick up the telephone to a son I've not seen since the day he was born, and then only as a bundle in the arms of a nurse carrying him from the room? But of course I can't. It's just too much of a risk.

She put the pictures under the dressing-table tray with the letter. Do nothing, she told herself. He said he wouldn't pester me.

By the end of June Laura had persuaded herself that Tom had done as he promised and was going to leave her alone. But he still occupied a lot of her waking thoughts, and sometimes her dreams.

One night she woke from a nightmare in which someone, a

nurse perhaps, held out her naked baby son to her. Full of love, she reached for him. But the woman turned and threw the baby into a basin. She watched as, arms flailing and legs kicking, he turned to liquid and ran down the drain. He was gone, irretrievably, devastatingly gone.

'Wake up, darling, it's just a bad dream.' Giovanni was shaking her. Gasping, half crying, she clung to him.

'What was it, sweetheart? Tell me.'

She shook her head, pulling herself together. 'It's nothing. I don't know. It's gone.'

CHAPTER TWELVE

For the next month there was no further word from Tom, and Laura had had several phone calls with Sophie in which neither of them had mentioned the letters. They had talked about the farm, and Laura's worries about Anna. Her granddaughter's problems pushed thoughts of Tom out of her mind at least for some of the time. On one of those calls, she said, 'Soph, why don't you come up for a few days? Or are you all too busy harvesting? It would be so lovely to see you.'

'I'd love to. And no. Harvesting isn't like it was, with us women making picnics for half the village up on Top Field. Now it's delivered pizza and a flask of tea and the men eat it on the tractors. How about the weekend?'

The day Sophie arrived was sunny and warm and she suggested a walk in the park.

'OK, but let's go to Regent's Park,' said Laura. 'The roses will still be out and the food at that café is marginally better than at the one in Hyde Park.'

They took the bus, got off at the zoo and walked across the park. Laura felt immediately better. Maybe it's the fresh air, she thought, or more likely just seeing her old friend.

They talked about the farm: Jake was really happy working for his father and was convinced there was a future for organic farming. 'Remember when he wanted to be a land agent because it's better paid and safer? But farming's in his blood, isn't it?' said Laura.

'Yes, and he's good at it. He's trying hard to get Hal to farm all three farms organically – you know, no chemical pesticides or herbicides. Surprisingly, Hal seems to be coming round. Talks a lot about sustainability. Though he won't go fully organic, I'm sure.'

'Pippa will be on Jake's side, though, won't she? She's a hippie at heart. And they must both be happy to know one of their sons will take over Chorlton one day. David would have been very proud of them.'

Sophie nodded, a shadow crossing her face. It was two and a half years since David, her husband and Laura's brother, had died. For thirty years before that, she, Hal and Pippa had managed the farms, but now she took a very back seat.

'Yes,' she said. 'The contracting business is huge now. We farm nearly all our neighbours' land, right into Warwickshire.'

They inspected the roses, mostly hybrid teas planted in municipal blocks. They chatted on, family discussions occasionally interrupted by the need to bend and press their noses to a rose, exclaiming at the depth of scent or complaining at the lack of it, commenting on a bloom's perfection or the sinister absence of greenfly, blackspot or mildew.

And then they got to Anna.

'I'm so worried about her, Soph. Angelica and Silvano are at the end of their tether. Oberon thinks she's still smoking a lot of marijuana. She did go on the drug course, but I doubt it's made any difference. And she completed her community service – or, at least, turned up for it every day. But only, I suspect, because the judge had told her bluntly she'd serve her suspended prison sentence if she didn't. She had to weed a churchyard with a lot of other offenders and clear litter from under flyovers and railway embankments. It took longer than normal to do the hundred hours because she was allowed two days off a week to work for Oberon.'

Laura said she had the impression the officers in charge turned a blind eye to their charges doing next to nothing. But at least Anna had got the requisite ticks in the boxes. 'Until next time,' she said. 'There will be a next time, I'm sure.'

'There needn't be, surely,' said Sophie. 'At least she's still working for Oberon. He's a sensible lad.'

'He is, but he can't stop her smoking dope.'

Sophie frowned. 'I feel out of my depth. I'm a doctor, but even when I was practising, I couldn't tell who was on drugs and who wasn't. Sometimes people function fine, despite booze or drugs, or at least appear to.'

'Sometimes she's full of beans,' said Laura. 'Other times she's sulky and moping, or angry about nothing. I'm sure these mood swings are drug-related.'

'She needs help, Laura. But how to get her to see it?'

'She also needs a better job, or another part-time one. I've not told Angelica but I've had to give Anna the odd handout. Oberon's business is getting busier, but it's not enough. Since she finished the community service she's been doing three days a week for him, two packing and one helping with the admin. At least he's paying her now. She used to do it for free. But she needs more.'

'What about the pub she was working in?'

'That's the other problem. She can't go back there, can't even show her face, because she's a witness for the prosecution of the man she gave the methadone to. He absconded but some of his friends were done for dealing as a result of her case. One's in prison. They must want to kill her.'

'Oh, God. How horrible. Poor girl. There's no boyfriend?'

'No, I don't think so. I don't think she's ever had one. No one that any of the family ever met, anyway. And I suppose that's a good thing if her friends are riff-raff and drug dealers.'

'I'm sure they're not. But she should get out of London, shouldn't she?'

'Except that her going back to Holly Farm wouldn't work. She and Silvano would be at loggerheads in no time.'

'She could stay at Chorlton,' said Sophie. 'I'd be happy to have her.'

'Oh, Soph, you're so generous. How can you be so forgiving? It was your prescription pad she stole!'

'I love her to bits, that's why. And she's your granddaughter.'

They walked across the lawns to the café on the Inner Circle and sat outside on the open terrace, where they ordered Caesar salads and a couple of glasses of Chardonnay.

Laura could feel the warmth of the sun through her shirt. She found herself relaxing, glad of Sophie's presence. Sophie has always had that effect, she thought, the ability to make you feel better.

Suddenly she wanted to tell her about Tom. 'There's something else.'

Sophie looked at her, her fork poised in mid-air, her face expectant.

'I've never told anyone except you why I gave away my first baby fifty-five years ago.'

Sophie nodded, her face serious.

'Giovanni doesn't know. He thought it was because we had no money and nowhere to live.'

Sophie waited, her eyes on Laura's. Then she said, 'What is it, Laura? Has something happened?'

Laura could feel her mouth trembling and she pushed her paper napkin against it. She felt the prick of tears, but she looked up, eyes open, until the danger passed. 'You know those letters you readdressed to me? They were from my son. That baby has reappeared. He's fifty-five and works in London, and he wants to meet us.'

And then it all came out. Laura told Sophie about her immediate repudiation of her son, then his letter, his promise not to pester her, and the photographs. 'I don't know if he looks like Giovanni or Marcin. I don't think he looks like either.'

'But do you want to see him?'

'I don't know. Sometimes I'm desperate to. Other times I'm just too frightened. But I can't see him, can I?'

'Why not? Everyone will accept him as Giovanni's son. Of course they will. It's over fifty years ago. No one is going to start counting months and days of gestation and questioning his paternity. What matters is if you want to see him or not.'

'But what if he blames me for giving him away?'

'Did he say he blamed you? Or sound as though he did?'

'No, he said he'd wanted for nothing.'

When they got home, Laura took the letters and photographs from under the tray on her dressing-table and gave them to Sophie. They sat side by side on the bed while Sophie read them.

When she'd finished, Laura said, 'Help me, Sophie. What would you do? What should I do?'

'I think,' said Sophie slowly, 'that you should show these to your husband and then you should decide together.'

That evening Sophie took Oberon and Anna out to supper, saying it would be nice for her to see her grandson and great-niece without the usual family tribe to contend with. She'd treat them to Sally Clarke's in Kensington Church Street. Laura knew she was tactfully clearing the house so that Giovanni and she could talk about their son.

For once Laura had no interest in cooking dinner. Instead she made smoked-salmon sandwiches and opened a bottle of Barolo.

When Giovanni came down from his study, he found Laura on the sofa with the newspaper. On the coffee-table in front of her was the tray of sandwiches.

'What's this?' he said, kissing her. 'Sandwiches? Are you on strike? Are we snacking in front of the TV like Americans?'

She smiled, trying to control her nervousness. 'Yes and no, *caro*. Yes to the sandwiches. No to the telly. I've something to discuss with you and I thought it would be easier if I didn't have to cook at the same time.'

'Discuss?' He frowned. 'That sounds ominous.'

Her heart banging uncomfortably, she handed him Tom's letter. 'You read this while I get the wine,' she said. 'You're going to need it.'

She went out of the door then stopped, turned and tiptoed back to peep round the jamb, her heart in her mouth.

At first, he read with a puzzled frown, then abruptly sat up and leant over the paper, reading with utter concentration. He put his hand on the arm of the sofa as though to push himself up. Then he reread the letter and fell back, a look of wonder, maybe even happiness on his face.

She crept downstairs and waited a few more minutes. Then she reappeared with the wine.

Of course he wanted to know how it had happened, and she showed him the previous letter from Jeannie MacDonald. Finally, she showed him the photographs. He studied them for a long time, his face a mixture of disbelief and astonishment.

Suddenly, looking at Tom's letter, he said, 'But, Laura,' he pointed at the date on Tom's letter, 'this is months ago. What did you reply? Why didn't you tell me? What—'

'I haven't replied. I just told the MacDonald woman that that date, the baby's birthdate, meant nothing to me and to go away.'

'You what? You told her to go away, Why, for God's sake?'

Laura gripped his arm, peering into his face. 'Oh, darling, I was too frightened. Frightened to meet him, but also frightened it would open old wounds between you and me. It took you so long to forgive me, and to this day I don't know if you really have.'

Giovanni spun round to face her. 'Laura, of course I've forgiven you. You did it for the baby's sake, and I finally understood that. What I've never understood is why you did it without telling me, without giving me a chance to dissuade you.'

Laura didn't reply. She couldn't, for the same reason that had stood between her and Giovanni all these years: she suspected the baby wasn't his.

Giovanni broke the silence. 'But, Laura, my darling, that old wound has had fifty years of happiness with you and Angelica to heal it. It is gone.'

How generous he is, thought Laura, a wave of love engulfing her. If only she'd had the sense to tell him the truth all those years ago. Why hadn't she told him that she and Marcin had slept together? When she and Giovanni had first made love, she'd allowed him to believe that it was the first time for her, never revealing that six weeks earlier she'd still been with Marcin.

Desperate thoughts flashed through her head. All the time she was pregnant, it had never occurred to her that the baby might not be Giovanni's. It was only when the doctor said she was due six weeks earlier than she'd believed that she'd realized she might be carrying Marcin's child. Probably was carrying Marcin's child.

Should she tell Giovanni now? No, of course not. If they did meet Tom, they couldn't tell him he'd only found his mother, not his father. It would be too cruel. And Giovanni would not be able to bear the humiliation. And neither could she.

'I don't know what to do,' she said.

'Don't you want to see him, Laura? Not see our son?'

'I don't know. Yes. Yes, I do. I've thought of nothing else since the letter came. But, darling, what if he hates us? Or, rather, hates me for giving him away? What if we don't like him?' She started to cry, the tears warm on her cheeks. 'It's all such a risk. I'm seventy-five, Giovanni, and you're nearly eighty. We've borne the loss of him all these years, and it will open up such deep wounds.'

She was crying in earnest now. Giovanni put his arms round her and kissed her hair. 'Shush, shush. It's all right, *cara mia*. Don't cry. We are going to eat our sandwiches, have a good glass of that wine, and then we will decide together if we see him or not.'

The next morning, when Giovanni had breakfasted and gone upstairs, Laura told Sophie about the night before.

'We've agreed to meet Tom,' she said. 'Giovanni is going to contact him, invite him here.'

'Laura, that's wonderful. I hoped you'd come to that conclusion.'

'I'm still horribly anxious, Sophie, but Giovanni's so excited there's no stopping him now.'

'It's the right decision,' said Sophie. 'If you'd said you wouldn't meet him, you'd be spending the rest of your life wondering.'

'Why didn't you say so when I asked you?'

'Because I thought it should be your decision. Yours and Giovanni's.' She paused, then put her hand on Laura's wrist. 'Laura, I've a revelation to make too. About all this.'

Laura looked at her, puzzled. 'I've met Tom,' said Sophie. 'And he is really, really nice.'

Laura's brain seemed to have stopped working. 'What?' she said. 'When? How?'

Sophie told her about the letter she'd had from Jeannie MacDonald, asking if the siblings Hugh, David and Laura meant anything, and how she'd agreed to meet her. 'I wanted to make sure she wasn't some sort of con-woman. We met in the Paddington Hilton and she brought Tom with her. I didn't want to give him your address because he might have crashed in without you wanting him, so I agreed they could write to Chorlton and I would forward the letters.'

Laura looked at her friend intently for a minute. 'God, you're a dark horse, Sophie. Have you told anyone?'

'Of course not. It's your story, not mine, and you should decide who to tell. Though he's bound to want to meet the rest of the family and they'll all want to meet him. He's delightful.' She smiled. 'Nice-looking too.'

CHAPTER THIRTEEN

Tom asked the taxi to stop at the top of the mews. He wanted to walk around a bit. Steady himself.

He paid the driver, waving away the change from a ten-pound note. The man grinned. 'Good on ya, guv,' he said. 'Must be my lucky day.'

Let's hope it's mine, thought Tom, as he set off down the cobbled street. As he rounded the bend, his eyes widened in surprise. On his right was a row of two-storey brick cottages, all painted different ice-cream shades. It looked totally un-English and made him smile. On the opposite side, by contrast, there were ordinary modern brick mews houses, with standard windows and metal up-and-over garage doors.

Number one was one of the coloured cottages, a pistachio green. He rang the bell and waited while he listened to someone clumping down the stairs.

The man who opened the door was bald on top with a pair of silver spectacles sitting on his smooth dome. The surrounding fringe of thin grey hair framed a lined but distinguished face: olive skin, deep-set brown eyes and good teeth revealed in a wide smile. Tom guessed he was about eighty.

'Tom?'

Tom had lost his voice. It took an effort to say, 'Yes. Tom Standing.'

'I'm Giovanni.'

Suddenly it seemed mad, to meet your father for the first time and find him in his dotage. Tom put out his hand, and Giovanni took it. They looked at each other for a moment, and then the old man pulled Tom into a hug. Releasing him, he said, 'So you are my son.' And then he let out a burst of laughter. 'My son,' he repeated.

Tom smiled, at once feeling a lot more relaxed. 'It sounds very strange to say I'm pleased to meet my own father, but I am.'

'Come and meet your mother,' said Giovanni, turning and climbing slowly up the straight flight of stairs into a large living room.

A woman, a little younger than Giovanni, got up from her chair. She moved, he saw, without the stiffness of old age. She had a strong face with wide-apart, watchful eyes, and hair not yet completely grey. As he took her hand, he noticed her short unvarnished nails. She wasn't smiling.

Giovanni was still chuckling. 'There's no accepted way to behave, is there? Laura, *cara mia*, this is Tom, our son.'

The woman didn't kiss him or say anything. She held onto his hand, and he put his other over both of theirs. Their eyes met, a little solemnly, then Laura turned away. As she sat down she indicated the sofa. 'Sit down, Tom.'

Giovanni opened a bottle of champagne. 'We usually drink prosecco,' he said, 'but even I, a good Italian, have to admit that, for a real celebration, you need champagne.'

Tom drank his rather faster than usual and was glad of its immediate effect. The anxiety lessened, and his spirit lifted.

'I made us *osso buco* and polenta for dinner,' Giovanni said. 'I hope you'll stay. Fifty-five years is a lot to catch up, don't you think?'

'Do you do the cooking?'

'Sometimes. But Laura is a good cook. She learnt to cook Italian food when we married. Now she's better than me sometimes, and I was a chef for years and years. There are lots of cooks in this family, and if they aren't cooks they're restaurateurs, caterers, or something to do with food.'

'Really? All in the food world? How interesting.'

'Mario runs our ice-cream business. His mother, my sister Carlotta, she's dead now, she was a great cook and she taught our daughter Angelica. Angelica used to write cookbooks and cook on TV, but now she's a caterer, doing parties. And she's married to Silvano, who has a gastro-pub in the Cotswolds.'

'Stop, stop, Giovanni,' interrupted Laura. 'The poor man can't take it all in.'

But Tom was impatient to hear more, so Giovanni told him about the Laura and Deli-Calzone chains.

'The Deli-Calzone chain!' exclaimed Tom. 'We practically live in the one in Docklands. Susan, my girlfriend, hates cooking, so we get most of our meals delivered from it.'

And then when Giovanni was explaining that Giovanni's was, despite the name, Laura's inspiration, Tom interrupted: 'Giovanni's? The restaurant in Notting Hill? Is that yours?'

'Well, yes,' said Laura. 'Giovanni's is my baby, I suppose. Do you know it?'

'I asked my wife to marry me in it.' Immediately Tom regretted saying this. It would lead to discussions and commiserations about the death of Clemmie and Charlie, and he didn't want to talk about that. Not yet anyway. But Giovanni was eager to get on with their own family history and didn't take him up on it.

'When you come again, you must meet more of us,' he said.

'I'd love to. Tell me about them,' said Tom.

Talking fast, Giovanni ran through the family: Laura, Giovanni and Sophie were the only ones still alive of the senior generation. The middle-aged were Hal and Pippa at Chorlton, the bachelor boy Richard, chef at Giovanni's, Angelica, Tom's sister, and her husband Silvano. And Mario, Silvano's brother. 'Mario's your age,' he said, 'and still chasing girls—'

'Mario is sixty,' interrupted Laura. 'Tom is only fifty-five.'

Giovanni did not seem to notice the interruption. He went on with a run-down of the younger generation – Jake and Oberon, Jake farming with his parents at Chorlton, Oberon and Anna working together on the recipe-box business.

Tom let the words wash over him, not trying to follow the family tree. I've found an enormous family, not just my parents, he thought. A close Italian family. And I'm part of it. Or I could be. It felt unreal, but hopeful and wonderful.

He tuned back in to hear Giovanni still talking about Oberon's business. 'It's mad,' he said. 'Only the English would pay to have their shopping done for them.'

'Just as well they do,' said Laura. 'It's giving Oberon and Anna a living.'

Giovanni snorted. 'But those two never cook themselves, do they? They order in disgusting pizza or they turn up here for proper Italian cooking. My wife, she runs a restaurant-for-free downstairs.'

Giovanni looked so fondly at her as he said this, Tom felt his heart give a little lurch and tears prick his eyes. My father and mother still love each other, he thought. After what? Nearly sixty years. His adoptive parents were never like that. He'd presumed they loved each other, but he never saw them laughing together, hugging each other. They didn't even talk much. Maybe they were disappointed in life. Maybe he'd been a disappointment. The truth was, he'd no idea.

Tom couldn't believe the mews kitchen. He was used to big bare kitchens of the type beloved of his rich friends, full of seldom-used expensive chef's kit and gleaming expanses of stainless steel. This kitchen was large too, but it was obviously used all the time. A pine table, big enough to seat a dozen, scarred and pale from years of use and scrubbing, dominated the centre. Tucked under it was an assortment of stools and chairs. Bottles, jars and spices were stacked on shelves or pushed into a corner of the worktop. An assortment of antique chamber pots stood on the windowsill, used as containers for growing herbs. Heavy wooden boards, a knife block stuffed with serious knives and an electric mixer cluttered the work surface while copper pans, frying pans and assorted cook's tools hung from butcher's hooks over the Aga. Family photographs, postcards, recipes clipped from magazines, reminders and notes were tucked into an old-fashioned notice-board, criss-crossed with elastic. The shelves of the big wooden dresser were hung with dozens of antique teacups and stacked with assorted plates and jugs. A squashy sofa, piled with magazines, and a bookcase stuffed with cookbooks added to the general air of comfortable family living.

The three of them sat at one end of the table. Two earthenware casseroles of *osso buco* and soft polenta sat on the Aga.

It was truly delicious, and Tom was aware that he was eating too fast. Laura offered him another helping. Too full to accept, he nonetheless couldn't resist an extra spoon of gravy on a dollop of polenta.

By the end of the evening, Tom and Giovanni were talking and laughing like old friends. Laura sat quietly, speaking little, watching Tom. It was hard to know what she was thinking. Poor woman, thought Tom. I must be a terrible shock to her.

Tom learnt a lot about the Angelotti side of the family, but little of the Olivers. He wanted to question Laura about her brothers, Hugh and David, about her parents, about Chorlton, about her early years, but Laura's near silence did not encourage questions, and he didn't want to press her.

As he left, Laura again put out her hand rather than offering him her cheek.

'When you come again, you must bring Susan,' she said.

It sounded more of a command than an invitation, but Tom agreed at once. 'I'd love to. And I'm sure she'd love to meet you.'

That's a lie, he thought. But maybe she'll get to like them. You'd need a heart of stone not to be charmed by Giovanni's warmth.

Over the following weeks, Tom found himself discovering a new world, one of noise, argument, laughter, and of hearty, fragrant Italian meals. Laura reigned over the commune, which, besides Anna and Oberon, consisted of Giovanni's nephew, Mario, and Laura's nephew, Richard, with his over-exuberant lurcher, Tatiana. Other friends and family came and went, and sometimes they would sit down ten or twelve to Sunday lunch or supper.

'That's why the kitchen is so big,' explained Laura. 'When Carlotta, Giovanni's sister, arrived with her two boys, Angelica was only little, and we wanted the children to grow up together.

Giovanni and his sister had always been close, and she became my great friend, so we knocked the two ground floors together.'

Tom visited his new-found parents regularly and started to take Susan with him. At first, he behaved with classic English reserve, waiting to be invited, making sure he arrived bearing gifts. But one day, when he'd been in Frankfurt on business for some days and hadn't telephoned, Giovanni rang him up. 'Eh, Tom, what's the matter? Why don't you come to see us? Anna is asking for you. Is this the way to treat your family?' His voice was loud with indignation.

'Oh, Giovanni, I'm so sorry. I love being with you all. I've been away, but also I feel we're imposing on you. You don't let us take you out to dinner and Laura is always cooking for us.'

'That is – how do you English say it? – bollocks. It is bollocks. My son does not have to ask to come to supper. He comes when he likes. But he has to like to come many times, not once in a month. This is not an English house. This is your home. Maybe not your house. But your home. You understand?'

He was almost shouting now, and Tom couldn't help laughing. Giovanni was such a stereotypical southern Italian, talking at full volume and waving his arms around. He even sang opera arias while cooking.

The upshot was that Giovanni forced a front-door key on him.

As a wet July gave way to an equally rainy August, Tom admitted this was the best summer he'd had since losing Charlie and Clemmie. He'd fallen in love with the whole chaotic, noisy Angelotti family. He basked in their affection and was surprised and gratified that they seemed delighted to have him a part of it.

To his surprise, even Susan seemed to enjoy the Sunday-lunch-party atmosphere with someone (usually Laura, but sometimes

Giovanni or Richard) cooking and everyone else chatting, drinking, helping with chopping, stirring, washing salad leaves or table-laying, as commanded by the cook. Susan, always impeccable in her perfectly tailored trousers, silk shirt or cashmere jersey, did not offer to help and stood apart, but not alone. The men, particularly Mario, found her fascinating. It crossed Tom's mind that what they saw in her was what had first attracted him, and now did rather less. He dismissed the thought, replacing it with satisfaction and relief that she was liked.

For all the informality and apparent ease of production, lunch was a serious business. There would be antipasti from Deli-Calzone, usually prosciutto, salami, olives, tomatoes, sometimes fresh figs or pears, served on a big board in the middle of the table and eaten with ciabatta and butter. Tom quickly learned not to treat this colourful banquet as lunch. There would be three or four more courses to follow.

The antipasti would be followed by pasta with seafood, usually *linguine alle vongole*, or perhaps large thin ravioli stuffed with crab.

The main course could be anything: a whole baked fish, a roast chicken scented with lemon and garlic, a stew of kidneys and mushrooms, fried sweetbreads or brains. Tom, who had never eaten offal and had assumed it would be revolting, was forced out of politeness to try some. To his astonishment it was utterly delicious, especially the brains. Susan wouldn't try anything strange, but no one seemed to mind.

Cheese would then appear, just one variety, usually a big piece of Gorgonzola or pecorino served with bread and maybe quince preserve.

Dessert was nearly always ice cream, with amaretti biscuits. Sometimes there'd be an almond cake too, or the currently fashionable tiramisu, from Deli-Calzone. Lunch was seldom over until four, occasionally five.

The only fly in the ointment, as far as Tom was concerned, was Laura's reserve. True, she wasn't Italian by birth, for all she cooked like an Italian, so maybe expecting her to be demonstrative was unreasonable. But Tom felt there was something more, as if she was holding back, judging him, perhaps. Occasionally he'd notice her eyes on him, anxious and sad.

One evening he arrived for supper on his own and Laura was alone in the kitchen, cooking. He pulled the cork from the bottle of Chianti he'd brought. 'Here's to you and Giovanni,' he said, handing her a glass, 'the best thing that's happened to me in years.'

She gave him a brief smile. 'I'm glad, Tom,' she said. 'Everyone loves you, especially Giovanni. He's very happy.'

'But not you?' There, he'd said it. He should not have asked her so directly. Quickly he softened the question: 'It must have been such a shock for you. I'm really sorry about that.'

'Yes, it was a shock. I thought you'd be angry with me for giving you away. But you're not. So that's good.'

She hasn't answered the question, he thought, then chastised himself for asking it. How crass to ask if she loved him. He must change the subject. But this was such an opportunity. He was almost never alone with her, and he needed to know. 'I'd love to hear about that time, Laura, when you had me. But perhaps you don't want to talk about it.'

'No, Tom, I don't. I can't.' Her face looked strained and closed, her mouth a tight line.

He felt like a torturer. 'I'm so sorry Laura, it doesn't matter.' She closed her eyes for a second, as though in pain.

He took a step forward and put his hands on her shoulders. He was immediately aware of her passive resistance, but ignored it, slipping his arms into a hug. 'You and Giovanni have been wonderful. Are wonderful.'

He stepped back, dropping his arms and looking into her frozen face. 'And, anyway, I know why you gave me away. Giovanni told me how brave you were, how much you suffered so that I could have a good start. I won't pester you again, I promise.'

She gave him a little smile and turned away, reaching for the olive oil to add a glug to her bubbling pot. 'Can you stir this pasta, Tom? It mustn't stick.'

CHAPTER FOURTEEN

Laura and Giovanni were in the mews kitchen when Giovanni handed her the *Evening Standard*, opened to the report on the latest announcements from Michelin of stars awarded to restaurants in the UK. Her heart sank. Yet again, Giovanni's had been overlooked. 'But why?' she wailed. 'We must deserve one. Thirty-five years!'

'It's because we're Italian. Michelin is French. They probably want classic French cooking.'

'No, it can't be. The Fat Duck has two stars and is hardly French. Heston follows his own rules.'

'Maybe it's the retro antipasti trolleys. Maybe they only like plated dishes.'

Suddenly Laura jumped up and picked up the telephone.

'What are you doing?' said Giovanni.

'I'm ringing Michelin. To ask why they haven't given us a star.'

Three days later Tim Black, the editor of *The Michelin Guide*, and one of his inspectors, were sitting in Laura's office with her, the maître d', Milo, the executive head chef, Dino, who now oversaw all the restaurants but had been head chef at Giovanni's for years, and Richard, who had succeeded him. Laura was nervous and regretting ringing the *Guide*.

'It is extraordinarily good of you to come,' she said. 'I rang you on the spur of the moment but didn't expect even to be put through to you.'

Tim Black laughed. 'Well, we don't often get calls from restaurateurs. Usually they love us to bits because we've awarded them a star, or they hate us because we haven't, but they don't ring us to say so. Anyway, it seemed only fair to come and see you in person. We've been watching you for years. And, personally, I'm a great admirer of your Laura restaurants. Few chains achieve that sort of quality.'

Laura felt a rush of pleasure at the compliment. 'That's very kind of you. Right now I wish you were also a fan of Giovanni's!'

'We do know Giovanni's is a very good restaurant.'

'But not good enough?' said Laura.

'Not so far, sadly. You've been very close, many times, but each time there's been a last-minute bad report from one of our inspectors.'

Laura caught Dino's eye. He frowned, shaking his head very slightly.

Laura turned to the editor. 'Go on,' she said.

'OK, let me explain how it works,' said Black. 'If we think a restaurant is close to getting a star, we inspect it two or three times before deciding. And the reports have to be consistently excellent across all areas – food, service, everything – to get the star.'

His voice was measured and his tone friendly. Laura liked him. 'So, what did we do wrong?'

Black turned to his colleague. 'Let's run through the reports. Maybe take the last two years.'

Laura sat in silence as the inspector examined a large folder, marked *Giovanni's* on the outside cover, and told them what they'd been criticised for. 'We believe you use the same oil for all the dressings on the first courses. It's excellent oil, Tuscan, we think, delicious on the Caprese and the grilled aubergines, but wouldn't it be better, and more interesting, to have a lighter oil on the crab or seafood salads?

'And then there is the bread. It has nearly always been excellent, but occasionally it has let you down. We look for consistency as well as flavour and I see that you got great praise for your sourdough in February last year, then suddenly you were producing a good, but not remarkable, focaccia instead. Then, let's see, in August last you were actually buying in part-baked French loaves and baking them – in one case under-baking them – on site.'

Laura listened in dismay. The man was absolutely right. It had never occurred to her to vary the oils. They'd had an excellent baker for years and when he'd retired they'd thought the pastry chef would be up to doing the baking, but it turned out that although he could bake good focaccia and grissini, his sourdough was a disaster. He'd managed to kill off the essential wild yeast starter that his predecessor had kept going for years, and when she'd remonstrated with him he'd quit. For two weeks they'd had to resort to buying in the part-baked baguettes.

The list went on. The deep-fried sage leaves on the tagliatelle with porcini were not as young as they should be and were consequently bitter. They'd been growing herbs on the flat roof of the kitchen, but soon discovered that herbs raised in the London air were tougher than those grown commercially in a poly-tunnel.

Then one of the wine waiters had been friendly to the point

of over-familiarity. Laura knew whom they meant. The man had been a cousin of one of the cooks on a week's trial. He hadn't been hired.

That evening she told Giovanni all about it. 'You know, darling, I've not felt such humiliation and shame, since I was a child ticked off by a teacher.'

Giovanni shook his head in sympathy. 'I'd no idea their inspectors were so knowledgeable. Did Dino and Richard respond well? Or were they on the defensive?'

'No, they were fine. Dino was as ashamed as I was about the olive oil. Richard was a bit upset, naturally.'

That night Laura lay awake listening to Giovanni's snoring. She didn't usually mind the rhythmic rise and fall of the sound. She found it somehow comforting and soporific. But tonight she couldn't sleep. Eventually, she gave up trying, lay on her back and stared at the invisible ceiling. Why couldn't she sleep? What was she anxious about? Was it the failings of Giovanni's in Michelin eyes? No, she could get a grip on that, she knew. It must be something else. Tom, she thought. I should be happy that Giovanni and Tom get on so well. Giovanni seems to have shed years.

Yet the closeness between her husband and son worried her. She could see no likeness between them and she became more and more convinced that Marcin, not Giovanni, was Tom's father. She tried to reason with herself. So what? No one need ever know. And the chance of Marcin hearing of the return of Tom, and deciding that he could be his father, then following it up and appearing on the doorstep, was remote, surely. Why should he? She had no idea what had happened to him and he'd probably be equally ignorant of her. He hadn't known of her pregnancy, and if he'd guessed he'd have assumed Giovanni was the father.

Laura shifted her thoughts to her other cause for anxiety, her granddaughter Anna. The drug-and-alcohol-awareness course that the judge had insisted on had been effective for a while, but she had slipped back to her bad old ways. She was drinking a lot again and smoking marijuana, making no effort to hide it. She makes me so cross, thought Laura. How can she be so stupid? She knows drugs and drink are bad for her, she doesn't look well, and she could do with losing a few pounds. She's still an attractive girl, but she used to be slim and care how she looked. Now she made no effort. Didn't she want to find a boyfriend?

Still, at least she appeared to be happier working for Oberon and living away from her parents. And she got on well with Tom, much better than she did with Silvano and Angelica.

Tom gets on with everyone, thought Laura. She couldn't help being proud of him. She wished she could just relax and love him like everyone else. But she couldn't. It was the fear of what might happen if the truth about his parentage came out. She'd lose him again, almost certainly. And she could lose her marriage, her husband, her happiness.

Susan was still in Paris, negotiating for the rights to some Cartier-Bresson photographs, and Tom rather enjoyed having the flat to himself. He sat on the sofa with a late-night whisky in his hand, considering what the next day held. His heart sank a bit as he mentally ticked off his morning meetings, mainly catch-ups with his colleagues or conference calls about deals in progress. His lunch was with a financial public-relations company. His three o'clock was a meeting with Ajax's auditors and four o'clock was

blocked out for him to read a long contract for the merger –
actually a takeover – of a rival firm.

I used to love all this, he thought. I found it exciting to have
ten balls in the air at once. I enjoyed the stress, the speed, the
cut-and-thrust of dealing, the huge amounts of money we were
playing with. But I don't want to do it any more.

He thought of the evening he'd just spent with the Angelottis.
Almost all the talk had been about the doings of the family or
of their businesses, but very little of it was about money. They'd
talked of the quality of the grass-fed beef now being supplied by
Chorlton, whether the fashion for certain foods would fade as
fads usually did, whether female chefs were held back because
their boyfriends and husbands wouldn't babysit at night. He
found he was more interested in their talk and happier in their
company than he was anywhere else.

For a long time, he'd found his younger colleagues a bit
tedious. They spent their money so obviously, on Savile Row
suits, Rolexes and sports cars. They talked of women in a way
that slightly embarrassed Tom, and their conversation usually
seemed limited to big deals, other people's bonuses, the gym
and personal trainers.

I think I'm heading for a decision here, thought Tom. I want
out.

Immediately his mood lightened. Maybe I could help the
family, *my* family, in some way. I'd love that. If I sold my shares
in Ajax, I'd be rich beyond the dreams of avarice. I could just
invest the money and live off the interest for ever. I could do
anything: buy a farm, read all those books I've never had time
for, learn a language. I'd like to learn Italian.

The question of how Susan would fit into this fantasy life

crossed his mind. He supposed she'd go on working. She'd no plans to sell her business and suddenly turn into a housewife at their wedding. Domesticity bored her. Well, he thought, whatever she does, I'm going to quit. I shall start planning my exit tomorrow.

CHAPTER FIFTEEN

When Tom and Susan arrived at Holly Farm for a weekend in November, an SL 500 Mercedes was parked in the drive.

'Isn't that Mario's?' asked Tom.

'Is it? I wouldn't know.'

'It must be. Only Mario would drive such an impractical car.' Suddenly Tom burst out laughing, 'Look, Susan. At the number plate!'

She laughed too. A little reluctantly, he thought. 'Good Lord,' she said, 'you must be right. MARIO A1. It probably cost him a fortune.'

'Maybe he's down here in pursuit of you,' he said lightly. 'Silvano must've told him we'd be here. He's such a flirt. Can't blame him for trying, just so long as you aren't keen on him.'

She smiled, pleased at his teasing.

On the Saturday, Mario suggested they went to Frampton for the meet. Neither Susan nor Tom had ever seen a hunt in action and agreed with alacrity.

Angelica and Silvano declined. 'It's in the Frampton Arms yard,' Angelica told Tom, 'and since we used to run that pub and loved it, it holds rather mixed memories for me.' She explained that Cousin Jane had pretty well kicked them out, deciding that she could run the pub better herself.

'But you go,' said Silvano. 'It'll be fun. It's a lovely frosty day and the whole scene will look like a Christmas card. You'll love it.'

It *was* fun. The inn yard was packed with elegantly dressed riders on gleaming horses, and as many followers on foot. The huntsman kept the hounds, a pack of perhaps fifteen couples, more or less confined to one side of the yard. You had to weave in and out of the crowd of riders, followers, hunt staff and hounds, avoiding the muddy puddles and hoping the horses wouldn't kick. There was an almost palpable atmosphere of excitement and anticipation – rather like the feeling you got before skiing down a steep run, Tom supposed. Hastily he turned his thoughts away. He hadn't skied since Clemmie and Charlie's death.

'It does look like a Christmas card, doesn't it?' he said quickly. 'One you can smell and hear as well as see.'

'Oh,' said Susan, 'I have to get a red jacket like that. Aren't they gorgeous?'

Mario whispered in her ear, 'You'd better say pink, not red, if you want to be accepted in the horse world.'

Tom watched her smiling up at Mario. She looked wonderful. She was dressed as if she already belonged to the county set in long black boots, tight pale leggings, tweed jacket, Barbour over her arm. He'd never seen any of that kit before. She must have bought it for this weekend.

Young people, presumably pub staff, were carrying trays of drinks round. Riders reached down to help themselves.

'What is it?' Susan asked one of the servers.

'Stirrup cup,' the girl replied.

'But what's in it?'

'I think it's whisky and milk. Or you can have port.' She smiled cheerfully as she handed Susan a drink, then turned to swap a rider's empty glass for a full one.

There were perhaps a dozen children on ponies, the small ones on a leading rein. One little girl couldn't be older than four, Tom thought. She was dressed exactly like her mother in black hard hat, tweed hunting jacket, white shirt, string riding gloves and a tie held with a brass pin of a horse's head. She even held a miniature riding crop.

Tom had had two glasses of port when, after a nod from the master, the huntsman, with an almost imperceptible movement and a quiet word or two, gathered up the hounds. They obediently trotted out of the yard and into the lane followed by the whippers-in, the master of foxhounds and other hunt staff. Tom's little party had to stand clear as the rest of the field followed, eager riders jostling for position behind the field master, others straggling.

Mario led them up the track behind the pub from where they could see the hunt trotting down through the village. They watched from their vantage point until the hounds disappeared into a copse. The sound of the huntsman's horn carried across the still air, encouraging the hounds. The fields, trees and farm buildings looked like a stage set against the pale blue sky. The ridge-and-furrow fields glinted in the winter sun, the alternate stripes of bare earth and frost apparently raked by a giant's comb.

Mario put his arm around Susan, rubbing her arm as though to warm her. She was looking up at him, eyes alight. The thought crossed Tom's mind that she was deliberately flirting to make him jealous. He didn't feel jealous but her need for attention irritated him.

When they got back from the meet, Susan went for a walk with Mario, saying she could do with the exercise. They were forty minutes late for lunch and Angelica was obviously put out. 'I could kill your brother, Silvano,' she said. 'He's the first to complain if food isn't up to scratch. If he says my Yorkshire pud is dry, or the beef is overcooked, I hope you'll have a go at him.' Tom thought he'd quite like to have a go at Susan, but he knew he wouldn't. He didn't have the energy for a quarrel.

They played backgammon in the afternoon, then Silvano and Angelica took them to the Crabtree for supper. It was packed, and the restaurant had a fashionable buzz about it, which, Tom noticed, put shine and excitement into Susan's eyes. She invited Mario to sit next to her on the banquette and spent a good deal of dinner talking to him, rather than to all of them. I wonder if she even knows she does it, thought Tom. Suddenly he felt deeply weary. I'm too old for games.

When they got home, mellow after a good dinner and excellent claret, Anna was climbing out of her car, parked next to Mario's.

Angelica jumped out. 'Darling, what's up? Are you OK?'

'No, I'm bloody not.' She yanked the basket that doubled as her handbag off the passenger seat and slammed the car door.

'How about "Hello, Mum and Dad"? Or "Hi, Mario, hi, Tom. Nice to see you Susan"?' said Silvano.

Anna looked sullenly at her father but did not respond. Neither did she acknowledge the others. Angelica went up to her and put her arms round her. Over her daughter's shoulder she said to her husband, 'Darling, could you bring in Anna's case?' To Anna, she said, 'Come on, let's get you into the warm.'

Once inside, Angelica went up to Anna's bedroom with a cup of tea, while Silvano made an effort to be jovial, offering nightcaps or another glass of wine. Tom could see he was worried about his daughter.

Tom and Susan's bedroom was next to Anna's. As he returned from the bathroom, toothbrush in hand, Tom could hear Silvano and Anna. He couldn't make out what they were saying, but the pitch and intensity rose rapidly. Within moments it was obvious father and daughter were having a blazing row.

Susan was already in bed, reading a magazine. She looks, Tom thought, younger and more vulnerable without her makeup. 'Silvano has no idea how to handle that girl,' he said. 'Why can't he see that, whatever the matter is, now is not the time to challenge her?'

Susan frowned. 'Not your problem, Tom.'

He decided to ignore the irritation in her voice. 'No, but I believe she's a clever, talented young woman. I hate to see the waste.'

'Anyone would think she was your daughter. It's none of your business.' She tossed the magazine on to the floor and wriggled down under the duvet, pulling it over her head crossly.

Tom wondered what had got into her. He looked at the hump of her body under the bedclothes. He suspected he was supposed to stroke it, apologize for something, make a fuss of her, but he was too tired for drama, or for sex. He climbed into bed and lay on his back, thinking that he'd had better days. He didn't trust Mario and, if he was honest, he didn't really trust Susan either. And he was worried about Anna. Poor girl, for all her anger she'd looked absolutely exhausted, her eyes glittery and desperate, the skin round them shadowed.

Susan was right, it wasn't his business, but he couldn't help feeling sorry for Anna. He felt a real connection with her, perhaps because they were both adopted. He felt he understood her in a way that her dad couldn't. Silvano, usually such a sensible, calm sort of guy, became so emotional, so *Italian* about his daughter.

Soon he heard Susan's breathing change as she fell asleep. Well, he thought, whatever she was cross about, it can't have been serious.

The next morning Tom left Susan sleeping and went down to breakfast. He found Silvano already on toast and marmalade and Angelica at the Aga, stirring porridge.

He kissed her cheek. Her eyes were proof of a sleepless night. He sat down next to Silvano.

'I'm so sorry about our daughter, Tom,' said Silvano. 'I despair of her.'

'Which you shouldn't,' snapped Angelica. 'She's unhappy. We should be helping her, not despairing of her.' She turned to Tom. 'But it's so dispiriting. She seemed at last to be happy. Getting on with Oberon, working hard. But now she's blown it again.'

'What happened?'

'She got herself sacked, can you believe it?' said Silvano. 'There could not be a gentler, more understanding young man than Oberon, but even he couldn't put up with her smoking pot with the casual help. They missed a delivery completely because they were all high as kites. Of course I despair of her.' He stood up. 'Tom, forgive me, I must go to the office for a couple of hours, but I'll be home for lunch.'

When he'd gone, Angelica sat down, pushing the cafetière into Tom's reach. 'He doesn't really need to work, but it's better he's not here when Anna wakes up.' She lifted her head to look directly at him. Tom's heart went out to her: she seemed so forlorn and exhausted. 'You must have heard them rowing last night.'

Tom nodded. 'I wish I could help. Maybe talk to her.'

'Tom, that's kind, but I don't know that anyone can help her. She won't take advice. Won't go into proper rehab. Won't see a counsellor. Won't go to uni. She's unhappy, conflicted about something. But what?'

Anna was still in bed when Angelica took the rest of them on a tour of local villages, which mostly meant a quick look at the church and a cup of coffee or a beer in the pub. When they got back Anna had gone, leaving a note on the fridge door: *Sorry about last night. Going to a party in Chipping Norton. Back late. XX A*

That afternoon Tom declined Mario's suggestion of a visit to Frampton to see the hunt kennels and to have tea with Jane. He had met her once but hadn't warmed to her. Relations between her and Angelica seemed cordial enough on the surface, but rather cool for such a demonstrative and affectionate family. He knew that once upon a time Silvano and Angelica had run the Frampton Arms, and Angelica had started her catering company there. Jane had refused to renew their lease and decided to run the business herself. The pub had survived the transfer, but Frampton Feasts had petered out, mainly because Angelica's customers had abandoned it when Angelica left and followed her when she'd set up Angelica's Angels. Not surprising, really, thought Tom. She was a great chef, full of enthusiasm and 100 per cent customer-friendly, all traits that Jane seemed to lack.

Angelica didn't want to go to Frampton either, but Mario was keen to go and Susan wanted to see the grand house and grounds, and meet the aristocratic Jane. Mario and Susan went together, and Tom spent a peaceful afternoon reading by the fire. He almost felt guilty at the pleasure it gave him.

When they got back, Susan looked positively glowing. They both did. It might have been the winter cold, but that wouldn't explain her merry mood and Mario's air of satisfaction.

This is ridiculous, thought Tom. I should tackle her, or him. But I do nothing. Later, at supper in the Angelottis' kitchen, he decided he'd invented the whole thing. Susan sat next to him and directed her slow gaze and wide smile at him, told the table how interesting the kennels were and how beautiful she found Frampton. She was all charm and hardly looked at Mario. Under the tablecloth she put her hand on Tom's thigh and told Angelica about their plans to marry the following summer.

They made love that night, and Susan was the eager initiator. It was good. Maybe, thought Tom, drifting into satisfied sleep, we both just work too hard. We need more weekends away.

At four in the morning, they were woken by the telephone ringing downstairs. They heard Silvano in the corridor, followed by his footsteps hurrying down the stairs then Angelica's. Their voices were raised, sounding distressed, but Tom couldn't hear what they were saying.

He pulled on his dressing-gown. 'Where are you going?' Susan said.

'There's something wrong,' he said. 'Anna, I expect. I'll see.' He pulled the door shut behind him. He didn't want Susan telling him it was not his problem. He was fond of Anna, and maybe he'd be able to calm Silvano, who was bound to overreact.

'What is it, Angelica?' he called.

She turned, her face distraught. 'Oh, Tom, it's Anna. That was the police. They've got her in Chipping Norton station. Silvano is going to collect her.'

'Hold on, Angelica. Let me speak to Silvano.' He ran down the stairs and found Silvano pulling on his coat. 'Silvano, wait. Please. Tell me what happened.'

Silvano's face was rigid and he spoke through clenched teeth. 'Anna was found slumped in a nightclub loo, too drunk to stand. They called the police. But when they tried to get her out, she punched the nightclub owner. They arrested her for disturbing the peace and slung her into a cell. But the nightclub boss doesn't want to bring charges. I'm going to fetch her.'

'Listen, Silvano, I wouldn't collect her now if I were you. Let her sober up in a police cell. You can't reason with anyone when they're drunk. Why don't you let me collect her? By the morning she'll be sober, and I'll meet her and give her breakfast. Try to talk to her.'

In the end Silvano saw the sense of what Tom was saying. They rang the police station back and agreed to collect Anna in the morning.

As Tom climbed back into bed, Susan said, 'You're mad, Tom. She's trouble and you'll end up responsible for her. Stay out of it.'

Tom, trying to recapture the afterglow of last night, took Susan's face in his hands and kissed her. 'I dare say you're right. But she's family, isn't she? And I believe in her. She'll come good, you'll see.'

Tom was shocked at the change in Anna. The furious girl of yesterday had turned into a washed-out waif. She was pale and dishevelled, last night's makeup under her eyes. The police sergeant handed them a clear plastic bag containing her handbag and coat, which she had to sign for.

'Where's your car, Anna?'

'In the pub car-park. Where the party was.'

'OK, I'll drop you off later and you can collect it. Right now you need breakfast.'

Tom drove her to the Frampton Arms and ordered them both a big fry-up. Anna, relieved not to be going home, cheered up a bit and went off to the Ladies to wash her face and brush her hair. 'Can we stay here until Dad's gone to the Crabtree?' she asked. 'I can't face him right now.'

'OK, but you'll have to sooner or later.'

She pulled a face. 'I know. Just not quite yet.'

Tom suggested they check out Frampton church. 'A lot of our family are buried there.'

They looked round the little church first and Tom showed her a memorial plaque on the wall behind the medieval font. It was a plain white stone rectangle. Carved under the RAF badge in relief at the top, were the words:

In memoriam

Wing Commander Hugh Lyon Oliver
55th Squadron

Shot down over the Channel

18 October 1942, age 35

'This was Laura's big brother, Hugh,' said Tom. He studied Anna's face as she read the inscription. She was frowning. 'What does that mean?' she asked, pointing at the Latin script in the RAF badge.

'Per Ardua ad Astra. By adversity to the stars.'

Anna nodded. 'Only 35. Poor Nonna.'

'Let's look round the churchyard. I'll show you Hugh's brother David's grave. You must have known him. He died on Millennium night.'

'I was there. It was awful.'

They went out into the sunlight and walked past ancient tombstones to where the headstones were less covered in lichen and more legible. They found the grave, a shallow mound with a plain headstone.

David Oliver

1917–2001

Beloved husband to Sophie,
father to Hal and Richard

Anna looked closely at the headstone. 'I missed his funeral,' she said. 'I had a ticket for India and I was desperate to go travelling. I decided Uncle David wouldn't mind.'

'What was he like?'

'Amazing. He never complained about anything. And he was stuck in a wheelchair.'

They continued their tour of the graves. 'But you must have come to the church, or walked in the graveyard before?'

'I suppose I must have. As a child.'

'But you didn't come to visit your uncle David's grave?'

She frowned, puzzled. 'No, why should I? It's all meaningless, Tom. There isn't a God. What's under here is just bones. Visiting them is a bit sick, I think.'

They strolled on, round the corner of the church to where the graves were covered in lichen and much more difficult to read. They found the graves of Tom's grandparents, Maud and Donald Oliver.

'They're your great-grandparents,' said Tom.

'Except I'm adopted.'

'So am I, but it makes no difference. If in law you're Angelica and Silvano's child, you're also the great-grandchild of these two. They came here from Yorkshire between the wars. He was an air commodore in the RAF. You probably know he drove Laura out of the house when she was pregnant with me. Maud was more forgiving. I don't think she had an easy life but, by all accounts, she kept the family together.'

'Lots of Maxwell-Calders, aren't there?' said Anna, peering at the larger, more ornate tombstones.

'Well, Maxwell-Calders have owned the Frampton estates for donkey's years. I expect you know we're related.'

Anna looked blank, so Tom went on, 'Distantly, but there is a connection. After your great-uncle Hugh Oliver – the pilot with the plaque in the church – was killed, his widow Grace married George Maxwell-Calder, the last Earl of Frampton. Her daughter is Lady Jane. Both George and Grace are buried over there somewhere. They died many years apart, but she's buried beside him.'

They found the graves and Anna peered closely at the inscriptions. 'I remember coming to her funeral,' said Anna. 'I was fascinated because the earl had died years before from eating poisonous mushrooms. She'd eaten them too, but she survived.'

To the left of Grace's grave, they found George's parents, the earl of Frampton and his countess, Geraldine. 'She was the first female master of foxhounds in the country,' said Tom. 'Also chair of the Oxfordshire WI. A formidable woman, according to Laura.'

Anna smiled. 'I've never been interested in all this family stuff, but I admit it's better than going home and getting a going-over from Dad.'

Tom sat down on the little wall that enclosed the earl and countess and gestured to Anna to sit beside him. 'Anna,' he said, 'let's try to talk sensibly about you.' He put out a hand to prevent her getting up again. 'No, listen. It's important.' She sat back, resigned and resentful.

Tom took his time, thinking of what he wanted to say and delivering his little speech quietly, looking at Anna's profile. She stared woodenly ahead.

'Anna, these people, the Olivers and the Framptons, were and are mostly good people. When I started to research them, I was struck by how stalwart and faithful they were. It's true that Donald gave Maud a tough time, not least over my appearance on the scene, but Maud managed to stay with him for fifty years, without ever abandoning her daughter. She was the glue that kept the family together, rather like Laura is now. Honest, tough, loving, reliable. Hugh died for his country, David was a solid farmer and faithful to both his wives. Their sons Richard and Hal both work hard and would do anything for anyone, including you.'

Anna looked up at him, her eyes tired. Almost bored, thought Tom. 'So, what has this to do with me?'

Tom smiled at her. 'Just hear me out,' he said. 'And then our Italian relatives are admirable, too, with the obvious exception of Mario. Giovanni and Laura worked all the hours that God gave to build up Giovanni's, Deli-Calzone and the Laura chain, and so did Silvano and your great-aunt Carlotta. Your parents are probably too close for you to see their merits, but Angelica and Silvano are chips off the Angelotti block: both obsessed with quality, good organizers, dedicated restaurateurs, and honest as the day is long. Loving and loyal, too. Angelica told me that the day you arrived was the happiest of her life.'

Tom paused, but Anna didn't respond. She looked steadily forward. 'They both adore you, Anna.'

'Dad doesn't. Sometimes I think he hates me.'

'No. He loves you. Which is why he can't handle you destroying yourself.' Before Anna could argue further, Tom held her wrist and looked into her face. 'Listen, Anna. One day they'll be in this churchyard along with all the others. A family that has made the most of the cards they were dealt and done a heap more good than harm. Do you want to be the drop-out of the family, the one who was too weak or lazy to take advantage of such a massive gift?'

She turned to look at him. 'What gift?'

'I mean the gift of love. No one in the world could love you as Silvano and Angelica do. But Laura and Giovanni come close. Sophie, Oberon, Richard, Hal. Me. Everyone is on your side, Anna. If you had no one, if you lacked intelligence and talent, if you were ill or ugly or screwed up, maybe the way you're throwing away your chances would be forgivable.'

He stood up, putting out a hand to pull her up. She shook her head.

'Take my hand, Anna,' he said. 'When you need help, and it's offered, it's plain stupid to refuse it.'

*

To Tom's relief and the family's astonishment, Anna joined Alcoholics Anonymous. Oberon didn't give her her job back immediately, but when she'd been sober for several weeks, he re-employed her.

Everyone held their breath, but the weeks passed without Anna falling off the wagon, taking drugs or lapsing into her old bouts of fury or misery. She seemed relaxed, if a little subdued, and talked openly about AA, how good everyone was to her. She'd made a few friends there and her twice-weekly meetings were the essential props that kept her together, she said.

Tom was gratified that Anna seemed to trust him. He became her online mentor. They emailed each other every day, Tom checking on her progress both at work and emotionally. Gradually her messages became lighter and funnier, more confident and happier.

And then one day she telephoned him. 'Can I come and see you?' she said.

'Of course. Are you in trouble?'

She laughed. 'No, absolutely not. But I want to ask you something. Not on the telephone or by text.'

When she arrived, Tom was surprised to see she had a briefcase with her. She accepted a cup of coffee, and then, in the manner of a salesperson, opened her briefcase. It was empty except for two sheets of paper. Tom repressed a smile. She was so solemn, and those two sheets could as well have been carried in her handbag or pocket.

'OK, shoot,' he said.

'Right. Well, these are last month's trading figures for Oberon's Recipe Boxes.' She handed him a sheet. 'And these are my projections for trading if we had more space to make up more boxes.'

She put the second sheet on the table before them. 'I want to ask you if you'll back the business.'

Tom could see at once that there was not enough information for any rational decision. No estimate of capital expenditure in the set-up of new premises; no evidence of growing demand, such as business turned down due to lack of facilities; no projections of running costs in new premises, such as rent, rates, utilities, none of which Oberon paid in his grandmother's house.

But he was impressed. This was a very different Anna from the one her mother had originally described to him: the irresponsible, drinking, druggy, partying but often unhappy young woman. Instead she was calm, upbeat, serious. Maybe Giovanni was right. He'd said that since Tom had been around Anna had been happier and more rational. Tom thought their both being adopted helped: she understood his desire to find his parents and he understood her feeling of not quite belonging in her adoptive family. Perhaps their talk in the churchyard had pushed her into action.

These thoughts ran through his mind as he pretended to study Anna's papers. 'Where do you stand in all this, Anna? Are you Oberon's messenger?'

'He doesn't even know I'm here.'

'So, why are you?'

'He works so hard, and takes it all so seriously, thinking up and testing new recipes to offer the subscribers. And he'd like it to be green and environmentally friendly, locally sourced and seasonal. But it's too small. He has to do everything himself and turn down business because he hasn't the space to get bigger. But he'd never ask you for help. He's got no collateral to ask the bank for a loan, and he feels he can't ask his mum because she's already been so generous. That's why I'm here.' She spoke earnestly and fast, her eyes fixed steadily on him.

'Are you in love with each other?'

She looked stunned, then barked into laughter. 'In love? With Oberon? No, no. Never.'

He looked at her laughing and made up his mind. He'd help them grow the business. Why not? He had the money and it might be fun.

PART THREE

2003

CHAPTER SIXTEEN

Susan persuaded Tom that a winter holiday in the sun was essential to replenish their energies before their big day in the summer, and also to celebrate his leaving Ajax, which he'd finally done just before Christmas. She had insisted on the fashionable St Barts and he'd had to agree: it was idyllic.

Tom had had to cross a few palms to get his hired sloop moored close to the quay. By the standards of the other boats in the harbour theirs was tiny, strictly for day sailing. This suited both him and Susan. She didn't like sleeping on yachts unless they were huge and comfortable, and Tom didn't want the hassle of a crew. He liked to do the sailing himself, and he could manage a twenty-five-foot sloop. They used it to potter round the island, often dropping anchor in Colombier to spend the day on the beach.

They'd rented a house belonging to a hedge-fund friend on Flamands Bay. Luckily, as cars were only permitted for residents, it came with a beach buggy to get around in. Every evening they'd drive into Gustavia, have a few drinks at the Select bar, stroll down the street admiring shop windows of designer beach bags, jewellery, beachwear and silk kimonos hanging from driftwood or arranged on beach sand. Even the flip-flops cost an arm and a leg. They'd have dinner in one or other of the shabby-chic restaurants, which were also fashionably expensive.

But the island had a half-asleep mood and gentle pace that Tom quickly adjusted to. In the past he'd worked such long hours at Ajax, his head full of the current deals, that he'd found switching off difficult. He couldn't sleep, and he woke early. Skiing or sailing weeks were fine, because he had something urgent to do, but beach holidays, with no requirement to sail a boat if he didn't feel like it, took at least a week to get used to, when it would be time to go home.

But this holiday was different, three weeks long and totally relaxed. And when they got home, he'd have no office to go to, and could deal with his personal investments (mostly safe equities, but he privately backed a few start-ups just for the fun of it) in a day or two a week. He could fit such minimal work round his occasional meetings with Oberon and Anna about Recipe Boxes and spend time with Susan and his new-found family.

Life's good, he thought, and I'm a lucky man. He was content at the prospect of his marriage in July. He'd have liked to be in love, to care for Susan more than he did, but that wasn't going to happen. He told himself he did love her, and the fact that his love for Clemmie, set in aspic by her death, would always trump any other, didn't matter.

Susan tanned fast and evenly, and she looked, Tom thought, better than ever. He bought her a necklace at what had quickly become her favourite shop, Imrie. It was a long platinum chain, with randomly spaced black and white pearls. She wore it most evenings, usually with one of her white or pale grey shifts, low-cut and casual. She was happy and relaxed, thinking a lot about their wedding, but with pleasure, not anxiety. In London it was all lists, menus, timetables and decisions. Here she seemed focused on him.

Tom, looking at the necklace lying on her tanned skin, the pearls rolling slightly on the swell of her breasts as she moved, felt the familiar pull of desire. It's the effect of plenty of sleep and no worries, he told himself. We'll be fine together if we just get enough holidays.

A week into their holiday, Tom was at the Select, fighting for attention at the bar when he felt a tap on his shoulder. Thinking it was some impatient customer, he stepped a little aside to let whoever it was get nearer to the bar.

'Tom, *amico mio. Come stai?* What are you doing here?'

Tom turned to see Mario, grinning, extending his hand, hugging his shoulder. 'Mario! What are *you* doing here?'

'Same as you, I guess. Sun, sea, sex. I presume Susan is with you?'

'She is. She's over there.' He waved to Susan at their table, and Mario hurried over to her.

Tom watched as she jumped up to hug him. Mario had his back to Tom as he enveloped the willowy Susan, her arms round his neck. It seemed an overlong kiss. But, then, Tom had always been aware of the frisson between the two.

Over the next few days he became increasingly irritated with Mario and angry with Susan. He didn't believe Mario's claim that their meeting was a coincidence. Mario didn't usually holiday in the Caribbean, and it was unlike him to go anywhere alone. And to land up on St Barts? He'd followed Susan here, for sure.

As Susan spent more and more time alone with Mario – walking along the beach, disappearing for a drink on someone else's yacht – Tom's anger was replaced with resignation and something like bitterness. How could he be such a fool as to think they were happy? Just because, stuck alone with him on holiday, she gave him more attention. He felt taken for granted, an old-fashioned cuckold. Does she think I'm blind?

One day the three of them had sailed round to Colombier and spent the morning on the beach. By two o'clock it was blisteringly hot, and Tom was ready to go home for a siesta or to read a book in the hammock slung under the pergola in the garden. 'Oh, let's not go home yet,' said Susan, 'I want another swim.'

'You go, Tom,' said Mario. 'I'll stay with Susan and we can come back later.'

'But how? I'll have taken the boat. You'll be stuck here.'

'We can hitch a lift. Someone will be going our way.'

'There's no road down to this beach. Everyone comes in by sea.'

In the end they left it that Susan would ring Tom when they were ready to leave and she and Mario would walk up the steep hillside to the road. Tom would fetch them from there.

Tom sailed back alone. The solitude and the sea soon calmed his anger. As he felt his shoulders relax and his lungs fill with the clean sea air, he forgot about Susan and Tom. It was heaven. There was just enough breeze to keep the sails filled and the boat running smoothly along, without yawing or floundering. Except when going about, Tom sat quietly at the tiller, watching the bow wave dissipating as it passed him, the water sparkling and clear. The brown boobies plunged seaward, skidding onto the surface of the water, where they bobbed serenely, like plastic ducks. He watched the gulls, wheeling and flashing. They seemed to follow his boat. Probably think I'm fishing, he thought, and about to chuck them a bucket of fish guts.

Wanting to prolong his solitary sail, Tom tacked out to sea a little, approaching the harbour in a wide circle. I'm not alone like this enough, he thought. And once we're married, will I ever be?

And yet that week, before the arrival of Mario, had been perfect. He'd had no doubts then. And he didn't, in truth, think Susan's flirtation with Mario meant anything. She probably did it just to get his attention. It most certainly made him cross. But in future, he resolved, he'd be tolerant, loving and blind. They were grown-ups. More than grown-ups. If Susan spent time with Mario, that was fine. Hadn't he just told himself how good it was to be alone?

But that evening his good resolutions went out of the window. Susan didn't ring, and as it got dark he became increasingly anxious. Something must have happened. Maybe one of them had been stung by a scorpion on the climb up to the road. Or trodden on a sea urchin in the shallows. But why didn't one of them ring? They both had mobiles. They knew he was expecting a call to collect them.

He drove to the bend in the road above Colombier, got out of the buggy and peered down at the beach. He couldn't see very well, but the sand looked deserted. The only boats still in the harbour were big yachts, their cabins lit, presumably housing their owners, who would spend the night in the bay.

Susan and Mario must have hitched a ride back to Gustavia by sea. Tom checked his phone for the umpteenth time. No message or voicemail from either of them. Slight anxiety had turned into genuine worry and now into mounting anger. Tom jumped back into the buggy and drove fast to the town. He had his phone on the seat beside him and half expected it to ring. But nothing.

He parked beside the harbour and walked to the Select. He stalked through the throng of people in its garden and went into the bar, which was even more crowded. He made himself smile and wave at acquaintances as he forced a path between them.

And then he saw them. They were sitting side by side at a table of six. Tom had no idea who the other four were. They were all laughing. Mario and Susan were sitting next to each other, he had an arm round her shoulders and she was leaning in close, looking at him in that enraptured way she had. Mario's eyes were on the others, relaxed, handsome, confident.

Tom felt the hot rush of fury. He strode over to the table. Susan saw him and at once sat up, disentangling herself from Mario's embrace.

Tom didn't say a word. He didn't trust himself to speak. He stood behind Susan, yanked her chair back and put his arms under hers to pull her upright. Then holding both her elbows from the back he frogmarched her out of the restaurant. It occurred to him, as he forced their way through the crowd, that he was using her like a battering ram. She was protesting, trying to turn round to face him, and the commotion made people fall away, giving them room to pass.

'For God's sake Tom, what's the matter?' It was Mario, following them into the pub garden.

Tom stopped for a second and turned enough to look Mario in the face. 'Piss off, Mario.' He pushed Susan through the gate into the street, grabbed her arm and pulled her to the buggy. He opened the buggy's passenger door. For a moment she hesitated, looking around. 'Forget it, Susan. Lover-boy has pissed off as instructed. No surprise there. He never had any staying power.'

She shook his hand off her elbow and got in. She'd quickly regained her dignity and control.

They drove back to the house in silence. On arrival, Tom poured himself a whisky but didn't offer Susan one. She sat on the arm of the sofa.

'So, didn't you think I'd be worried? Couldn't you have rung to tell me you were back? Did it not occur to you that I might join you for supper?'

'No, I didn't think you'd worry. Why would you?' she asked, cool as cucumber. 'It's patently obvious you'd rather be alone. You couldn't wait to leave us this afternoon. How could I know you'd suddenly had enough of your own company?' She stood up and poured herself a whisky.

Tom felt a wave of despair. Susan could never be in the wrong. 'I think it's more a case of you having had enough of my company,' he said, aware of the bitterness in his voice. 'Why don't you go the whole hog and move in with Mario?'

'Why would I do that?' She sat down, this time on the sofa, adjusting her skirt as she did so.

'Oh, come on, Susan. Ever since he arrived, you've been all over each other like a rash.'

'That's nonsense, Tom. Yes, I like Mario and he makes me feel good. But it's nothing serious. Not like you and your darling Anna.'

'Anna? What has Anna got to do with it?'

'Everything. If you think I'm flirting with Mario, what about you and Anna? You probably spend more time with her than you do with me. It's Anna this and Anna that. Non-stop. I don't like it, but I've not complained, have I?'

'Good God, Susan, Anna's a child. She's like a daughter, or a niece, to me. You must know that!'

'She's certainly too young for you. But it wouldn't be the first time an old man fell for a young woman.' She drained her glass and picked up a magazine.

For the rest of the holiday, they saw nothing of Mario. Tom was damned if he'd ask Susan whether he'd left the island. He didn't want to demean himself by showing any interest in the tosser. After two days of polite behaviour, in which they sailed round Nevis, anchoring in Oualie Bay, exploring the island and eating in different restaurants, they had regained a little of their earlier pleasure in each other's company.

On the third morning after the Mario debacle, Tom woke with Susan's body pressed against his back. He knew she wasn't asleep. She wanted to make love and make up.

CHAPTER SEVENTEEN

Oberon still couldn't believe his good fortune. In April, enabled by Tom's generosity, Oberon's Recipe Boxes moved to an industrial unit by the railway line in North Kensington. They could afford to hire permanent staff to help with the packaging and delivery on scooters, leaving him free to manage the day-to-day operations.

Tom was the chairman of ORB, Oberon the managing director and Anna in charge of buying and recipe development. She was becoming increasingly interested in food and cooking. She even rang her mother for advice and helped her grandmother when half the family descended on her for Sunday lunch. She would borrow her grandmother's Italian cookbooks too, and trawl through Marcella Hazan for recipe ideas for Oberon's boxes. She wasn't a director of the company, but she was at last on a decent salary. Oberon and Tom intended to make her a director as soon as they broke even – providing, of course, that she hadn't relapsed.

Oberon thought the world of Anna. He was amazed at how diligently she worked – the girl who had resisted everyone's efforts to make her take a proper job was now working a fifty-hour week and enjoying it. She'd stopped smoking – not even ordinary tobacco – and she was going to regular AA meetings. She hadn't touched alcohol since her first session. It was as if something had switched in her brain.

'I couldn't have done it without a lot of help,' she told Oberon. 'AA, obviously. They're fantastic. But it's not just them. There's you, Oberon. Who else would've given me back my job after I screwed up so spectacularly? And then Tom more or less insisted I grow up.' She told him about Tom collecting her from the police station and giving her a bollocking in the churchyard. 'He did make me see that I was being bloody *selfish*, complaining a lot and contributing nothing.'

One Saturday when he and Anna had got the last of the weekend orders off, stored the deliveries, hosed down the floors and yard and climbed out of their white overalls, they stood side by side in the office, looking at the rain streaming down the window and blown in swirling gusts across the car park.

'What a filthy day,' he said.

'Are you going straight home? We could share a taxi,' said Anna. 'I can't bear the thought of trudging through that.'

'OK. If you've got no plans, let's stop at Blockbuster and get a box set, order a takeaway and hole up for the evening.' Suddenly unsure, he added, 'Unless you have a date?'

Anna laughed. 'I do now.'

They'd both seen *Pretty Woman* before, but they watched it again, sprawling side by side on the sofa, eating Nando's with their fingers. Then they watched the news.

Oberon looked across at Anna and saw that she was asleep, her lips just parted, her thick lashes lying on her cheek, like a sleeping child's. She looked very young. On the spur of the moment, he leant over and kissed her just-open mouth. For a moment he felt her breath and the softness of her lips. Then he panicked. God, what am I doing? She'll jump up and scream or something. But she didn't move, apart from opening her eyes. He moved his head a little away from her, the better to read her expression.

It was gentle and amused. She smiled and, still holding his gaze, she slowly shook her head. 'No,' she said, her voice barely audible.

'Why not?'

She put her finger up to his cheek. 'Well, for one thing you're my cousin and my best friend,' she said. 'And for another, probably more important, I'm gay.'

Anna had known she was gay since school when she'd fallen in love with Jasmin, the rebellious – wicked, the nuns said – dark-haired rangy girl with short hair and olive skin. She was in the form above Anna's. She had first come to Anna's attention, and indeed the whole school's, when, as a sixteen-year-old assistant stage manager for the school production of Romeo and Juliet, she'd pushed the button that closed the stage curtains in the middle of the balcony scene. When questioned how she could have been so wicked, she'd said, according to the school grapevine, that the play was so awful she was saving the actors from shame and the audience from boredom. The gossip was that she'd have been expelled years ago, had she not been the school's only hope of winning any matches in hockey, tennis or netball. She was captain of hockey, in the first tennis team and the highest scorer in netball.

But what had captivated Anna was her voice. Jasmin was in

the choir and sang with a mellow, smooth and sweet-as-toffee alto. Anna's class sat right behind the choir stalls in chapel and she contrived, if she could, to sit immediately behind Jasmin. When Jasmin's voice, clear and rich, rose over the others, or rang out in the otherwise silent chapel, gathering force until it filled all the spaces in the air and in Anna's head with the most perfect sound, she would gaze at the back of Jasmin's, transfixed by the nape of her neck. Jasmin hardly moved when she sang. She stood very tall with her head slightly tipped back, as though to propel the notes towards the rafters. Anna would imagine what she couldn't see from behind: Jasmin's half-closed eyes and open mouth, her soft lips, her colour heightened by the sheer joy of singing.

When they sat down again to listen to some dull sermon or reading, Anna would deliberately ignore everything and concentrate on Jasmin's head. She wondered how it would feel to comb or brush the short hair at the back upwards, against the grain. She'd do it so gently and rhythmically, over and over, until in the end Jasmin would be forced, like a stroked cat, to stretch her neck with pleasure.

She remained silently, but utterly, in love with Jasmin for the whole year. Other girls talked openly about their 'pashes' on their heroines. They often had shared idols, becoming happy groupies, feeding together on their fixation with the same girl. But Anna told no one of her love, least of all Jasmin, who spoke to her only once.

Anna treasured that moment, went over and over it in her mind, reliving the glory of it. They'd been in the locker room, changing for afternoon sport, and Anna was late. She pulled on her shorts and netball shirt and was about to run after the others when she realized that the girl frantically rummaging in her locker was Jasmin. She stopped, heart banging. 'Hello,' she said.

Jasmin turned her head. 'You don't have any laces, do you?'

'Laces?' Anna responded, her brain refusing to work. 'Oh, laces. Boot laces. No. I mean yes. You could have mine if you like.'

'Could I? Really?' She looked at Anna's booted feet. 'Have you got extra ones? I've bust mine and the bloody bus is waiting. We're playing Haverdon Girls.'

Anna sat down and started rapidly unlacing her boots. 'What size are you?'

'Five, but I don't need the boots, just the laces. I can't—'

'I'm five too. Here.' She shoved the boots into Jasmin's arms. 'I hate netball anyway.'

Jasmin glanced around, then grabbed the boots, flashed a wide smile at Anna and turned for the door. 'You're an angel, whoever you are.' She was almost at the door when she shouted over her shoulder, 'What's your name, anyway?'

'I'm Anna. Anna . . .' Jasmin was too far away to hear her. 'I'm Anna Angelotti and I love you,' she said, very quietly.

Jasmin had left at the end of the term, without speaking to her again. But she'd left Anna's boots on her desk with a note; 'Thanks. You were a star. We won 53–26.' She had kept the note for years. From then on, whenever she thought of love, she'd imagine Jasmin's face, or the back of her neck.

It worried her that she didn't fancy boys. Everyone else seemed to, so she had to pretend. Like the other girls, she covered the underside of her desk lid with pictures of pop idols. Boyzone and Oasis were there as camouflage: the photograph of Sinéad O'Connor was what held her attention, the one she dreamed over.

She left school without having told a soul that she was gay. She felt inadequate and cowardly that she hadn't been brave enough to do so. She knew she had nothing to be ashamed of. Homosexuality was legal. There were gay clubs all over London, and there was even talk of changing the law so that gay couples could get married. Yet she couldn't do it. Couldn't announce to her mum and dad that she would never have a boyfriend, never marry a bloke. One day, she thought, when I have a partner I really love and who loves me, she'll give me the courage to speak out. She'll stand next to me when we tell them. She'll laugh off Grandpa's disbelief and Dad's distress. She'll make Nonna and Mum see that it's OK.

But that lover hadn't appeared. Of course she hadn't. In that year at the crammer she'd started to put on weight – all that pizza and beer with her mates and very little home cooking. And, somehow, she'd gained another stone since then. She felt fat and ugly, yet she took a perverse pride in deliberately not trying. Stuff the lot of you, she thought.

When her father banged on about how pretty she used to be and how she needed to smarten up to attract a boyfriend, or when her mother said she'd feel better about herself if she had a good haircut, it triggered a rush of anger. Why can't they take me as I am? she thought. I don't criticize the way they look.

In her quieter moments, Anna knew she was drinking too much and smoking too much pot. She admitted to herself that maybe what her parents had said about boyfriends might also apply to girlfriends. She knew she was attracted to girls who were squeaky clean, with short shiny hair, slim bodies, wide smiles. Girls like Jasmin. Or Sinéad O'Connor. But somehow she always reached for her worn jeans and trainers, her ancient T-shirt and sloppy cardigan.

She did have occasional lovers. Secret, of course, some for a single night, others for a few weeks, like Helen. There had been no misery at parting, no great drama, no recriminations. Those relationships had mostly been stress-free. Open and warm, funny and fun. That was one of the things that made her prefer women to men. They were friendlier, more open, less egotistical. Safer. Yes, that was it. Safer.

And then she'd endured that night in prison and the bollocking from Tom. He'd opened her eyes and made her see that being popular or unpopular, beautiful or plain was not the point. The point, Tom said, was to do something useful and positive, something that she could do well and take a pride in.

In the months since her talk with Tom in the graveyard, she'd met him almost weekly for a drink or lunch, and she'd found she wanted to have something positive to tell him. He seemed so convinced that she was intelligent, capable and bright, and would one day do great things. It was a bit like when she was at primary school – she'd been about ten and was so keen to please the teacher. Then there had been nothing better than to be praised for a good drawing or project, to be awarded a good-behaviour badge or be the best in the class.

She'd begun to feel more confident, to like herself more. She had Tom, like a benevolent uncle, Oberon as a best friend, a job she enjoyed and a much better relationship with her mother. And, she thought, I'm not twenty-three yet. Plenty of time to find the love of my life. Plenty of time to come out completely.

At least she'd made a start. Oberon knew, and so did most of her friends.

CHAPTER EIGHTEEN

Tom was faintly irritated at a message on his phone from the facilities manager of his apartment block asking him to 'pop by the office' when he had a moment. What can he want? he wondered. And why summon him to his office? Surely he should be asking if he could come and see Tom, not demanding Tom's attendance on him.

He rang the man back. 'Tom Standing here,' he said.

'Ah, Mr Standing. Thank you so much for calling back. I expect you received my voicemail.'

'I did. And I'm at home now if you want to see me. I need to leave for the office in an hour, so if you could come straight away?'

'Sir, I'm afraid the matter is delicate, and I'd be much obliged if we could discuss it in my office. There is something I need to show you.'

Curiosity overcame irritation and Tom took the lift down to the manager's basement office.

'I'll get straight to the point. You will understand that we use CCTV to monitor the garage. Security, as you know, is one of the chief advantages of this building, and the car bays are permanently under surveillance. Residents are given the code to lift the barrier, or a card to put in their windscreens that will trigger its opening. Visitors can only gain access if their name and car number are given to our security manager in advance, in which case they speak to the office on arrival and the barrier will be lifted.'

'Yes. I understand the system. But where are we going with all this?' said Tom.

'Sorry, sir. The thing is, someone not known to the office has been regularly parking in your bay.'

'Really? How odd. Do you know who it is?'

'No, not yet. We can find out, of course. We have the car registration. But before we investigate further we thought we should check if you or your partner has authorized it?'

Tom shook his head, frowning. 'Maybe it's just another resident too lazy to park in his own spot. Some of the bays are difficult to get into.'

'No, he's not a resident. If you come with me, I'll show you on the CCTV footage.'

Tom followed him through another office, then into the surveillance room with a long line of monitors on the wall, each showing a different black-and-white view – the front steps, the foyer, various passages and lift lobbies. Below the screens there was a long built-in desk with several swivel chairs. Only one was occupied, by a slightly overweight security man in a too-tight white shirt with epaulettes and 'Atlas Security' embroidered on the back.

'Jason, can you find the disc of the Merc, the SL 500, that parks in bay seven, please?'

Oh, God, thought Tom, suddenly feeling sick. An SL 500. Only one person he knew drove that car. 'What colour is the car?' he asked, keeping his voice steady.

'White.'

Mario. And if Mario was parking in his bay, that meant . . .

Tom was fighting to remain calm against rising anger. But he wasn't about to make an ass of himself in front of the facilities manager and the security guy.

One of the monitors flickered and then the image appeared of an SL 500 swinging into bay seven. The car stopped and the driver's door swung open. A man climbed out and shut the door, his body half turned towards the camera. As he extended his arm to click his key fob, his face was visible. Mario.

Tom's flash of fury almost choked him. His fists clenched and his instinct was to attack the monitor, obliterate the image. But he managed to stand stock still and remain silent while his mind raced. He could say he'd check with Susan and see if she knew the man. Or he could deny all knowledge and turn a cuckold's blind eye. Or he could tell this man the truth. No, that was impossible.

Looking at the screen, he said, 'Ah, yes. That's a cousin. Mario Angelotti. He's giving my fiancée Italian lessons. I'd forgotten we said he could park in one of our bays.'

The man appeared to believe him. Tom forced himself to continue: 'You're very efficient and thorough. I'm impressed. It's reassuring to have such good security systems. Thank you.' As they walked to the lift, he added, 'I'm sorry to have given you unnecessary trouble. We should have told you. I imagine Susan just gave him the code, which of course she shouldn't have done.'

Tom had to endure a little lecture from the manager about the purpose of the security rules, like not divulging codes. Then the man softened his tone, smiled (patronizingly, thought Tom) and said, 'At least we know it's not a terrorist. It would have been a pity to have that beautiful car impounded.'

As Tom rode back up to his penthouse, he thought how much he'd enjoy seeing Mario's pride and joy confiscated and crushed.

But soon Tom's anger subsided into a feeling of deep disappointment, almost despair. He sat on the edge of their bed without the will to stop his mind going over and over his relationship with Susan – which was now, he knew, irretrievably over. But his sadness was tinged with guilt. He hadn't loved Susan unconditionally, with the absolute certainty with which he'd loved Clemmie. He'd been fooling himself and, worse, fooling her. He should never have been so weak as to agree to marriage.

The thought of Susan setting off to work in the morning, then sneaking back to sleep with Mario in their bed revived the anger. How could she do that to the man she was about to marry? He might not have truly loved her, but he would never have treated her badly or been unfaithful to her. Perhaps she knew, too deep down to admit it, that he didn't love her enough. Maybe that insecurity had prompted the need for another lover, for more attention, for a second string to her bow.

The thought made him suddenly stand up. 'Stop brooding, you idiot,' he said to himself. 'It's over. It's sad, really, really sad, but more for Susan than for you. One day when your wounded ego has recovered, you'll be grateful. It's the excuse you need to walk away.'

He would have to have it out with Susan, but the prospect depressed him further. He'd have liked her to disappear without another word. He sighed. No chance of that.

Tom knew she would be home about six, and he made sure

he was there before her. He made her a cocktail as usual and waited until she was sitting down.

Then he sat opposite her and said, 'Susan, we have to talk.'

She looked up, frowning. Then she smiled her professional smile. 'That sounds serious.'

'It is. I know about Mario, Susan.' He held up his hand. 'Before you protest, let me tell you that I've seen the CCTV footage of him getting out of his car in my bay, and I know he's been parking there for months, ever since we came back from St Barts.'

'I . . . I . . . It's not what you think, darling.'

'No? What is it, then?'

Susan looked wildly around, as if hunting for escape. Tom felt a moment of sympathy for her, but when she fixed her eyes, huge and earnest, on him and he knew she was going to come up with a lie, he told himself not to be so damn soft. 'I'm sorry I didn't tell you, Tom, but you're so stupidly jealous about Mario that I didn't dare. I did let him have the entry-code so he could park in our spaces. He has some business in the area, and it saves him looking for parking.'

'Susan, don't embarrass yourself. Mario has no business anywhere. He only has a job at Gelati Angelotti because Giovanni is too kind to sack him.'

Susan's eyes were wide and pleading. 'I don't know what the business is, Tom, but you must believe me. I'm telling the truth.'

No, you're not, thought Tom, but you're one hell of an actress. That look, the big shiny eyes, the full trembling mouth. 'Give me a break, Susan, I'm not an idiot. What kind of business only happens on days I'm away? And if he did have any business in Canary Wharf, every building has a car park under it. There'd be no need to use ours.'

She didn't say anything more, just looked at her lap, a composed, tragic figure. But the sight of her didn't move him. It's not going to work, Susan, he thought. I'm not fooled any longer.

He stood up. She was crying now, or at least wiping under her eyes. She's manipulated me for so long, he thought, that I'm impervious to it. 'Susan, I've had enough. I'm through. I imagine you were going to break off our engagement anyway.'

Her head jerked up. 'Break off! No, Tom, don't say that. Of course I wasn't. I love you.'

He shook his head in disbelief. 'Funny way to show it. But, anyway, as I said, I'm through.'

'But, Tom,' she shouted, jumping up, 'we can't cancel the wedding now. Everyone's coming, the hotel is booked, the honeymoon . . .'

He stood there, looking at her urgent face, waiting for her to run out of steam. Eventually she stopped, her voice dropping away to silence. 'Susan, listen to yourself,' he said quietly. 'You're suggesting I marry a woman who's cheating on me and has been for months. Would you marry me if I had another woman?'

Susan's head came up and her eyes regained some of their fire. 'But that's exactly what you do have, Tom. I wouldn't have listened to Mario if I wasn't so unhappy about your obsession with Anna. It's more your fault than mine.'

Suddenly Tom felt really, really tired. 'You don't believe that, Susan. You're just thrashing about looking for a way to blame me. Well, go ahead, blame me if you like, but one thing is certain. We aren't getting married. It's over.'

CHAPTER NINETEEN

It took Anna twelve minutes to run to Paddington station and she only just made it. She threw herself, panting, into a seat and almost immediately the train moved off. It took her a few minutes, eyes shut, listening to her heart gradually slowing, before she'd recovered enough to open her computer.

By the time the train reached Charlbury she'd finished her blog on the evils of waste and how home cooks could avoid it. She had six thousand followers now, many of them reading and commenting on her adventures with organic vegetable boxes, recipe invention, and her battles with flea beetle, cabbage fly, drought and flood.

Anna closed her Mac and looked out at the Oxfordshire countryside. It was only August but some of the fields were already yellow stubble or deep brown plough. The trees had that heavy look of late summer, the vibrant green of spring long since replaced by a duller, deeper colour. But it was still beautiful with the sky pale and the clouds white and high. She smiled at the sight of a foal cantering to keep up with its mother's trot.

Anna now spent at least a day a week in the country, working with her mother on their smallholding, growing organic herbs and vegetables for the catering company and her dad's restaurant, the Crabtree. They'd even started a weekly delivery to some of the Angelotti London businesses. She usually went by train so she could write as she travelled.

She'd been working with Oberon for eighteen months now, and he'd encouraged her to take on their recipe testing and writing the leaflets that went into the boxes. Anna looked back on her old life and wondered that she could have been quite so unhappy. She felt a different person now. Oberon was great to work and share a house with. After that day when they'd eaten takeaways in front of the telly and he'd kissed her, she'd worried that maybe her rejection had hurt him. But he'd been wonderful, confessing that she'd looked too delicious, asleep on the sofa, to resist, but it wasn't really love, just a combination of affection and sex. He was pleased and flattered, he said, that she'd told him about being gay. And he'd become truly her best friend, someone she could talk to about anything.

I am extraordinarily lucky, she thought, to have Tom and Oberon, both of them with my interests at heart. It was just so comfortable, like having an uncle and an elder brother.

The only problem with not coming out to her family was that they were all endlessly on the lookout for a 'nice young man' for her and frequently asked if there was anyone special. It was embarrassing. And it made her feel awkward and deceitful. But she couldn't tell them that there wasn't a snowball's chance in hell that she'd hook up with a man.

Maybe one day she'd just arrive with a lover and let them work it out for themselves. But she couldn't imagine doing that either. If she had met the woman she wanted to spend the rest of her life with, maybe she'd summon the courage to do that. She'd have to tell them sometime. But not now.

Her mother met her at the station and they drove straight to the fields behind the Crabtree. Angelica glanced at her daughter. 'I'm longing to show you the new shed. You were quite right to insist on it. It's made a huge difference.'

A new sign had been fixed to the fence beside the gate. 'Crabtree Organic Vegetables', it read, with a telephone number, and chalked on a blackboard propped against the fence: *cauli; purple sprouters; tomatoes; butternut; heritage carrots; courgette flowers; baby beets; Bramleys.*

Anna felt a little lift of excitement. It was just a wooden shed, but a classy one. It had a shaded veranda, and wide steps led up to the double doors, now open so that customers could see inside and be tempted to go further. It served as office and farm shop and at one end there were stacks of empty boxes, brown paper packets and trays, but as yet not much produce. The exception was two huge baskets, overflowing with Bramley apples.

'I know where they come from, Mum,' said Anna, smiling.

'You're right. That tree is a marvel. It produces more apples than I can cope with. But at least now I can flog some into the business. Mind you, I still end up giving half the crop away. There's a box outside our gate at Holly Farm saying, *Help yourself. Free Bramleys.*'

Anna was examining the row of jars behind the counter. 'You're still making apple jelly, I see.'

'Yes, but now we're selling it instead of giving it to the church bazaar. The bestsellers are the unusual flavours: rosemary, lemongrass . . . I can't keep up, really.'

'I've been thinking about that, Mum. The value-added stuff makes us so much more money than the raw produce. One day we should add a kitchen and make apple pies, rhubarb crumbles, vegetarian curries. What do you think?'

'I think we need to decide if we're running a farm shop for the public, in which case you're right, or a wholesale veg operation for restaurants and caterers, in which case we should maybe concentrate on that. We seem to be going in two directions at once.' Angelica linked her arm through Anna's. 'But right now, let's see how the boys are doing.' She looked at her watch. 'They should be just about done.'

Two of the lads – Mike and Angus – who did waiting shifts in the Crabtree also harvested vegetables and delivered them to customers. Three times a week, Angelica would email the head chefs of the Laura's restaurants, Giovanni's, the Deli-Calzones and her catering business with a list of what vegetables would be available next day. The chefs would then leave voicemail orders on the telephone in the farm shop. When they came into work next morning, Mike and Angus would listen to the messages, then pick, cut or dig up what was needed, plus extra for the shop. Behind the shed there was a long trestle table with a trough and a pressure hose to prepare the produce – chopping off outer leaves, tying bunches, blasting the mud off the roots. The weighing, pricing, wrapping and packing were done in the shed. Then they'd load the boxes into the van and deliver them. The chefs, even those at the most distant Deli-Calzones in the East End of London, had their orders by noon, harvested less than four hours before. Anna knew of no other supplier who could do that.

They walked round the smallholding, stopping to talk to

Roger, who was hoeing between the rows of cabbages. He'd come to them after a lifetime as a glasshouse man in the Vale of Evesham, and there was nothing he didn't know about growing vegetables. He spoke with a broad Worcestershire accent of the kind one only heard on the stage.

'What are these for?' asked Anna, squatting to examine the card collars round the cabbage stalks.

'They keeps them cabbage flies from laying their eggs. Those critters love cabbages, they do. And so do cutworms and flea beetles and all sorts. But I knows their ways and I ain't letting them at my cabbages.'

Angelica turned to Anna. 'Roger is amazing. Even when he worked for the big growers, who sprayed chemicals on everything, he grew organically in his allotment, didn't you, Roger?'

Roger nodded. 'It's how I were brung up, but we didn't call it organic. It's how everyone grew vegetables. My dad couldn't afford that fancy artificial stuff. It were just muck for fertilizer and getting out most evening to kill them pests, squashing 'em between our fingers.'

'Do you still have your allotment?' asked Anna.

Roger shook his head. 'Not since I got this 'ere job. Mrs Angelotti, she lets me take what I needs from here.' He grinned, showing yellowish teeth, one broken. 'I gets paid for growing my own vegetables now. But even if I had to pay good money I'd not go to that supermarket. There's never any holes in them vegetables. If the bugs won't eat 'em, why should I?'

They laughed. 'Your veg hasn't got many holes in it, Roger,' said Angelica. 'Which is just as well, or the chefs would complain.'

Roger walked round with them and Anna found the old man fascinating. He explained that he grew marigolds to deter beetles, comfrey to make compost, and dill next to the brassicas because it attracted a wasp that ate the cabbage fly.

Mike and Angus were lifting carrots, and in one corner of the big barrow there was a pile of pink fir apples, their knobbly bumps making them look more like stones than potatoes, a mound of salsify and a pile of Jerusalem artichokes. At one end of another barrow lay a deep pile of young leeks, neatly arranged.

'We've not got the baby beetroot yet – they want a lot of that – and we need three celeriac,' said Mike.

Anna and her mother helped the boys to prepare the chefs' orders and to place the shop vegetables in the racks. Then Mike set off in the van with the boxed orders while Angus oiled the forks and shears they'd used that morning, tidied and swept the packing area.

It's a proper little business, thought Anna, and Mum and I, we're partners in it. What's more, we don't fight. Extraordinary!

CHAPTER TWENTY

It was nine months since Tom had retired from Ajax and five since he'd broken up with Susan. He didn't regret either. He didn't feel lonely or lost without an office to go to. He relished the lack of responsibility. He spent a good deal of his time doing the things he'd never been able to do but always said he would. He walked all over London, became a frequent visitor at Tate Modern, trying to get a grip on contemporary art, and went to concerts on his own. Sometimes he just lay on the sofa with his Bang & Olufsen speakers filling the flat with Beethoven.

But what gave him the most pleasure was his new family. He found their various businesses interesting and they seemed to like talking to him about them.

One day, Tom was observing an event Angelica had organized for the Slow Food Movement's annual meeting and fair. He knew little of the hospitality world but she'd asked him to run his businessman's eye, and his sophisticated customer's eye, over the operation.

It was taking place in a big marquee on the field between the Crabtree and the market garden, surrounded by the morning's food market. All the stalls were from local growers or makers, some members of the Slow Food Movement, determined to persuade the public to reject cheap manufactured fast food and opt for the real thing.

Tom was finding it hard to take his eyes off the young woman behind the buffet. She was expertly carving a ham while, at the same time, responding to the customers. She was startlingly beautiful, tall and slender with satiny brown skin and fine features. Above the smooth high forehead, her hair was plaited in fine corn-rows to the back of her crown where it was held in some sort of band from which it exploded in a curly pony-tail. But what transfixed Tom's attention was the animation of her face. As she put two wafer-thin ham slices on each plate, she was eagerly answering the questions of every customer, nodding and smiling with what looked like genuine pleasure.

Eavesdropping, Tom learnt that the ham came from a Middle White pig raised by the Angelottis on Holly Farm a few miles away, that it was cured by the local butcher. And, yes, it was she who'd slow-cooked it in a waterbath to tenderness, skinned it, glazed it with marmalade and mustard, studded it with cloves and roasted it.

She wore no makeup. She didn't need any. Her lips look stained, he thought, as though with berry juice, and as she talked, her large dark eyes seemed to flash with pleasure. Her wide smile showed faultless teeth, almost as white as the collar of her chef's jacket. No rings on her fingers, he noticed. But that doesn't mean anything, he thought, she probably takes them off because she's cooking. Her only adornments were pearl studs in her ears. He'd never noticed anyone's ears before, but hers were exquisite: small, delicate, like a complicated sea-shell. She should be painted just like that, Tom thought, with carving knife and fork poised over the ham, looking up and smiling.

'Tom, what's up?'

It was Angelica. He wrenched himself out of his reverie. 'Oh, nothing. I was watching that young woman carving the ham. I can just imagine her as the subject of an old-master painting. Who is she?'

'She's called Sebele. She's Eritrean. She had two Michelin stars as head chef of Belgrave Place. But the owners closed it when the rent doubled.'

'Two stars? She must be terrific. What's she doing now?'

'Freelance cheffing until the right job comes up. She doesn't want to run another top kitchen, though – too much worry and not enough time actually cooking, she says.'

'Does she work for you a lot? I've never seen her before.'

Angelica laughed. 'You're quite taken with her, aren't you?' She pushed him gently in the midriff.

Embarrassment made him awkward. He felt caught out, like a teenager. He forced a smile. Angelica went on, 'I hire her for the big parties, if I can. She's brilliant. I wish I could employ her full-time.'

Tom reluctantly pulled his eyes away from the scene at the buffet. He couldn't go on staring at the girl: he was supposed to be familiarizing himself with Angelica's catering business.

Earlier that morning, once he'd watched the marquee being set up, Tom had visited the kitchen, had a look at Angelica's office procedures, then toured the stalls, manned by farmers, growers, cheese-makers and beekeepers. Not one of them will ever make any real money, he thought. They'll never defeat the likes of McDonald's and Cadbury's. They're lovely people, and admirable, but mad.

Late in the afternoon Angelica and Tom drove back to Holly Farm together.

'I've asked Sebele to supper,' said Angelica. 'You'll like her, Tom. She's really interesting.'

Tom felt a little stab of excitement. Ridiculous, at his age. But he couldn't help it. 'Really?' he said.

'Oh, she's amazing. She came here as a refugee when she was fifteen. She lost her whole family in the war of independence. She had no English, no money, nothing. Her first job was flipping burgers.'

'Good Lord. How old is she?'

'I don't know. Maybe thirty, thirty-five?'

Sebele arrived wearing an emerald green dress. Just a long loose tube with a deep scooped neck, but it was perfect on her. Tom had to make an effort not to gawp at her body shifting under the thin fabric. Her flawless African skin, so smooth it seemed polished, looked marvellous against the green. She'd swapped the pearl earrings for gold ones and a green and gold scrunchie held the loose hair at the back of her head. It looked, thought Tom, both elegant and jaunty.

They sat at the kitchen table, eating cassoulet. Tom watched the two women reminiscing about some catering drama they'd shared, when a bride's mother had wanted her daughter's wedding cake to be topped with roses out of her garden.

'I picked perfect blooms,' said Sebele, 'pale yellow buds, open roses and a few glossy leaves. They looked really good, didn't they?'

'They did, but when the couple came to cut their cake it was covered with tiny black creepy-crawlies.' Both women were laughing. 'They'd come out of the flowers to binge on the icing.'

Sebele wiped her eyes with the table napkin. 'It wasn't so funny at the time,' she said.

'What did you do?' Tom asked.

'Well, only the bridal pair and a couple of waiters had noticed,' said Angelica, 'so we just carried the whole cake out to the kitchen, shook the remaining creepy-crawlies out of the flowers, dusted the ones on the cake off it, put the roses back and proceeded with the cake-cutting. The bride thought it was hilarious, thank God.'

During dinner, Tom tried not to stare too obviously at Sebele, but he mostly failed. When she'd been carving the ham, her neck had been largely hidden by her chef's collar. Now he marvelled at how slender and elegant it was. Like Cleopatra's, he thought. A thin gold chain followed the hollow of her neck and the swell of her breasts. He imagined slipping his hand into the neck of her dress, feeling the warmth of her skin, caressing her slender shoulders, plunging his hand down her bra to hold one of those full round breasts.

God, he thought, this is ridiculous. I'm lusting after her like a teenager, and I'm old enough to be her father. He made an effort to join the conversation, which had moved on to Silvano's pigs.

Angelica had started keeping Middle Whites for the pork and bacon, and also because she couldn't bear the food waste generated by her catering company and Silvano's restaurant. The pigs lived on leftovers and the unsold vegetables from the market garden.

'We're going to try making prosciutto and salami,' said Silvano. 'We don't have the ideal climate for it, but some people are making a go of it, drying the hams in breezy barns or with electric fans.'

'As if you hadn't enough to do already!' exclaimed Tom.

Silvano smiled. 'I know. But this would be for fun. A hobby. An experiment.'

'My family used to keep pigs,' Angelica chipped in. 'Mamma said killing one in the autumn was a village event. Everyone helped, and it was quite a party.'

'You still get that in parts of Italy, in the *campagna*,' said Silvano. 'But it wouldn't be allowed here now. Since the local abattoir closed, beasts are trucked miles to slaughter.'

The talk, about Angelica's Angels, restaurants, the organic movement, the foodie explosion, was mostly conducted by the Angelottis and Sebele. Tom listened to the three of them, impressed. They really care about good food, he thought. Making money is secondary.

Sebele was particularly vocal on the subject of street food. 'I'd love to start an African street-food market,' she said, 'with specialities from Algeria, Morocco, Tanzania, Namibia, everywhere. The traditional Eritrean or Ethiopian dishes are delicious. I go to an Ethiopian restaurant in Battersea for an occasional fix of the food I remember eating as a child.' She looked round them, eyes shining. 'You must all come. My treat. Or I could cook for you. I'd make *tsebhi*, which is a stew. You eat it with *injera*, a sourdough flatbread made from *teff*, the grain grown all over Eritrea and Ethiopia. It's amazing, really nutritious, full of iron . . .'

Animated, she talked on about her street market, selling food from Marrakesh to Cape Town. And Tom watched her like a star-struck kid.

*

When Sebele said goodbye, she hugged Silvano and kissed Angelica. She put her hand out to Tom. As he took it, he had the fleeting desire to clasp her to him, to grab her mass of hair in his other hand and pull her head back so he could kiss her mouth. He swallowed, and politely dropped her hand. 'Goodbye,' he said. 'It was really good to meet you.'

How lame he was being. But she grinned, looking into his eyes. 'Ditto,' she said.

Two weeks later Angelica telephoned to make a date for them to discuss Tom's ideas for her business. 'I thought you might like to come on the nineteenth. Sebele is coming down to organize a street-food party. She's persuaded one of our clients that it would be more fun than salmon and strawberries.'

Sebele had dominated Tom's thoughts for the past fortnight and now his heart leapt, although the fact that Angelica had noticed his interest in Sebele did bother him a little. He had no business lusting after a woman twenty years his junior.

'Sure,' he said, too embarrassed to mention Sebele. 'I'd love to.'

They had their meeting in Silvano's office, above the garages at Holly Farm, and Tom tried to resign himself to not seeing Sebele at all. She'd be working up at the catering kitchens behind the Crabtree. But then, in the middle of a discussion about the relative merits of hiring or owning kit such as marquees, crockery and cutlery, Silvano's secretary came in with a mobile phone in her hand. 'It's for you, Tom,' she said. 'Sebele.'

He took the phone, looking across at Angelica, who was smiling.

'Sebele?'

'Hello, Tom. Angelica told me you were down for the day. I'd like to pick your brains about my street-food idea. I was wondering if we could have supper together, maybe in a pub.'

'Great idea. I'd love to.' Angelica was listening, and he made an effort to sound casual.

'Let's go to the Kings Arms in Milton,' said Sebele.

Tom found Sebele sitting at the bar. She was wearing a long-sleeved top with horizontal green stripes and the same green and gold scrunchie she'd worn for supper with the Angelottis.

He kissed her cheek. 'You look great,' he said. 'You obviously know green suits you.'

She smiled, puzzled. 'Why do you say that?'

'Because you were wearing a green dress when we last met, and that green thingummy in your hair.'

She put her hand behind her head to check. 'So I am. And, yes, I like green. But you are a strange man to notice what a woman wears.'

I'm in danger of flirting here, thought Tom. And she's much too young to be interested in me. He ordered white wine for her to turn her glass of fizzy water into a spritzer, and a beer for himself.

'Tell me about your street-food plan,' he said. 'I'm flattered you think I can advise you but I know nothing about cooking and the food world.'

But she wanted advice about money. 'When I ran a Michelin-starred kitchen, I had a couple of customers keen to back me in starting my own business. But neither of them would be interested in street food, or indeed any catering. They want to back a restaurant so they can show off to their trendy friends.'

Tom smiled. 'I recognize the type. But the street-food thing, have you calculated the set-up costs? And are you sure there's a market for it?'

At dinner they talked about Sebele's dreams, as yet neither costed nor researched. By the end of the main course they had agreed that she should go on working for Angelica while she continued her trials and researches, and Tom would help her draw up a business plan that might interest investors.

The conversation turned to Tom's background. Under Sebele's genuine interest, Tom found himself talking about Ajax, about Clemmie and Charlie, and even about 9/11. It was astonishing. She made it easy to talk of these things, which he never did. She listened intently, and silently, except to ask him direct questions. He didn't talk at all about his feelings, just stuck to the bald facts, yet he felt she understood the cost to him. Her face was serious, her gaze direct, but there was sympathy in her eyes.

When he tried to turn the tables and find out about her, she was flippant. 'Oh, I was born in Eritrea, but I went to school in England and became obsessed with cooking. Usual route: catering college, apprenticeships, climbing the greasy kitchen pole.'

Tom watched her. God, she was lovely. Everything about her. Her neat straight nose, her tiny ears, high cheekbones, the wideness of her smile, above all those eyes. And the way she was utterly absorbed in their conversation. It was intoxicating.

Over coffee, she put her hand on the table, temptingly within reach, and when he put his over it, she looked up slowly and held his gaze for a long silent moment. But he forced himself to rub her hand in a friendly manner, then withdrew.

He sensed that she would sleep with him if he pressed her. He was sure of it. He could see the commitment in her eyes, alternately excited, teasing, tender, always focused on him. And her willingness was confirmed in the unhurried soft kiss she gave him as they parted. It was all he could do not to pull her into him, devour her.

But he moved away and opened her car door for her.

Over the next few weeks he forced himself to take it slowly but he was obsessed by her – by everything about her. She was attracted to him, too – or was she just excited by the idea of an older man, a rich one, so different from her? He mustn't rush her. He couldn't bear it if she thought of him as a casual lover, to enjoy and discard.

He decided to woo her in the old-fashioned way. He took her to the theatre, to the movies, to a concert at the Wigmore Hall, out to dinner. The more time he spent with her, the more admirable and desirable she became. He could not believe that a fifteen-year-old refugee orphan, coming to England with no education and no possessions, could somehow turn herself into this bright, knowledgeable, successful businesswoman, apparently without hang-ups.

He told Sebele that, after the death of Clemmie and Charlie, he'd been certain he'd never love again. And how, when Susan had come along, he'd felt somehow guilty, as though he were being unfaithful to Clemmie because he'd allowed his animal need for sex to swamp his judgement.

'But why did you ever feel guilty? You weren't hurting anyone. You were single and free.'

'I know, but for some reason I often felt a sort of uneasy anguish. Maybe because I was allowing Susan to lead us up a garden path, which, in my heart of hearts, I knew would not be flower-strewn. It was almost a relief to discover she was having an affair with Mario.' He gave her a rueful smile. 'I should have sent him a thank-you present.'

His only anxiety, and it was diminishing fast, was that Sebele was so young.

Towards the end of September, perhaps six weeks after they'd met, they were in the sitting room of Tom's flat, picnicking on the rug by the window. They'd ordered antipasti from the Deli-Calzone downstairs and the food was on a tray between them.

Tom watched Sebele's long fingers deftly arrange prosciutto, Pecorino and a slice of quince cheese on a small piece of ciabatta. He watched as she took a bite, thinking, as so often, how perfect her teeth were. She popped the rest of her creation into his mouth, and as she withdrew her hand he held it in his and looked into her eyes.

'What?' she said, her smile teasing.

'I want to know where you think this is going. Us. Where we are going?'

She continued to chew slowly, frowning a little. Then she swallowed and asked, 'Where would you like it to go, Tom?'

'I'd like it to last for ever. But mostly I want to know that for you it's not just a bit of fun with an old codger.'

'Tom, you're not an old codger! I have never been so consistently happy. I wake up happy.' She looked deadly serious, her former merriment completely gone.

He shifted closer to her on the carpet and pushed the tray aside. 'Then why so solemn?'

'Waking up happy is new for me. I'm used to having to force the smile to my face until it takes hold and I'm fine.' She paused, her eyes anxious. 'I'm damaged goods, Tom. I have terrible nightmares. I wake up screaming sometimes.'

'Oh, my love, what do you dream about?'

And then she told him about the teenage soldiers who had killed her family. 'They were so young. And quite mad. Full of dope, I suppose, and drunk with killing. They shot everyone except the boys. They took them away to be soldiers.' She spoke quietly, matter-of-factly. 'They clubbed the babies with their rifle butts. "Don't waste ammunition on the children," one shouted.'

Her voice faltered occasionally. She explained that when the government forces had got to her burnt-out village, they'd thought everyone was dead. Everyone was, except her. They'd found her under a pile of bodies in the family's hut. The corpses were her parents, siblings, aunt and grandmother. Her younger brother was missing, presumed kidnapped.

'I don't dream about any of it exactly. Not the killing. I wake up before that. I dream I'm at home in the village, and gangs of soldiers come in, and I know it is the end. Or I dream about my sister being raped and then cut up with a machete. Just hacked to pieces. I saw that. It really happened.'

Sebele was trembling all over now, and as Tom reached for her, she began to shake. He held her and then she was crying. He rocked and shushed her like a baby. He could hardly hear what she was saying through her sobs and hiccups. After a while the crying abated a little and she tried to smile. 'I'm so sorry, Tom. I've not talked about any of that for so long. Not since I first arrived in England.'

'Who did you talk to then?' He was lifting her hair, loose around her face, to stroke her tear-streaked cheeks.

'My foster-mother. She'd worked a lot with traumatized children and she knew, I think, that talking helps.' She was smiling and sniffing at the same time now.

She talked on and on, sometimes hesitantly or too fast, as she forced herself to be calm. She told him about the hospital she was taken to, and then the charity that had sent her to England. When she got to the story of her foster-parents, Molly and Edward, an English couple in Oxford, the tale turned into a fairy story. Tom fetched them both a glass of whisky, and later cups of tea while Sebele continued, unhurriedly and fluently now.

'They were unbelievable. They had two of us foster-children. The other was a silent boy, Evan, about ten. He was English, from Manchester. He'd been abused by his parents for years. He never spoke, but they believed he would one day, and they talked to him just as they did to me, all the time.'

'And did he ever speak?'

'No, but he's a chef too now. They taught us both to cook. I learnt to make hollandaise in my first month with them. I think they believed cooking had healing powers.'

'Maybe it does,' said Tom. 'I'm sure Angelica would agree with that. Go on.'

'At first I couldn't bear school. It frightened me. I couldn't speak English, I was the only non-white child and I wasn't learning anything. So they taught me at home until I'd learnt the language. They're an amazing couple. They took us to concerts and read us the classics. I had two years of secondary school and then I went to Oxford Brookes to do a hospitality degree.'

'What a remarkable couple. I'd like to meet them.'

'You can. They're retired now. I love them to death.'

CHAPTER TWENTY-ONE

Angelica had put in an advance order for the new *Michelin Guide* from Amazon. When it arrived, she opened the package at once, eager to find out whether her mother's restaurant had at last got a star. Laura, she knew, was determined not to retire until she'd achieved her lifelong ambition. They had done exactly what the Michelin boss and inspector had told her, and she and Richard had gone through every dish, making sure each ingredient was the best they could find, that the way they cooked it and put it together ensured the freshest, most authentic taste.

Please, God, thought Angelica, let Mamma have got her star this time. She opened the book at the list of newly starred restaurants and ran her eyes quickly down the page. The Fat Duck had risen to three stars, and more restaurants now had two, then there was a list of one-star establishments. Suddenly she saw it. The Crabtree Restaurant. For a moment she looked at the words without quite taking them in. Then it hit her: they'd got a star! For the Crabtree! She swung round, looking wildly for Silvano. A star after two years. It was amazing. She felt faint, and realized she was holding her breath. She sat down and reread the page. Yes, it was definitely their Crabtree. She let the knowledge wash over her. They'd certainly dreamt of getting a star one day, but not so soon.

She must tell Silvano. She picked up the guide and set off to find him. Then she remembered. What about Mamma? She's been trying for a star at Giovanni's for so many years, it will be awful for her that we've got one so quickly.

She looked at the list of restaurants again, running her eyes further down the list. And then she was jumping up and shouting, 'Yes! Yes!' and punching the air like a footballer. Giovanni's had been awarded a star too.

Two weeks later the Angelottis, senior and junior, had a joint celebratory dinner. They held it at the Crabtree, and the whole extended family – the Angelottis from London, including Mario and Tom, and the Olivers from Chorlton – were there. Dino, the head chefs and the managers from both restaurants came too.

When Anna asked, 'Why on earth are we inviting Jane the Pain to the dinner?' Angelica found herself on the defensive. 'Don't be unkind. She's all on her own in that great mansion. We could hardly leave her out.'

'But, Mum, she's such a snob and you know what she's like. She'll either be all dignified and gracious and make the chefs and managers feel like shit or she'll be rude. And what has she got to do with our restaurants? Nothing. And she's hardly family.'

'I'm afraid that's not true, darling. She's a major shareholder in Giovanni's. She inherited the shares from George. He backed Mamma and Papa when they started the business after the war. And, anyway, she's family. Her real father was your great-uncle Hugh, remember? Jane was born an Oliver.'

Anna's face, truculent before, softened. 'I suppose I did know that. Tom showed me their graves in the churchyard. They sounded OK. But that doesn't mean their daughter is. She's horrible.'

Angelica was firm. 'Darling, sometimes you have to just grin and bear it.'

They had the smaller of the two dining rooms to themselves and Angelica had had the tables pushed together to make a big one. There was a party atmosphere from the start with impromptu speeches and a lot of laughter. Laura spoke in praise of Silvano and Angelica and the great job they'd done with the Crabtree. Angelica jumped up to sing the praises of her mother and father with the Laura and Deli-Calzone chains, and their wonderful Giovanni's, which should have had a star twenty years ago. And then Mario, quite drunk, suddenly got to his feet and made an incomprehensible speech about the unbeatable Angelotti family.

'Anna here,' he said, tipping his chair sideways to put an arm drunkenly round her shoulders, 'is a marvel. She has slain her demons, and proved herself a true Angelotti, producing organic veg for half the week and running Oberon's recipe-box business for the rest.'

Anna threw his arm off her shoulders as if she was tossing away a pillow. Mario didn't notice. He went on, 'But my hero is my brother, Silvano. He's my best friend and I forgive him for stealing Angelica from me. One big happy family.'

Mario was swaying over Anna and she pulled him down by his shirt-tail. 'Shut up, Uncle Mario. You're pissed and you're embarrassing us all.' But she was laughing.

Mario shook her off. 'What does it matter if I'm drunk? *In vino veritas.* This is the best family in the world. Three generations of Olivers and Angelottis in the good food business.' Turning from one to another as he spoke, he reeled them off: 'Farmer Hal, chef Richard, Oberon with his boxes, Angelica's party catering and her veg business with Anna. And now two Michelin stars! The Queen should give Uncle Giovanni a knighthood.' He stopped and sat down to a lot of laughter and applause.

Angelica looked across the table at Jane, who had not joined in the general merriment. Suddenly she felt annoyed with her. Couldn't she just relax and be kind for once? Jane looked, she thought, positively hostile. 'What's the matter, Jane? Are you all right?'

Jane returned her gaze without a smile. Indeed, she looked contemptuous. 'I was just thinking that all this self-worship is seriously over the top. I hate to be rude, but you do seem to forget that this famous family has had considerable help on the way. None of you Angelottis would have jobs if it wasn't for my father's investment.'

Anna thumped the table with her glass. Angelica noticed her daughter's tell-tale blush. Oh, God, she thought, this could turn ugly.

'You hate to be rude?' said Anna, glaring at Jane. 'I think you glory in it.' She turned to Angelica. 'I told you not to invite her, Mum. I knew she'd have a go.'

'Shush, darling.' Angelica tried to smile. She turned to Jane. 'Oh, come on, Jane, you know my father was always grateful for George's backing. And George did well out of it too. He'd be thrilled about Giovanni's star. Don't be a such a party pooper.'

Jane sat back, apparently unmoved. 'I've no intention of spoiling anyone's fun. I'd forgotten that you volatile Italians draw your swords over nothing. But admit it. You're like the Mafia. You all employ each other and there's always an excuse for boasting.'

'So you don't think two Michelin stars in the family is worth a celebration?' Anna demanded.

'Certainly, but a bit of modesty wouldn't go amiss. How would you have managed on your own, Anna? Tell me that,' she drawled. 'Your cousin employs you, your grandmother houses you, your new-found uncle funds your business, your mother and father buy your produce, bail you out of jail, send you to rehab. Aren't you the lucky one? And then they all think you're brilliant for staying on the wagon and drug-free for five minutes.'

It was too much for Angelica. She could feel her control flying out of the window. 'How *dare* you, Jane? As if you hadn't had help from your family! You've been handed everything on a plate, and if you weren't given it, like the Frampton estates, you just took it, like my catering operation.' Warming to her theme, Angelica ignored Silvano's signals. Face flushed, she charged on: 'Talk about biting the hand that fed you! Who gave you a job when you lost your father? Who taught you about outside catering? We did. The Angelottis. And by way of thanks you cancelled our lease and chucked us out so you could steal the business. We had to find a new pub and catering premises and start all over again.'

Suddenly aware that the whole table was silent and staring, Angelica could feel the tears coming. Oh, God, she thought, as she struggled to her feet, I've got to get away. As she pushed back from the table, she looked across at Jane. The woman was smiling.

CHAPTER TWENTY-TWO

Anna had been attending her AA meetings regularly for well over a year now. She had good friends in the group. She trusted them and knew that they helped to keep her anchored and off the booze.

One cold November evening she was walking home from a meeting with her friend Martha. Anna had been grateful to her since her very first AA session. She'd stumbled down the basement steps into a room full of alcoholics and as she'd stood, hesitating, in the doorway, a big-boned, fresh-faced woman had walked swiftly towards her, her hand out. 'Hi, I'm Martha.'

Anna half turned away, considering running up the steps again.

'You just want to bolt, don't you?' Martha had said, half laughing. She was older than Anna, mid-thirties, she guessed. 'My first time I did bolt. Which is why I like to get to newcomers quickly, before they get a chance to make a run for it.'

Martha and Anna had become firm friends. Martha knew all about her, including her origins in Romania and the fact that she was gay, but single. Anna knew that Martha was divorced from an abusive husband and had started drinking when she'd lost their child. Now she had a high-powered job at the BBC.

Tonight they were heading for Martha's pad in Ladbroke Grove for a late supper. 'I want you to meet Cassia, my little sister. She's staying with me at the moment – she's between flats – and cooking supper for us. I think you'll like her.'

Cassia had very short white-blonde hair, a small neat head like a boy's, with slanting blue-grey eyes and no makeup. Her slim body was clad in cut-off jeans and a plain white T-shirt.

She had Martha's open friendliness. 'I guess you guys aren't allowed a proper drink. How about lime juice? Or elderflower? Or tea?'

Anna accepted lime juice, thinking how totally unalike the sisters were. Cassia caught her looking from one to the other. 'I know, we don't look like sisters, do we?'

Martha chipped in, 'Sadly our parents are both dead, so we can't cross-examine them.' She laughed. 'We could do a DNA test, I suppose.'

'Oh no we couldn't. I'd hate that,' Cassia said quickly. 'What if we discovered we weren't related at all?'

She looked so stricken that Martha laughed and put an arm round her. 'It wouldn't change anything, you idiot.'

When Cassia put a fish pie on the table, it wasn't great. The juices had overflowed the dish and the messy edges were burnt. 'Oh, God, I'm sorry, Anna. Martha says you're in the food business. Why am I trying to cook for you? I'm terrible.'

'Don't be daft. I'll eat anything and, anyway, it smells delicious. And it's like a picture in a cookbook. Rustic and messy is all the fashion now.'

It tasted a lot better than it looked, and they ate it with a green salad. Cassia was funny and talkative, telling them about her day in the art gallery where she worked. They had an enormous Jackson Pollock on the ground-floor, which attracted a lot of attention. They'd already been offered over two million for it from a collector in Japan, but Cassia's boss was holding out for more. An American gallery curator was flying in to see it tomorrow. 'And this morning,' she said, 'a guy came in selling these'. She got up, rummaged in her bag and pulled out a postcard. She handed it to Anna. The picture was of a woman wearing a cook's apron, completely covered with brightly coloured food spatters and streaks. She was holding a frying pan with red sauce dripping from it, while a small boy, also spattered, stood looking up at her. The caption was *Jackson Pollock's Mother.*

'Don't you think it's brilliant?' asked Cassia.

'Yes, I do. But I bet your boss wasn't amused. Did he show the poor guy the door?'

'No. He thought it was funny. He ordered a box of a hundred. He often sends art postcards to clients, just to be friendly and keep in touch. But this'll be the first jokey one.'

They talked until about eleven o'clock, and all the time, Anna examined Cassia, thinking how perfect, gamine and lithe she was. She wondered if she was gay, then, if she was, if she was single. She'd given no hint of the attraction being mutual.

The next morning, she rang Martha. 'Thanks for last night, Marty.'

'A pleasure. What did you think of my little sis?'

Oh, God, thought Anna, she knows I fancy her. And then she thought, But what the hell? 'Cassia? She's lovely. I liked her a lot.'

'Do you mean a-lot-a-lot?'

Anna laughed. 'Well, yes.'

'That's a bit of luck. She's pretty taken with you too.'

'What? Really? You mean she's . . .'

'Yes, dumbcluck. She's gay. Always has been, though the girl-friends have been pretty dire.'

'Hey, stop, are you telling me . . .'

'I'm telling you she fancies you. Why do you think I asked you to supper? I had to take a hand in her affairs. Do a bit of matchmaking.'

The following week Anna and Cassia met at a pub in Shepherd Market and held hands under the table. Cassia drank red wine and Anna had no difficulty in sticking to Coke. They talked until closing time, then walked the streets for another hour, still talking. It was cold, but Anna felt warmed by some internal fire. Adrenalin, possibly. When they got to Martha's street, Anna drew Cassia to her and kissed her.

'I'd ask you home,' Cassia said, 'but it's Martha's flat and she doesn't approve of instant intimacy.'

Anna surprised herself by agreeing with this. Good old Marty. Looking out for her sister. 'I have a similar problem. My cousin Oberon, who's also my housemate and best friend, would slaughter us both if he didn't approve.' She took Cassia's head in her hands, her palms to Cassia's cheeks and kissed her again. 'We'd better get to know each other first then,' she said. 'How long would make it respectable, do you think?'

'Six weeks?'

Actually, it was four. By which time Martha had seen them together twice, once at her place and once when Anna took Oberon and the two sisters out to the Notting Hill Brasserie. Anna noticed that Oberon was a little cool at first, but Martha's warmth and Cassia's sweetness quickly won him over.

'I don't blame you, Cassia,' he said, 'but I'm a bit jealous.

You see, I'd have fallen for Anna if she'd let me. But she has me relegated to best friend. Which is fine. If you make her happy I'll love you too.'

A month after they met Cassia moved into her new flat in Maida Vale. It was in a red-brick Victorian mansion block and the flats had high ceilings, large rooms and wide corridors. They used Anna's car to move her stuff from Martha's. As yet she had no furniture other than a futon, bed linen and towels from Ikea, a lot of paintings and antique mirrors and a small marble sculpture of two chubby women dancing cheek to cheek. They stopped at the hardware store on Westbourne Grove and bought a bucket, broom and cleaning things.

Between them they manhandled Cassia's possessions up the front stairs, along the corridor, into the lift and along another corridor into her one-bedroom flat. Then they spent the afternoon cleaning.

At seven o'clock Anna ordered pizza and they sat on the futon eating it. Then Anna managed to get the boiler working, and Cassia climbed into the shower.

Anna returned to the bedroom, intending to wait until Cassia was done, then go home, leaving her to luxuriate alone in her new flat.

But suddenly she thought, This is ridiculous. We both want it. Why wait? She stepped out of her clothes, leaving them in a heap on the bedroom floor, and joined Cassia in the shower.

Soaping Cassia under running water was the sexiest thing Anna had ever done. Cassia cuddled up close, so Anna could feel her breasts, stomach and thighs against her own while her hands went slowly up and down her back and bottom. She could barely breathe. They kissed, and it was glorious, but then, drawing breath, a stream of water had Cassia choking, and they were both laughing. They stumbled out of the shower and dried each other feverishly and not very well. Then Anna took Cassia's hand and led her back to the futon.

CHAPTER TWENTY-THREE

Sebele stood behind Tom, leaning into his back, her arms round him. He was sitting on a high stool at the kitchen counter, looking out over the river, the spotless glass wall dropping thirty storeys from his feet to the square below. She dropped a kiss on the top of his head, then rested her chin on it to look at the barges and boats on the Thames. They looked tiny from up there, like toys.

He ran his hands up and down her forearms, stroked and folded her fingers. I love the way he does that, she thought. It's like he loves every bit of me, even my cook's arms with oven burns on the wrists and horrible nails from peeling beetroot and chopping onions. She closed her eyes the better to feel.

'Can I buy you a ring?' he said, caressing her ring finger. 'Any kind you like – vulgar great diamond, emeralds, sapphires?'

Her eyes jerked open and she laughed. 'I'd love a ring, but I'd prefer it to be glass. Or plastic. The responsibility of real jewellery would kill me. I'd leave it on some kitchen sink or wear it and get it all gunked-up with bread dough.'

He swivelled his stool to face her and put his arms round her waist. 'OK, no ring. But why won't you move in here? It's crazy, you paying rent in Hoxton when we spend every night here.

We've been together over a year, darling. You want us to live together, don't you?'

'Of course I do, you idiot. You're saddled with me, like it or not.'

'Why not, then?'

She hesitated a moment, conscious that what she had to say might hurt him. 'I don't know. I feel somehow if I move my stuff in here, that will be that. We'll be here for ever. This place is wonderful, so stylish and grand, but it's somehow *corporate*, not personal.'

'You really don't like this flat, do you?' He didn't sound offended, just interested.

'I do. I sort of admire it intellectually. I can see it's amazing. But it's Susan, not me. I'd like a house we'd found together, one that was comfy and colourful and didn't feel like it was out of an architectural magazine. A house for us to grow old in.'

'For me to grow old in, you mean. But, my love, if that's what you want, that's what we'll have.'

Sebele set out to look for a house, and eventually found, at eye-watering expense, exactly what she wanted in a back street in North Kensington. It was a wide Victorian two-storey building that had once been a rope-making factory and more recently a photographer's studio. The red brick had mellowed and the roofline was interrupted by two Dutch-looking gables. Between them, in the middle of the roof, there was a jolly little turret from which you could see over the surrounding rooftops. According to the estate agent, it was originally a lookout for the factory owner to keep an eye on the workers in the yards at the back. Those yards were now a jumble of disused sheds, dead cars and rubbish.

They hadn't discussed the property in front of the agent, and during their tour Tom was inscrutable. He showed neither delight nor consternation. But once they were back in the car, Sebele burst out, 'Oh, Tom, isn't it just perfect?'

Tom shook his head. 'It'll take for ever – years. Clearance, planning permission, new plumbing, wiring, everything . . .'

'But it's wonderful,' she exclaimed. 'And it would be such fun to do. We aren't in a hurry, are we? Tom, it's absolutely right.' Sebele's excitement was interfering with her speech. She knew she was gabbling, the words and thoughts coming out a muddle, but she couldn't stop. 'It's such a pretty building, big spaces we can do what we like with. It's near the family. I love the area, Portobello market, and the new Sainsbury's. I could have a huge kitchen and we could fix the sheds, let them to artists or start-ups, or we could have a garden . . .' She stopped, suddenly anxious. 'Oh, Tom, say you like it. Please, please, can we buy it?'

He took her by the shoulders and for a horrible moment she thought he was going to say no. 'If you love it, my darling girl, I love it too.'

Sebele couldn't believe her luck. Tom had completely changed her life. Not just because he was rich and spoilt her, but because he pulled her so completely into his life and his involvement in his new-found family. At the same time, he entered wholeheartedly into his love affair with her, worrying about how hard she worked and wanting to know every detail of her every day. Such attention was intoxicating.

He still spent a couple of hours a day in his study, managing his investments, but he regarded this as housekeeping: it had to be done but it didn't hold the excitement and interest for him it once had. He didn't seem to miss his old life in the City. He'd describe himself as retired, but to Sebele the description was laughable. If Tom was retired he took the title very seriously, she thought, filling his day with walks, museums, music, books. And he was so obviously not slowing down. He was speeding up, interested in everything, project-managing the house conversion, helping Oberon and Anna, and learning Italian.

Sebele had always been energetic, able to work a twelve-hour day and go dancing at the end of it. Now she felt invincible. So this is what love does, she thought. She'd told Tom she woke up happy. It was true. Her eyes shot open as she thought of him, or the house, or her work, and sometimes she literally jumped out of bed, eager for the day.

One day Tom emerged from his study with a sheaf of papers. 'We need to talk,' he said, sitting down at the dining-table.

Sebele assumed the papers concerned the new house. She sat down next to him and peered at the cover of the top file. It had *Plan for the Expansion of Angelica's Angels* scrawled across the top.

'Remember when we met,' he said, 'I was down in the Cotswolds to have a look at the catering business?' Sebele nodded. 'It was obvious that Angelica's Angels was passing up a lot of revenue by hiring in so much. They get the profit on the food and drink and almost nothing else. Everything, from the marquees to the last teaspoon, is hired from specialist companies.'

'And I remember,' said Sebele, 'that you concluded it wouldn't be worth owning the marquees or the equipment because customers would sure-as-hell want the tent or the tablecloths or the style of glassware that we didn't have.'

Tom smiled. 'True. But since then Angelica has gone through the invoices for the last two years to get an idea of the most popular styles of tent, crockery, et cetera, and the frequency of the hirings. And I've been doing sums. Even allowing for breakages and maintenance, the business should own the most popular ranges. They would easily pay for themselves in a single summer. And the good news is, the same goes for a big white marquee to seat two hundred people.'

'But how can they afford it? Angelica is always strapped for capital.'

'Well, OK, here comes the second part of my plan. You join Angelica's Angels full-time, and you build up the street-food side of the business, which you'll be a partner in, with fifty per cent. I'm certain there's a real future in that. It fits the modern desire for speed, informality and new, different food. You'll manage the hire side too. And the hiring of photographers, singing waiters and discos. We should make a big thing about themed parties and get into the London market with them, maybe eventually hire a designer to concentrate on that side of the business. If you joined Angelica at once, you could do all the research and planning in the slow months of January and February. I'll fund the investment in exchange for shares.'

'Stop, Tom, stop, for heaven's sake. Let me get this straight – you're going to be a partner in Angelica's Angels?'

'Yes, a junior one.'

'And I'm to join the company full time?'

'Yes, the whole idea is to give you the job you want.'

Sebele was dumbfounded. Yes, it made sense. She'd love it, of course. But she was also angry. Tom was assuming he could map out her future without consultation. And if he was a partner in the overall business, and her street-food bit was a subsidiary, she'd be working for him. He'd be her boss, or one of them.

She sat silent.

Tom turned to look into her face. 'Oh, Sebele darling, don't look like that! You're super-efficient, Angelica will love having you full time, and you need your own business again. You don't want to be a jobbing chef for ever.'

'No, Tom, I don't. But I'd quite like to be consulted about my own career.'

'But that's what we're doing! Consulting. Before we put it to the Angelottis. If they agree, and I'm sure they will, it would be wonderful, wouldn't it?'

'You don't get it, do you? I'm upset because I would have liked to be in on the process from the start. I could have contributed something. But you didn't even tell me you were planning this. What kind of partnership is it, when you do the thinking, make the decisions, then expect me to fall obediently into line?' As she talked, Sebele became increasingly emotional. 'The trouble with you, Tom, is, you've been too rich for too long.'

She knew she'd gone too far, was losing control, but she couldn't stop. 'You're used to offering investment to desperate entrepreneurs and have them fall at your feet in gratitude.' She was shouting now, and she could feel the prick of tears behind her eyelids. 'I'm not here for the money, Tom. I'm here because I love you. But we have to be equals. I'm not your daughter to be handed my future on a plate.' Suddenly, she was crying. She stood up and headed for the lift. 'Sorry,' she spluttered, 'I can't explain. And you'd never understand anyway.'

Tom watched her go in horror and amazement. He had looked forward to her excitement and delight. Indeed, he'd deliberately not involved her before because he wanted to present her with a finished plan. An offering to a princess.

He walked to the window and waited for her to emerge from the lobby down there in the square. He hoped she wouldn't appear because that would mean she'd changed her mind and was on her way back. But there she was, pulling on her bright yellow raincoat as she walked down the shallow steps of their building. Thank God for that coat, he thought. He couldn't miss her in it. They'd bought it together and it was lined with fake fur. She must have picked it up while she waited for the lift. He watched her walk across the square towards the pier where a ferryboat was just arriving. Please don't let her get on it, he prayed.

She didn't. She waited and watched the ferry, then went inside the little shelter, out of Tom's view.

Tom's pulse slowed as he stood at the window, waiting for Sebele to return. It was hard to distinguish individuals from so far away, but that yellow mac was unmissable among the City workers' black and grey.

As he stood there, he began to see that he'd got it all wrong. His approach was old-fashioned and arrogant. Probably sexist. Certainly patronizing. But, dammit, he thought, it was still a good idea. She must see that.

It was the first time they'd had anything approaching a quarrel, and it made him anxious. Maybe it was his age. Maybe he just didn't understand young women. But then he realized it was nothing to do with age or sex, it was to do with arrogant presumption. If someone had made a similar proposal to him, not asking what he thought of it, not prefacing it with an enquiry about whether he'd be interested or not, he'd be indignant too. She's right, he thought. I've been in charge too long.

After ten minutes Tom went down to find Sebele. She was still in the ferry shelter, staring at the river. He sat down next to her and took her hand. She leant her cheek against his shoulder.

'Can we start again?' Tom said. 'Would you ever consider going into business with me?'

All the Angelottis spent Christmas Day with Laura and Giovanni. Sebele had met almost everyone before, but never so many of the family together. Now she understood how Tom had fallen in love with the whole chaotic Italian tribe. Oberon and Anna were there, and Anna was looking good, slim and boyish in stylish black dungarees with a multi-coloured striped shirt. While he dispensed drinks, Giovanni sang along to Pavarotti, Mario and Silvano joining in for the chorus of 'Toreador'. Giovanni still had a rich baritone voice of considerable power, and Mario and Silvano were tenors. Sebele longed to join in but was too shy.

Everyone was friendly, glad that Tom had a girlfriend and, as always, pleased to be in Laura's cluttered but somehow efficient kitchen, about to get some truly great cooking. Only Susan was cool.

When she and Mario arrived, well after everyone else, Sebele found it strange that Tom's former girlfriend should be there. She thought Susan beautiful, though, and felt a twinge of jealousy. But she went boldly up to her and put out her hand, smiling. 'You must be Susan,' she said. 'I'm Sebele.'

Susan didn't smile. 'I know who you are,' she replied, and looked round the room, over Sebele's shoulder.

Mario chipped in: 'I've been wanting to meet you for months, but my cousin here,' he punched Tom lightly in the ribs, 'has kept you to himself. I do see why.' Susan frowned and soon drew

Mario away to get a glass of prosecco from Giovanni at the other end of the kitchen.

Sebele felt Tom's arm snake around her waist and she leant into him gratefully. 'Are you OK, darling?'

'I'm fine. I love your family. But I don't understand why they welcome Susan back. Don't they know what she did to you?'

'Probably not. I didn't tell them. Only that we'd broken up, though I'm sure they guessed. But, darling, they're Italians. Family is everything. And Mario, like him or not, is family. So for him the door will always be open, whatever he does.' He squeezed her waist. 'I'm sorry she was rude to you.'

Sebele smiled. 'She wasn't exactly friendly, but it's understandable. The stupid woman lost a good man and now has a distinctly dodgy one.'

Laura at first refused Sebele's help in the kitchen, but Angelica insisted. 'Come on, Mamma, you know she's a pro. If we throw all these boozing, singing men out, make them go upstairs, the three of us will have the prep done in no time.' She lowered her voice: 'With any luck they'll take Susan with them.'

So, everyone went upstairs, as ordered by Laura, who promptly set Angelica to laying the table and Sebele to helping her with the cooking.

They were preparing an Italian Christmas with no less than five courses. They'd start with classic antipasti, the platters like something out of a coffee-table cookbook.

Watching Laura cook was a lesson in itself. It was hard to believe that she was seventy-seven. Or that she wasn't Italian. Only her accent gave her away. Sebele felt she should be taking notes as Laura browned the veal and put it into a big pot with sliced fennel and potatoes. She added a good slug of oil, another of wine, half a dozen skinned and halved tomatoes, and a sprig of rosemary. There's nothing complicated or unusual in any of this, thought Sebele, but somehow, it's very special. Laura does everything efficiently and fast, without fuss, and using only the best ingredients. She watched her put on the lid and give it a pat. Job done. 'There,' Laura said. 'We'll cook it slowly and eat it when it's just faintly pink.'

The pasta was a lasagne, the usual meat layers replaced with thin slices of fried aubergine. Sebele was given the task of semi-cooking the lasagne sheets and layering everything in a big ceramic dish. First a layer of lasagne, then tomato sauce, then fried aubergine, then cheese sauce, then one more layer of everything, ending with the second layer of cheese sauce. She sprinkled grated Parmigiano and breadcrumbs on top. It would go on the top shelf of the oven, above the pot-roasting veal.

'I had to order the veal from a farmer in Devon, who's trying to buck the trend and get people to eat it. None of the butchers round here stock it.'

'Why don't the British eat veal?' asked Sebele. 'That looked beautiful meat.'

'I don't know. Partly out of sentiment. Though why it's OK to eat a little woolly lamb and not to eat a calf, I don't know. There was a terrific scandal in the eighties when dairy calves were being shipped to Europe to be raised in horrible crates so narrow they couldn't move. The problem is that calves from milking herds don't grow up to make profitable beef. The male calves are mostly killed at birth.'

Sebele frowned. 'But that's just awful.'

'I know, and they'd make good veal, if only we would eat it.'

To follow would be a whole Pecorino, served with Laura's *cotognata*, and afterwards a ball of ice cream the size of a large coconut that Mario had contributed. 'It's our new pistachio and honeycomb *cassata*, covered in dark chocolate. You'll love it.'

'Pity he didn't tell us he was bringing it,' said Angelica. 'I ordered that big panettone.'

'Doesn't matter, darling,' said Laura. 'They'll be great together and they'll both keep.'

Sebele tried not to eat too much, but somehow the genial insistence of Giovanni and Laura, and the matchless aroma of fennel, rosemary and roast veal, made it impossible to resist. By the time they got to coffee and chilled *vin santo* with *biscotti* to dunk in it, she was too merry to care. She'd never been at a meal like it. It seemed disorganized and unplanned, with all the men laughing and drinking while they ate, the women somehow getting the food on to and off the table while continuing a shouted conversation.

Sebele was sitting diagonally opposite Tom, and saw Laura come up behind him with another bottle of *vin santo*. She seemed to hesitate for a second, then leant forward and put her arms round Tom's shoulders, her cheek next to his. She whispered something in his ear, and straightened up, put the bottle down and turned away.

What struck Sebele was Tom's expression of delighted surprise. He put his hands on the arms of his chair, as if to rise and follow Laura, then seemed to think better of it. He sat back smiling.

Lunch wasn't over until five o'clock, and Sebele and Tom drove slowly home. It was already dark, and the streets were eerily quiet. Canary Wharf was like a ghost town with restaurants shuttered and almost no one on the pavements.

Sebele made tea, and they sat in the living room with the blinds open, looking out on the river, shining and smooth as glass, with nothing moving on it. The apartment block to the east had every floor outlined in blue neon, but nearly all the windows were dark, their occupants gone home to Mum and Dad for Christmas. They'll be all over the world, thought Sebele, not just the UK, but America, Europe, the Far East, and they've taken the urgency and bustle of Canary Wharf with them. It was extraordinarily peaceful.

'Why don't we go to bed?' said Tom. 'Snuggle up to watch a box-set? *The Sopranos* maybe.' He put out a hand and ruffled her hair, today in a loose Afro-cloud around her head.

But Sebele wasn't listening. 'When Laura hugged you after lunch, when she brought the extra bottle of *vin santo*, what did she whisper in your ear?'

Tom smiled at her. 'You noticed? Yes, it was quite something for me. You know how she's never really shown me much affection, as if she couldn't accept that I was her son? Everyone else has been wonderful, but Laura has stayed quite cool. Not cold or frosty, just a bit indifferent. Well, tonight she said the loveliest thing.' He paused, shaking his head a little, as though in wonder.

'What?'

'She said, "I love you, son." Just that. "I love you, son."'

PART FOUR

2005

CHAPTER TWENTY-FOUR

Jane opened the Chorlton farm office door and stepped in. Jake was there with his secretary.

He stood up. 'Hello, Jane,' he said, kissing her briefly. 'To what do we owe the pleasure? I doubt you're here to get me to turn Frampton organic.'

'Not a chance. I came to see your mother. Or Hal. Are they here?'

'I think so, yes. We had breakfast together.'

'They're not in the house. I went into the kitchen and yelled. No reply.'

'Mm. That's odd.' Then Jake's brow lightened. 'Oh, I know. They'll be in the attic. Mum said she was going to turn out the loft. Mad idea. There must be a hundred years of junk in there. Well, seventy at least.'

Jane returned to the house and climbed the stairs to the top floor. She had hardly been up there since she was about nine. God, she thought, that's fifty-something years ago. She went into the bedroom where she'd slept for six years after her father was killed in the war. Everything was the same, but the room looked so small and dingy. Her child's bed was still there, and the chest of drawers her mother was always nagging her to tidy, and the big toybox, shaped like a treasure chest. She opened it now, half expecting to see a jumble of wooden toys, but it was empty.

She walked across to the window and looked down on the yard behind the kitchen. How did Mum bear it? she thought. Us, the poor relations, stuck in the attic and expected to be grateful. She opened the cupboard door. On the back her height measurements were still there. They started in 1943, on her third birthday when she was two foot eleven inches, then every year until her mother had remarried and they had gone to live at Frampton in 1948. Surrounding the neat lines and dates recording her growth, there were paintings of frolicking farmyard animals: a fat sow with dancing piglets, a cow jumping over the moon, a billy-goat with balloons tied to his horns, a pony rearing with a delighted little girl clinging to his back. She felt suddenly emotional. Her mother had painted these, and the little girl was her, the pony her adored Snowdrop. Maybe I was happier here at Chorlton, she thought, than at Frampton, for all its luxury. She shook off the idea. What nonsense. Frampton was beautiful. And it was hers now, all its rolling acres, its farms and the village. I have a lot more than these smug Olivers, so pleased with each other, such a tight-knit tribe.

Thoughts of the Olivers brought her back to the reason for her visit. She must find Hal and Pippa. She left her old bedroom, glancing briefly into the next-door room, once her mother's, and set off down the corridor. At the end she found a wooden ladder up to the open trapdoor of the loft. Gingerly, she climbed up.

She proceeded cautiously towards the sounds of scraping, thumping and muffled voices at the far end. The loft was stacked with furniture, old beds, mattresses obviously infested with mice, suitcases and trunks, boxes and boxes of books and papers. She picked up a cushion and its fabric gave way, releasing a cloud of feathers.

Hal was sorting books on the floor. He hauled himself up by pulling on a rafter. 'Hi, Jane, this is a surprise.'

'Good Lord, Jane. What are you doing up here?' Pippa looked up from stuffing old clothes into a black bin bag.

'I'm looking for you two but, more to the point, what are you doing?'

'Trying to get rid of years and years of junk. It's rather fun.' Pippa, still willowy, red-blonde and beautiful at fifty-something, stood and stretched, her hands on her back. 'If you want anything, help yourself.'

'No thanks. I've got an attic full of my own junk.'

'We've earned a coffee break,' said Pippa, picking up one of the many black bags. 'We'll come down with you.'

Hal passed Jane a bag. 'This one's not too heavy. Can you manage it, Jane?'

I'm only ten years older than you, she thought. She took the bag. 'Of course I can. I'm not decrepit yet,' she said. 'I can just about manage a bag of cushions.'

They had coffee in the kitchen and Jane said, 'I'm going away for three weeks. To get some winter sun. I came over to ask if you'd keep an eye on Frampton for me. Of course, the staff are there, but you know what they're like. Once the cat's away . . .'

'I'm sure they'll manage perfectly,' said Pippa, 'but we'll step in if necessary.'

'Thank you. It's just that if we have a big freeze, I don't want to come back to burst pipes and flooding, which has happened before. And they might need advice, or authority to do something. You remember when that wretched old cat cost me a fortune in scans and vet's hospital fees because no one wanted to do the sensible thing and put the creature down? You'll have my number and you can always ring me.'

'Fine. Of course. But hasn't the estate office got your mobile number?'

'Yes, but they know I don't like to be bothered on holiday. So I've told them to ring you.'

Pippa changed the subject. 'Jane, are you sure you don't want to have anything from the loft? There are a lot of your mum's paintings and drawings, which I'm sure you'll want to keep.'

I doubt it, thought Jane, as Pippa went on: 'They're yours, of course. But there are a couple I'd love to keep if you agree.'

'Go ahead. Mother kept too many of her paintings, and Frampton is stuffed with them. Help yourself, but they won't have any value.'

'And there are boxes of stuff we think belonged to her,' Hal put in. 'And Hugh's old air-force uniforms and things. We've got them down as far as the dining room. If you've got time, you could have a rummage now.'

Jane thought she might as well. It could be interesting, and she didn't have anything better to do.

When Hal and Pippa went back to their labours upstairs, Jane settled down to go through the pile of boxes in the dining room. As she suspected, there was nothing she wanted. What would I do with Dad's uniforms? she thought. And Mother painted far too many pictures. Pippa was welcome to the lot.

Hal had told her that he'd yet to go through the pile of papers on the dining-table. They were mostly old photos and letters. He'd told her to have a look if she liked but said she might want to wait till he'd sorted them a bit, separated the stuff that was nothing to do with her, like the children's school reports, his farm accounts, boxes of ancient invoices. Most of it would need chucking, he'd added.

But Jane thought she'd have a look anyway. She leant over the table and opened a box. The contents, farm accounts, were ragged from the ravages of mice. She dumped the box in the corner. Hal could lug them to the bonfire later. She dealt the same fate to about six more cardboard or wooden boxes, which had similarly been home to generations of mice.

Next was a heavy metal trunk that had managed to keep out rodents. It was full of shoeboxes of photographs and photo albums. One album was labelled '1950–73' and she flipped through it, thinking it would have pictures of her. But it was devoted to the Olivers, full of pictures of Hal and Richard as children. Sophie, who'd married David after Jill had died giving birth to them, had always dressed them in identical clothes when they were little. Jane, intrigued in spite of herself, turned the pages. There were photographs of the boys, often with David, on tractors, in wheelbarrows, on ponies, at birthday parties, swimming in the river. As they grew up they became more distinguishable from each other. No longer dressed the same, Hal was generally casual and scruffy, Richard neat and tidy. On the last page there was a formal portrait of the boys side by side in Eton uniform. They must have been thirteen.

Finally she found a packet of photographs, mostly black-and-white, of her own family. Some she recognized from similar pictures at home, like the ones in the baby book of her as an infant.

There were a lot of black-and-white snaps of her at three

or four, at Frampton after her mum had married George. But there were earlier unfamiliar pictures too, perhaps taken by her grandmother, Maud: one of Jane sitting up in an old-fashioned pram, pushed by her mother outside Plumtree Cottage where they'd lived when her father was alive, snaps of him in RAF uniform holding her hand as she, perhaps eighteen months old, took wobbly steps, some of him pushing her on a trike, and a Christmas meal with her grandparents at Chorlton.

She stared hard at a picture of her as a teenager, grinning over her pony's back as she settled his saddle on his back. That was the day, she thought, that Angelica fell off her horse and ended up in a coma. And that was the summer the Angelottis spent with us, and I taught Mario and Silvano to ride. I was so happy then. When did I start being unhappy?

Her back was beginning to ache. What am I doing drooling over Memory Lane? she thought. Do I want any of this stuff? Probably not.

She turned her attention to a mini-trunk in metal, obviously mouse-proof. It was heavy, but Jane lifted it on to the floor so that she could sit down next to it and examine its contents in comfort. Inside she found a shoebox of letters, which obviously belonged to Sophie. They were in neat bundles. They were from the boys to her when they were at school, from 1973 to 1978, then from Richard at Oxford and from Hal in Australia. Getting bored now, she put the box back into the trunk. Sophie's problem.

As she was about to close the lid, she noticed a packet of letters labelled 'Laura 1946–50'. 1946? That was just after the war, when Laura was banished from Chorlton because she was pregnant. When she ran away with Giovanni.

She couldn't resist. She slipped the packet into her handbag. I'll sneak it back when I've had a good read, she thought.

Almost as soon as she arrived home, Jane read the letters. It was fascinating stuff. Unfortunately, there were no copies of Sophie's to Laura, but it seemed Sophie had kept all Laura's. At the beginning the letters were brief and anguished, just telling Sophie where she and Giovanni were living, that they were working in a café, that they had a room in a Paddington house with a grumpy landlady. And then there was a gap. When the letters resumed, Laura told Sophie she'd lost the baby. And then there was a letter from Giovanni.

Dear Sophie,

You are Laura's friend and you must help her. Laura had the baby in early January. It was nearly two months too soon. We had nowhere to live then, only hostels, but not together, and we had no money. The doctor at the hospital, he made Laura give the baby away to some rich people. Now it is nearly spring, and she is still very unhappy, so sad. She misses her mother, I think, and Chorlton. Please come to see her.

Giovanni

After that, the letters came thick and fast, Laura so relieved to have her friend Sophie in her life once more, telling Sophie of her excitement at being pregnant again and her recovered happiness with Giovanni, asking her advice about her pregnancy, begging her to come to her wedding, and then to be there at the birth.

Jane, although excited to be reading her aunt's intimate letters, was both irritated and jealous. There was Laura, to all intents and purposes an outcast, as happy as she could be, beloved of her husband, doing well in business and with something Jane had never had: a best friend. A true best friend who would always be there and always love her.

She skimmed through the rest of the letters, mostly short, covering the next few years. She wondered why she was bothering to read them. And then she found a long letter from Laura to Sophie dated 31 January 1952.

Darling Sophie,

I just wanted to put on paper something I've always wanted to say and have always been too ashamed to. I only admitted the truth about my first baby last week in Kensington Gardens, because you'd guessed. I'm so, so sorry, Sophie. It was no way to treat my best friend and confidante of all my life's secrets but up to that moment I couldn't tell anyone, not even you.

I wanted to, of course. I knew you would be what you always have been, wise, kind, on my side. But I was too mortified by what I'd done.

The truth is that I slept with Giovanni almost as soon as I met him. And only weeks after I'd sent Marcin packing. When I discovered I was pregnant, of course I thought the baby must be Giovanni's. It never occurred to me that it could be Marcin's. Even if it had, I'd have dismissed the thought – we used that contraceptive stuff, Volpar.

It was only when the doctor said the baby would arrive so early that I realized it might not be Giovanni's. Of course, I never saw the baby. I only know it was a boy because the nurse referred to 'he' as they rushed him out of the room.

I've never said a word to Giovanni, and of course he's never fully understood why I gave the baby away. But, Sophie, I had to. He thinks it was because we had no money and nowhere to live, but really it was because he might turn out to be blond and blue-eyed, and obviously not Giovanni's.

Darling Giovanni has forgiven me now and is utterly in love with Angelica. But I think of the boy still. Of course I do. He'd be five now. But I can't tell you what a relief it is to have no more secrets from you.

Laura

With no clear idea of why she was doing it, Jane walked through to her study and photocopied the letter. Then she returned the original to the packet in the right place and flipped through the rest of the letters, but there was nothing particularly interesting in them.

She put on her Barbour jacket and slipped the packet of letters into the poacher's pocket in the lining, then drove back to Chorlton. There was no one about. Maybe Hal and Pippa were still up in the loft. She returned to the dining room and replaced the letters in the shoe box. I could just sneak out now, she thought, but then decided she might as well be seen to be doing what she was meant to be doing. She sorted both photographs and papers into three separate piles: Angelotti, Oliver and Frampton, and boxed them up neatly. It made her feel virtuous and altruistic. No one was paying her to do the boring sorting, were they?

*

A fortnight later Laura and Giovanni came to see her. They were staying at Chorlton for the weekend and they'd invited themselves over for a cup of tea on the Sunday.

Jane felt some satisfaction at this. So, she thought, they're coming to 'pay their respects'. They know I still matter to the family. She wasn't just a spinster neighbour in need of a charity visit, which was how she felt when Pippa arrived with half a cake or a branch of sprouts or some other ridiculous offering. Giovanni and Laura knew how important her father had always been to the family fortunes by backing Giovanni's businesses, and giving Chorlton the contract to farm the Frampton land. And they knew she was important to them now.

But Jane was irritated too. She'd suggested Saturday instead of Sunday, but that didn't suit the Angelottis. She had to give way and agree to Sunday afternoon when her servants were off. At some moment of weakness, she'd agreed to letting the cook, butler and groom all have Sunday afternoon off. These days, people expected to be paid exorbitant wages and choose when they would work. There'd be no one to open the door to visitors today or bring in the tea. It wasn't right that she should be bustling around like a kitchen maid.

They arrived promptly at four thirty, Giovanni with his usual bonhomie, and Laura kissing her on both cheeks, saying, 'Jane, dear, you look like a model in *Country Life*.'

She did look good, she knew. At almost sixty-five she was as trim as ever and her habitual uniform of well-tailored jodhpurs, shirt, cashmere sweater and tweed jacket suited her excellent figure. Whereas Laura had let herself go, stupid woman. All that pasta and cake. And she could do with a decent haircut. That mop of curls, now mostly grey, was ridiculous on someone in her late seventies.

They talked for about an hour and then, when they were just about to go, Laura suddenly said, 'Jane, dear, I really want to say something, which I'm sure you don't want to hear, but I think you must. In the last hour, you have criticized your gardener, the cleaner, the cook. You've complained that the girl-groom is insolent, that Hal doesn't agree with you over pesticides, that the hunt master doesn't know how to run a hunt, that Pippa is interfering with the flower rota for the village church, and a whole lot more that I can't remember.'

Giovanni cut in, 'Darling, I don't—'

'I'm the only one who will ever say it, Giovanni.'

'There's more, is there?' barked Jane. 'Well, go ahead, I'm listening.'

Laura sat forward in her chair, leaning towards Jane, her face earnest and troubled. 'Your mother was the gentlest, kindest woman in the world. And your father the most honourable, generous friend. And they were both happy by nature. I don't think I ever heard either of them being rude or unkind about anyone.'

'And you're telling me that I don't match up?'

'Yes, I suppose I am. Jane, it really worries me that you're so unhappy, so discontented when you have so much, that you're so critical of others, always looking to find fault in everything. What can we do, what can I do, to make you see the world in a brighter light?'

Jane was more stung by this kindness than she had been by Laura's forthrightness. 'It's none of your bloody business, Laura. And I think you should leave.'

As Jane stood, Laura got up and went to her. 'Come here, Jane. I want to show you something,' she said, getting behind her and taking her shoulders to steer her to stand in front of the tall gilt mirror.

'Look at yourself, Jane,' she said. 'Look. Just look. You're a handsome woman. If you smiled, you'd be lovely. But you seldom smile. You have the downturned mouth of someone who is always discontented, always miserable.'

She let go of Jane and said, 'Dear Jane, no one means you harm. If people are unfriendly, it's because you've snubbed them, or been rude to them, or ridden over their feelings. Wouldn't life be better for you too, if you were less critical?' When Jane said nothing, just stood with her arms crossed, looking angry, Laura went on, 'Just give being nice a try, Jane. It's not too late.'

And with that the pair of them left.

Jane was upset. She tried to maintain her anger. How dare Laura take it on herself to give her moral lectures? She, who had lied to her husband for fifty years. And she was quite wrong about people hating her. The servants probably adored her. She paid them enough, God knew.

Jane stood in front of the mirror again and looked hard at her face. Yes, she was handsome. Not pretty or beautiful, but strong and handsome. She went to the stairs and examined her portrait as a young woman, the last in a descending line from the second floor, with all the Maxwell-Calders and their wives from the seventeenth century. It had been painted when she was eighteen and the artist had obviously copied the 'girls in pearls' photograph that had appeared in *Tatler* about the time of her coming-out ball. She remembered that she had flatly refused to sit for the portrait because it would have interfered with training for the Frampton point-to-point and competing in the Cotswold horse trials.

She stood for a long time, her image staring back at her with the confidence and bloom of youth. Slowly, her eyes filled with tears. What a waste, she thought. What a total waste.

Wiping her eyes on the back of her wrists, Jane sat down on the stairs. Laura had implied that she, Jane, had everything. But that was rubbish. Laura had sailed through life, getting everything she'd ever wanted, lovers, husband, children, family, career. By contrast here she was, with none of these. She doubted if she even had a true friend.

Abruptly she stood up. Of course I'm tough, she told herself. I have to be. I'm on my own and I'm mistress of a huge estate. All I ask is proper respect. And one thing I don't need, she thought, is sanctimonious lectures on behaviour from Laura bloody Angelotti.

CHAPTER TWENTY-FIVE

A lot of the time now, Anna was dizzy with happiness. Her only problem, which she hadn't yet the courage to tackle, was her family. She wanted them to know she was gay, she longed to introduce Cassia to them, and wanted them to love her as she did, but she was terrified of their disapproval. And she knew that if they didn't accept Cassia, she'd lose them all. She decided she needed Tom's help.

When Anna arrived at the pub, Tom was sitting at a table in the corner. She gave him a kiss on the cheek as she slid onto the banquette opposite him.

She hadn't seen him for a while. Since she'd been going to AA, and was enjoying her job so much, they'd been less in touch, presumably because he felt she needed less mentoring, less avuncular advice. But she missed him and had suggested brunch.

They talked mostly of Sebele, then Giovanni's and the Crabtree's Michelin stars, and then about her work with Oberon. She told him that almost every girl they hired to help with the boxes fell for him, and how hopeless he was at resisting them, then at telling them he wasn't looking for love.

'I'm becoming his gatekeeper,' she said. 'I have to hint to

Arabella or Samantha or whoever that she's not the only one, that he's unreliable boyfriend material. And, of course, they think I'm warning them off because I have designs on him myself.'

'That's understandable. You remember I thought there might be something between the two of you?'

Anna face cracked into a grin. 'I do. I love him to bits. He's like a brother. Or a cousin. Which of course he is. But I don't fancy him.' She stared into her soup bowl for a bit, twirling the floating croutons around with her spoon. 'He did kiss me once, but I wasn't up for it. The thing is, I'm gay, Tom. Always have been. I've known ever since school.' She kept her eyes on his, looking for shock, disapproval, any hint of disgust. But his gaze didn't waver, and his expression was as usual. Interested, affectionate.

He smiled. 'Really? Do you have a girlfriend?'

Anna nodded. 'Yes, I've found someone now. She's called Cassia. She's wonderful.'

Tom's face opened in a delighted smile. 'That's great, Anna. How lovely. Do your parents know?'

'Most of my friends know I'm gay, of course, but none of the family. Except Oberon, and now you. Oberon knows Cass and thinks she's great. I don't want to hide anything any more. Oh, Tom, I can't tell you how good it feels just to have told you.'

'You need to tell your parents, Anna.'

'I know. I want to, but Mum and Dad will be upset, maybe horrified. But I don't want to have to keep Cassia a secret.'

'Absolutely right. Who do you think will be most worried? Your mother and grandmother will be OK with it, I reckon. I think Silvano and Giovanni may find it hard to take.'

They talked for an hour, half of which was taken up with Anna singing Cassia's praises. Tom watched her with pleasure. It was just good to see her so happy.

They agreed that the best way to tackle it was to start with Angelica, then take her advice about telling her father and grandparents.

Anna and Cassia drove down to Holly Farm on Cassia's Honda 250 motorbike. Cassia had driven bikes ever since she was old enough to get a licence and she loved them. For February it wasn't a bad day, but Cassia insisted Anna wear thermals and jerseys, thick socks and leathers against the wind – she had a second set and a second helmet for passengers. Anna sat on the pillion with her arms round Cassia's narrow waist, thinking how love changed everything. She'd never have thought she'd want anything to do with motorbikes, or someone whose magazine subs went to *Art Historian*, *Antiques Now*, *Classic Bikes* and *Biker's Weekly*.

Cassia dropped Anna at the gates to Holly Farm. She would drive on to the Crabtree, where no one would know her, get a cup of coffee and wait for Anna's call.

Angelica was at her desk, absorbed in her computer, and didn't hear her daughter until Anna said, 'Hi, Mum,' from the door.

As her mother swung round, her face alight with pleasure, Anna felt a sinking fear that her new-found good relationship with her mother was about to sunder.

'Hello, darling! I wasn't expecting you till Friday.'

'I know, Mum. But I need to talk to you and I wanted to catch you alone. I've something important to tell you. Something I should've told you ages ago.'

She saw her mother's open face change at once to anxiety, fear even. 'You're not pregnant, darling?'

Anna almost laughed. 'No, Mum. It's good news.'

Angelica stood up and hugged her. 'You're in love?'

'Well, yes, but . . .' she hesitated, thinking, Here goes, say it '. . . but it's with a girl. A woman. I'm gay, Mum.'

For a moment Angelica, still with her arms around her daughter, looked blankly at her. 'A woman? What woman?' Then she dropped her arms and spun round as though distracted, not looking at Anna.

'Mum, it's OK. It's good. I'm happy.'

That seemed to get through to her. 'Oh, God, darling, I'm sorry. It was just the shock,' said Angelica, once again putting her arms round Anna and looking into her eyes. 'That's what matters, isn't it? Does she really make you happy? Happiness is everything.'

After twenty minutes, during which both women became increasingly relaxed, Anna rang Cassia, and Angelica got into the car and went to tell Silvano. She'll pass Cassia on the road, thought Anna, but it will never occur to her that the biker is my lover.

Cassia arrived almost half an hour before Angelica returned with Silvano. In that half-hour, they sat on the sofa, holding hands, hugging and telling each other over and over again that this was good. Better to be out of the closet than in. Better to take some prejudice and abuse than lie to everyone.

Anna was the first to hear her parents' car and she went out to meet her father, leaving Cassia in the kitchen. Silvano just put his arm round her and said, 'It's OK by me, *cara*, as long as this woman of yours is worthy of you.' They walked up to the house and he leant in to whisper, 'But I swear I'll kill her if she messes you around.'

*

The worst confrontation, predictably, was with Giovanni. Anna went to see him and Laura without Cassia because she wanted to protect her from her grandfather. Poor Grandpa, she thought, he'll think that somehow his own machismo will be damaged by one of his own being gay. Anna had always been closer to Nonna than to Giovanni. She gazed at her grandparents, noticing for the first time that they were looking properly old. Laura's hair was almost completely white, and her skin sagged round her neck. She seemed a little shrunken, sitting on the sofa next to Giovanni. Her grandfather's strong, handsome face was mottled with age and his shave was a little patchy. His paunch challenged the buttons of his shirt.

Anna, telling herself to be brave and just get on with it, took a deep breath and said, 'I have to tell you both something, and I don't think you'll like it. I'm gay, and I'm in love with a girl called Cassia.'

For a minute no one said anything. Then Laura leant forward. 'Gay? You mean homosexual? You like women, not men?'

Anna nodded. 'Yes, Nonna. That's what I mean.'

There was another stunned silence, followed by a blizzard of disbelief, questions, protestations and appeals from Giovanni, his voice rising as he stoked his own anger. 'It's not natural,' he stormed. 'Women were made to have babies and men were made to give them the babies. What can two women do? It's not right. It's wrong.' He went on in this vein while Anna, determined to keep her cool, let him rant.

When at last he gave her space to speak, she had trouble keeping her voice steady. 'Grandpa, people have argued for centuries about homosexuality. In ancient Greece it was common for men to have wives and male lovers. It has existed in every civilization. In all single-sex institutions – in convents, in the army, in boarding schools – homosexuality goes on, however hard they try to stamp it out. Which makes me think it's part of human nature. That maybe everyone has a bit of male and female in them. Maybe even you, Grandpa, could love a man if the circumstances were right.'

'Never! Never!' shouted Giovanni. 'Under no circumstances.'

Laura put three fingers on Giovanni's lower arm. '*Caro mio*,' she said gently, 'the main thing is she has told us. She knows we can't have secrets in this family, and whatever anyone in the family does, we'll never reject them. You may think it is wrong, and I can't say I wouldn't rather she came home with a nice boy, but I don't think she has hurt anyone. I think she is very brave to tell us. And I want to meet this girlfriend of hers. How can we judge someone if we don't know them?'

As always, it was Laura who found the way to peace. 'Let's just invite her for Sunday lunch, eh, Giovanni? Then you can see if you like her. Or you can tell her what a mortal sin homosexuality is, if you like.' She smiled at him, teasing. 'But I think you are too kind to do that.' She kissed his wrinkled old cheek, and Anna thought that old people kissing, which she used to find disgusting, was really touching. And she was as sure as she could be that Laura would love Cassia. And Giovanni would come round one day. Of course he would. No one could fail to like Cassia.

CHAPTER TWENTY-SIX

It was three years since Tom had so wonderfully crashed into their lives and Laura often thought how like Giovanni he was: kind, honest, loving, straightforward. At first his reserve, his determination not to rock the Angelotti boat by his very existence, had worried her. It was almost as though he felt guilty, when she was to blame, not him.

Giovanni had quickly committed to loving Tom, but she'd been too scared. She'd trodden cautiously, frightened of him discovering somehow that he might not be Giovanni's son.

His extreme wealth had made her uncomfortable too, and she didn't approve of Susan, whom she thought hard and shallow. A son of hers should not be blinded by beauty. But Tom had gradually loosened up, had proved not to be in love with Susan anyway, and he'd made Giovanni enormously happy. And then he'd found the wonderful Sebele. The girl was every bit as beautiful as Susan and much, much nicer. She was energetic, hard-working, fun and funny. And she could cook.

Since Tom had first brought Sebele to meet them and they'd cooked Christmas dinner together, they often came, sometimes just for a drink or coffee, but mostly for supper, when she and

Sebele would chat in the kitchen while Tom talked to his father. She'd come to love Sebele and knew, with absolute certainty, that in spite of differences in age, background and culture, she was the right woman for her son.

And at long last – it must be almost two years – Tom and Sebele had announced they'd decided to marry. Sebele had shown her, proud and laughing, a purple and orange plastic ring like a knuckle-duster, on her left hand.

'Are you sure, my darling, that Tom is not too old for you? He must be twenty years older than you.'

'Eighteen, actually. But if it was forty I'd still marry him. I can't not, Laura. Your son is the most wonderful thing that has ever happened to me, and I'm not letting him get away.'

Laura decided to have a party for them. Sebele insisted on helping her do the cooking.

'You must be sick of Italian food all the time,' Laura told Sebele. 'If I knew how to make Ethiopian food, I'd do that. But I don't, so we'll honour Tom with the food of his childhood.'

They had an English buffet of salmon, rare beef on the bone, salads and hot boiled potatoes, followed by treacle tart, sherry trifle and a round of Stilton.

Laura had laid places at the huge kitchen table, enlarged with trestle tables at each end. She'd set up the buffet on the work surface along one wall. The whole family was there: everyone from Chorlton, Jane from Frampton, and all the Angelottis, including Mario and Susan, Anna and Cassia. And Sebele had invited her foster-parents, Molly and Edward, now in their seventies. She'd asked Molly if she should invite Evan, the silent chef who was once her foster-brother, but Molly said, no, he still found a large crowd intimidating. 'We'll introduce him to Tom one day, with just us.'

Laura watched Anna remove her salmon *en croûte* from the oven. That girl has really come good, she thought, thanks largely to the influence of Tom, whom she adored. Not content with doing a simple poached salmon and serving it cold, she had sandwiched the whole boned and skinned fillets with a hard-boiled-egg-and-caper-sauce mix, wrapped them in wilted spinach leaves, then covered the whole thing in puff pastry and baked it. The crust was shiny brown and latticed with fine back-of-the-knife marks.

Everyone clapped as Anna put it in the middle of the buffet spread. 'You slice it, please, Nonna,' she said, 'And, Grandpa, will you carve the beef?'

'How did you stop the bottom going soggy, Anna?' said Laura, cutting into Anna's creation to expose perfect layers of spinach, salmon, egg and pastry.

Anna laughed. 'I pre-baked a strip of pastry, covered it with a layer of semolina to soak up any juices, and put the raw salmon on that. It's Mum's trick. That's how she stops the bottom crust of a plate pie sogging up.'

'And then you wrapped it in the pastry?'

'Yes. It's only frozen puff. I don't think I'm up to making the real thing.'

'I'll show you one day.'

Tom put his arm round his mother's shoulders. 'Don't you women ever stop talking about cooking?

They were still around the table at midnight, having sat down three hours earlier. Almost everyone was a bit drunk, and every-one, thought Jane, sourly, except me, is having a high old time.

Jane was sitting next to Susan. Typical, she thought. I'm the spinster round here so I have to sit next to another woman. Why couldn't it be Sophie? She's a spare female too, but she's tucked up between young Jake and that Edward fellow.

She turned to Susan and said quietly, 'Doesn't it get on your tits that this family is always so pleased with itself?'

Susan looked at her, frowning a bit. Then she smiled. 'Well, yes, I agree. I've never met a family so in love with each other. Even Mario adores the others, though they all think he's the black sheep.'

'What are you girls talking about?' asked Giovanni, on Susan's right. When he didn't get an immediate answer – Jane felt caught out by the old man – he went on, 'Yes, Mario is a bit of a black sheep, but we all love him anyway. You love him, don't you, Susan?'

Susan smiled, her mouth wide but her expression aloof. 'Maybe I do.' Jane admired her cool. Susan was beautiful and unimpressed by anything.

Giovanni, not quite satisfied with Susan's answer, sat back and looked round the table. A king surveying his happy subjects, thought Jane. 'Me, I love them all.' He banged his empty glass with a spoon and conversation fell away.

'Go on, Papa,' called Angelica. 'Speech!'

Giovanni took his time while the whole family waited respectfully. Then he cleared his throat. 'This has been a momentous three years for the Angelotti family. I am so proud of you all. Hal, Pippa and Jake have turned the Chorlton estates into model organic farms. Like Prince Charles, hey, Jake?' He laughed at Jake's discomfiture at the praise. He lifted his glass in toast to the Olivers. Then he went round the table, lauding Silvano and Angelica, then Anna and Oberon. 'And my lovely granddaughter has stopped being the wild child of the family and she and Oberon have made a new modern business that I never thought would work. But it has. I am very proud of them.'

Really, thought Jane, irritably, all the girl has done is get a job packing boxes for her cousin. She's hardly Businesswoman of the Year. And he's not so proud of her lesbian ladyfriend. Not a word about Cassia, I notice. But, then, she's not an Angelotti or an Oliver, is she?

Giovanni resumed his panegyric. 'Even Mario here,' he went on, 'whom Susan has just described as the black sheep of the family, has sold more ice cream this year than ever before, and developed new and delicious ones like this *cassata* here. Wasn't it good?' He looked round to nods and smiles. Jane nodded too. It was about the only thing he'd said that she could agree with.

'And then, the most wonderful thing of all, our long-lost Tom is returned to us.' He looked down the length of the table at Tom, and, thought Jane, smiled like only a besotted old Italian could. 'Only Laura, and maybe Sophie here, knows how hard it was for Laura to give up our baby. I expect you all know the story, but you should hear it from ... How do I say? The horse's mouth?'

This is nauseating, thought Jane. He's going to blub. And, indeed, Giovanni had to wipe under his eyes with the back of his hand as he spoke. 'We were without a home and living in separate hostels. In those days getting a baby before you were married was such a bad thing no hostel or rooming house would have us both together. We had no money, and the only way to give the baby a good life was to give him away. We never saw him. Not until three years ago when he found us. And that was the happiest day of my life.

'Tom has had many tragedies in his life. But now he has found the lovely Sebele. She also had a terrible start in life, but thanks to Molly and Edward here, she has turned out just fine. Better than fine. Perfect. And Tom will, at last, get what he deserves, a wonderful wife and a wonderful life. And at last he knows that he is an Angelotti, our son, part of our family.'

Crying openly now, Giovanni staggered round the table to hug Tom, who, obviously moved, stood up to return the embrace.

Jane looked round the table. Every one of them was smiling, smugly pleased at this sentimental diatribe, even Cassia who gazed adoringly at Anna. They look like an advertisement for cornflakes or something, all smiling happy families.

Suddenly Jane could stand it no longer. 'Except,' she said quietly, but audibly, dropping her words carefully into the silence, 'Tom is not your son, Giovanni. He's the son of a Polish prisoner of war called Marcin.'

The silence was more confused than shocked. They all looked at each other. Sophie's mouth dropped open in horror. Laura looked directly at Jane, who went on, 'Isn't that so, Laura? Isn't that the reason you gave the baby away?'

The silence seemed to go on for ever, and Jane had a moment of regret. Should she have kept quiet? But then her spirit kicked in. It was ridiculous for them to be living under this pretence. And pricking the Angelotti bubble of self-satisfaction felt good. She must hang on to that feeling.

Giovanni, confused and dismayed, looked from Laura to Jane, and back to Laura. 'What does she mean, *cara mia*?'

Jane had to admire Laura's calm. She looked up, her face ashen but eyes dry. 'What she says is true, Giovanni. I don't know how she knows, but it's true.' She turned to her son. 'My darling Tom,

I don't know who your father is. I had a Polish boyfriend before I met Giovanni. He could be your father.'

Jane watched Giovanni's face, contorted first by anguish, then horror. For a moment there was silence, and Jane looked round the table. It was like a scene in a play, she thought, everyone frozen by shock. She felt a little thrill at her power to do that. Then Giovanni came to life. He stood up and, with his hands on the table, leant across it towards his wife. 'And you, Laura,' he said, his voice rising in anger, 'you never told me. Never! You've deceived me all our lives, Laura. Fifty years. More even. All our lives together.' He turned to Tom, his voice dropping. 'You'd better go, Tom. It seems you are not my son.'

Tom was already on his feet, taking a step round the table to his mother. Sebele stood too and put a hand on his shoulder. Then Tom looked, for a long beat, into Giovanni's face and saw the rigid features, hard eyes, chin jutting towards him. He turned and walked out of the kitchen door. Sebele hurried after him.

In the stunned silence, they heard the front door close, then Tom's car start up and drive away.

Jane looked round the table. Would they turn on the messenger? But she'd only told the truth and they should know the truth, surely.

Giovanni, without looking at Laura, pushed past everyone to stagger up the stairs. Angelica and Sophie both hurried round to comfort Laura, who sat unmoving, rigid and pale.

Finally, someone spoke. It was Anna, her face pink with anger. 'God, you are such a bitch, Jane,' she said. 'Why don't you bugger off out of here before one of us throws you out?'

Jane decided it was beneath her dignity to respond to such vulgarity. But then Angelica joined in: 'Why does it give you so much satisfaction to ruin other people's happiness, Jane?' She leant across the table. 'You've always done it, and every time we've forgiven you because you're part of the family, which, worse luck, you are, for all you like to pretend you were born Lady Jane of Frampton, silver spoon in your mouth. You forget you're really just an Oliver who struck gold when her mother married the son of an earl. I'm through with you, Jane.'

Jane was dismayed to see nods around the table and that impudent Jake actually clapping at this ridiculous outburst. She stood up. 'Fine,' she said. 'I can see you'd all prefer not to know the truth.' Jane's mind was scrabbling around, looking for a winning exit line. 'Well, I'm off, and, Hal, you can whistle for the Frampton contracts next year, but you won't get them.'

No one answered, and no one followed her out. She collected her coat from the pile on the wooden seat in the hall. As she pulled it off the heap, all the others slid to the floor. She left them there and stepped into the mews.

She walked halfway up Praed Street without seeing a single taxi. Her mood of elation, almost triumph, at the reaction to her pronouncement was turning to uneasiness. She thought of Laura's words about how good her parents were, and the knowledge that they would have disapproved of what she'd done intruded. Her father would have thought 'meddling', as he called it, unworthy of a Maxwell-Calder. Well, she thought, too bad. There can't be anything wrong with telling the truth. But she wasn't sure he'd have agreed.

At last a lighted taxi gave a welcome reason to quit this train of thought. 'Eaton Square,' she said.

CHAPTER TWENTY-SEVEN

Even when his beloved Angelica had fallen in love with the ne'er-do-well Mario, Giovanni had not felt like this: empty, hollowed out, utterly miserable. He couldn't even deflect his misery into rage against Jane; he couldn't make himself get up, move, talk to anyone. He just lay on the bed without even the energy to weep. All his efforts, such as they were, were concentrated on trying not to think.

Yet thinking was the one thing his brain would insist on doing, though it brought him no relief. How could his darling Laura, the light of his life for fifty-plus years, have so comprehensively deceived him? How could she carry someone else's child, pretend it was his, allow him to listen to its heartbeat through her bare tummy as they lay in that cold bed in the Paddington rooming house? How could she allow him to be so happy? Above all, how could she be so happy knowing all the while she was deceiving him?

After two or three hours – he had no idea how long – he had to go to the bathroom, and heaved himself off the bed. He hadn't noticed anyone leaving and he didn't know where Laura was. Or Sophie, or Angelica and Silvano for that matter. They had all been staying with them for the night, but everything was quiet downstairs. He stared at his face in the bathroom mirror. God, he looked old. For the first time in his life, Giovanni thought death would be a relief. How could he go on with this pain, this treachery, this falsehood, the knowledge of fifty years, a whole life, wasted on the woman who had caused it all?

And how could he have been so bewitched by someone else's son?

He lay on his back, wide-eyed. Gradually his thoughts shifted to Tom. Poor Tom. That man hadn't deserved this. Not deserved a mother who would lie about his father, then give him away to be brought up by strangers. Tom had truly been dealt the harshest of blows: the loss of his first wife and his young son, the tragedy of 9/11 killing his colleagues. There'd already been enough sadness in his life without this. And just when it was all coming right, when he'd thought he'd regained his parents, been welcomed into the family, found fresh purpose in helping his relations in their businesses, and fallen in love with a wonderful girl, it turned out his father was that oaf Marcin, the Polish PoW, who had not been seen for at least half a century. Well, he and Tom were both victims of Laura's deceit and there was no comfort in knowing she'd hurt Tom as well as him.

Laura knew it would be useless to talk to Giovanni, though of course she'd wanted to. When he'd blundered off upstairs, she'd asked everyone to leave, and most of them had. Sophie, Silvano and her daughter were staying the night, and Anna sent Cassia and Oberon home without her, telling them that she needed to stay with Nonna.

'Sit here, Mamma,' said Angelica, almost pushing her into the sofa. 'Don't go near Papa yet.' She went upstairs, shut her parents' bedroom door and came back into the sitting room, closing the door after her. 'He's asleep, I think,' she said, 'Anyway, he's in bed and I've closed the doors so we won't disturb him.'

Silvano and Sophie were clearing up the kitchen and Laura, welcoming the distraction, tried to rise to go and help them, but Angelica wouldn't allow it. 'Sit down, Mamma. Anna will get us some tea.'

Laura drank it gratefully. If I was Italian I'd have a coffee and a brandy, she thought. But Englishness will out. A cup of tea is strangely comforting.

'Thank you, Anna darling,' she said. It was the first time she'd spoken since she'd confirmed the truth of Jane's accusations.

'Tell us what happened, Mamma,' said Angelica, a hand resting on her mother's knee.

Laura sat between her daughter and her granddaughter and had a conversation she'd never have believed three generations of women could possibly have. She told them about her love affair with Giovanni, which came, she said, as a revelation after Marcin's insensitive and bullying behaviour. She told them how they'd slept together very soon, and that she hadn't told Giovanni about Marcin.

'He knew he'd been my boyfriend. They even had a fight behind the pub one day. But he didn't know I'd slept with Marcin.'

'But of course you had,' said Anna. 'Surely he'd know that.'

'Oh, darling girl, it wasn't like now, with everyone openly sleeping with anyone they've just met. You see, in those days, we really believed that if a boy knew you were not a virgin, he'd leave you at once. Certainly, he wouldn't marry you. I was too ashamed to tell Giovanni about Marcin.'

'But,' objected Angelica, 'surely, Mamma, when you knew you were pregnant, you must have known it couldn't be Papa's.'

'You have no idea how naïve we were then. I didn't do any calculations. Your father and I were overcome with joy at the thought of having a baby together, and when my father tried to kick him out, Giovanni was so wonderful, staying calm and polite but determined. We both thought the baby was his.'

'When did you discover it wasn't?' asked Anna.

'I never knew for certain. I still don't. But when I was in a hostel for unmarried mothers and about to have the baby, the doctor told me it would be born soon after Christmas. I'd thought it wasn't due until February. Then I realized it could be Marcin's.'

'And you still didn't tell Papa?'

'How could I? He'd be furious I'd slept with Marcin, and that I'd never told him. And he was so excited about the coming baby.'

They were silent for a while, Laura with her eyes closed. She was remembering the agony of decision as though it were yesterday. 'I suppose I just hoped it would turn out right.' she said. 'Giovanni would get a job and find us a flat and we'd manage somehow. But that didn't happen.' Her voice cracked, and she made an effort to control it. 'In the end I didn't have much option. The hostel would only take me back and care for me after the birth if I gave up the baby for adoption. We had nowhere to live, no money, and Giovanni didn't have a job. I'd have been on the streets a few hours after the birth. The doctor at the hospital persuaded me it would be best for the child.' Laura swallowed, wondering that she could control her voice to speak so matter-of-factly. She felt as bleak as midwinter. 'So I gave him away.'

'Didn't Papa object?' asked Angelica.

'He was devastated when he found out, but we weren't married so I didn't need his permission.'

Granddaughter and daughter persuaded Laura to sleep in the twin-bedded spare room, with Sophie in the other bed. Silvano and Angelica had the other spare room and Anna slept under an eiderdown on the sofa.

Next morning Laura came down to find Giovanni, in his dressing-gown, making coffee, something he seldom did. She reached to relieve him of the cafetière, but he shrugged her away. He didn't speak.

She laid breakfast for everyone in the usual way, putting out cereal, yoghurt, cut-up fresh fruit, bowls and the wherewithal for toast and marmalade. Giovanni didn't look at her or acknowledge any of her activity around him. Neither did he greet any of the others as they drifted in. He sat down, drank his coffee, ate a piece of bread with honey, then went upstairs again.

'We have to leave him for a bit,' said Sophie. 'Laura, love, he'll come round. But he's like a wounded lion. He's licking his wounds. Just try not to fret about him, darling.'

It was easier said than done, but Laura tried to believe Sophie, her daughter and granddaughter when they said that she'd behaved as any woman would have at that time and in those circumstances, and one day Giovanni would understand.

CHAPTER TWENTY-EIGHT

A few days later, Pippa came out of a cubicle in the farm shop's Ladies to come face to face with Jane. There was no one else in the room and both women stared at each other in the mirror over the basins, without speaking. Then Pippa lifted her chin and turned to Jane. 'How could you do that, Jane? Blow Laura's life apart? And how do you know your accusations were true anyway?'

'I think I've done her a favour. At least she's no longer living a lie. And Giovanni's so soppy he's probably forgiven her already.'

'You're wrong there. She's wretched. But how did you know what Giovanni didn't?'

'Oh, that's simple. I found a letter Laura had written years ago to your beloved mother-in-law, the do-gooding Sophie.'

Pippa frowned. 'A letter? How did you get hold of a letter to Sophie?'

'That day I was helping you sort the attic? Remember? Plenty of secrets in attics, you know.' Jane was chuckling as she swung out of the door.

A week after Jane's disastrous revelation, Giovanni was still barely speaking, and Laura was hollow-eyed from lack of sleep and anxiety. Anna went to see Tom and Sebele. She didn't fore-warn them, just arrived and got the porter on Reception to buzz up and say she was there.

Tom was alone. Sebele was out, he told her, searching in junk-yards and reclamation places for stuff for their new house. He opened his arms and Anna walked into them for a hug. 'It's good of you to come, Anna. Would you like a cuppa?'

He made them tea and they sat together on the sofa. 'The thing is, Tom, over the past few years, I've pretty well always listened to your advice, haven't I?'

Tom smiled. 'Yes, Anna, I think you have.'

'Well, do you think you'll listen while I give you some?'

Tom laughed, a little awkwardly. 'I'll certainly listen. Whether I take it . . .'

'That's fine. As long as you listen. It's perfectly simple. Giovanni loves you like a son. He's desolated to find you might not be his. You love him too. In fact, you love all of us, the whole family. And they love you and Sebele. So what's the fucking problem?'

'Er. I think it could be that I'm not Giovanni's son. No?'

'So, where does it say you have to share DNA to love some-one? I love Dad and Mum, and I have none of their DNA because I'm adopted. You love me, ditto. No DNA connection. You love my nonna, your very own mamma, and if you're not careful you'll lose her, too, in spite of a ton of DNA in common. And she really, really loves you. It took her for ever to accept you and now we know why. She was so conflicted, so sure she'd get hurt. And, bingo, she finally does accept you. And then gets *really* hurt.'

'Anna darling. I'm with you. But I'm not the problem. I feel like an interloper. I believed I was Laura's *and Giovanni's* son. I confidently gate-crashed the family with that certainty, that pass-port if you like. Now I've no right to barge into the Paddington house any more. That passport, as least as far as Giovanni is concerned, is withdrawn.'

'How do you know? Yes, everyone was upset that night. It was such a shock. But they're miserable now, not because you might be someone else's son but because they've lost you. I've never seen Nonna so down. She's bereft, Tom. Giovanni won't speak to her. He won't forgive her, not because you aren't his but because she never told him. You have to come back to us, Tom. You have to.'

'I've thought of trying to see Laura, and I'd dearly love to, but that would upset Giovanni, and make him even angrier with her. He plainly doesn't want me anywhere near. Understandably so.'

'Understandably? Whoever's to blame, Tom, it's not you. That's nonsense.'

'It's very Italian. Family, real family, blood, DNA, the lot, means everything.'

'Well, that's nonsense too.'

They were briefly silent. Then Tom ran both hands through his hair and shook his head as though to clear it.

'Anna, you know I'd give anything to undo what that med-dling bloody Jane did that night. But it's not my call. Did you see Giovanni's reaction? If I did insist on seeing my mother, it would be so disloyal to him. He'd ban me, I know he would.' He looked into her eyes. 'Anna, I'm not man enough to bear that.'

Anna took her mission to her grandfather. She found him in his study at the end of the corridor. He wasn't working. He was staring at his empty desk and he did not look up when she came in. She pulled a chair up to the desk opposite him and sat on it. 'Hello, Grandpa. I think we need to talk.'

He looked up then, his eyes expressionless. 'Talk about what?'

'You know as well as I do. Do you want to ruin this family, Grandpa? I thought we meant everything to you.'

'Don't be impertinent, Anna. You don't know what you're talking about.'

'Yes, I do. Your hurt pride is about to break up the best of families.'

'Hurt pride? Is that all you think it is? You don't begin to understand, Anna. And, anyway, it's none of your business.'

'It's all of our business, Grandpa. Nonna is utterly miserable, of course, and so is Tom. Can you imagine what it's like? To finally find who you believe are your real parents and then, when you truly love them, to lose them again? None of this is Tom's fault, is it?'

'No, he's a victim, just as I am. Of your grandmother's duplicity.'

'God, Grandpa, how can you be so harsh? Can't you put yourself in her shoes? She was eighteen. Until you appeared she'd persuaded herself she was in love with the Polish guy. All young girls do that. And, by the way, getting pregnant "out of wedlock", as your generation would say, wasn't unusual. I've been mugging up on it and it's thought that nearly half the births in the latter years of the war and immediately after it were illegitimate. The fact is young people were doing what they always have, bonking.'

'Don't be vulgar, Anna.' Giovanni tried to wave her to silence, but she ploughed on.

'OK, they were making love, sleeping together. The problem was that contraception was ineffective and abortion illegal. And the morals of the time were so hypocritical, pregnancies were hushed up and babies born in secret and given away. Poor Nonna was so ashamed of herself for giving in to Marcin that she never told you. She thought, if you knew, you'd reject her as a slut. And, Grandpa, this is the important bit, so listen up.'

Anna was into her stride now, and she sensed that she'd got her grandfather's attention at last. He was watching her intently. She went on, her voice low but earnest. 'Grandpa, you have to understand that Nonna was so in love with you, and so happy about the baby, it never *occurred* to her that it might not be yours. She says she never gave the Pole a thought, and if she had she'd have dismissed it because they'd used some sort of contraceptive gel. In your day there were no routine check-ups. When she was five months pregnant she thought she was three months. It wasn't until she was in that hostel, when she thought she still had a couple of months to go, that a doctor told her the situation. You were living somewhere else, and everyone was pressurizing her to give up the baby. Can you imagine what it was like for her? She thought you'd reject her and the baby, if she told you. Or at best it would ruin your relationship. She was so full of misery and guilt she couldn't imagine you understanding. And you probably wouldn't have, would you?'

Giovanni was silent. Then he shook his head. 'I don't know. I hope I would have.'

Anna came round the desk and took both his gnarled old hands in hers. 'Grandpa, it's not too late. You love Tom. We all do. And he's your wife's child, even if he's not yours. He's family.'

He was looking at their hands, squeezing and caressing hers absentmindedly. But he was shaking his head.

She pulled her hands away slowly and kissed the bald patch on his head. 'Talk to Nonna. Please.'

Giovanni looked up at her and put out his hand to hold her bare forearm. He kept it there for a long beat, then gave her a weak smile. 'Bless you, *cara*,' he said.

Two days later Laura was in the kitchen, washing all her antique cups and saucers, and bits of bric-a-brac she'd collected since she was a girl. As she gently lowered bone china cups into the sudsy water she thought how trawling antique shops had always been her secret indulgence, and how, when unhappy, she'd polish the old silver and brass and wash the china. Angelica cooks when unhappy, she thought. Giovanni goes out walking, which is where he is now.

Then she heard his key in the front door. She expected him to walk past the kitchen, straight to his study upstairs. She heard him drop his stick into the umbrella stand in the hall. And then the kitchen door opened and he came in. 'I need to talk to you, Laura,' he said.

Her heart lifted. But then she told herself that just because he wanted to talk it didn't mean he'd forgiven her. 'Of course,' she said. 'Shall I make some coffee?' She didn't wait for an answer but put the kettle on and spooned good Italian coffee into the cafetière. It gave her something to focus on before the attack came.

They sat down at the corner of the big table, coffee and a bowl of *biscotti* in front of them.

'I've been thinking,' he said, his eyes on his *biscotto* as he absentmindedly dunked it in his coffee.

'Me too. I wish I could stop. Thinking is horrible.'

'I've come out of that phase,' he said. 'I've decided something.'

Laura thought that whatever he'd decided it was unlikely to

put things right. He might have deigned to speak to her, for the first time in a week, but she could still feel the hard knot of resentment inside her. How could he be so hard-hearted to his wife of fifty years? This past week she'd been just a servant, dishing up food, with not even a mumbled thanks as he'd left the kitchen.

She didn't encourage him. She sat silent, waiting. If he said they had to divorce, would that make it better or worse? At least, if she wasn't with him, she could contact Tom. Would Tom want that? Her thoughts were flying in all directions.

At last he looked up. His eyes looked strained and tired but for once she felt no sympathy. Join the club, she thought.

'Laura, we have to go after Tom. Ask him to come back. I don't give a shit if he's Marcin's son. As far as I'm concerned, he's ours.'

For a long moment she just looked at him, unable to believe what he'd just said. And then they were both crying. And Laura got a chance to get out all her resentment, guilt, everything.

'The thing is, Giovanni, it has been my cross to bear all these years, not yours. I've so often wanted to tell you, just to have you comfort me. But of course you wouldn't have done that because you'd have been so angry. I've had years and years of thinking about that boy, of where he was, what his home was like. I've followed him in my mind as he grew up, wondering if he was married, if we had grandchildren, if he was happy, years and years of it, Giovanni, and on my own. While you lived in blissful ignorance.'

He put his arm round, her, held her tight and tried to shush her, 'It's over now, *cara* . . .'

But Laura, having started was compelled to finish. 'Then, when Tom found us, I felt so torn. I replied to the first letter from the agency woman saying I'd no idea what it meant. I wanted the whole thing to just go away. But he didn't give up and at first I ignored his letters. I was terrified it would all come out. And then when we did meet him, I found it hard to accept him. At first. But, Giovanni, he seemed so like you, so strong and loving and loyal, I had to love him.' Her voice, caught by tears, faltered. 'I needed you so much, Giovanni, and I couldn't call on you.'

Laura's sleeves were pushed up over her elbows and her bare forearms, lightly sprinkled with old-age freckles, lay on the table. Giovanni put his hand on her arm and rubbed it up and down. God, she thought, it feels good to have his touch again. She went on. 'Yes, I deceived you, but I also spared you the anxiety and unhappiness I bore. You'd probably have rejected the baby anyway, and he would still have ended up adopted.'

'Would I have rejected him? I don't know. I hope not.' He shook his head fractionally. 'But probably.'

'And rejected me too?'

'No, I'd never have done that.'

'I wouldn't have blamed you if you had. But we'd both have been wretched. As it was, in the end we were happy, weren't we?'

'We were, *cara mia*.'

'And Tom got a good home.'

'Yes, thank God.'

They stood up and looked at each other. For the first time in a week, they both smiled.

'Tom might be your child,' said Laura. 'We don't know. We could do a DNA test.'

'Why bother?' He put both his arms round her and held her close for a long time. He whispered into her hair, 'As I said, I don't care. I just want our son back. And I want him to change his name to Angelotti.'

CHAPTER TWENTY-NINE

Sebele kept waking up. She never slept well in hotels and latterly she'd got used to the comforting sound of Tom's gentle snore. But it wasn't the unfamiliar bed at the Birmingham Exhibition Centre or the absence of Tom that kept her awake. It was anxiety. She was scared of tomorrow. The Street Food Show would be the biggest test of her career and she'd had no rehearsal for it. That was the problem with event catering: no job was like any other, every night was a first night.

She knew perfectly well that everything seemed worse in the middle of the night than it really was. She'd organized everything like a military operation: she'd hired the right staff, gone over the delivery schedule with a fine-tooth comb and spoken personally to every stallholder. But, all the same, things could go wrong, couldn't they? What if the fire officer decided the gas wok was a hazard? What if the chocolate fountain didn't work? What if the Burmese acrobats didn't arrive? As she sat up to check the time yet again, she couldn't convince herself she was fretting unnecessarily.

At four thirty she gave up on sleep. She pulled on the hotel's bathrobe and made herself a cup of tea. She sat down at the dressing-table – there wasn't a desk – and opened her laptop.

As she went through the running order, she felt a familiar calm replace the anxiety. It would be fun. In fact, it would be wonderful: the first street-food exhibition of any size in the country, and Sebele's Angels were staging it.

If all went well (and why shouldn't it?), they'd make a shedload of money and garner a whole lot more clients.

Her street-food division of Angelica's Angels had been going for a year now and had become the fastest-growing part of the catering company, and the most profitable. She'd started out with simple stalls and two vans that could be adapted to whatever street food the customer wanted. They could be adorned with bunting, objects and decorations denoting the food on offer and its nationality. Chinese pancakes stuffed with Peking duck, Vietnamese *pho*, Thai fishcakes, Napoli pizza, Chicago sliders, fish and chips, whatever. Now that they owned a barnful of props, carpets, hangings, cooking gear, tepees and tents, their stalls were more authentic and they'd become expert street-food cooks for a score of nationalities.

Sebele had let about a third of the stalls to other street-food traders and another third to equipment and food suppliers. Tom had questioned the wisdom of letting rival caterers in, but Sebele had argued that she'd vetted them carefully for quality and it would be useful to know more traders as she sometimes had to subcontract. Besides, she said, competition was good for everyone. If they couldn't beat their rivals, they shouldn't be in business.

At five thirty Sebele was looking forward to the day. It was still too early to go to the exhibition centre and she knew she wouldn't go back to sleep. She showered and dressed, made another cup of tea and pulled out her file of house plans. She'd had the plans for every room blown up to A4 size, so she could work out in detail where all the built-in and free-standing furniture should go. The builders had been in the house for almost a year now, and it was nearing completion. The house was ridiculously big for the two of them, but she justified the size and expense to herself: she and Tom needed a study each, and she needed a big kitchen for testing recipes, entertaining friends and Tom's sprawling family.

The kitchen would be her pride and joy. Tom had encouraged her to spend as much as she liked, and she'd gone for the best of everything. It was, she thought, to be as lived-in a kitchen as Laura's, but quite different. She loved the bustle and clutter of the Angelotti kitchen, but hers would be super-efficient, all whisper-quiet drawers, machines that popped up magically to counter height, American refrigeration, French chef's range, the lot. A wooden dining-table sat in the garden bay, with sliding glass walls and roof. At the touch of a button the diners would be in the garden. The kitchen designers had been astonished at her attention to detail. Most of their clients, they said, didn't cook at all, even though they wanted state-of-the-art kit.

The kitchen, she knew, was a huge extravagance, but the rest of the house was furnished, Tom said, on a shoestring. He'd expected her to hire a designer, but Sebele would have none of it. They'd trawled markets, bought furniture and carpets at auction, and ended with an eclectic mix of modern and antique, quirky and traditional. She didn't see the point of a six-thousand-pound glass coffee-table from a fancy shop, when one bought from a junk yard for fifty and re-chromed for £150 would look every bit as good.

Now she checked carefully through all the rooms, deciding which would have shutters, which curtains, which blinds. She checked, not for the first time, that the electrical plans showed sockets everywhere they needed them and in a few places they probably didn't, but just might.

She made a few notes, then texted Tom: *It's 6.30 and I'm working on the house, and am SO HAPPY, mainly because I love you. See you lunchtime? S*

By six forty-five she was walking from the hotel to the exhibition building and was pleased to see that the directional signs to the Street Food Fair were well displayed and easy to follow. She was greeted by her manager and the PR team, all smiling, confident and excited. Everything seemed under control.

Their own stalls were at the heart of the show, and they were arranged, not in the grid pattern of the rest of the exhibitors but in five higgledy-piggledy villages. The Far Eastern one was strung with lanterns, the stalls were shaped like pagodas and they sold Vietnamese, Thai, Chinese, Burmese and Japanese take-aways. She watched a young man making Sri Lankan hoppers in a bowl-shaped frying pan, like a mini-wok, swirling the paper-thin rice-flour batter with a practised flick of his wrist, then breaking an egg into the well. He looked up. 'Good morning, Sebele. I'm just checking everything works. How about a hopper for breakfast?'

'Well, I might just have that. Thank you. It smells delicious.'

He slid the hopper onto a paper plate. 'What would you like on top?' He indicated the row of bowls along the edge of the stand.

Sebele helped herself to a scattering of ground prawn powder, chopped chilli, sliced spring onions and a few fresh coriander leaves. Then she added dark soy sauce from a bottle and carried her hopper to one of the tables in the communal space. The tables and chairs were necessary for the non-handheld food and they knew from experience that customers would buy a beer or some juice more willingly if they had a free hand to hold it.

Sebele ate quickly, then continued her tour.

In the next section Mexican tacos vied with every kind of North American fast food, Texan burgers, Chicago barbecued ribs, Canadian pancakes, cupcakes and muffins, hot chocolate chip cookies and New York donuts.

Two genuinely French girls, dressed in stripy T-shirts and jaunty berets, were mixing the batter to make crêpes to order on twin griddles, and positioning big jars of almonds and sugar next to the giant praline pan in which a block of butter was ready to melt. The Euro village also had Italian ice cream, German *wurst*, Belgian *moules frites*, British fish and chips, and much more. The Whitstable oyster man would be walking the floor, selling oysters from the bucket suspended on one hip, opening them as he chatted to the customers, offering condiments from bottles attached to his midriff and collecting the empty shells in a second bucket on his other hip. Everyone looked ready to go.

All in all, thought Sebele, we're organized and up for it. It's going to be a great day.

By ten o'clock the hall was heaving, and by lunchtime they were forced to close the doors, sending visitors away because they were in danger of breaching the maximum limit to satisfy public safety regulations. It was upsetting, but at least it meant they had a success on their hands.

Sebele, satisfied that her 'villages' were all working well – though fewer people were eating the traditional Cornish pasties and the toffee apples than they'd expected – went to investigate the stalls she'd let to other traders. The most popular, to her surprise, were the Mexican ones: ceviche expertly cut and marinated, then served with guacamole on crisp tortilla chips. Next to it a cocktail bar offered nothing but margaritas and caipirinhas. The queue stretched across the front of the adjacent stalls, which was causing a problem. To speed up service Sebele volunteered a couple of her waiters to sell the drinks, ready-made, from trays to the queue.

'Señora, you are an angel from heaven,' called the owner of the Mexican bar.

'No problem.' Sebele laughed. 'I just hate to see lost sales. Next time bring a few more staff.'

Tom turned up at lunchtime and they ate Indian curries. The thalis, on which they were served, were made of paper, but they looked like traditional brass plates.

'You see, Tom, we've learnt a lot from subletting some stalls. I'm going to add Indian thalis, ceviche and margaritas to our range, for sure.'

Tom was tremendously proud of Sebele. She was so good at her job, efficient and confident, yet with none of the strident bossiness he associated with powerful women. And the way she supervised the builders and decorators, with a mix of friendliness and firmness, impressed him.

He'd thought at the start that the house was probably too big for them, but now it was almost finished, he questioned why they needed all those huge rooms. Four were marked as guest rooms on the plan, but they rarely had guests and never to stay.

This is a perfect family house, he thought, perfect for children. He remembered Clemmie's total joy in Charlie, and he found himself wanting Sebele to have that joy. And he wanted it for himself too. And the more he thought of it, the more important it seemed. Once the idea of having another child after Charlie was anathema to him. Now it became a recurring desire.

Sebele had said she didn't want children, that she was a career girl. She didn't like the idea of being a full-time working mother, she said, leaving children to au pairs and nannies, sending them to boarding school. And she was, she said, too selfish to give up working. She loved her job, and the freedom she had.

But, thought Tom, she'd no idea of the joy a child can bring. She'd dismissed something she knew nothing about. She'd no idea what they were missing. They'd been together for two years now and he loved her more every day. And, of course, they could live perfectly happily without children, but the thought nagged him. He would love to have a child with her.

One evening, as they were walking along the Thames, he suddenly said, 'Darling, are you absolutely sure we shouldn't try for a baby?'

Sebele stopped in her tracks. 'Why do you say that? You don't want a child, do you? I thought after Charlie . . .'

'I didn't at first, I couldn't even think about it. And it was a huge relief that you didn't want children either. But now I keep thinking what a wonderful mother you'd be. And, yes, I'd like another child, I'd like us to have a child together.'

He held her by the shoulders and looked into her face. He saw her eyes fill with tears. 'Tom, it's not going to happen.'

'Why not, darling? Are you so dead against it?' She shook her head.

'You're still young,' he said.

Again, she shook her head. 'I'm forty, Tom. If I was going to

275

get pregnant it would probably have happened by now. I came off the pill six months after we met.'

There was silence as he absorbed that. Then he frowned, baffled. 'But you told me you didn't want children.'

'I know. I didn't then. I wanted you to myself.'

'But you changed your mind too?'

'Yes, I'd have loved a baby. I'd still love to have your baby, Tom. But I didn't tell you I'd stopped taking the pill because I knew you'd said you didn't want another child. I just hoped I'd get pregnant and then, somehow, you'd come round. I was sure you'd accept your own baby, and I knew you'd make a wonderful dad.'

Tom hugged her. 'You cunning thing! . . . I seem to have lost my fear of another tragedy.'

'Well,' Sebele said, moving out of his embrace, 'it's academic now, darling. Every month for over a year I've secretly hoped I'd be pregnant. You've no idea how badly I wanted to tell you, to share the sadness of repeatedly failing.' Her voice cracked a little. She fished a tissue out of her pocket and blew her nose. 'But you know what? I'm reconciled now. I have you, a great career, and we're going to have a wonderful house. It's plenty, Tom, really.'

'But it could still happen, surely. Plenty of women have babies into their forties.'

'I don't think I'll be one of them. But we're happy, aren't we, Tom? Life's good, isn't it?'

'Of course it is. And I'm too old to play cricket on the lawn anyway.'

CHAPTER THIRTY

Anna, Cassia and Oberon were having supper at the Cow Shed, the trendiest new café-cum-restaurant in Golborne Road. Everything was delicious, especially the burgers. Over coffee they chatted to the owner, Simon, who told them how difficult it was to have a constant supply of organic produce. 'It's not so much that it's more expensive than non-organic stuff, but the supply is so unreliable. Those burgers you had were not technically organic. They come from a farm that's on its way to organic certification with another year to go. But their beef is grass-fed and not pumped full of antibiotics. It's good, don't you think?'

'Delicious,' said Oberon. 'What's the breed?'

'Dexter. Another reason it's expensive – they're slow-growing and small.'

'Another reason they're so delicious,' said Anna. 'But how come you can serve them rare? Most burger places tell you that Health and Safety requires them cremated.'

Simon grinned. 'True, but we get around that by keeping the meat in the piece until it's ordered. We never have mince sitting around.'

Over the apple and apricot crumble served with Jersey cream,

Oberon said, 'This place is heaving. Look, not an empty table anywhere.'

'I know,' said Anna. 'I've been wondering if we could have a proper farm shop – not just a shack selling a few veg like now – with a café in one of the barns behind the Crabtree. The veg could come straight off our field. Pippa could increase her laying hens. Half the Chorlton land is organic now anyway, and we could use their grass-fed lamb and beef. I bet Pippa would be up for it.'

Oberon laughed. 'Anna, it's nearly midnight. Do you never stop?'

'No,' said Cassia, 'she doesn't.'

'But listen, Oberon,' said Anna. 'We needn't have a proper menu. We could just sell what we can get hold of. The Crabtree could provide good bread, and we could serve soups, salads, burgers and a few puds.'

'Anna, I'm sorry, but I'm knackered. Can we discuss it in the morning? Or, rather, can you talk to your mum about it? She's your business partner, and I've enough to do with the boxes. I'll just be a wet blanket.' He pushed back his chair. 'I'm off.' He kissed Cassia, then Anna.

But when Anna put her idea to her parents, Silvano was clear: no, he couldn't let them have a barn for a café. It would take the coffee and cake business away from the Crabtree and, anyway, they were planning to move Angelica's whole catering operation out of the Crabtree yard and onto the land currently occupied by her market garden. That field was to become an industrial estate housing all the catering-company kitchens and stores, equipment for hire, marquees, vans and refrigerated units, plus Sebele's stalls and barbecues. 'It's a nightmare. I want to clear the Crabtree yard for a car park for the Crabtree customers. Hal's agreed to let a bit of land to you and your mother for your veg, isn't that so, darling?' he said, looking at Angelica.

Angelica nodded. 'I was going to tell you, sweetheart. We'll need to move our whole operation to Chorlton over the winter. It will be good, because we'll have a third more land.'

'And, Anna,' Silvano cut in, 'if you really want a café and farm shop, you should talk to Hal and Pippa. Chorlton has plenty of main-road frontage.'

Pippa jumped at the idea. Chorlton could do with a farm shop, she said, and a café would be great, providing she could run it.

Two weeks later, when Anna and her mother were planning the winter planting on a plan spread out on the Holly Farm kitchen table, Anna looked up. 'Mum, I've had an idea.'

'Please not,' said her mother. 'No more bright ideas. We have enough on our plates, don't you think?'

'Yes, but this might help, although I haven't discussed it with Oberon. Maybe Oberon's Recipe Boxes could move to Dad's new industrial estate. We're bursting out of the unit in North Kensington. Neither Oberon nor Cass and I would need to live in London. Oberon could go back to Chorlton – he often says how jealous he is of his brother living there. And Cass and I could rent a cottage somewhere.'

'Whoa, whoa, Anna! I'd love that, of course. But doesn't the box business have to be in London? Isn't that where the customers are?'

'Yes, but they're mostly in West London, and we have the boxes packed and ready to go by eleven o'clock. They're all afternoon deliveries, and they might as well sit in a refrigerated truck on the way to London as in a big fridge in London. True, we'd still need a yard or something in London where the deliveries are loaded on to bikes. The best way around London is still pedal power.'

CHAPTER THIRTY-ONE

Tom was enjoying his freedom from Ajax, especially not having to get up at dawn and be at his desk at seven. He could sometimes, not often, persuade Sebele to have a lie-in too, and she was almost always home in time for supper. They often dined with the senior Angelottis and spent odd weekends at Chorlton or Holly Farm.

He and Sebele had moved into the house a month ago, and a lot of his time over the past few months had been delightfully spent in nesting. He loved to see the pleasure Sebele got from the blinds going up in the bedrooms, from lighting the suspended wood-burning stove for the first time, hearing the Sonos system blast Beethoven at full volume through the whole house. She'd walk along the rack of upturned saucepans over the old fireplace in the kitchen, almost lovingly touching each one. She stroked the long wooden table and the sleek marble tops. She was besotted with her kitchen.

Under his instruction, the builders had dug up the yard and he'd spent many freezing but happy hours there, first taking lessons from the bricklayer, then physically laying the bricks for the raised beds and paths. He would come in exhausted and stand under a hot shower, feeling again the pleasure of well-earned relief he'd not experienced since his skiing days. Now he was enjoying supervising the delivery of tons of horticultural sand, compost and top soil that he'd mix and dig into the compacted London clay. In the spring he and Sebele would plant it up themselves, without the services of a poncy garden designer. He smiled, thinking unkindly of how many interior designers, *feng shui* gurus, lighting experts, even life-style consultants Susan would have employed.

The house was finished, and soon the garden would be too. All it would then require would be a bit of weekend mowing, watering and weeding. What would he do then?

Up till now Tom had backed Anna and Oberon's box business and Angelica's catering company. He found both interesting and fun. But they were small beer and he'd recently begun to feel the odd restless stirring. He didn't want to go back to the City, rejoin the competitive deal-making, but he felt under-employed. He missed the buzz of business, and knew he needed something more, but what? I'd like, he thought, a bigger challenge, something I could run, rather than just advise on.

He was fascinated by the family's various enterprises, and a little jealous. They were all constantly full of ideas. As soon as they had one project off the ground, they'd start thinking of another. Even the quiet Silvano, steadily building up the Crabtree, was on the hunt for a bigger hotel. The Crabtree was a restaurant with rooms but now he wanted a country hotel with maybe thirty rooms and a top-end restaurant.

All the family businesses were well run by people who really cared about them and about their customers but, he thought, they could be improved with a bit of modern business efficiency.

Angelica would sometimes ask for his advice but would seldom take it. She was a traditionalist, like her father. She was suspicious of online banking, of overt marketing or advertising. She said advertising special offers, or advertising at all, smacked of desperation. 'Advertising is for the likes of Pizza Hut,' she said, 'not for the Ritz. I'd rather we behaved like the Ritz than Pizza Hut.' She couldn't, or wouldn't, understand that marketing could be subtle, almost subliminal, and targeted to exactly the people she'd like to attract.

Silvano was much the same. The little industrial park behind the Crabtree was nicely designed with good-quality buildings and several trees, which would one day soften the look of the place. Although he'd taken Tom's advice to construct the units as and when he had tenants to fill them, he seemed in no hurry to fill the empty lots. Silvano believed giving good service was enough to bring in more tenants.

A month later, Tom was still intermittently considering what to do to satisfy his inner entrepreneur when Hal asked him to visit Chorlton to discuss, among other things, an abattoir.

Tom didn't know Hal well, but he seemed a nice enough chap. He'd been a farmer all his adult life and, like most farmers, he generally had a lot to moan about. Either it was the weather or the bureaucracy, the labour shortage, the cost of machinery or the lack of subsidies. Always something. Tom was surprised when Hal told him he and some neighbouring farmers and landowners had together bought the old Walford Minor slaughterhouse, intending to restore it and operate it as a cooperative.

An abattoir was about as far away from his areas of expertise as you could get but Tom was intrigued. Over a cup of coffee in the Chorlton kitchen, it quickly became clear to Tom that he'd underestimated Hal. He was as enthusiastic as any member of the clan and he clearly loved his job.

'We're doing well, Tom,' Hal said. 'Hard to believe. Farming is usually a relentless round of hard work and disappointment. But it turns out there's a market for organic crops and they fetch a premium. I wish I'd listened to Jake years ago. And raising animals isn't quite as expensive as I'd feared. Our pasture isn't organic yet but we can sell grass-fed beef and free-range chickens to good butchers, hotels and restaurants at better prices than we'd ever get from a supermarket or wholesaler.'

'Who do you sell the produce to?'

'The crops go mostly to organic food manufacturers for breakfast cereal, or to wholesalers. On the meat side, four major supermarkets stock the Chorlton brand, but the only product they take is pork sausages, which sell like hot cakes.' He jumped up and went to the fridge, returning with three packets of sausages. 'Here. This one, our Traditional, with just a bit of onion and sage, is the bestseller. Then we have these two, Leek and Thyme, and Black Pepper and Chive. No dried onion powder, no phosphates, no colouring. We add nothing to the meat other than ten per cent breadcrumbs, salt, pepper and real flavourings.'

'OK, OK! I've got it!' Tom laughed. 'I'm sold.'

Hal sat down again, smiling. 'Sorry, I get overexcited. Pippa's going to cook them for lunch, so you'll see for yourself.'

In the next hour Tom learnt a lot about Chorlton. Most of the profits, he was told, came from contracting: cutting hedges and verges for the council and farming for other people. Hal farmed five thousand acres in Oxfordshire and Gloucestershire, only twelve hundred belonging to Chorlton. Contracting was comparatively safe because he got a fee for doing the work, then a slice of the sales of the crops. If a crop failed, he still had the fee. If his own crop failed, he got nothing.

His next best income stream was from sales of meat to the family businesses, to Giovanni's and the Crabtree, the Laura's restaurants, Angelica's catering company and Oberon's Recipe Boxes. They even sold milk and eggs to Mario's ice-cream business. 'Though I wish we didn't,' said Hal. 'Getting Mario to pay is a constant battle.'

They talked on and eventually Tom asked, 'OK, Hal, so what do you want to show me?'

'Let's look at the abattoir.' Hal plunged on, excited as ever: 'The thing is, I've set up a local cooperative to take over the old slaughterhouse in Walford Minor. We've bought it and got planning to rebuild it, but we need a loan to do the work. It's been closed for years, since the rules and regs made it hard for small abattoirs to survive. You remember, after the mad-cow disease epidemic? But then the obvious dawned – that processing huge amounts of meat in large slaughterhouses that send products far and wide might be a highly effective way of actually spreading disease.'

'But that doesn't mean an unhygienic old-fashioned abattoir is going to do any better, does it?'

'No, but now it's possible to get a licence, providing you can prove that every stage of the killing and packing process is safe, that all the animals are traceable, that their meat is not mixed with any other animal's.'

'I can't imagine many people seeing this as a brilliant business opportunity,' said Tom.

'You'd be surprised. Farmers hate sending their beasts off on day-long journeys to get killed. They'd much prefer a half-hour ride and the knowledge that the animals won't be panicked or stressed.'

They talked on, Hal explaining who his partners in the scheme were. 'Almost all the closest farmers, including big landowners like Jane, are in.'

'Jane's part of the cooperative? I'm surprised. I'd have thought . . . I mean, after she cancelled the Frampton contracts? That must have been a huge setback?'

'To be frank, Tom, it's turned out to be a blessing. Jane's combination of high-handedness and lack of knowledge was a pain. Frankly, she's an idiot. Thinks she knows everything and knows f-all. Now I'm free to take other contracts to the north where the land is better and the owners a lot more agreeable.'

'But won't she be a pain as a partner in the abattoir?'

'I don't think so. She won't take any part in running it, thank God. She's the biggest producer of both beef and lamb round here. We could hardly leave her out.'

Hal and Tom climbed into Hal's old Discovery and drove to Walford Minor to see the slaughterhouse. It was in a large yard at the edge of the village, behind what had been the village butcher. 'Until about 1990, they killed all the animals for miles around,' Hal told him.

Tom looked at the small rooms, now empty. Behind them was a large yard with wobbly wooden fences enclosing pens. Some rails had been patched with scaffolding poles or old farm gates, while the concrete was cracked and potholed. Tom found it a depressing sight and said so.

'I want to transform it. I've seen abattoirs so brilliantly managed I think you could show them to schoolchildren. Ours is going to be like that. Organically certified and a model of its kind. If you're going to eat meat with a clear conscience, you need to know that the animal died with minimum stress and no pain. Really.'

'But how can you possibly manage that? They must panic, surely.'

'Absolutely not. We'll rebuild this yard with covered pens attached to the building and gates with rubber bumpers to stop clanging. There will be deep, clean straw bedding and water. The animals, who are all used to being handled anyway, will soon settle down.' He smiled. 'I'm seriously thinking we may play them soothing music too.'

'But won't they smell what's going on? Blood or anything?'

'No. That's why it's vital the ventilation is controlled so the air moves from the live animals into the facility, not the other way. You'll see, Tom. My ambition is that the cattle will be contentedly eating or sleeping until they're moved, calmly, into the crush where they're slaughtered with a bolt to the head.'

On the drive back, Tom was silent, thinking about the abattoir. He'd eaten meat all his life and had never given a thought to where it came from, or how the animals he ate had been treated. Hal's concern for the beasts, his conviction that the system should change, was admirable. Sebele always insisted on meat from a known provenance, genuinely free-range chicken, sustainable fish. Until now he'd acquiesced because he loved her and they could afford it, so why not? Now he realized it was an important issue, not a fashionable fad for the rich.

Still, he thought, it'll be difficult to make money. Hal had explained that you had to pay for two government vets to clear every animal as healthy before slaughter. Also, the fees they could charge for slaughtering could not be much higher than those of the big abattoirs. And how could you guarantee that the beasts would come in a steady flow? He didn't express his doubts.

They picked up Jake at Chorlton and set off on a tour of the farms. Tom had often been for walks with Sebele or Sophie on the home farm, to the bluebell woods or up to Top Field from where you could see for miles. But he'd never been given a proper tour of the whole estate with business in mind.

Pippa's farm shop and café were so busy no one had time to talk to them, apart from Pippa shouting across a counter that she wouldn't be able to get home to fry the sausages so Jake or Hal would have to do it.

They decided to skip the sausages and instead picked up a couple of beef and mustard wraps from the shop, then went to inspect what Jake called his compost field.

Jake was clearly obsessed with the soil and talked non-stop while they gazed at a huge concrete field on which long, parallel mounds (called windrows, said Jake) of compost were being turned by a giant machine tall enough to straddle the rows. Tom soon became bemused by Jake's talk of what made for good soil: micro-organisms, nutrients and the balance of acidity, temperature and oxygen levels, and lots of nematode worms.

Hal detailed the capital cost of concreting and machinery, and the running costs of labour and transport.

'So how do you make it pay? It can't be just the better yields from well-fed fields, can it?'

'No, we charge for taking green waste from councils, food waste from supermarkets, muck and straw from stables and farms. And we sell bagged organic compost.' He reached down to rub a handful of compost from the nearest windrow in his fingers. 'Feel this. Two years old, ready to go on the fields. Beautiful, isn't it?'

Tom took the handful of compost. It was damp, but friable, dark brown and soft. He sniffed it. It smelt fresh and loamy. He smiled, beginning to see that, to a farmer, it could indeed be beautiful.

They went on to have a look at the dairy operation. They climbed out of the car and leant on the fence. 'They're Jersey Shorthorns,' Jake said, 'ninety-four of them.' Tom watched the way Jake studied them, methodically checking them all. The cows walked towards them, the nearest standing side by side. Jake idly scratched the poll of the closest.

'The pasture's good here,' said Hal, 'with plenty of clover, chicory and ryegrass. These girls will give fifteen or sixteen litres of milk a day.'

'Is that a lot?'

'Well, it's only about a third of what those poor beasts on factory farms can produce. They're stuffed full of antibiotics and fed on high-protein pellets – the sort of food cattle are not designed to eat – but they're finished after two lactations. They're lucky if they see their fifth birthday before they're slaughtered. Ours give a lot less milk, but they seldom need a vet and they keep going for nine or ten years.'

They inspected the new milking parlour where one man could milk the herd in an hour. 'Is it profitable?' asked Tom.

'Not always. Depends on the milk price. Jake would like to make cheese, yoghurt and butter, but we'd a need a separator to take off the cream and a much bigger herd. To say nothing of the cheese-making gear.'

Tom climbed into his car with a familiar sense of excitement.

He liked new challenges, and this would certainly be one. It was clear as daylight that farming was a risk, but he could see there was something satisfying about the wholesome, practical, almost primitive means of producing good food. And doing it with the least damage to man or beast – or planet.

He told himself he was getting soft in his old age. But then, as he drove home, the feeling of well-being expanded. He'd look at the figures carefully, do some digging about abattoirs and the dairy trade, even see if anyone was making proper money out of compost. But he knew he'd invest if he could. Unless it was positively mad to do so, he'd put the money Hal needed into Chorlton. Sebele would approve, he was sure.

His mind filled with an image of her cooking some unheard-of dish in her dream kitchen. He smiled to himself. I'm as besotted with that woman, he thought, as the first day I saw her, behind a counter, carving a ham.

PART FIVE

2008

CHAPTER THIRTY-TWO

Anna and Cassia were at Bicester discount village, shopping. When they had fallen in love, four years ago, Anna had had little interest in clothes. She mostly lived in T-shirts, jeans and scruffy trainers she'd had for years. But as happiness lit up every aspect of her life, it became increasingly enjoyable working with Oberon, growing organic vegetables with her mum and inventing recipes, her clothes became better and brighter. She took more pride in turning out funny and informative blogs too.

She and Cassia occasionally awarded themselves a jaunt to Bicester to buy heavily discounted designer stuff, mostly for Cassia, who, with a size-eight figure, a gift for putting clothes together and a job that required stylish dressing, always looked amazing.

They'd had a good morning. By noon, they'd bought Cassia two Issey Miyake pleated tops, a skirt from Commes des Garçons, and an Yves St Laurent business suit. Now they were waiting to pay for an Escada yellow jacket for Anna. It was reduced to £150 from nearly a grand, and it fitted her like a glove. Anna was having her usual tussle with Cassia about desire versus extravagance.

'I know it's a terrific bargain, but should I really buy it?'

'Yes.'

'But I don't need another jacket, do I?'

'Yes, you do.'

'And it's yellow. What will I ever wear it with?'

'Oh, Anna darling, just buy it. It's beautiful. It'll make you happy.'

Cassia was right. Anna pulled out her credit card. The business paid her a decent salary, and she was a director. She could afford £150.

They were looking unsuccessfully for an empty table at one of the cafés when Anna's mobile rang, and she scrabbled in her handbag to find it. It was Oberon.

'Anna, I'm sorry to ruin your day off. But can you come in? Something dreadful's happened. I think we've poisoned some customers.'

'What? We can't have!'

'I know it's hard to believe, but we need to get to the bottom of it.'

'I'm on my way.' Anna stuffed the phone into her bag and took Cassia's arm. 'We have to go back, darling.'

It took ages to get out of the car park, and while Cassia drove, Anna rang Oberon for more details. It seemed that one of Monday's customers, who'd had the bang-bang chicken, had been ill last night. They had delivered a large order to a house in Kensington, a Mr Stevens. At first Oberon thought it might be nothing to do with the recipe boxes, but when Mrs Stevens rang again to say another of their friends was ill, so seriously that he'd been taken to hospital, Oberon saw they had a major problem.

'Oh, my God, what have you done so far?'

'Nothing yet. I only just got the second call. I tried to get Tom, but he's not picking up.'

'Ring my mum, Oberon. She'll know what to do. There's a procedure for suspected food poisoning.'

By the time Anna and Cassia drove into the yard, just after one o'clock, Oberon had carried out Angelica's instructions. He'd telephoned the council and they were sending an environmental health officer to inspect the premises and collect samples.

He'd then had the grim task of ringing or emailing everyone who'd had the chicken dish. Mrs Stevens gave him the telephone numbers of all her guests and, to his horror, everyone he managed to contact had been affected, some really badly. Besides the man in hospital, two women had seen a doctor. All he could do was apologize and tell them the council were trying to establish the cause. He then telephoned all the other customers who had ordered the same box. To his surprise, and relief, none of the other forty-three recipients of bang-bang chicken had been ill.

That's strange, thought Anna. Why is it only that delivery? She told the two cooks working in the kitchen what had happened and asked them not to talk to anyone about the incident. Rumours would endanger the business. Meanwhile they were to continue as normal.

The EHO arrived at two. He was affable and efficient. He pulled a white coat out of a plastic bag and put it on with a blue net hat and latex gloves. Anna watched as he took swabs from the walk-in fridge shelves, the sinks and the worktops, inside the refrigerated van and the door handles of the van and loos. He removed and bagged two raw chicken breasts from the batch they'd used for the bang-bang and the leftover shredded vegetables, then put them into a refrigerated box in his car. He took photographs of the anteroom where the staff's white coats, disposable hats and overshoes were kept, the kitchen and the inside of the van.

He was taking off his white coat when Lucinda, who manned the phones and worked in the office on Anna's day off, appeared at the door. 'The *Express* want to speak to you, Oberon.'

'The *Express*? Why?'

'I don't know,'

'I'll take it,' said Anna, following her to the office. She picked up the phone. 'I'm Anna Angelotti, a director of the firm. What can I do for you?'

'Anna Angelotti, did you say? Are you related to Giovanni Angelotti, the restaurateur, by any chance?' His voice was friendly, relaxed, very polite.

'I'm his granddaughter.'

'I'm a huge fan. Giovanni's has been the best Italian restaurant in London for years.'

'Yes, it's good, isn't it? But can I help you? I'm afraid Oberon is unavailable.'

'Ah, yes, I'm sure you can help. We're running a story in tomorrow's paper and we wanted to give you the opportunity to comment.'

'A story? What about?'

'Well, it seems a High Court judge, Lord Twinsdale, is in hospital as a result of food poisoning from eating a chicken dish delivered by your company, Oberon's Recipe Boxes.'

'Oh, God! No. No. That's not true.' Anna's brain was floundering.

'But we understand that you delivered the food to Mr Stevens in Kensington Church Street on Monday.'

'Look, we don't know that it was our chicken. We're trying to find out. We run our business to the highest hygiene standards, and as soon as we had the complaints, we called the council and they—'

'Complaints? Has there been more than one?'

'Look.' Anna put her hand over her eyes, trying to think. 'I'm sorry, I can't talk to you now.'

'Environmental Health have been, have they? Did they confirm—'

'They've only just arrived. Really, you can't run a story when no one knows anything yet. You can't—'

'Don't worry, Miss Angelotti, we won't say anything that isn't true. Thank you.'

He terminated the call and Anna stood, her heart pounding. A paragraph in the paper about Oberon's Recipe Boxes poisoning a judge could kill their business. She racked her brain, trying to remember exactly what she'd said.

Oberon came in. 'The EHO says he'll get the results as soon as he can from the lab and from the hospital where the judge is. We'll know later today if they're closing us down or if we're free to deliver tomorrow's orders.' He sat down heavily in his chair. 'I can't understand it. I remember that order. It was for a new customer, who wanted a dish for ten or twelve people for a party.'

'Oh, yes. We had to go out to buy bigger bags for the ingredients, so he wouldn't have to open ten little packets of everything.' Anna sat on the table next to Oberon's chair. 'Oberon, the *Express* has got hold of the story.'

'Oh, no.'

'I hope I put them off.'

'But why? How did they get to know? A couple of people throwing up is hardly national news, is it?'

'According to them, one of them, the guy in hospital, is a High Court judge and a lord to boot. That paper loves gossip from high places. I expect one of the guests rang up the gossip column.'

That evening, at about seven, Anna had a text from Oberon. 'All clear. Bug counts good everywhere. Including the chicken and the veg. It must have been something else they ate. They're going to get the London health guys to check the Stevenses' place.'

Anna's relief was marred by her anxiety about the *Express*. She tried to get hold of someone at the newspaper to stop them running the story but the only staff still at their desks were the news reporters. She was put through to one but got nowhere.

'Who do you want to speak to?' The voice was bored, or tired, or both.

'I don't know his name. He rang me this afternoon. About a case of food poisoning.'

'I can't help you if you don't know his name.'

Anna tried to keep the desperation out of her voice. 'But the story he's probably written is not true. I just want to correct it before it goes to print.'

'What page does he write for?'

'I don't know. News, I suppose. Or maybe the gossip column.'

'Well, this is the newsroom and I don't think we have any food poisoning stories. I'll put you through to the Rich and Famous column.'

The phone rang for ages and Anna's heart sank. Eventually it went to voicemail, and she hung up.

Cassia put her arms round Anna's neck. 'Poor love. What a nightmare.' She kissed her. 'I guess this is one time you could have done with a proper drink.'

Anna shook her head, forcing a smile. 'I do remember the

relief from the first pull on a pint or gulp of wine but I don't crave it any more. A cup of tea would be good, though.'

Next morning Anna emerged from the shower to hear her mobile ringing. She went through to the bedroom and picked it up. It was Silvano. 'Anna, darling, have you seen the *Express*?'

Anna sat down, her heart contracting. 'No,' she said. 'Read it to me, please, Dad.' He did so.

'High Court Judge poisoned.

> *Lord Twinsdale, the prominent High Court judge and privy councillor, famous for his successful defence of six prostitutes charged with soliciting in Park Lane in 1970, was rushed to hospital in the early hours of Wednesday morning with suspected food poisoning. He is not in intensive care, but in view of his age (he is 89) and general frailty he is considered too ill to receive visitors and is expected to stay in hospital for a week at least. His relatives have been informed.*
>
> *'Lord Twinsdale is believed to have been poisoned at a party catered for by the trendy online company Oberon's Recipe Boxes, which delivers fashionable food to those who like to eat "from scratch" but are too busy to shop for themselves. It is understood that the peer's hosts on the fateful evening were John and Sue Stevens, who had ordered bang-bang chicken (a spicy chicken salad flavoured with peanuts and chilli). Mr Stevens was also taken ill. Mrs Stevens, who is vegetarian and did not eat the chicken, was not affected.*

> *'Yesterday afternoon, men in white coats from the local
> council descended on the Oxfordshire premises of Oberon's
> Recipe Boxes and took away samples for testing. It is not
> known how many other party guests were poisoned.'*

When Anna arrived at work, Oberon and Tom were both there.

'I'm so sorry, Oberon,' she said. 'If I hadn't admitted the council were involved . . . and there was only one man in a white coat . . .'

'Don't worry,' said Tom. 'It's not your fault. What we need to do is make sure all our customers know we're in the clear, as soon as possible. If we handle it right, we'll be fine.'

'But are we in the clear? Nine out of ten people at the Stevenses' were sick. We can't tell anyone anything until we know what really happened. And why anyone was ill.'

That afternoon the EHO was back with his draft report. Anna and Oberon sat with him while he explained that his London colleagues had examined a bowl of leftover chicken from the Stevenses' kitchen and found it to be badly infected with salmonella, the same strain that the hospital and the doctors had identified as the cause of the diners' illness.

I can't bear it, thought Anna. I thought we'd been exonerated. How come the chicken in our fridge is fine and the chicken in the Stevenses' isn't? She opened her mouth to interrupt but the EHO kept talking. He explained that Mrs Stevens had made up the dish for ten when the boxes arrived on Monday. Her dinner party wasn't until Tuesday, but she'd wanted to get ahead. She'd shredded the cooked chicken breasts and mixed the meat with the julienned vegetables, the peanut and chilli sauces, and had arranged it all on a big serving platter. When she found the finished platter was too big to fit on the fridge shelf, she'd put it out on the balcony, reckoning that as it was winter that would be as good as a fridge. She'd covered it with an upturned plastic box to protect it from neighbouring cats and weighted it with a doorstop. It had spent the next day there, until she'd brought it in to serve at dinner.

'But even in winter,' he continued, 'the sun beating down on a plastic box for four or five hours – and Tuesday was very sunny – will have a greenhouse effect, warming the chicken to dangerous levels. I'm sure that was what caused the problem.'

'But,' said Oberon, 'doesn't that mean there must have been salmonella in the chicken to start with?'

'Yes, but there's no evidence it came from this kitchen. Your chicken showed no sign of it, and neither did the swabs from your premises. I suspect that Mrs Stevens put it there with not-quite-clean equipment – the spoon she used to mix it or some such. We don't know for sure. What we do know is that you're in the clear.'

When he'd gone, Oberon emailed all their customers:

Some of you may have read an article in the Express alleging that a dish delivered by us had caused the illness of one of our customers. I'm happy to tell you that West Oxfordshire Environmental Health, whom we immediately asked to investigate, have tested our provisions, inspected our premises and checked our processes, and assure us that we were not responsible for the complainant's illness.

Obviously, such rumours can be very damaging to a small business and very unsettling for customers. I hope, if you had any doubts about us, you are now reassured and will continue to buy from us. If you would like to speak to me or Anna, please do call.

Anna read it over his shoulder. 'That's fine. Not sure if it will help but we have to try.'

Oberon pressed 'send'.

CHAPTER THIRTY-THREE

Tom stared at the television screen. It couldn't be. He must have misread it. He jumped up, fumbled in the sofa for the remote control, found it and turned up the volume. The newsreader confirmed what he'd just read in the newsflash moving beneath the screen.

'Lehman Brothers filed for bankruptcy protection this morning. Since then the Dow Jones has been in freefall, recording its fastest losses since 9/11.' He sat down slowly, his eyes fixed on the screen. After a while he was aware of Sebele standing behind him, looking at the television over his shoulder. He put his arm out to draw her to sit beside him on the sofa.

They watched as various pundits attributed the disaster to Lehman's reliance on sub-prime lending – giving mortgages to people who had no hope of ever paying off their debts; to the naked greed of hedge-fund managers taking enormous risks because their personal bonuses could be so high; on the mis-selling of mini-bonds as 'low risk' to people when they were only judged 'low risk' because they were backed by Lehman's, one of the most respected banks in the world.

During the following weeks, everyone watched with horror

as the contagion spread to other financial institutions, first in America and then in Europe. The FTSE 100 followed the way of the Dow Jones, with companies wiped out overnight. The Icelandic banks failed, and in the UK there was a run on Northern Rock, previously the most successful of the building societies. For a while it looked as though HBOS, Lloyds and even Barclays could fail, but a combination of government bail-outs, write-downs and banks merging or consolidating kept them afloat. But now they dared not lend to anyone and were desperately calling in every loan they could. In the space of a few weeks, the British economy, which had, only months before apparently been thriving, was now in deep recession.

Giovanni suggested a family meeting to discuss the situation. Nearly everyone had a stake, not just in their own businesses but in each other's and all were affected by the crash.

Everyone came, except Jane. Giovanni couldn't bear to speak to her so Silvano had emailed her with a bald notice that the meeting was taking place and, as she was a shareholder in the Angelotti restaurants, she was entitled to come. But she replied coolly that she would be in Scotland. She seemed unaware of how serious the crash was, asking him to let her know how her investments in the restaurants were affected. No one expressed the relief they all felt that she wasn't there.

They arranged to meet one morning at the usual venue for family pow-wows – Laura and Giovanni's big kitchen table. Tom and Sebele were the first to arrive and they helped Laura put out assorted mugs for coffee. She'd made a huge cake too.

'Oh, Laura, I do love you!' exclaimed Sebele. 'This is a crisis meeting, not a celebration, but here you are, serving us coffee in your royal mugs.' She held up a Silver Jubilee mug in one hand and a Charles and Diana wedding one in the other. 'And you make cake.'

Laura nodded. 'There's no situation that can't be improved by cake. And this is Angelica's favourite. Orange, almond and polenta. Try it.'

But Sebele stopped her cutting it. 'Let's wait for everyone else,' she said.

Tom sat down next to Laura and took her hands in his. She gazed into his face. She looked drawn and exhausted. She's desperate for me to tell her all will be well. I wish I could, thought Tom.

'It's Giovanni I'm worried about,' she said. 'He sees his life's work crumbling to nothing. He's so proud of what everyone has achieved. But now there are not enough customers and Angelica's clients are cancelling parties as fast as they can.'

'Things are seldom as dire as they seem. Let's wait till we know the facts.'

But the facts were worse than Tom had feared. Giovanni did his best to keep order and to chair the meeting in a business-like way, but things got out of hand almost immediately.

'I suggest we go round the table and each of us gives a quick business report. Mario, let's start with Gelati Angelotti.'

Mario gave a short, forced laugh. 'Well, as I'm officially the black sheep of this family, you won't be surprised to hear that Gelati Angelotti is finished. We can't pay the wages.'

No one spoke for a few moments, then everyone did at once, protesting or demanding information. Giovanni banged on the table for silence. 'Mario, we need an explanation.'

'I've emailed the spreadsheets to you, Uncle, but I can tell you they don't make happy reading. Basically, there's practically no money in the bank, and what there is is in Northern Rock, which, I'm sure you know, is in the shit.'

'You moved the company accounts to Northern Rock? Without consulting me? We've banked with Barclays for ever, Mario. Why, for God's sake?'

'Because they were offering the best interest rates, and because they agreed to a loan.'

'But why did you need a loan?' asked Laura. 'Your sales this summer were the best ever.'

Hal chipped in: 'Yet you haven't paid our bills for six months. What's going on Mario?'

'And, what's more, you still haven't delivered last week's ice-cream order for the farm café,' said Pippa, her Australian accent intensifying with her indignation. 'We've had to buy from the bloody supermarket, mate.'

Everyone was talking at once and gesticulating. Like an Italian comedy show, thought Tom.

Mario stood up and the clamour died away. 'Well, I'm off. Good luck, everyone. I'm sure the lovely Tom here, who has never lent me a penny, will bail you all out as usual. Goodbye.'

No one responded or tried to stop him. Tom looked at Giovanni, who had his head in his hands. Laura, next to him, had an arm round her husband's shoulders. 'It's all right, darling. We did our best,' she said. 'Even his mother knew he was a wrong 'un.'

Giovanni looked at Tom. 'Do you think you could take charge of this meeting for me, son? I'm not up to it any more.'

'Sure, Giovanni, if everyone agrees.' There were nods around the table. 'OK, then,' he went on. 'I think it's safe to assume that Mario will have run up some debt we don't know about too.

I'll look into it. But to a happier story. You're doing all right at Chorlton, Hal, aren't you?'

Hal looked round the room. 'I think we'll be fine. It should be good news. We haven't felt the effects of recession on trading yet. The prices for this year's crops were fixed at planting time. The contracting side is fine. Landowners can't just stop planting and reaping. Dairy sales, especially for yoghurt, are up. The abattoir is on track to break even next year. Even the compost-making is contributing a bit. Pippa's café has had a terrific year, and sales are holding up.'

'All good, then?'

'Yes, for the moment. It's next year we need to worry about, I suppose, with the fear that prices might be down.'

Tom had become fond of Hal in the last two years. It had been good working together on getting the abattoir and the cheese-making parlour up and running. He watched Hal, relaxed and confident, sip his coffee.

'I'm a bit worried about the large bank loans for machinery and the new milking parlour,' said Tom. 'If we were forced to repay now, we'd be done for, wouldn't we?'

Hal put down his mug. 'Don't worry. I've spoken to the land agent and he's confident that the bank will honour the deal for a ten-year payback. We've not heard a peep from them, so I guess he's right.'

Tom was making notes. He turned to Angelica, who said her catering company had had a good summer, especially with Sebele's street food and themed parties. But, all the same, they would run out of money in six months if they didn't pick up some big parties to replace the cancelled autumn ones. 'We'll have to let a lot of experienced staff go, and that will make next summer, if business recovers, very difficult.'

It seemed the London restaurants were suffering the most. 'We're so reliant on the American tourist trade, that's the problem,' said Laura. 'All the Americans who were in London in September promptly flew home and now they aren't travelling at all. Hotels are empty, and restaurants are going bust all over the place. Laura's isn't losing money but revenue is down nearly twenty per cent. Giovanni's is in the red for the first time since 9/11, when we lost money for four months. Only the Deli-Calzones are doing well.'

'The bad thing,' put in Giovanni, 'is that we can't invest. The group will still make a decent profit this year, thanks to the Deli-Calzone chain, but we had plans to redo some of the Laura's, which need facelifts, and to give Giovanni's a new kitchen. But we don't dare spend the money.'

Tom turned to Silvano. 'What about you? You're less dependent on Americans, I guess?'

'True. But half our customers are tourists, and we have much the same problem – some cancellations, few new bookings. Then three of the industrial-park units aren't let. No one's risking expansion or new ventures. But most of our staff are seasonal so we'll be OK on running costs.'

He stopped and looked at the table, then seemed to straighten up and take a breath. 'However, we do have a huge problem and I think it will be the end of us. Most of you know, I think, that we're committed to buying a big country hotel, Westland Park, in Shropshire, with an eighteen-hole golf course. For three million. It will need another three million spent on it. I had arranged a bank loan of four million, but now the bank has reneged on the deal. They won't lend us a penny.'

Angelica reached out and took Anna's hand. Mother and daughter both looked at Silvano, Angelica with sympathy and understanding, Anna confused.

'Which bank?' asked Tom.

'Barclays.'

'I still don't understand why we can't just pull out too, Daddy,' said Anna.

Poor girl, thought Tom. It's probably the first time her father has seemed anything but solid as a rock.

Silvano shook his head. 'Anna darling, I told you, there's no way. We signed the deal and the vendors aren't going to be so stupid as to let us off now. They'd never get that price today. And, of course, we couldn't sell it on at that price either. It would be a fire sale and we'd lose enough to bankrupt us.'

It took a while for everyone to understand what had happened. Then Tom spoke directly to Silvano. 'Are you really saying, Silvano, that you've agreed to pay three million for a hotel without making payment conditional on the bank providing the money?'

'I know, I know, Tom. You suggested I get a top-notch lawyer to hold my hand and I thought it would cost too much. It never occurred to me that the bank would pull the rug.'

Tom turned to Oberon. 'Finally, last but not least, Oberon, do you want to say anything about your boxes?'

'Not much to say. We're struggling, no doubt of that. Everything had been going really well, but then we had the rumour that our chicken had given a customer food poisoning. We tried to scotch it, but I think a lot of people believed it. We saw a real drop in orders. And on top of that, as with everyone else, the bank wants its money back.'

The discussion moved on to general complaints of being unable to borrow for investment in equipment or improvements, while at the same time being harassed by lenders for the repayment of loans originally intended to be long term, but which turned out, on examining the small print, to be repayable on demand.

Tom began to feel they were going around in circles. 'I've got a suggestion,' he said. 'It seems to me that, apart from Hal and Jake with the farms, your businesses have a lot in common. They're all catering of one sort or another, all good basic businesses but with a cash-flow problem. We don't know if the problem will be short or long term. It would be safer to assume the worst, in which case everyone needs to cut costs while selling more. Never an easy combo. And somehow we need to replace the called-in bank loans.'

'And your suggestion?' asked Silvano.

'I'd like to see if we could consolidate the businesses to save some money. Maybe put all the finance departments together, share some senior positions, delay all but absolutely essential expenditure and, I'm afraid, lose some staff. Do some cross-marketing between the restaurants, for example. It might also be easier to borrow money as a bigger conglomerate than as individual small businesses. I don't know if it will work but if you'll let me take a closer look at everyone's finances, and we put our heads together, then maybe . . .'

'I think that's a good idea,' said Angelica. Everyone nodded, but without much conviction.

Laura stood up, 'Now, will someone please eat a piece of cake?'

CHAPTER THIRTY-FOUR

Jane woke to a cold but bright autumn day. Well, she thought, I suppose going to lunch with my accountant on my birthday is better than going nowhere. She'd considered driving to London and insisting on some friends coming out to dinner with her but decided she couldn't be bothered – at such short notice only the least jolly of her circle would be free to accept. Besides, she'd have to pay, and it felt slightly shaming that no one had asked her out to celebrate. She'd had precisely three birthday cards, one from a friend, one from Laura and one from her housekeeper. Sad, really.

She sat at her dressing-table, brooding. She was sixty-eight. *Sixty-eight!* She didn't feel that old. She narrowed her eyes and examined her face. She did look grumpy, as Laura had pointed out to her so unkindly. But, dammit, she didn't look two years off seventy.

Shaking herself out of her lethargy she decided to go for a hack, maybe ride all the way to the Crabtree where she was to meet Erikson, her 'man of business', as she preferred to think of him. She had thought of telling him to find somewhere else – she wasn't keen on giving the Angelottis any business. She'd hardly seen them since that long-ago dinner when she'd told them the truth about Tom and Laura, and Anna had been so rude to her.

But the Crabtree was the only half-decent place for lunch. Her own pub, the Frampton Arms, had a new manager given to arguing instead of doing as instructed, and going there would hardly be a birthday treat. Silvano won't be at the Crabtree anyway, thought Jane. He'll almost certainly be in Shropshire, where the gossip had it he was overstretching himself buying some huge pile with a golf course. And Angelica wouldn't be in the pub either. Her catering company had moved to that hideous industrial estate they'd built behind it. How they got away with that I'll never know, she thought. Especially as I objected. You'd think the biggest landowner for miles around would have some influence, but these days the planners give permission for any monstrosity, as long as it provides jobs.

Until a fortnight ago, she hadn't ridden for months, and last season she'd barely hunted because she'd been in the Caribbean most of the winter. But this year she had a new mare, Popcorn, and she'd hired a girl-groom, who'd been getting Popcorn fit for the season. The combination of horse and groom had somehow revived her enthusiasm. Now she'd been out riding several times to get her bottom and thighs used to the saddle again and the mare used to her. She'd join the hunt for the next meet.

Jane had grown up with the hounds kennelled at Frampton. Her grandmother, the fearsome Geraldine, had been the master. Her grandfather had first taken her hunting when she was still on a leading rein. As she grew up she was accorded proper respect as the daughter of an earl and, more important, she thought, as an excellent horsewoman, never known to balk at a fence or a wall. When the last master died, there had been a suggestion (no, it was more a natural assumption) that she'd take over, but the idiot hunt committee had rejected the idea.

Of course, they'd never have dared reject her if she'd been allowed to inherit the earldom. But the ridiculous succession rules meant daughters of earls couldn't become countesses. The 'Lady Jane' she used was a courtesy title. She'd got the lands and the money, which counted for something in the county, but the title should have been hers too.

It still smarted. Why shouldn't she be the countess? And why hadn't she been made master? She was a far better rider than anyone else. She'd had the best horses in her stables. The hounds had been kennelled at Frampton for free and the huntsman was on the Frampton payroll. How dare the committee decide she was 'not the best person to lead the hunt', and that some bloody little land agent was?

Anyhow, she thought with satisfaction, she'd had the last laugh. She'd kicked the hounds out of the Frampton kennels and they'd had to rent some barns near Chipping Norton. And she didn't have the expense and the constant complaints about broken gates, trampled verges and hounds in people's gardens that she remembered her father being unnecessarily apologetic about.

Now she just paid her membership fee and hunted when she felt like it.

She rang the stables and left a message for the groom. *Bring Popcorn round at ten, please. Make sure she has a headcollar. You needn't come with me. I'll ride alone.* She went through to her dressing room and slid back the doors of her spacious cupboard. She chose a pair of pale jodhpurs from a rack ranging from almost white to black, via every shade of fawn and brown. Then she surveyed the row of eight or nine pairs of highly polished leather boots – long black hunting ones and short brown jodhpur boots. She chose an old pair of long ones, soft and comfortable. A crisp white shirt, a quilted down waistcoat and her favourite tweed hacking jacket completed her outfit. 'I've still got the figure of a girl,' she said to herself, as she turned in front of the long mirror, admiring her narrow waist and the lift of the split tails of her jacket.

In the kitchen the breakfast things were laid out for her. She helped herself to the porridge sitting in a double boiler on the Aga and poured a cup of coffee from the cafetière.

At precisely ten she walked out of the front door, collecting her riding hat and crop from the boot room on her way.

Popcorn was a nicely schooled animal, willing, obedient and quiet. When Jane had been young she'd loved to ride skittish horses that danced on the spot and travelled sideways, tossing their heads. Now she just wanted them to do what she demanded, at once, without fuss.

It was a glorious day. There was still some warmth in the sunshine, and no wind. Jane kept up a good pace, alternately walking out, trotting and occasionally breaking into a collected canter. Popcorn walked quietly and without fuss, even when they passed the abattoir in Walford Minor and a big cattle truck suddenly and noisily dropped its ramp. The clang made Jane jump, but Popcorn just pricked her ears and walked on, while two large bullocks clattered slowly down the slope.

Jane called angrily to the cattleman. 'For goodness' sake, man. Have some consideration! This is a young horse.'

The man stared at her, then shrugged. 'Your problem, lady, not mine.'

'You should unload deeper into the yard, not right in the entrance with your truck halfway into the road.'

'Who says?'

'I do, damn it. And I own this abattoir!' That isn't strictly true, Jane thought, but I do own a share in it. And he's not to know.

The man and his colleague were guiding the beasts further into one of the holding paddocks. He shouted over his shoulder, 'Well, then, you shouldn't be so rude to your customers, should you?'

Jane couldn't respond: he was now out of earshot. She rode on, out of sorts. She felt she'd been bettered in that exchange. Such insolence! She was used to proper deference from these people. But after ten minutes the glorious weather and Popcorn's eager obedience lifted her mood. The horse advanced and backed to open gates, and passed a huge machine spreading muck in a field without a second glance. 'Well, madam,' said Jane, patting the mare's neck, 'you might even be worth the fortune I paid for you.'

She arrived at the Crabtree at noon, used the head collar and rope to tie Popcorn to a post at the far end of the car park, loosened her girth and crossed the stirrups over the saddle. A young gardener was adding compost and peat to the beds in front of the terrace and Jane called, 'Excuse me. Would you give my horse a bucket of water, please?'

The gardener looked up, startled.

God, it's not rocket science, you idiot, Jane thought. 'If you wouldn't mind,' she added. That did the trick.

'Yes, madam. I'll get a bucket.'

He walked off, and Jane went inside. She ordered a spritzer in the sunny window seat of the bar. Erikson (she never called him by his Christian name – she didn't even know it) soon joined her.

Over fishcakes and salad, Erikson, in his usual punctilious way, explained Jane's finances to her.

'It's not all good news, I'm afraid, Lady Jane. As you know, I'm sure, the recession is biting hard, and shows no sign of abating. Your stocks and shares have taken a real tumble. But we mustn't lose our nerve. Of course, they will recover.'

'I don't need to sell anything, anyway, do I?' said Jane. 'I have plenty of cash, I think?'

'You do indeed,' Erikson replied. 'Your father always believed in the third, third, third principle and I've stuck to that with your fortune ever since. A third in equities, a third in land and a third liquid. In his day your father liked to keep a good deal of money available because, as you know, he was very entrepreneurial and liked to back enterprising businesses. In the twenty-five years since his death, those investments in businesses have paid handsomely.' He pulled a printed spreadsheet from his folder and handed it to her. 'Though, in common with the rest of the tourist trade, the Angelotti restaurants in London have been badly hit this year, I'm afraid.'

He went through lists of investments in equities and property and Jane feigned more interest than she felt. She cut him short. 'So overall, it's been a bad year,' she said.

'Yes, indeed it has. But your South African investments have done very well, and your cash position is strong.'

'How far have land prices dropped?'

'Not much in the Cotswolds, at least for the moment. I expect you know that the Chorlton estate is likely to go under?'

Jane felt a little burst of satisfaction at this news, which she hadn't heard till now. No one tells me anything, she thought. But she didn't like to admit this to Erikson. 'But if, as you say, land prices are holding up, they'll be all right, won't they?'

'Ah, but unlike you, Lady Jane, the Olivers have borrowed a lot against the value of their land and now they can't repay the loans. Their move towards organic has been their undoing. It's an expensive business, waiting two years for your fields to be certified organic while you refrain from increasing the yield with fertilizers and pesticides. They were doing very well, selling organic crops to specialist muesli manufacturers and health-food shops, but then they decided to raise the stock organically too. And you don't get much more money for organic beef than for grass-fed. The public doesn't understand the difference.'

'But what has changed? They were so optimistic a few months ago. People still have to eat, don't they?'

'What has changed is the attitude of the banks. For the last few years they've been falling over themselves to lend to farmers, and Chorlton borrowed a lot – for the new milking parlour and organic cheese business, to buy all that machinery to turn compost, and to build new grain stores and driers, which they need now since they no longer farm your land and have access to your barns and equipment.'

Jane felt a little thrill. Serve them right. She'd told them often enough that the organic business wasn't viable.

Erikson went on, 'Now the banks want their money back. About the only thing they didn't finance was the abattoir, which, as you know is a farmers' co-op – you have a share. Tom Standing made them a loan for that'

'But the banks can't go back on their deals, can they?'

'Unfortunately, they can, and if the Olivers can't pay up, they'll foreclose.'

'Foreclose? Make them bankrupt?'

'Precisely.'

Jane was thinking fast. 'What do you think Chorlton is worth, Erikson? Now, I mean, at today's prices?'

'I don't know, because I don't know what it consists of. But land prices round here are, ironically, up about ten per cent to around three thousand an acre – maybe because land is something of a safe haven for money when stocks and shares are all over the place. Houses, in contrast, are slightly down. The farmhouses on Chorlton – there are three farms aren't there? – might fetch between three and four hundred thousand, the big house twice that. And the cottages a quarter of a million.'

'Would you make it your business to find out exactly, Erikson? If I have the funds to buy Chorlton, I'm sure it will be a good investment in the long term.'

And it would give me exquisite pleasure, thought Jane. Hal, that sanctimonious freak, would be working for me. And none of Chorlton would be organic.

CHAPTER THIRTY-FIVE

Anna was standing by the huge roll-up doors to their wonderful new packing shed, watching Oberon manoeuvre the fork-lift to pick up a pallet of recipe boxes. God, he's thin, she thought. He's always been slim, but now he looks skeletal, his face strained and grim, his mouth set in a hard line, his eyes tired. Poor darling Oberon. I wish I could do something. Or say something. But there's nothing anyone can do. The business is failing, and we can't pay our debts.

Orders were still coming in, but nothing like they had been before the crash. If we'd stayed in west London, she thought, we'd have been able to ride this recession. But with Tom's help and a big loan from the bank, they'd built the brilliant facility at Crabtree. She looked round at offices, packing shed, cold store, loading bay and two shiny ORB delivery vans, painted all over with brightly coloured pictures of chefs carrying trays of veg, filleting fish, rolling pastry, chopping herbs. On the sides and back of the vans were the words

OBERON'S RECIPE BOXES

We deliver

www.orb.com

She felt her eyes filling with tears. They had both worked so hard, and were so proud of the business, especially since they'd gone fully sustainable.

When the van was packed, and Oberon had joined her for their usual morning cup of coffee and review of tomorrow's orders, she decided she had to speak. They could no longer ignore the elephant in the room.

'Oberon,' she said, looking into her mug rather than at him, 'the meeting this afternoon. It could be the end, couldn't it? Tom isn't going to bail us out, is he?'

'I don't know. He might. It's our only chance, and he's put in so much money already, first to move us to the London depot, then here, and for the website.'

Later the three of them sat at the table in the meeting room. How ironic, thought Anna. We built this room for our future expansion, to have meetings with suppliers and to interview prospective workers. But the expansion has reversed, accelerated by the food-poisoning scare, the new staff have been sacked and the recent meetings with suppliers have been about *their* cash-flow problems.

Anna studied Tom's face. But he was looking down, calm, inscrutable. Perhaps he's about to offer to take over the bank's loan and save us, she thought. Or maybe he'll tell us it's all over. Oberon will be thinking the same thing. She looked at him, but he was looking at Tom.

'Oberon, Anna,' Tom said, 'I think we have to call it a day. I could put in more money, and I was tempted to, because I think you're running the company well and doing a great job.'

'But?' said Anna.

'I've been looking at all the family businesses. You remember we agreed I would at our meeting in September? Sadly, this is the most vulnerable because we're faced with the perfect storm: the recession, too much debt and massive competition all at once. The worst is not the debt or the crash, because if I put more investment in we could ride it out – the slump won't last for ever. It's the competition that's the killer.'

'We've always had competition,' interjected Oberon. 'We just have to be better than our rivals.'

'Which we're good at,' continued Tom, evenly, 'but I've been doing some homework. We know from our testing that our immediate rivals, the small businesses started by keen cooks are not too much of a threat. They come and go. But Simply Fresh is something else. It's huge. It was started in the Netherlands, spread to Austria and Germany, and in six months they're almost a household name in the UK. The operation is very slick, they undercut us on price, and most of all they spend millions – and I mean millions – on marketing. They're not even in profit in the UK yet, but the parent company knows what it's doing. It pours money into leafleting outside tube stations, offers deep discounts for first orders, advertises on hoardings and in bus stations. Next spring, they're going nationwide with television ads featuring celebrities – top pop stars and sportspeople. And, basically, their offer is the same as ours.'

Anna had been shaking her head and trying to interrupt, but Tom had denied her with a raised hand while he had his say. Now he stopped talking and she burst in hotly, 'But they're nothing like us. They're not organic and the customer just combines cheap meat with pre-made sauce and microwaves it.' Her eyes ablaze, she ended, 'It's rubbish, Tom.'

Oberon smiled weakly. 'But most exhausted commuters – and

that's our market, Anna – just don't want to shop or lug the shopping home. Most of them don't care if it's organic or that we bother to source the best French tarragon or the best Alfonso mangoes.'

'If we close down now,' said Tom, 'and rent out the building, we'll have enough money to pay the staff and the suppliers, and we can fold honourably.'

'But we can't do that!' exclaimed Anna. 'The recession can't—'

'Anna,' interrupted Oberon, 'Tom's right. If we leave it any later, the staff will get nothing, and the suppliers won't be paid.'

Tom's heart went out to Anna. The girl didn't want to give up.

She scowled at him. 'But there must be someone out there who'd want to buy us and let us go on running the show? The business itself is healthy, with good premises and staff. Someone in the same sort of line but looking to expand.'

Tom shook his head. 'No one would take on the bank loan – and, anyway, you two wouldn't want to sell to a company who'd immediately junk the organic status, would you?'

Anna watched Tom and Oberon calmly discussing cash-flow and expenses, deciding when to declare bankruptcy and who would speak to the staff. Suddenly she couldn't bear it. She pushed back her chair and jumped up. 'I can't do this,' she said. She could feel the tears coming and hurried out of the room along the corridor to the Ladies. Once inside, she stood in front of the mirror, trying not to cry. Her face was flushed and her eyes desperate. It was all her fault. If she hadn't persuaded Oberon to sell only organic vegetables certified by the Soil Association, insisted on grass-fed beef, free-range organic eggs and chicken that cost three times that of supermarket birds, they wouldn't be going broke.

She put her hands over her face, but the tears came anyway,

wetting her palms and leaking through her fingers. What would happen to Oberon now? His family had supported him from the start with the Paddington cottage. Tom had helped them with their west London premises and, along with the bank, had invested in this place. Now Oberon would be riven with guilt and beholden to everyone.

After a while, Anna stopped crying and leant against the wall, thinking. It was such a bitter blow. Until a few months ago, they'd been riding so high, confident of repaying everyone and making a success of it. Now it would all go for nothing. The carefully designed packing shed, expensive refrigeration and shiny new vans would belong to someone else, doing something else. What a criminal waste of time, effort, money.

Who would have thought business could be so emotional? What I really, really need right now, she thought, is a drink. She met her eyes in the mirror. 'No, you don't,' she said aloud. 'You need to find Oberon and put your arms around him.'

A few moments later, nose blown and face washed, a smile forced to her face, she found him. He was back in his office, sitting at his computer.

'Look,' he said, pushing the screen round so she could read it. She went behind him to lean on his back, her arms around his shoulders.

There were two lines, blown up to fill the screen.

Fain would I climb yet fear I to fall.

If thy heart fails thee, climb not at all.

Anna read them and came round to look into Oberon's face for an explanation.

'Sir Walter Raleigh,' he said, 'ambitious to rise in the Elizabethan court, but scared of losing favour – and possibly his head – is supposed to have scratched the first line on a window pane. When the Queen saw the words, she added her response.'

'It's beautiful. And she was right.'

He stood up and closed the computer. 'Anna, be proud. At least we tried.'

CHAPTER THIRTY-SIX

Tom was alone in the house. Angelica had slimmed her workforce down to the bare minimum after the crash, but now there was a sudden rush of Christmas parties and Sebele was working for the third night running.

As he made himself an omelette for supper, Tom smiled wryly to himself. Serves me right, he thought. I told them to shrink the payroll. He tipped the omelette on to a plate and carried it through to his study, where he ate it while watching the financial news. Then he clicked off the TV and sat back, thinking.

The family, especially Giovanni and Angelica, had responded well to his austerity measures. No one was happy, but they had all knuckled down and were controlling costs as best they could. They'd cancelled planned expenditure and cut staff to the bone, which had been horrible. For people used to an expanding business in which good staff could be rewarded well, and new people hired, the hardest thing was to say goodbye to blameless employees and to ask colleagues to take a pay cut.

He'd spent months looking in detail at all the businesses and was convinced they were basically sound. If they could just tighten their belts and keep ticking over, and if business began to improve in a year, they'd be fine. And within a year he'd be able to help more.

So far, his investments in his family had not turned out brilliantly. He'd lost his stake in the recipe boxes, but that had always been a risk.

He wouldn't see any return on the abattoir or the Chorlton cheese unit for a while and, anyway, they were only loans, and at a pretty modest interest rate.

He'd also chipped in the money to keep the ice-cream business afloat. Not because he wanted to bail Mario out – he didn't, and happily Mario had left anyway – but he had to try to lift the cloud of misery that Giovanni sat under. The ice-cream trade was inherently highly profitable (or would be with a good boss) and there had been no dip in sales. It seemed that, whatever happened to world economics, people still ate ice-cream. But the loan to Gelati Angelotti was just that, an interest-free loan to his dad. The only real earner for him was Angelica and Sebele's catering company – in which he had a share. They'd ride the recession, he was sure.

Well, he thought, catering's not as profitable as playing with other people's money in the City but, still, if he could have done more, he would. He'd have liked to repay everyone's bank loans, give Giovanni's and the Laura's restaurants their planned refits, help Silvano get his luxury hotel and golf club. The lot. But that would amount to something like ten million and he didn't have that kind of cash in his back pocket. Most of his money was tied up in long-term investments and he couldn't get it out for months, in some cases years. And this was a terrible time to sell investments.

He had about two million in cash, but how to prioritize?

Which business should get help? The most urgent problem was Silvano. He needed three million for that hotel. Maybe they'd take less when they realized the bind Silvano was in. He rang Silvano and suggested they went together to talk to the owners.

'It's kind of you, Tom,' said Silvano, 'but what's the point? I haven't got the money.'

'I've an idea. But we need to stall. Get a delay.'

On the drive up to Shropshire, Tom told Silvano his plan – a mixture of reduced and delayed payments and the owner retaining a small share in the business. 'The thing is,' concluded Tom, 'he's not going to get three million from anyone right now. If he needs money, he must be willing to negotiate.'

Silvano didn't answer, and Tom looked across at him. His face was rigid, stressed, grey. He looked terrible. 'Tell you what, Silvano, how about you leave the talking to me? I'll be your man of business, and we'll see where we get.'

Silvano gave a fleeting stiff smile and nodded. 'Thanks, Tom. That would be great.'

The Westland Hotel and Golf Course had magnificent wrought-iron gates hanging from classical pillars with stone balls on top. The gates were open, and they drove down a long, gravelled drive neatly edged with lawns. At the end a Georgian stone mansion was flanked by magnificent trees and surrounded by parkland.

'My God, Silvano, this is a bit grand,' said Tom.

'Mm. But it needs a packet spent on it all the same. They keep the entrance looking good, but the bedrooms need refurbishing – some don't even have bathrooms. And look,' Silvano said, pointing at the roof gutters, where healthy tufts of grass, and even a small holly tree, were growing.

The owner, Clive Gilbert, a cheerful chap wearing yellow-brown tweeds, showed them into his office. It was a large, untidy room stuffed with files, books and too much furniture. He waved Tom to a chair and cleared another of newspapers and magazines for Silvano. 'Tea? Coffee? A snifter?'

They talked pleasantries until a waiter arrived with coffee, then got down to business.

'The thing is,' said Tom, 'Silvano hasn't got the money to honour your contract. The bank reneged on his loan.'

'So I understand. My sympathies.'

'I checked various sites yesterday and spoke to an estate agent. In today's climate you'd be very lucky indeed to find a buyer at all, even at two million.'

'True,' Gilbert smiled, 'but then I already have a binding contract for three.'

'With someone who hasn't got the money and cannot borrow it.'

Gilbert looked at Silvano. 'I hate to be blunt, Silvano, but that's your problem, not mine.'

'Not entirely,' said Tom, evenly. 'If you put Silvano into bankruptcy, which you can certainly do, and he has to sell all his assets to pay you, you won't get three million. You won't even get two. His house and the Crabtree are mortgaged, and he has no other real assets. You might get a million, and obviously the process will be expensive. Bankruptcy proceedings don't come cheap.'

The smile had left Gilbert's face, but his voice remained pleasant. 'What do you suggest?' he asked.

Tom opened his briefcase and brought out a document. 'The outline details are here, which I know you'll need time to consider so I'll leave them with you. But, in essence, we're offering two million pounds: one million down, half a million in six months, the remaining half-million in a year. You retain the property, and of course any profits, until the two million is paid. At the end of the period Westland will transfer to Silvano but you will retain ten per cent of the shares. If Silvano is successful in transforming the business as he plans to – and you're welcome to see the business plan – you might eventually do a lot better than your current, unachievable, deal.'

Gilbert, having thought briefly about it and studied the single sheet of paper, attempted to negotiate the figures upwards, but Tom politely refused.

'You need to talk to your advisers, I'm sure,' he said, standing up. 'No hurry. We'll wait to hear from you.' He put his business card on the desk in front of Gilbert. 'I think you have Silvano's contact numbers. Call either of us, any time.'

Two days later Gilbert's lawyer emailed Tom with a counter-proposal of three million over three years, but Tom refused. 'I'm afraid it's two million over eighteen months and ten per cent of the business, or you make Silvano bankrupt.'

A week after that, Gilbert rang Silvano. 'OK, Silvano, I agree. That Tom of yours is pretty persuasive. He speaks quietly and wields a big stick.'

Tom's next concern, with the most urgent need, was Giovanni's. He talked to Laura.

'Laura darling, I've got enough liquid cash to help Giovanni's, I think, but I need you to be happy about it. You see, just covering losses will get nowhere. I'm not sure that even if the recession lifted tomorrow Giovanni's would be back in profit.'

'But it made money before. It's only been in the red since the crash.'

'I know, but the profits have been slowly declining for the last ten years. What do you think of asking all our customers, and former customers, what they like and don't like about Giovanni's?'

'Oh, we couldn't do that, Tom. It would look desperate. A mail shot? That would be vulgar, wouldn't it?'

'With an online anonymous survey, yes, it would. But an email or a letter, from you to your customers, saying we're about to do a major refit – to celebrate the restaurant's fortieth birthday, say – you could ask them to help you get it right. Could they let you know what they like about Giovanni's and what they don't?'

'But, Tom, we hardly get any complaints. They love it. It's a good restaurant.'

'Yes, it is. Of course it is. But I've asked my old business colleagues and I get the impression that some of them think it's in a bit of a time warp, not informal enough, too grand.'

'But we have a Michelin star, Tom. We've got to be smart.'

'Laura darling, there has to be a reason for the fall-off in business. Look at the new restaurants all over town, which are packed. We need to know what they have and Giovanni's doesn't.'

In the end, Laura and Giovanni agreed to Tom's survey idea. And what came back from the customers was satisfaction, even delight, with the quality of the food but plenty of complaints about it being too rich, too expensive, taking too long to come to table. The older customers tended to like everything just as it was. Younger ones wanted faster service, more interesting décor, a bigger bar serving more interesting cocktails with tapas-like plates of food. They didn't always want to eat three-course meals on a white tablecloth.

Tom collated the results, sent them to Giovanni and Laura, then went to see them.

They sat at the kitchen table and Tom looked from one to the other. 'So, what do you think?'

'That word "time-warp" came up too often to ignore,' said Laura. 'We have to do something.'

'But will a refit help?' asked Giovanni. 'Maybe our time is just up. The restaurant, like us two, is slowly on its way out. Maybe it should be allowed to retire gracefully. We could just shut up shop. Quit while we're ahead.'

Tom took a deep breath and said, 'Giovanni's is too important to the group. It's the flagship, and if it went under it could be damaging. Besides, it's a London landmark, and we need it to be here in a hundred years, like Rules, or the Savoy. I propose that we close it as soon as possible and give it a complete refit, kitchen, bar, everything. Meanwhile, Laura and Richard work on new menus, *cicchetti* for the bar and new cocktails.'

That night, Tom and Sebele ate avocado on toast with a garlicky dressing.

'I've never had avocado on toast before,' Tom said.

'It was all there was. But it's good, isn't it?'

'Mm. I think this is the sort of snack we should sell at the new bar at Giovanni's. *Bruschetti* with different, modern toppings.'

'You're finally becoming a foodie, Tom. And you look really happy.'

'I feel happy. I like deals. And making stuff happen. And making money, And I think the new Giovanni's will be great if we keep the old-world atmosphere in the dining room and make the bar area much more informal. And when Silvano finally gets Westland in a year's time I will, I hope, have the money to refurbish it and that will be a real money spinner. The golf club already makes good money. It's just the hotel that needs a refit.' He lifted his glass to her. 'So why wouldn't I be happy? Plus I love this house. And I love you. And it's high bloody time you married me. OK?'

She held his gaze for a long beat. 'OK,' she said.

CHAPTER THIRTY-SEVEN

Being old, thought Laura, is not just a matter of concealing aches and pains so that your family aren't bored to death with your multiple complaints. It's also accepting that it's downhill from now on, with increasing doses of death and sadness. Both of her brothers had died years ago: she barely remembered the thirty-five-year-old Hugh other than as a glamorous pilot in an air-force uniform. By contrast, David had lived to eighty-three, spending nearly thirty years in a wheelchair from which he watched, and sometimes interfered with, his son's management of his beloved Chorlton.

Laura found her mind repeatedly returning to the long-gone past – which now seemed to her sun-filled and happy – and then to the current intractable problems of the world. She felt weighed down and lacking in hope, which was unlike her. Of course she'd been sad, even heartbroken, before. Who hasn't suffered in a long life? But this was different. No one had died, no one was ill or on drugs or even much in pain.

Laura made a deliberate effort to count her blessings. They had Tom. Thank God for Tom, she thought, feeling a familiar glow of warmth, no, of love, run through her. Ironically, Tom and Giovanni were even closer now than before Jane had made her revelation. And for her the lifting of that weight of secrecy and guilt after fifty years had been truly cathartic.

She had much to be grateful for, much to be happy about, but still she could not shake off the gloom. I'm known for my energy and cheerfulness, she thought, and right now I can't summon either.

It wasn't just the Angelotti enterprises that were in trouble. Hal had come to London for an early meeting with the bank about Chorlton, and it had gone badly. He'd turned up in her kitchen at eleven, dishevelled and exhausted. 'It's too bad,' he said. 'At our last meeting round this table I was the most confident of all of us that we'd survive the recession. But, Laura, now we could lose Chorlton. Barclays wants its money back.'

'What? I thought you said they were honouring the loan?'

'Yes, well, that's what the local manager told us. But now he's been told to call in all loans, no exceptions.'

'Oh, my poor, poor Hal. What are you going to do?'

'We have until the end of the year to pay the money.' He ran his fingers through his hair, gripping a fistful and pulling it. 'If we don't find a white knight the bank will foreclose. We'll be bankrupt.'

'They can do that, can they?'

'They can, and they intend to. It'd mean the end for us, and the vultures would pick the carcass clean.'

'Whoa, whoa, Hal,' exclaimed Laura. 'The property must be worth a fortune. If we have to sell, surely we'd raise enough . . .'

Hal shook his head. 'You'd think so, but we've borrowed so much for the milking parlour and everything. And the receiver won't come free. There'd be his fat fee, then the tax man would get first dibs, and the bank would come next. The rest of our creditors, suppliers and staff would be lucky to get fifty pence in the pound. God knows what there'd be left for us.'

Laura shook her head in disbelief. The loss of Chorlton would be hard for everyone, but it would be devastating for Hal. No one could have worked harder or done a better job. Farming is seldom easy, and her nephew had proved as resilient, and even more imaginative, as his father.

'The worst of it,' said Hal, 'is that a bunch of bureaucrats, who'll know nothing of farming, will take over Chorlton.'

'Oh, my darling Hal,' Laura reached up to put her arms round his neck. He was big and bulky, and old age had made her smaller. A flash of memory took her back to hugging him as a skinny lad. Now here she was, an old lady, trying to comfort a grown man.

She leant back to look at him. 'Is there no hope of getting another bank to take over the loan?'

Hal straightened his shoulders and stepped out of Laura's embrace. He made an effort to smile at her. 'I've tried every bank I could think of. The only option is one I'd rather die than accept.'

'What's that, love?'

'Jane. I don't know what's the matter with that woman. She's always had it in for the Olivers. Anyway, she's made an offer for everything, the three farms, all the houses and cottages, everything . . .'

'But shouldn't you . . . At least . . .'

Hal shook his head. 'It's a completely ludicrous offer, but she knows we're in dire straits. It would be a fire sale – she isn't even offering current value. The bait is we keep the house and I keep my job. I become her farm manager.'

'And you'd have that dreadful estate manager of hers for a boss, would you?'

'Yes. He talks posh and wears tailored tweeds, so he can do no wrong as far as Jane's concerned. I couldn't do it. I'd rather see Chorlton go under than go to her.'

Laura longed to talk to Giovanni about it, but he had enough to worry about with the Angelotti businesses. Besides, he'd taken himself on one of his long, solitary walks round London, something he'd increasingly done of late. It was as if he could not bear to be still for fear of his anxiety overwhelming his mind.

Laura's worry centred on Chorlton, a four-generation farming business and her childhood home. If it went, where would Hal and Pippa live? And Jake? And Sophie?

Maybe Hal should accept Jane's offer. Where was he going to find another job, at fifty-eight, in the middle of a recession? Of course it would be hard. It would be horrible. But bankruptcy was worse, surely.

That afternoon, the doorbell rang. Laura looked out of the bedroom window to see Tom at the door. She was tempted not to answer. She didn't want to see anyone, not even Tom. But then, as she heard the door open, she remembered Giovanni insisting he have a key. '*La mia casa è la tua casa,*' he'd said.

She smoothed her hair, lifted her chin and went downstairs, smile at the ready. As they kissed, she suspected that Tom, ever observant, could see she was putting on a brave face. Once in the kitchen he took her by the shoulders and looked into her eyes. 'What is it, Laura?' he said. 'You're not yourself.'

Suddenly she felt like a child, on the verge of tears. She put her hand up to her mouth, trying not to cry.

Tom led her to a chair and sat down next to her, still holding her hand. 'Tell me.'

Once she started talking she couldn't stop. She told him about Hal, how his only chance was to sell Chorlton to Jane; how utterly miserable Giovanni was at what Mario had done. Not so much because Tom had had to make good the losses, but because Mario had besmirched the Angelotti name. He'd been using Gelati profits to finance a fancy car, designer clothes, almost a playboy lifestyle. 'Mario may look confident,' she said, 'but really he's insecure. He'd have been so desperate to impress Susan.'

Tom let her talk, seldom interrupting, and Laura hung on to his arm as she blurted it all out. The drop in London restaurant customers was playing on Giovanni's mind, and he hated to see his granddaughter so distraught over the failure of the recipe boxes.

And then there was poor Pippa, whose shop and café were doing so well, but they'd go down with Chorlton. So would Angelica's market garden, now that it was on Chorlton land.

'The trouble is,' said Laura, her voice catching, 'Giovanni is used to helping the family, occasionally with money, but always with reassurance and advice. Now he can do nothing. He can't bear to see all of us, recently so happy and successful, in such trouble.'

She was openly crying now. 'Oh, Tom, it's all so awful. We've worked so hard, paid our taxes and treated our staff properly. We've fed our customers honestly – we've really, really, done a good job. And we're going to lose it all, including Chorlton.'

Tom reached for the kitchen roll and passed her a couple of sheets. Laura pressed them to her eyes. 'I'm so sorry, Tom, weeping all over you. I know worse things happen at sea. And we won't lose this place or anything. If the worst came to the worst we could all live in these cottages and start again.' She straightened her back and forced a smile. 'I should brace up. It's just that I thought my life was going to end well. Not in the destruction of everything we've all worked so hard for.'

When he didn't respond, Laura said, 'Say something, Tom. Is it too late to save Chorlton? Do you think we should just let it go?'

Tom was thinking fast. The thought of Jane taking over Chorlton was too horrible. If only he could release the money he had locked in other investments, he could buy it himself, or pay back the bank. He needed time. Which he didn't have.

'Laura, darling, I wish I could wave a magic wand, and believe me, I will do my best. But I just don't have the cash to bail everyone out. I have some, but . . .'

'You don't have to do that, Tom. You've been so generous to us already. No one is expecting you to—'

'Laura, we're family, aren't we? And the hospitality businesses are good. They'll all survive a period of austerity somehow. But Chorlton is a real worry. The property will one day be worth a fortune, a prize for some rich City type or foreign millionaire. But not now. Did Hal say what Jane is offering for it?' He went on before she could reply: 'I'd have thought it would fetch several million if we had time to mount a decent sale, use a good agent, advertise . . . Land prices haven't fallen like everything else, at least not in the Cotswolds.'

'Hal said Jane's offer was derisory,' said Laura, 'but he thought other bidders would be just as tough, knowing it was a distressed sale. And he hasn't time anyway. The bank has given him until the end of the year. That's only six weeks away. It's repay or go bust.'

Laura made tea and produced a tin of biscuits. When Tom said how delicious they were, Laura said, 'They're *baci di dama,* lady's kisses – Giovanni's favourite. I made them in the hope of cheering him up, but he hasn't eaten one.'

They sat in silence while Tom, his elbows on the table and his fingers on his frowning forehead, did some thinking.

He straightened up. 'Laura, I think Hal should negotiate in earnest with Jane, but not sign anything until he has to, after Christmas. A sale to Jane now would be a better bet than bankruptcy. At least the family could still live there. Jane would probably keep Pippa's farm shop and café going as they make good money. Hal and Jake would have their jobs, and Sophie will still have somewhere to live.'

Laura was looking at him, listening, but her eyes were without hope.

'If we can just get the bank to give us a little longer,' Tom went on, 'I might be able to raise the cash, but I'm not sure I can. And I don't want to raise everyone's hopes. I don't want to tell anyone I'm trying.' He smiled and rubbed her forearm briefly. 'But I can't keep secrets from you.'

Laura nodded. 'We have to persuade Hal to accept the Frampton offer then,' she said, her voice dull with defeat.

'I think so. Even if Jane proves to be the frightful landlord we all suspect she might be, it will buy Hal time to think of some future way of life.'

When Tom kissed her at the door, he said, 'You know what, Laura? We should all concentrate on having one last wonderful Christmas at Chorlton.'

Laura was eighty-one, and it was a long time since she'd been on a train by herself. She would never have admitted it – she had a reputation for energy and independence to maintain – but she felt a little nervous stepping over the gap as she boarded the train at Paddington. She hadn't told anyone she was going down to see Hal, because that would have led to a discussion of Chorlton's future, and she could not trust anyone, not even Giovanni, to feel quite as she did. She'd telephoned Chorlton only that morning and spoken to Jake, telling him that she was coming down to see his father.

Once settled in her seat, she rather enjoyed the trip. She watched the countryside slide by and thought about the seventy-odd years they'd travelled this line. As a child there was the excitement of going up to town for a Christmas panto or a rare shopping trip with her mother to Liberty's or Swan & Edgar. And then, as a teenager during the war, she would stand on the platform at Moreton-in-Marsh to meet her father or her big brother Hugh. She was so proud of them, stepping off the train in RAF uniform.

But there were grim memories too, like that first flight with Giovanni in 1946. They'd fled from Chorlton and her irate father, and spent the night tucked up in Giovanni's single bunk in his fruit-pickers' dormitory. Then they'd caught the train to London in the morning, with no idea where they'd sleep that night, where they'd live, what work they could get.

And later there'd been her desperate train trip home in the vain hope of reconciliation, only to be banished again by her father. And the train ride with Giovanni, Angelica in her arms, for Grace and George's wedding in Frampton church when her father, yet again, had dismissed her.

But after that, when the families were finally reconciled, there'd been excited family trips to Chorlton or Frampton for Christmas or the summer holidays, for the opening of Silvano's first restaurant at the Frampton Arms, to see what David and then Hal had done on the farms, and latterly to admire Silvano's Crabtree, Anna's vegetable smallholding and Pippa's farm shop and café. Chorlton was woven into the warp and weft of the Oliver and Angelotti families. She could not believe she was on a mission to persuade her nephew to sell it.

Pippa met her at the station, and as they took the Frampton road home to Chorlton, Pippa talked of the success of the farm shop and café, Jake's new cheese to be called Chorlton Blue, Hal's compost fields, the good harvest safely in and sold already. Neither mentioned the cloud hanging over everything.

When they walked into the familiar old kitchen, Laura saw at once that there were coffee things and cake for a lot more than two people.

'Laura,' said Hal, 'I guess you want to talk about the future of Chorlton, so I've asked the others to come. We all have a stake in the place. And, anyway, they all want to see you. It's been weeks.' Half an hour later Laura found herself making her case to Pippa, Jake and Sophie as well as to Hal.

'I'm conscious that what happens to Chorlton isn't strictly my business,' she said. 'I have a small share in the estate, as you know, but it doesn't affect my livelihood like it does yours.' She paused, organizing her words in her head. 'The thing is, none of us want Chorlton to go under. It's my childhood home, just as it's been yours, Hal, and Jake's and Oberon's too. And Sophie, you've lived at Chorlton for, what, almost sixty years?' She smiled across at her friend. 'You spent your whole childhood running round the place with me. Even you, Pippa, you're the newcomer, yet you've been here more than half your life.'

There were nods round the table. 'I'm sure none of you want

to work for Jane,' Laura went on, 'but I think the alternative would be worse. You'd all have to find somewhere else to live and another way to earn a living. It's highly unlikely that another buyer would want you all to stay. At least Jane wants the business to continue with Hal farming it.'

'Except she'd go back to pouring pesticides and herbicides on the fields. She'd scrap all the organic stuff,' said Pippa. 'I don't want to be part of a farm or a shop and café if they aren't sustainable.'

'But, Mum,' said Jake, 'Jane won't necessarily want to mess with your café and farm shop. They make money *because* they're sustainable, selling stuff you can't get in the supermarket. And if Jane buys Chorlton and we continue to run it, isn't there at least a chance that, at some future date, we might be able to buy it back? That manager of hers has taken the profitable Frampton estate to a loss-making one in two seasons, hasn't he, Dad? If he continues like that, who knows what might happen?'

The debate went on for a very long time. Hal did concede there was sense in staying on as Jane's employee rather than losing the roof over their heads. Jake was for going to see Jane in an effort to persuade her to keep the organic status but Hal thought that would be a waste of time. Jake said he'd go anyway. What was there to lose?

At the end of the week, Hal emailed Laura, copying Tom and the rest of the family.

Sad news. Yesterday we agreed a deal with Jane to sell Chorlton to her on 31 December, the day we must repay the loan or go under.

Good news. You are all invited for Christmas at Chorlton. If it's to be our Last Hurrah, let's make it a good one. No excuses accepted. Hal and Pippa

CHAPTER THIRTY-EIGHT

Tom went to see Malcolm Drury, Barclays' chairman, a friend since they'd cut their teeth together at Merrill Lynch. Malcolm, portly and jovial, came round his near-empty desk, to shake Tom's hand and clap him on the back.

They sat on a sofa and talked of Malcolm's sons and Tom's planned re-marriage, then Tom set out his stall. But he completely failed to persuade Malcolm to extend the loan period to Hal.

'I just can't do that, old chap,' said Malcolm. 'I can't override a manager's decision when he's obediently sticking to the policy I've set. Which, frankly, is to be brutal. To get the loans back, no exceptions. And it would set a precedent, with every branch pleading special cases.'

Tom had been about to protest when Malcolm held up his hand, 'But maybe I could give you, Tom, a personal loan and then you use it to pay back their debt, and when, in six months, you can scratch together the cash, you can repay us.'

Tom had wanted to laugh. 'Malcolm, what makes you think I'd be a better bet than Hal Oliver? He has a working profitable farm and I'm somewhere between unemployed and retired.'

'Well, I know you for a start, and second, it doesn't mess with the system. You know how these things work, Tom. Logic doesn't play a huge part.' He paused, then suddenly chuckled. 'Although there is some logic in it. A short-term loan to you at a whacking profit is a lot better than a long-term one to a farmer at piddling interest rates.'

Tom borrowed five million, and immediately used half of it to pay off Hal's loans. The whole thing only took two days. Wonderful what a nod from the chairman could do. The interest rate for his six-month loan was exorbitant, but Tom didn't care. The cash would be enough to get on with everything urgent, and in six months he'd be in the money, with investments paying out, and they could get on with the planned, and abruptly cancelled, restaurant refurbishments.

Tom walked through the palatial lobby of Barclays, and out into the City drizzle with a barely suppressed grin. He felt like jumping down the steps and clicking his heels together, like Fred Astaire. How funny, he thought, I've done hundreds of deals in my life, all of them bigger than this one, but scuppering Jane's plan to buy Chorlton is giving me a bigger buzz than any of them.

Rescuing the Chorlton estate would not have made sense if he wasn't part of the family. Farming in the Cotswolds, where costs were high, fields small and sloping, and the land poor, was never going to be a gold mine. But, hell, he thought, it's not all about profit. And he had to hand it to Hal: Chorlton was diversifying to stay ahead of the game. These days, unless you were a great big agri-business in the flat and fertile eastern counties, it was innovation or bust.

He didn't even tell Sebele that he'd managed what he'd set out to do. Of course everyone knew that he was financing the refit of Giovanni's and had engineered a deal so that Silvano would not lose Westland Park, but they would all be at Chorlton tomorrow and he wanted to make his proposal for the future, then.

When Tom and Sebele arrived, Laura had been at Chorlton almost a week, helping Pippa and Angelica get ready for the biggest family party in years.

Tom was astonished. Every bit of the ground floor was decorated, with fresh holly and ivy over the pictures, twisted into garlands above the fireplace, in tubs and buckets in the corners. Christmas cards were pinned to long ribbons that hung from the picture rails. A great bunch of fresh mistletoe hung from the entrance-hall ceiling light. Big church candles burnt on mantelpieces, tables and window sills. The whole scene was magical. A picture-book Christmas Eve.

Richard's lurcher, Tatiana, an old lady now, slept on the rug in front of the fire, right in everyone's way. There was a huge Christmas tree, cut from the estate and positioned in the corner of the drawing room. It reached nearly to the ceiling and the decoration was almost done. There were already fairy lights, glass baubles and dozens of other decorations in place. Jake and Oberon were adding the finishing touches with shiny Quality Street toffees suspended with cotton loops, which Laura, sitting on the sofa, was making.

'Oh, Pippa,' said Sebele, 'the whole house looks beautiful. Old-fashioned and real and obviously not designed by some fancy stylist.'

'You can say that again.' Pippa laughed, then went on in her still-evident Australian accent, 'Some of that clobber is fifty years old. Sophie says Richard and Hal made the little Santas and the cardboard stars when they were kids. My first Christmas here, before Oberon and Jake were born, I did suggest we chuck them out and begin again, but they're such a sentimental lot, the whole family objected like I was proposing to junk the Crown Jewels or something.'

Jake reached up to point out a battered little angel, tinsel crown askew and with only one paper wing. 'I made that about twenty-five years ago. It was never great and now it's just a crumpled bit of paper. We should have ditched it ages ago.'

'Just wait till you have children of your own,' said Laura. 'Then you'll understand.'

Over tea, the conversation turned, inevitably, to Chorlton's troubles. 'I'll be amazed if Jane sticks to any of the promises Jake extracted from her,' said Hal.

'What promises?' Silvano asked. 'Did she come up with a deal you liked?'

'Well, yes, sort of. She said she'd give our strategy for sustainable farming a go for two years. I don't believe her for a minute. You know Jane. Reliable as a snake. Yesterday she was making noises about pulling out of the abattoir cooperative, because, she says, she didn't realize it wasn't making money yet.'

'Hey, you two,' said Laura, sharply, 'we had a deal, remember? No business talk, no recession talk, no rehearsal of our woes. Above all, no talk of Jane! Nothing but goodwill and Christmas cheer.'

'OK,' chipped in Anna, 'but I need reassurance from Sophie that she hasn't invited her for Christmas lunch.'

'Relax,' Sophie replied. 'I think the risk of her ruining a good party is just too high. I'd hoped she'd be in the Caribbean, but she's at Frampton.'

Tom was tempted to come in with his news, but they weren't all in the room and he wanted enough time to discuss the ramifications, so he said nothing.

That evening they ate a sort of flat pie Angelica had invented, with a filling of smoked salmon and goat's cheese, followed by a salad with plenty of avocado in it, then tangerines in caramel sauce with ice cream. It was very informal, and after supper, everyone went back to work preparing for Christmas dinner or laying the Christmas table, or trying to wrap presents without the recipients seeing. Someone had put ABBA on the player and, although there were objections at first, in the end everyone was singing, and Anna, Cassia, Oberon and Jake were dancing.

Next morning Laura and Sophie went to the Christmas Day church service, leaving Richard in charge of the cooking while the rest of them went for a brisk walk up to Top Field. It was a beautiful morning, crisp and cold, and Tom stood looking down over the cluster of ancient farm buildings, dusted with snow, and felt deeply glad that he'd been able to prevent the sale to Jane. But a lot of his content came from belonging to a family capable of being so relaxed and merry, despite believing this was their last Christmas at Chorlton. He hugged his secret to himself, aware that he had in his pocket a Christmas gift that would go some way to repaying what he owed the Angelottis. Without them he wouldn't have known the complicated richness of his new life or have met Sebele. He owed them everything.

By noon everyone was home. Hal, opening the champagne, asked Tom if he'd bring in some more logs. 'I'm so sorry. I meant to do it last night. They're in the little barn, through the kitchen and round to the left.'

Tom filled a double-handled basket with logs and, thinking it would be quicker to go back through the front door, set off to walk round the side of the house. As he approached, he heard a car skidding on the gravel. He rounded the corner to see Jane struggling out of her Audi and slamming the car door. Oh, God, he thought. She knows.

He set down the log basket and ran to her. He caught up with her just before she got to the front door. 'No, you don't, Jane,' he said, as he took her by the shoulders.

'Leave me alone,' she shouted. 'Get off me.'

'You are not going in there,' he said. 'Shush, Jane, be quiet. They don't know anything about it.' He spoke urgently, but softly.

She turned to him, her face ugly with rage. 'You utter bastard, Tom. How *dare* you interfere? We had a deal.'

She was still shouting, and Tom feared that even carols at full blast on the CD player would not drown her out. 'Do I gather you've learnt that Chorlton is no longer for sale?' he said.

'Too right I have. I found a message on my answerphone this morning from my lawyer saying Hal wasn't selling and the bank had their money. That can only be you – the interfering bloody guardian angel of all the Olivers and Angelottis.'

She was still trying to shake off his grip as he tried to steer her back to her car. 'Go home, Jane. You're really not welcome here.'

'Who says? Get out of my way. I want to speak to Hal.'

'This is not the time, Jane. I haven't even told them I've paid off the loan.'

'You upstart interloper! You think you can do anything!'

'I can absolutely stop you going in there. And I will. Go, Jane. Just leave.'

His calmness seemed to infuriate Jane further. Her rage contorted her face almost unrecognizably. Unable to free herself, she suddenly screwed up her mouth and jerked her head at him. A gob of spittle landed on his cheek.

A shiver of revulsion went through him, but he would not give her the satisfaction of showing it. 'That's an odd way for a lady to behave,' he said. He had to release his right arm to extract a tissue from his pocket. As he wiped his cheek, she wrenched herself free and sprinted for the front door.

Tom lunged after her just as the front door opened and Anna and Cassia appeared. 'Let me through!' yelled Jane, and barged into the house, knocking the astonished Anna sideways into the doorjamb.

'Ouch!' exclaimed Anna, looking from Jane, now disappearing into the drawing room, to Tom. 'What's going on?'

'I'll explain in a minute. But we need to get her out of here.'

They hurried into the house to find Jane standing in the middle of the room, surrounded by most of the family, looking astonished or bewildered. 'You knew, didn't you, Hal?' she shouted. 'You probably all knew.'

'Knew what?' demanded Jake.

'Don't play the innocent with me, young man. Your dad has just stitched me up, the bastard.'

Everyone was talking. Angelica and Anna were shouting at Jane. Laura went up to her and tried to take her arm, but Jane pushed her off angrily. Laura, old enough to be a bit unsteady anyway, staggered and fell. As she went down, her head struck the edge of the coffee table.

Angelica rushed to her. She and Pippa pulled her up and helped her to the sofa. Laura's face was contorted with pain and Pippa called, 'Richard, get Sophie.' Giovanni sat down beside his wife, his arm round her, his face anguished.

The room had gone deathly quiet. Richard headed for the kitchen, calling for Sophie. She hurried in and knelt in front of Laura.

Sophie soon established there were no broken bones. Laura was fine and tried to wave everyone away. 'No, Sophie darling, no pain, no dizziness, nothing. I've got a fine bump coming up on my noddle, that's all.' She smiled up at Giovanni. 'I'm all right, *caro*. Really.'

Tom, watching, was surprised at the relief he felt. If she'd been really hurt, he thought, I hate to think what I might have done to Jane. He leant over to stroke his mother's arm. At her age, a fall like that must be a shock, if nothing else. What a stalwart old bird she was.

He turned his attention back to Jane. He could see at once that the fight had gone out of her. As he looked at her, her eyes filled with tears. Poor bloody woman, he thought, she's her own worst enemy. 'I think you should go, Jane,' he said quietly, and ushered her to the door. No one spoke to her or tried to stop her.

As she ducked into her car, Tom said, 'We don't want to have an enemy for a neighbour, Jane, but, frankly, we're all too old to dance to your tune. If you decide to be civilized, you're welcome. Right now, I'm afraid you're not.'

Tom watched her progress down the drive, the car jerking and kicking up gravel. Poor stupid bitch, he thought, she has no idea how to be happy.

Tom picked up his abandoned basket of logs and returned to the drawing room. He was met with a clamour of questions.

'OK, OK, I wanted to tell you this at the table, but now is fine. Only let's all sit down.'

As silence settled on them again, Tom said, 'Right, here goes.

Last week I went to see the chairman of Barclays. We made a deal that meant I could pay off your loan, Hal.'

No one said a word. They all stared at Tom, faces blank. Then Hal said, 'You've what? You got them to change their minds?'

'No, they refused to reverse their decision. They still wanted their money back. But they gave me, personally, a loan for six months, by which time I will have enough money for us to do what we want with all of the businesses. I paid off your loan yesterday, Hal. That's why Jane is so incandescent.' He looked directly at Hal. 'What I propose is complicated and maybe you won't agree, and that would be fine by me. At least we've bought a little time and you won't have the pressure of a forced sale and have to accept a ludicrous price because the estate has been made bankrupt.'

'What do you propose?' said Hal. He doesn't seem relieved, or pleased, thought Tom. He seems almost suspicious. Poor man, he's been through such hell of late, he doesn't trust good news.

'OK, here is my plan.' He looked round the circle. 'Almost every one of your businesses has been hit by the recession, but they are mostly good, sound enterprises and I'm sure they'll do well in the future. The cooperation of the restaurant businesses and the informal consolidation we've done so far has started to pay dividends already, but we could go further. What I propose now is that we put all the companies, the Angelotti restaurants, Angelica and Sebele's catering businesses, the organic veg business and even Chorlton into one big company. And I will chair the group.'

No one said anything, and then, once again, everyone was talking at once. 'But how would that work?' asked Richard. 'Right now I own twenty per cent of Giovanni's, but that's all. Would I . . . ?

'Everyone will hold shares in the new company based on the value of their current businesses and their share in them,' said Tom. 'We'll get a valuer in to independently assess everything. And my very first action as chairman will be to try to buy Jane out. She still owns a good bit of the Angelotti business and the sooner she doesn't, the better, I think.'

Laura became emotional, pushing herself up and hurrying round to hug Tom. She started to speak, then became tearful and couldn't. Tom stood and guided her back to her chair. 'Hang on, Laura darling, I've not finished yet.'

'Sorry to be blunt,' Oberon said, 'but you are a businessman, Tom. Kind and generous. But, still, a businessman. Can I ask what's in it for you?'

'Good question, Oberon.' Tom then explained. 'In effect, I will be the banker, but I will charge only one per cent above bank rate for loans. And for that, and for being a very active chairman, I'd like a slice of the action. Say ten per cent of the consolidated company.'

He looked around the room. Mostly, the faces still bore signs of shock. 'We'll manage the businesses as efficiently as we can,' he went on, 'and when the good times return we can take the company public and all make some money, or we can decide to carry on as a group, or even split up again.'

At last Tom saw some tentative smiles. Then, quite suddenly, everyone was talking much too loudly. Tom held up his hand and raised his voice. 'Just one more piece of the jigsaw. Sadly, this has all come too late to save Oberon's Recipe Boxes. But working with Oberon showed me just what a talented business-man he is. He's already agreed to work with me on my own investments and future adventures. If you agree to this proposal,

I hope Oberon will also develop the social marketing for the group and be the internet consultant for us all. That could work, couldn't it, Oberon?'

Oberon, at first surprised, grinned. 'Yes, certainly. I – I think. Er, I'd love that. If you'll have me.'

Tom looked round them all. 'So that's my proposal. Have a think. Everyone should consider the offer and talk to each other, and obviously to me, if you like, before deciding.' He took a deep breath and dropped into a chair. 'God,' he said, 'keeping all that in for the last forty-eight hours has been hard. Hal, any chance of another glass?'

The excitement of Tom's announcement and the relief at not losing Chorlton stoked the general Christmas cheer through the resumption of present opening and through Christmas dinner.

Laura turned out Anna's giant Christmas pudding and stuck some holly in the top. Richard poured warm brandy all over it and set it alight to a lot of cheering and clapping.

'Don't choke on the five-pence pieces,' said Laura. 'We really need some children to maintain the excitement of finding a silver coin. Oberon and Jake, are you two ever going to find wives and make me a *bambino* or two? Or Tom and Sebele, how about you? I need great-grandchildren.'

By the time they went to bed, everyone had told Tom they loved him, and that it all sounded too good to be true. Oberon, flushed with slightly too many beers and another in his hand, said, 'Tom, it feels like a new beginning. I think it could be so good.'

'I agree,' said Tom, 'but what about you, Anna?'

'I'm happy, Tom. I was sad about the boxes, but I do think you made the right decision.' She looked across at Angelica. 'And I like growing veg with Mum.'

'You should do more than just grow veg,' said Tom. 'Don't stop the blogging and environmental campaigning, Anna. You're good at it.'

'She is,' said Cassia. 'I think she should do an environmental degree.'

'Good idea. You could do sustainability studies or something. Part time? With the Open University?'

Anna leant up and kissed his cheek. 'Give it a rest, Tom. You sound like my dad.'

'Well, your dad is right. Has been right all the time.'

'I know,' said Anna, 'but don't tell him I said so.'

Before they went to bed, Sebele suggested to Tom that they walk up to Top Field.

'We walked up there this morning!'

'I know, but let's go again. It's a lovely night and it'll clear my head,' she said.

They put on their wellies and walked, just the two of them, arm in arm and in silence. When they got to the top and looked back on the farm, the yard lights bright and the house lights golden, Sebele said, 'Tom, you know you promised Giovanni you'd change your name to Angelotti. Where has that got to?'

'Well, I've registered my change of name,' said Tom, 'Giovanni has formally adopted me, and I owe him that much at least. But actually *using* the name would be too confusing.'

'But what's so difficult? Millions of women change their names on marriage, and they manage fine. You don't have to be called Standing.'

Tom frowned, amused. 'Where are you going with this, dar-ling?' Sebele took hold of his jacket lapels and pulled him close to her. He shut his eyes the better to breathe her in. She smelt delicious, familiar, very sexy.

'You have to start using Angelotti,' she said. 'You know what Laura said about us having a duty to make babies?'

'Oh, Sebele, I hope that didn't upset you. I thought it might ...'

'No, darling. But we're about to make her wish come true. Tom, there's to be a new Angelotti.'

ACKNOWLEDGEMENTS

I know most readers don't bother to read the acknowledgements page, but I'm compelled by a host of kind people to whom I owe great thanks to write one nonetheless.

First, as always, Jane Turnbull, my agent, and Jane Wood, my editor at Quercus: they combine that vital mix of brutal forthrightness and great encouragement. Then, also as always, I must thank my PA, Francisca Sankson, for endless reading and checking, and my husband John Playfair for making me cups of tea and doing the shopping, washing up and lots else, so I could keep writing. But also, this time, I need to thank him for allowing me to steal his experience of post-war adoption and of his search for his birth mother and father, without which I would not have written this tale.

All writers need kind friends who know about subjects of which they are ignorant, and who are prepared to check, correct and advise so that the author looks like an expert. My list of such friends includes Julia and Richard Beldam, especially Richard, whose experience includes surviving an avalanche while skiing; Johnny Secombe, who has been down the Cresta run more times than his wife PJ cares to think about; Jamie Hooker who is a hunt master and knows all there is to know about the arcane traditions of the English hunt; Helen Browning, CEO of the Soil Association for help on organic farming yields etc., Clare Scheckter, married to Jody, who between them run the famous Laverstoke Park organic farm and know about how an abattoir should be run and how to operate compost windrows; Clare Mackintosh, bestselling novelist and ex-copper, who helped me on police procedure; Debbie Toksvig who read and approved my chapters on a lesbian love affair; Anthony Peters for advice on 9/11, as well as the 2008 crash and other city matters; Tom Hall on wealth management, investment banking and City behaviour; Charles Arkell, William Colbatch-Clark and Mark Charter who dug out figures for me on historic land and property prices; Caroline, the Countess of Harrowby, for setting me right about aristocratic inheritance rights and Richard Imrie for inside info on St Barts Island in the Caribbean.

Looking at the list above you could be forgiven for thinking that I knew very little about anything. But at least the story is my own, and I know it's the better for the help of my friends.